THE LIGHTNING AND THE FEW

*Jox McNabb Thrillers
Book One*

Patrick Larsimont

Also in the Jox McNabb series
The Raiders and the Cross
The Maple and the Blue
The Vulcan and the Straits
The Wire and the Lines

THE LIGHTNING AND THE FEW

Published by Sapere Books.

24 Trafalgar Road, Ilkley, LS29 8HH

saperebooks.com

Copyright © Patrick Larsimont, 2022

Patrick Larsimont has asserted his right to be identified as the author of this work.
All rights reserved.

No part of this publication may be reproduced, stored in any retrieval system, or transmitted, in any form, or by any means, electronic, mechanical, photocopying, recording, or otherwise, without the prior written permission of the publishers.
This book is a work of fiction. Names, characters, businesses, organisations, places and events, other than those clearly in the public domain, are either the product of the author's imagination, or are used fictitiously.
Any resemblances to actual persons, living or dead, events or locales are purely coincidental.

ISBN: 978-1-80055-863-2

For Alison, the first person to call me a writer

PROLOGUE

Dunkerque, March 1990

Doctor Melanie McNabb was freezing and wished she had worn a jacket over her Imperial War Museum overalls. The sea breeze was tugging at her clothes and her mouth was gritty with blown sand. She always liked to look the part; IWM logo on her breast and hardhat, the word STAFF emblazoned across the shoulders, but this get-up was far from warm, waterproof or any good at keeping out the blasted sand. Her Hunter wellies had sprung a leak and her left foot was squelching in a cold, damp sock. This was the least of her worries.

Lucien, the Neanderthal crane driver, in between leering looks, was being far too rough with the controls of the crane's extendable arm. He seemed to struggle to understand that this was an archaeological dig rather than some hole on a building site. The dig was of historical importance and if her research and calculations were correct, could prove to be the final resting place of the Luftwaffe's top twin-engine fighter ace of the Battle of Britain. *Hauptmann* Otto Werner was *Kommandeur* of ZG 26 and one of the first recipients of the Knight's Cross of the Iron Cross with Oak Leaves. He was personally responsible for destroying twenty-seven British and Allied aircraft, before his death in July 1940, a notable achievement since all of his victories were against single engine Spitfires and Hurricanes, rather than the multiple victories achieved later in the war by other Messerschmitt Bf 110 aces, taking down Allied bombers in a night fighter role.

Peering into the impressive hole, Melanie could see where the burning aircraft had impacted all those years ago. It had hit the ground at such a velocity that it burrowed a good fifteen feet, charring the sand and leaving a trail of black carbon through the pale granules. There shouldn't be much left of the Messerschmitt *Bf 110 Zerstörer* or Destroyer and yet, here it was, like some giant fossil of a flying pterodactyl or marine plesiosaur. It was huge, accommodating a two-man crew, armed with a 20mm cannon and machine guns to the front and rear. Twelve metres long compared to the Spitfire's eight, it had twice the wingspan and three times the weight, but for all that, it had still been reduced to this rusting wreck.

Melanie's deputy, Bobby Brown-Stuart perched precariously on the remains at the bottom of the pit. Above him, peering over the edge was the man from the French Ministry of the Interior, cold, windswept and thoroughly fed up. Clipboard in hand and *Gauloise* at his lip, there was no risk of him doing anything even vaguely helpful. He was simply satisfied with muttering to the gaggle of local functionaries and the site owner's minders who were gathered nearby.

'Just a bit lower, Mel,' said Bobby. 'Let me grab the chain and I'll try to get it around the fuselage. I'll hook it up behind the wing stubs.'

Melanie waved her hand at Lucien, indicating what she hoped he'd understand as 'low and slow.'

For once, he appeared to be concentrating on her hand signals rather than her rear end and the chain lowered inch by inch.

Bobby grabbed it with padded work gloves and using the slack, he looped the chain under the fuselage, clipping it up through a hinged D-ring. He indicated 'All stop. Hold tight,' then scrambled around the wreck, carefully loosening the crust of charred sand and debris that had embraced it for the last five decades. He had a shiny trowel in his hand, and it took a while before he was satisfied that no damage would occur to the fragile infrastructure as it was extracted. He clambered up an aluminium ladder, a look of sheer delight on his face. He was as excited as Melanie about this recovery.

Once clear of its damp grave, the wreck groaned as unfamiliar pressure bore on joints, bolts and welding unused to movement for years. The pair from the IWM held their breath as it slowly rotated, before emerging into the light.

Once clear of the surface, Lucien skilfully panned what looked like the carcass of an ancient dragon over to a large white tarpaulin pegged out on the windblown surface of the beach. Lumps of wet sand fell, splattering loudly and making them both jump. Melanie recognised the faded outline of the white *Hahn* or cockerel, emblem of the 9th *Staffel* on the aircraft's shattered nose. Down the side of the fuselage were the faint remains of the aircraft's identifier letters, and on the ragged tail assembly the stripes of several victory bars.

Melanie's breath quickened as she realised the evidence was mounting up. Her heart pounded as the rusting frame was lowered. The man from the Ministry leant forward, as Melanie turned to give Lucien the biggest smile she could muster. Against all expectations, he'd managed the extraction without damaging her precious cargo.

There was very little left of the aircraft's canopy. No struts, no Perspex, nor even the usual rear-facing MG 15 machine gun. Handled by the aircraft's *Bordfunker*, the radio man and air-gunner, it was usually there to pack a nasty punch to any attacker approaching from the rear. Here the *Bordfunker* in question was twenty-one-year-old *Gefreiter* Rudi Watmacher, who had jumped clear of the burning aircraft, landing in the dunes with burns and a shattered leg. He'd recovered and survived the war, going on to live in Leipzig as a cabinetmaker before finally succumbing to cancer the previous year at the age of 72. It was his testimony, recorded by the IWM, that had first indicated that the grave of his illustrious commander, *Hauptmann* Otto Werner, may not be in the depths of the English Channel, as had always been believed, but rather inland, here amidst the grassy dunes within the perimeter of the ArcelorMittal Steel works, west of Dunkirk.

The watching group stood back as the structure was lowered onto the tarpaulin. Peering into the rear cockpit, Melanie could see the soft materials of the seat had been destroyed by a combination of fire and the passage of time. She noted the rectangular slot that usually encased the rear gunner's parachute was empty, suggesting it hadn't burned in situ — in other words, it had been used before the crash.

Equally compelling was the debris in the forward cockpit. Whoever had flown here had not escaped and there was a good chance of finding identifying evidence amongst the black sludge on the cockpit floor. Melanie picked through it gingerly with the medical forceps she had clipped onto her overalls. Any items of potential interest were carefully bagged and labelled for later inspection. Amongst them were charred material and leather, fragments that looked like damp sticks but were possibly bone, and then small white pebbles, which on closer inspection were definitely teeth. The police would now have to be involved.

Melanie began to feel guilty about her ghoulish enthusiasm. Down the left side of the cockpit, she found a metal disc covered in cracked glass. She wiped it gently against the sleeve of her overalls, recognising the remains of a wristwatch. The hands and hour pips had been lost to the flames, but within the recessed date panel, the number 27 was clearly visible. Her heart leapt at this new piece of tangible evidence.

'Bloody hell, have a look at this, Bobby,' she said, holding it up with a trembling hand. They both knew *Gefreiter* Rudi Watmacher's aircraft was shot down on 27th July 1940.

Peering closely at the item in his palm, Bobby looked up with a beaming smile. 'It's a match, Mel. It's a bloody match!'

Her curiosity piqued, Melanie began to rummage furiously.

'Take it easy, Mel! We don't want to damage or miss anything important.'

'I'm sorry. You're right. I'm a bit over-excited,' she mumbled, continuing to search.

Amongst the debris of the left footwell, there was something wedged beneath a charred foot pedal. It was an unimpressive black Teutonic cross about two inches wide. She wiped it carefully to reveal the date 1939 and at its centre found the unmistakable sign of the swastika. The cross's edges were trimmed with rolled silver and across the top edge, there was a little loop attached to a bulbous shape. She gently brushed the finger of her glove across it, wiping away the accumulated soot to reveal the delicate shape of an oakleaf.

This was it! A Knight's Cross with Oak Leaves, *die Ritterkreuz des Eisernen Kreuzes mit Eichenlaub*. Originally created on 3rd June 1940, up until 15th July 1941 it was the highest military honour that could be bestowed upon any German serviceman. Ordinary Knight's Crosses had existed before and were highly prized, but the addition of the Oakleaves was the supreme honour and was closely associated with the Battle of France and the beginning of what the Germans called the *Kanalkampf*, and the British, the Battle of Britain.

There was no doubting now, this was *Hauptmann* Otto Werner's aircraft. She had found her missing ace, but that wasn't why the smile that lit up her face slowly dissolved as her eyes filled with tears.

This was a historically significant find but was also an important personal milestone for Doctor Melanie McNabb. The man who had inspired her from earliest childhood, telling her she could achieve anything she dreamt of, was undoubtedly looking down at her right now. To Melanie, he was Grandpa Bang-Bang, but to the rest of the world, he was Group Captain Jeremy A. E. McNabb GC, DSO, MC, DFC & Bar or more simply put, the legendary fighter ace Jox McNabb.

When still a pimply nineteen-year-old on 27th July 1940, he had battled for his life against an awesomely skilled and monstrously huge enemy, and then against all conceivable odds, the terrified boy had emerged victorious.

Her grandpa was never credited with this aerial victory, but Melanie knew it was a fight which had haunted his memory to the end of his days. The most terrifying contest in Jox McNabb's very long war.

CHAPTER ONE

Dollar, Scotland, June 1939

'This will not do, McNabb. Your time with us has been exemplary and Mr Mar tells me you've been a diligent house prefect, but this behaviour is completely unacceptable and cannot be tolerated. If it had been just you, a sixth former, letting off a little steam after the exams, we might have shown some latitude, but with inebriated younger boys involved, my hands are tied. I have no alternative but to send you down,' concluded the rector.

And that was it. Jox McNabb was expelled from the Dollar Academy, the school he'd attended since he was four years old. He'd never liked the place much, but it was the closest thing to a home he'd ever had. His mother had died when he was a boy and overcome with grief, his father had thought boarding school was the only way he could cope. Now he was a big noise in the Indian Civil Service, Jox knew him only as a rather cold and haughty man who saw his son as an irritant, a sad reminder of the past. He would certainly be unimpressed by his only son's expulsion, not least since their last exchange of letters had focused on his singular lack of ambition for the future.

It had started innocently enough. He, his friend Andy Allen and some of the other sixth form leavers had decided to sneak out of their boarding houses to meet up for a quick drink in one of the sleepy pubs, away from the town of Dollar in Clackmannanshire. After all, they would soon be men about town, most of them eighteen, and it was a perfect summer's evening, just two weeks before the end of term. He hadn't thought it was a great idea when a couple of fifth formers joined them, but he'd always liked Ralph Campbell, a lad in his boarding house, who was good for a laugh and was next year's cricket captain. For all his sporting prowess, though, Ralph proved no match for the couple of frothy pints they'd enjoyed in the beer garden overlooked by the Ochils, at the back of the Woolpack Inn in nearby Tillicoultry.

It was still light, not even nine, when they jogged back to Dollar in high spirits and probably making too much noise. Ralph giggled most of the way, but suddenly stopped, turned quite pale and then did just that, ralph. Anxiety levels rose immediately as they realised the young cricketer was paralytic and they'd have a job sneaking him back into the house unobserved. With scouts posted, a burly pair of them frog-marched him along, finally managing to get him tucked up in one of the locker rooms.

Leaving Ralph to sober up, they scattered to be as far away as possible if he got spotted, trusting the schoolboy code of honour that he would never 'clype' on the others.

It was only once all the miscreants were rounded up that Jox learnt of the path to his ruin. Ralph had been marched into the house master's front parlour and had promptly thrown up on a prized Paisley patterned carpet. After threats of losing his cricket captaincy were made, Ralph sang like a canary.

Which explained how Jox found himself in the rector's office the following morning, sweating alcohol from every pore, under the unwavering eye of the rector, Harry Bell OBE.

'Leading younger boys astray is quite unacceptable. Your time with us may be over, but I consider your behaviour in regard to young Campbell and the other boys as wilful sabotage of promising school careers and indeed their future prospects. Your father will have to be told and I will be drafting a telegram this afternoon. I understand you have an aunt in Stirling, Mrs Jane Easton, with whom you will be staying. I'm disappointed things have come to this, McNabb, and sincerely hope this unpleasantness will act as a shock and set you onto the right track. Your country and the empire needs educated young men with vigour, but always tempered with self-discipline and respect. I am assured you possess the former, but sadly not yet the rest. It is time for you to buck up!'

Jox was given until teatime to clear his lockers, pack up his trunk and have it ready for collection by the porter. Mr Mar would ensure he had a single fare train ticket to Stirling and enough pocket money for a hackney carriage at the other end. In the meantime, he was encouraged to say his goodbyes and bid a final farewell to the familiar grounds that had been part of his life for so long.

The rector escorted Jox down the stairs from his office to the impressive bronze doors through which all leavers left the Academy. Jox turned and shook hands with both Masters for the first and last time, and the bronze doors clanged ominously shut behind him.

Feeling pretty low, he slunk towards the school war memorial. Casting a final look back at the school, he wondered what the hell he was going to do.

Maybe the Navy? But as soon as the thought entered his head, he knew it was a non-starter. He'd got sick on the school fishing trip on Loch Leven and had always hated the interminable passenger liner journeys when visiting his father in India. Whenever he returned to school ill, people always thought it was some tropical disease, but it was seasickness which caused his pallor, rather than malaria, bilharzia or dengue fever.

'What about you?' Jox asked the pleading boy on the sandstone plinth of the memorial. 'What do you think I should do?' The youth looked beseechingly into the gloriously blue sky filled with fluffy white cumulus. 'What would you know? Look at where your advice led these poor fellows.'

Jox knew the names of all a hundred and eighty-three men listed on the monument by heart. All of the pupils did. The list was for the Argyll & Sutherland Highlanders, the regiment most closely associated with the school. He'd once written an essay about Lieutenant-Colonel Gavin Laurie Wilson, winner of the DSO at Ypres, the MC at the Somme and a *Croix de Guerre* and Palm from the grateful French, who died of Spanish flu at the age of twenty-four at the military hospital in Étaples. He was a local Tillicoultry boy with a father who was a Master at the school.

'What do you think, Gavin? You knew what you were about; a colonel at twenty-four.'

A throaty sound made Jox start. The beseeching look on the youth's face remained unchanged, as clouds slipped through his open fingers. Jox cocked his head as the noise grew louder and he turned to find it. He caught a movement between the statue's outstretched arms, as he recognised the distinctive sound of a Rolls-Royce Merlin engine.

Flying very low over the school was a Hawker Hurricane Mk.1. It swooped as the pilot tried to impress some schoolgirl sweetheart or perhaps amuse a younger sibling. The sight of an aircraft practising aerobatics in the summer skies above the school had become more frequent, a response to tensions following Mr Hitler's annexation of the Sudetenland last year and then the rest of Czechoslovakia, just a few weeks ago.

The aircraft was directly overhead and Jox ducked at the impressive roar. His mood lifted immediately, seeing the glorious warbird execute a breath-taking series of rolls to the delight of the boys and girls scattered across the playing fields. Others filed out from their classrooms to witness the display, all waving and cheering enthusiastically. The pilot waggled his wings and the bright sun reflected from the distinctive hump of his Hurricane. The engine backfired dramatically as he pulled up, then swooped back down over the school, to the delight of his young audience.

Jox's eyes didn't leave him for an instant. He felt his heart swell. Perhaps it was fate calling, but that was when he noticed, on either side of the red, white and blue RAF roundel, picked out in bright yellow, the aircraft's identifying letters: *JX-M*.

As in Jox McNabb!

He knew his destiny was set.

A few months later, Jox was in London, face to face with Patrick McGonigle, Chairman of the RAF Pilot Selection Board.

'Jeremy Argyll Easton McNabb, is it? Your school housemaster seems to think rather highly of you, Mr McNabb,' said McGonigle.

'Ah ... he does?' replied Jox, somewhat thrown.

'Well yes, I flew with Laurence during the last war. A very fine aviator. Transferred from Naval Air Service to join us in the Royal Flying Corps. You seem surprised.'

'No, sir. Mr Mar is an excellent English Master and I've learnt a great deal from him, but I ... ah ... wasn't aware he'd been asked to provide an opinion on my application.'

'We like to canvas views on our candidates,' said the chairman, peering through the gold-rimmed spectacles on the tip of his nose. 'It says here, "Jeremy is a lively young chap. Independently minded, non-conformist but bright, technically astute and an excellent role model to the younger boys. He's a fine rugby player and cricketer, an excellent shot who has competed for the school regularly at Bisley. He will undoubtedly do well in his Higher Examinations." There, what do you have to say?'

'Well, that's very kind of him, sir.'

'And how did you in fact fare in your exams?'

'Three As and five Bs, sir.'

'Maths and Sciences?'

'Yes, sir. All three and Maths. I got As in Biology, English and French.'

'*Vous parlez donc français?*'

'*Oui, monsieur, un peu.*'

'On your application here, you say, "I want to serve my country and explore the freedom of the skies." Are you a poet, McNabb? "I wandered lonely as a cloud" and all of that?'

'Well, no, not exactly sir,' replied Jox, his heart sinking as he was making such a mess of things. 'It's the freedom of solo flight which appeals to me. Being in control of my own destiny. I hoped my aptitude for mechanics and being a good shot might perhaps make fighters a good fit.'

'I see,' replied his inquisitor. 'You are aware that volunteering for the RAF, should you be successful, may well require going to war? It's no secret Germany is threatening Poland's sovereignty and should they attack, Great Britain and France will have no choice but to declare war. This is no "Boy's Own" adventure you're embarking upon; this is brutal bloody war.

Sadly, I speak with some experience of the carnage of the last war.'

'Yes, sir, I understand. I want to do my duty for my king and country.'

'Good lad. I see your father is in the India Office?'

'Yes, sir.'

'He supports your application, I presume? You do seem rather young to me.'

'Yes, sir, absolutely,' lied Jox.

'Well, thank you for your time, Mr McNabb. Please hand this slip to the sergeant outside. He will advise you of the arrangements. If you do see Laurence, please pass on the fondest regards of Paddy McGonigle and be sure to be grateful, my boy. Good day to you.'

Jox looked at the blue slip of paper in his hand, unsure of its significance. He stuttered, 'Yes, sir, I will, sir. Thank you. Good morning to you.'

The rest of the day was spent wandering the corridors of Adastral House in Kingsway and being prodded, evaluated and tested. Jox's principal recollection was of queuing up bollock naked as a succession of men with clipboards viewed the candidates from various angles. Once deemed physically fit, competent and FFI (Free From Infection; principally of the venereal kind), he was allocated a number, 41276, a pay book and an advance on his pay.

He was ordered to make his way to No. 18 EFTS (Elementary Flying Training School) at Fairoaks Aerodrome, near Woking in Surrey, during the last week of August 1939. The initial flight training for candidate aircrew had been outsourced to civilian aviation companies, in this case Universal Flying Services, since during the Great War the RAF had learnt the costly consequences of sending half-trained men to the front to learn flight skills at a squadron level. Volunteers would now learn to fly first on biplanes, taught by civilian instructors.

CHAPTER TWO

Sitting in the back of the jolting lorry which picked them up from Woking Station, Jox appraised the other four chaps he'd met at the station. George Milne was the son of a wealthy sheep farmer. He was tall and had big hands and a surprisingly feminine face, with big eyes, long eyelashes and a shy smile. He spoke quietly and had an accent from somewhere in the North of England. He appeared to be great chums with a cheeky chap called Morgan Chalmers, nicknamed Mogs, whose people owned coal mines in Northumberland.

Chalmers was shorter, with a big nose and reddish blond hair, and was full of energy and seemed a bit of a rascal. Sandy Bullough was the youngest of the group, younger even than Jox, and looked it. He was small, underweight and rather twitchy, with dark hair and teeth that were too big for his mouth. He came from South Africa and seemed very knowledgeable about what the next ten weeks would bring. He was the only member of the group with any actual flight experience, with his uncle apparently high up in the RAF and his family 'pillars of the Jewish community in Durban.' They also owned a biplane to fly on the weekends.

The last chap was called David Pritchard. He was a Londoner and had curly dark hair, blue eyes and a bristly square jaw, reminding Jox of Biggles, the flying comic book hero who was all the rage at school. Jox had always rather fancied himself as a bit of a James Bigglesworth character, since he too was born in India and was the son of an administrator in the Indian Civil Service, but sadly, compared to Pritchard he wasn't even close. Irritated, he was determined not to like him.

Pritchard didn't help the case by making them wait for him and then in a rush, hurling his canvas kitbag into the back of the lorry, winding Jox in the process. Adding insult to injury, he shoved up against him saying, 'Move over, shorty, big lad coming through. Sorry to keep you waiting, boys, I needed a pee.'

There weren't many things Jox was sensitive about, but one was perhaps his height. He wasn't tiny like Bullough, but he had to acknowledge he was shorter than many of his peers. He was stocky enough to be a useful hooker, but tall he wasn't. Otherwise, with straight brown hair, a pronounced widow's peak and pale green eyes, he held his own in the looks department, but this bloody Biggles-chap was in another league.

Jox tried to ignore him, but on the way up the road, he soon fell for the stream of jokes, tales and commentary delivered by Pritchard in an endearing mock-Cockney twang. He was a Londoner through and through, but from well-to-do Wimbledon and had been to school at King's College. A few years older than the rest, he was full of tales of West End girls, South London gangs and the year-long tour of Europe he'd just completed in his father's four and a quarter litre 1936 Bentley. He spoke of the 'black shirts' he'd seen in Italy, the torch-lit Nazi parades in Germany and the columns of exhausted blue-clad soldiers he'd seen marching along the tree-lined roads of France.

'These are interesting times, my boys, and I reckon we're heading for the best place to live them. Hold on tight and we'll be flying over momentous events,' he said with infectious enthusiasm.

Jox was excited by the prospect but wondered if he would be up to playing his part in what the gathering storm clouds of war promised. His thoughts darkened as they made their way through the woods of Horsell Common and approached the aerodrome. According to Sandy Bullough, who had all the gen, it was originally called Dolly's Farm when requisitioned by the Air Ministry in 1936. Out of a motley collection of fields and an old farmhouse, the airfield now had grown to two hangars, a control tower, some offices and a parachute tower. There were also workshop facilities and a flight of bright yellow Tiger Moths to provide elementary flight training for prospective RAF pilots.

'Gentlemen, let me speak plainly,' said the chief flying instructor in his welcome speech. 'You are not yet in the RAF, in spite of what your pay books may suggest. Some of you may make it, but others will not. Look around and ask yourselves whether you measure up.'

The sixteen of them eyed one another surreptitiously.

'You are probationary pupil pilots and have fifty hours of flying time on the DH 82 Tiger Moths parked outside to prove your worth. There will be lectures to attend, exams to pass and our expectation is that after ten hours of dual-control flight, you will fly solo. You will then use the balance of your flight time to gain experience and develop skills before your final tests. You will be evaluated weekly and there are final written examinations too. The weeding out process begins now and will be overseen by myself and the chief ground instructor, Mr Brownlea.' He indicated a rotund gentleman in tan overalls worn over a shirt and tie, with stern eyes and a piercing gaze. 'It will be our task to dispense the bowler hats to the least deserving amongst you.'

In the evening, back at their surprisingly luxurious accommodation at the nearby Ottershaw Park Estate, the gang assembled to discuss this peculiar reference to headwear.

'Don't you know anything about the service?' asked Bullough disparagingly. 'Being handed a bowler hat is RAF jargon for getting the boot and being sent back to civvy street.'

'Crikey,' said Pritchard. 'Doesn't bode well. Well, best of luck lads, I think we're going to need it.'

The following morning, they made their way on foot to their new home for the next ten weeks. The airfield was waking up to a new day and the smells, sounds and activity were exhilarating. Jox loved the heady combination of doped canvas, aviation fuel, oil, leather and exhaust fumes. The firing engines and spinning propellers pulsated in his ears. As he walked between the yellow Tiger Moth biplanes, his heart was thumping and he felt more excited than ever before. He knew he was embarking on a great and noble endeavour.

First, he was issued with his flying kit: overalls, a one-piece Sidcot padded flying suit, a leather helmet, split goggles and elbow high flying gauntlets. At least now he looked the part. Next, he was introduced to Newitt, his flying instructor, a short intense man with a thick moustache, a pipe and tatty RFC wings sewn onto a civilian jacket.

They circled his allocated aircraft with Newitt pointing out the flaps, ailerons and a flurry of other terms which went in and out of Jox's ears in short order. He explained how the controls on the Tiger Moth worked and the rudiments of flight.

'You pull the column back to climb,' said Newitt. 'Push forward to dive. This is how the rudder bar works. I will explain the effect of airflow over the wing surfaces and then what this allows you to do with the aircraft.'

Jox was given a parachute, had a five-minute chat about what to do in case of need — 'Jump, count to three, pull the ring,' — and was then told to hop into the back seat, and strap in for a spin. The propeller was swung by a mechanic and the engine coughed to life. As the aircraft gathered speed, it rattled and bumped along the grass runway, and Jox hung on, absolutely terrified.

I'll never get the hang of this, he thought. *Why did I think this was for me?*

The furious bumping and vibrations suddenly stopped. They had left the ground. Still terrified, he looked down and saw they were well and truly airborne. The ground receded and the sensation of travelling at speed vanished, as a breath-taking view unfolded before them. Far below were the leafy woods of Horsell Common, and in the mid-distance Chobham and further away Woking. They banked over Ottershaw Manor, beyond which he could see the smoky smudge of the outskirts of London. The sheer beauty of the landscape unfolding before him and this unfamiliar perspective on the world filled Jox with an exhilarating sense of independence. He knew this was his calling and now he just had to fulfil his potential.

A voice in the speaking tube interrupted his rapture. 'Not too shabby, eh? Not feeling ill? It's a lovely day for a spin,' said Newitt. 'Right then, if you're comfortable, let's see what you've got. I'll talk you through the controls, demonstrate what they do and then you'll have a go.' Newitt looked back at him and gave a thumbs-up.

Jox swallowed and nodded back.

'Take the stick gently and follow what I do. Note the effect which each action has on the aircraft. Try to feel it in your body, through your buttocks.'

Jox seized the stick and the plane juddered and dropped.

'Take it easy, lad! I said follow me through the stick, not wrestle the bugger off me! She's a flighty mare. Now calm down. Do things smoothly and gradually. Everything is slow, relaxed and in minute increments.'

This set the tone for the next several days. They were first applied to flying straight and level, then attempting take-off, followed by circuits of the airfield, then bumpy, often very bumpy landings. Jox was taught to spin, to avoid, then to deal with stalls. Next everything went back to the beginning, but this time with greater precision and instructor scrutiny. It was a steep learning curve, particularly when diving, looping and banking were added to the mix. Mistakes were common, and panic-inducing since the actions to retrieve a situation were often counterintuitive. Instinct snatched at the controls, causing overcorrections and any lapses in concentration could have lethal consequences.

Newitt repeatedly explained, 'The secret is to stay relaxed. Avoid any sudden movements and try to settle yourself into the fabric of the machine. Become part of it.'

Jox soon discovered Newitt's 'tell' for when he was feeling anxious. He would tersely address Jox as 'Mr McNabb,' but when relaxed a plume of blue smoke from his pipe blew back from the front cockpit. Jox would forever associate the smell of 'Mellow Virginia' with success.

The first bowler hat went to a chap called Llewellyn. Blond and pale, he was a nervous fellow, too heavy-handed with the controls. After three bone-crunching landings in a row, his instructor refused to continue and he was sent on his way.

The second sacking hit much closer to home. Their little gang from the lorry ride had become a tight clique, each with an unofficial role. David Pritchard was the joker and George Milne the earnest conscience of the group. Morgan Chalmers was the rascal, whilst Sandy Bullough was the insider and know-it-all. Finally, Jox was considered the fearless one, ready to take on any challenge. Unified by their ambition to become pilots, they had become a tight unit.

Which was why what happened to Bullough was such a shock. He was the one they all thought was a shoo-in to pass but was the first amongst them to be weeded out. He hadn't done well in the written assessments, thinking them all rather beneath him. His real downfall, though, was thinking he knew it all. This 'inability to take instruction' finished him off. One moment he was there, the next he was gone.

'You were warned this would be brutal,' said Mr Brownlea. 'More of you will fail than succeed. Mark my words and get on with it.'

After a particularly nauseating session of aerobatics with Newitt, they were practising recovery from spins and Jox was discovering the stomach-churning reality of aerial combat. They had practised several landings and take-offs in a row, when they pulled to the side of the taxiway.

'Feeling all right, Mr McNabb?'

Jox was instantly on edge, replying nervously, 'Yes, sir.'

'Don't switch her off. Put the brake on while I get out, then you take her up for a spin.'

He was going solo.

Newitt clambered out and stood back from the Tiger Moth, his hands on his hips. Jox trembled in the cockpit. His mouth was parched, and his mind had gone completely blank of everything he'd ever been taught. He didn't know how long he stared at the dials in terror but was shaken out of it by a punch to the shoulder and Newitt shouting over the noise of the engine, 'Get a bloody move on! I haven't got all day. Taxi out and line her up properly, then take her once around like we've just done. Bring her back in one piece. You can do it, lad. On you go.'

The Tiger Moth fish-tailed up the grass runway. Jox's take-off was ragged and bumpy. Once free from the ground, he rose smoothly and swung around the airfield as he had dozens of times before. His landing was rather heavy and involved three thumping bounces, but with a flick of the stick, he got her down.

He taxied shakily back to the apron where Newitt was waiting and gave him the thumbs-up. Jox switched off, clambered from the cockpit and slung his parachute over his shoulder. Newitt had a grin on his face, his pipe in his mouth and his hand extended towards Jox. They shook and walked to the crew room, where Newitt would sign his logbook to confirm his solo.

They entered the hut in high spirits, but found the others clustered silently around the wireless. The clock on the wall ticked past eleven in the morning.

'What's going on?' asked Jox.

'Shut up! Just listen,' replied Pritchard.

A well-spoken voice came over the scratchy airwaves. Jox recognised the 'received pronunciation' of Prime Minister Neville Chamberlain.

'I am speaking to you from the cabinet room at 10 Downing Street. This morning the British ambassador in Berlin handed the German government a final note stating that unless we heard from them by eleven o'clock, that they were prepared at once to withdraw their troops from Poland, a state of war would exist between us.'

The anxious listeners glanced at each other nervously.

'I have to tell you now that no such undertaking has been received, and that consequently this country is at war with Germany.'

CHAPTER THREE

Jox had forgotten how bloody cold Scotland could get, especially this windswept corner of east Forfarshire, exposed to the very worst of the November gales rolling straight in from the North Sea. RAF Montrose at Broomfield Farm was about the bleakest spot to learn advanced flying as you could possibly choose. Officially No. 8 Service Flying School, when Jox and his companions arrived from sunny Fairoaks in leafy Surrey, the prospect of flying at this 'dreich' field, buffeted by wind and rain was far from inviting.

'Aye, Baltic right enough,' said the corporal at the gate.

To the blue-lipped, numb-toed acting pilot officers it might as well have been Mars. Jox, the Scotsman amongst them, was expected to know his way around, but was as lost, wet and thoroughly dejected as the rest.

Only nine of the original sixteen had made it through solo flight to pass the twenty-two 'air experience' stages required to complete 'Elementary Training.' They had then spent two weeks at RAF Uxbridge, west of London, enduring hours of drill, physical fitness training and lectures on the short illustrious history of the RAF. These were followed by classes on the administrative duties and protocols expected of prospective RAF officers.

Jox took to the marching, polishing and discipline well enough, since in truth it wasn't so different from school. He'd been issued with a rough woollen blue uniform, a pair of shiny black boots, a web belt and a forage cap with a white band. He felt hungry all the time, generally lacked sleep and slowly became irritated by the belligerent nature of the training cadre, but knew better than to open his mouth.

They were led by a Cockney flight sergeant, whose words of welcome had not boded well. 'Right, you 'orrible little 'erks. Since we are at war, the RAF has deemed you have what it takes to become officers and gentlemen. I for one cannot see it, particularly since it's taken me twelve years to earn these 'ere stripes and crown on my arms. You will therefore understand I am hardly impressed that you rabble are already sergeants. Over the next few weeks, it will be my task — alongside my staff, real corporals and sergeants, mind — to ensure you earn those bloody stripes. And believe you me, they will be bloody!'

And they were, but at least the torment didn't last too long. It was a rite of passage to be endured and with the war looming, suffering in common did much to bring the recruits together. There were lighter moments too, for example when bespoke tailors arrived to measure the fledgling pilots for their officers' uniforms. The rough old airmen's blues were soon to be replaced with tailor-made slate-blue uniforms fit for officers and gentlemen. In addition, as Uxbridge was one of the RAF's larger stations, they were allowed access to the excellent officers' mess, leading to well-lubricated laughter-filled evenings spent together.

When their postings were finally announced, by some miracle, Jox's little gang of David Pritchard, George Milne and Morgan Chalmers were all assigned to No. 8 Service Flying School at RAF Montrose in Scotland. The four of them were to be joined for the trip north by Roy 'Digger' Callendar, a jovial Australian, and Maurice 'Moose' Grant, a dark-haired giant from Ontario, Canada.

Just before the train journey via London, their new uniforms were delivered, still devoid of coveted wings but with a thin pilot officer's stripe at the sleeve.

Feeling rather smart and with a new-found swagger, the gang boarded at King's Cross through clouds of swirling steam and the stink of burning coal. They were in a single compartment and settled down for what was going to be a long journey, especially with 'phoney war' anxieties over enemy attacks on rail and transport hubs. When the chatty ticket inspector checked their travel warrants, he was respectful of their new uniforms, but warned of delays due to 'shenanigans' up the line. He saluted them, like the old soldier he undoubtedly was, saying, 'My apologies, sirs. I'm afraid it's the war.' He added sadly, 'Christ, I never thought I'd have to say that again in my lifetime. My heart goes out to you. Bless you and God speed.'

Jox felt like a fraud and was embarrassed to be called sir by someone older than his father. It was an uncomfortable novelty, but made him wonder what the future had in store for his little gang of chaps.

No one was expecting them when they finally arrived at the airfield. It took the corporal of the guard quite a while to find anyone willing to take responsibility for the new arrivals. In the meantime, they stood out in the rain, self-conscious in their sodden new uniforms, no longer 'glamour boys' but rather drowned rats.

They were surrounded by vintage hangars from the Great War, which they later discovered were known as 'Major Burke's sheds', named for the airfield's first CO. Made of slatted wood, they formed a semi-circle facing the beach and the North Sea. In sunnier climes, this coastline might have been inviting, but here it was flat, windswept and bleak.

RAF Montrose was the oldest military airfield in Scotland, created in 1912. It had two track runways which crossed over and a taxiway roughly in the shape of a sock, its heel to the sea. There were newer steel-clad hangars with tall sliding doors, plus maintenance sheds and a control tower creaking in the buffeting wind. Invisible from above were deep bomb shelters, hidden ammunition stores and a network of concrete pillboxes dotting the beach front, defences against seaborne and airborne threats. This was home for No. 8 Service Flying Training School (FTS), as well as No. 269 Maritime Patrol Squadron, who were rotating out and No. 603 (City of Edinburgh) Squadron due in from January.

The training school was equipped with Avro Ansons for twin engine instruction and North American Harvard Mark 1s for single engine fighter training. When leaving Uxbridge, those selected for fighter training were grouped together: Jox, David Pritchard, Maurice Grant, George Milne, Morgan Chalmers and Roy Callendar.

Chalmers teased Grant, saying, 'Look at the bloody size of you! How on earth are you going to fit into a fighter? Now me, I'm perfectly proportioned to be a fighter pilot, but how's a big lunk like you going to manage? Makes no bloody sense!'

'Don't worry about me, little man,' replied the placid Canuck. 'Concentrate on getting through the next phase of training. Think of the poor chaps who didn't make it and were sent home. We're lucky to still be in it. I reckon things will get a whole lot tougher and the pressure's on. To the RAF we're still civilians and have sixteen weeks to prove ourselves. That's what you should focus on.'

After a good hour exposed to the worst of the elements, the new arrivals were taken in hand by an unsmiling warrant officer whose Scots accent was incomprehensible even to Jox. They were marched off in squelching parade shoes to a metal hangar, then told to wait.

Almost immediately, they were startled by the WO's snarl: 'Attention! Get on yer feet, you bleeding shower. Station Commander on parade.'

An older gentleman with neat grey hair introduced himself as Wing Commander Robertson. He had RFC wings on his tunic and medal ribbons from the Great War and Colonial service across the Empire. He spoke through a peppery moustache which curled up at the tips, but seemed to struggle to stand still, with a stooped back obviously giving him trouble. In his speech he covered what they should expect from the forthcoming weeks and what would be required of them. It flowed from a stern welcome to a more encouraging pep-talk. He spoke with candour, integrity and a deep understanding of the subject matter. He concluded by asking for their dedication and wished them well.

'Good intentions, enthusiasm and rigour will take you a long way, gentlemen, but be vigilant at all times. Our weather here is treacherous. The cemetery at Sleeping Hillock is filled with airmen who trained here during the last war and this. I received a letter from an American pilot the other day, who trained here in 1918, recalling, "a crash every day and a funeral every week". So be warned, the wind is unforgiving and you are learning your craft on unfamiliar steeds. Be very careful, my boys. We need you to stay in one piece to face our enemies. Thank you and my very best wishes.'

After a hot meal and a change of clothing, Jox was allocated a warm room with Pritchard, and it wasn't too long before he started feeling human again. Sleep eluded him, though, with his mind racing, anxious about what the new day would bring.

When Jox joined the others for a hearty breakfast of porridge and eggs, Chalmers and Milne were squabbling as usual. To interrupt them, Jox said, 'George, why did you sign up?'

'I dunno.'

'Well, I was disappointed in love,' declared Callendar unexpectedly. 'Yeah, bit of a cliché, but the girl I was gonna marry decided she preferred someone else. I had a great engineering job in Sydney and we were all set for a life together, when she decided I wasn't exciting enough and ran off with some bloke in the Navy. It was the flashy uniform, I reckon.' He laughed bitterly. 'Right, I thought, I'll show her. What's the most glamorous thing I could think of? Becoming a pilot, I reckoned, so I did my basic back in Oz, then hopped on the boat to Blighty to be here with you blokes. Apart from the weather, I'm delighted to be here. Not keen on this cold, mind.'

'That's as good a reason as any, Roy,' Milne said. 'I'm just a farmer who loves this land. Our land. I'll probably end up doing the same as my old dad and my uncles, working with the sheep, but before then I wanted to see the world a bit. Defend our country if needs be, and fight for the right to live how we want. I don't know too much about these Nazi fellows, but I'm told they're keen on bossing others about, so it's a good enough reason for me to stop them. If I'm going to fight, though, I won't be doing it down in the mud like in the last war. I'll do it up here.' He pointed a long finger at the leaden skies outside the window. 'That's me. What about you, Jox?'

Jox sighed. 'I'm here rather by accident. Got thrown out of school for something silly and was facing a world of recriminations from my father. I needed a plan for my life, when frankly I just didn't have one. I looked up and saw the answer. I'd become a pilot in the Royal Air Force. No one could ever say I wasn't good enough then. Not my father, not anyone. Sounds rather silly saying it out loud, but there you have it.'

'If you think that's daft, listen to this,' said Pritchard. 'I've spent the last year gadding about Europe, having the time of my life. No real plan, simply thankful to have the funds to enjoy myself. I know I'm fortunate and rather entitled, but hey, not my fault.' The tone of his voice suddenly changed. 'But I saw some frightening things in Europe. Aggression and soldiers everywhere. Bullies shouting and mindless oppression. The people here at home really have no idea what's happening over there. The French have been mobilising for a while, but we're still dawdling. You only need to read the headlines to see what Germany is up to.'

'What about you, Mogs?' asked Milne, turning to Chalmers.

'You know my story, Georgie, but I don't mind telling the fellows,' Chalmers replied. 'My people own coal mines. Essential industries, you see. Like old George, I'm pretty much expected to follow in their footsteps, but unlike him, I hate it. Can't think of anything worse than spending a lifetime down those filthy tunnels, building grimy pit towers and worrying about shifts, wages, output and things like that. I want to be free, up in the air, doing something exciting. Maybe I'm just being selfish, but I want to do something for myself.'

'I don't reckon it's selfish to put your life on the line for your country,' said Grant in his deep, accented baritone. 'My father came to Canada from the old country when he was young. He made a life for himself, a good life with my mother, a *Métis*, but he never forgot where he came from: Kilmarnock in Scotland. He returned only once, during the last war with the Canadian Expeditionary Force. He fought at Vimy Ridge and Passchendaele. My father came when the old country called and brought me up to do the same. You've called again and my duty was to come. That's all I've got to say about that.'

'Crikey, Chief. I had no idea,' said Chalmers.

The big man's eyes flared. In a slow, even voice, he said, 'Don't call me that, little man. I don't like it. You call me Moose; I'm big enough and I don't mind.'

'I didn't mean to upset you.'

'You didn't upset me. I'm just saying it like it is.'

After breakfast, they were issued a new flying kit. Everything had an added level of technical sophistication compared to Fairoaks. The soft leather flying helmet had a face mask wired with a microphone and plug-in leads, the flying gloves were silk-lined, the flying overalls and padded Sidcot suit were a good, comfortable fit and even the boots were soft and snug.

After being given parachutes, the recruits were taken to the training block where a pile of books awaited each of them, as well as a locker in the crew room. They were then told to form up outside the block, to meet Flying Officer Brian Carbury, a RNZAF officer, who was to be their Flight Commander. He was attached to No. 603 (City of Edinburgh) Squadron, an Auxiliary Air Force unit, as their training officer, tasked with bringing the 'weekend warriors' up to speed. He would also be overseeing their training flight's progress. He was a Spitfire pilot, an experienced flight instructor and an expert in the modern RAF's fighter doctrine.

'I firmly believe in a tight formation flying to ensure mutual protection. I also value individual aerobatic skills, to get you out of trouble should you need it, but close formation flying will be the norm. We will teach you the art of deflection shooting, to deliver the killer blow when required. So far, you have focused on learning to survive flight; now you must learn to make your aircraft into an offensive weapon. My task is to evaluate your progress, trying to get as many of you as I can over the finishing line. Teaching and training will be up to your individual instructors, who you will meet shortly. I wish you good fortune, gentlemen.'

A softly spoken voice asked from behind Jox's back, 'Are you Mr McNabb, sir?'

Jox turned to find a stocky, bull-necked man with weary sky-blue eyes. He had an Edinburgh accent, large rough hands, bandy legs and dark hair with a pronounced bald patch.

'Yes, sir. That's me,' replied Jox.

'You don't call me "sir". I'm Flight Sergeant Waugh. I'll be your instructor at No. 8 FTS.'

'Good morning, sir,' spluttered Jox. 'Very nice to meet you.'

'No, no. I call you sir. You call me Flight Sergeant or just Flight. Are we clear, sir?'

Jox nodded, not trusting himself to get it right.

Waugh sighed in a way that said he'd seen it all before. His pale gaze and the crow's feet spreading across weather-chapped cheeks, spoke of years in open cockpits around the world. Jox knew he could learn a lot from this man, who held his fate in his hands.

'Right, let's go have a gander at your Harvard,' said Waugh, setting off without waiting for an answer.

Lined up outside the hangar, a shiny line of sleek mono-winged North American Harvard trainers waited.

'This is a much faster, more modern and advanced aircraft than you are used to. She has a retractable undercarriage, flaps and a constant speed airscrew.' Waugh was throwing a baffling array of jargon at Jox. 'It's pleasant enough to fly, but has to be treated with respect, especially at lower speeds and of course in this wind.'

Jox instantly felt intimidated by the stubby, pugnacious stance of the aircraft. It was a menacing scrapper which looked like it wanted to take a chunk out of him.

'Come on, then, hop into the front,' said Waugh.

As Jox clambered into the roomy cockpit, he was confronted by a bewildering array of dials and switches, warning lights with taps and knobs.

Waugh's quiet voice came through the earphones of his flight helmet: 'It looks rather complicated, but you'll get a hang of it. It's a bit gusty today, so I'll do most of the flying. You just listen and follow what I'm saying. It's important you pay attention,' he stressed. 'The Harvard has killed a lot of people. You've got to respect it. She bites and will sort the boys from the men. Now, d'you think you can handle it?'

'Yes, Flight Sergeant,' Jox answered warily.

'Well, let's see about that, laddie.'

CHAPTER FOUR

The pace set during No. 12 Training Course was relentless, and the struggle to fly against the merciless wind was soul-sapping and utterly terrifying. Back in Surrey they'd been patronised, treated like schoolboys, but here it was up to them to learn, develop, execute and survive.

There were new faces to get to know, amongst the forty or so beginning the course. Split into two groups, Jox and Pritchard were in A Flight, the other Fairoaks graduates in B. Amongst their new course mates was a short, taciturn Irishman, who had grown up in Richmond, so correspondingly had the same 'sarf' London accent as Pritchard. His name was Brendan Finucane, rather predictably known as Paddy. A good-looking chap, he had crinkly dark hair parted in the centre. In lessons, he was strong at mathematics and aviation theory, but had a tendency for heavy-handedness with his flight controls.

This was in stark contrast to Andrew Salvesen, known to everyone as Sally, the aristocratic scion of a wealthy Edinburgh family, who was a superb technical pilot. At first, he seemed somewhat haughty and aloof, but the class came to realise this was just a cover for his shyness. He soon proved a very useful pal indeed, given his many connections with the well-to-do families of Forfarshire, especially those with daughters with an eye out for bachelor aviators.

There was also tall Tom Neil, who, with his shock of red hair, soon became known as Ginger. Ginger was a trainee bank clerk from Bootle, near Liverpool, with a quick wit and a knowing grin on his face. Completing the group was Jack

Benzie, a charismatic ex-infantryman from Winnipeg, Canada, who had learnt to play the bagpipes as a 'pongo' and often played at parties.

They were a close-knit mob and soon became firm friends, all depending on each other to scrape through the ordeal of earning their coveted wings.

Jox had his first real fright at seven thousand feet. Told to practise 'recovery from a stall', he knew the theory of what to do by heart. Check the sky was clear, including down below. Ease the stick forward towards the dashboard, apply opposite-rudder, throttle back then raise the nose up to the stalling point. Then to recover, apply full rudder, get the nose down then throttle up the power and as air speed increases, level the aircraft off.

That particular spring morning, the wind was howling from the North Sea and unbeknownst to Jox, he was actually flying sidewise almost as fast as he was moving forwards. When his engine failed to restart, he faced the prospect of a glider landing in horizontal wind.

Attempting his first approach, metallic fear rose in his throat and his pulse pounded in his temple as he strained at the stick, trying to keep the aircraft level as it was buffeted by the fierce wind. He looped around the field a second time and could hear sand from the beach lashing against the Harvard's metal skin, like the drum roll before an execution.

He finally came down with a gut-wrenching thump, the Harvard skidding sideways before trundling off the runway and grinding to a bumpy stop on a grassy apron of sand.

Jox slumped in the cockpit, drenched with sweat and knowing full well it had been a damned near thing. He had very nearly bought it, but what horrified him the most was the speed at which things had gone wrong; he'd moved from being in control to utterly helpless. Nothing, he realised, could be taken for granted in aviation.

It was a failure which stung for a while, but with it, Jox felt his ability grow and eventually his confidence. His classmates found the going tough too, and every few days another disappeared, his services 'no longer required'. It was the sight of one of the other A Flight candidates, sitting in his civilian clothes, tears streaming down his cheeks as he waited for transport to town, which put a spectral face on a fate more terrifying to Jox than any danger lurking in the skies.

It was a relentless weeding out process which continued through the early spring of 1940, as the 'phoney war' began to warm up. On an unusually balmy February afternoon, A Flight worked through equations with their books, whilst B Flight looped the airfield in their Harvard Mark 1s. The throb of the engines overhead, the ticking of the crew room's iron stove and the kettle hissing to the boil were all soporific. It was a sudden change in the pitch of the sounds which made Jox glance up from the tedium of his textbook. A louder rumble had him lurching up from his chair and running through the door of the Nissen hut. Outside, barely two hundred yards away, he was stunned to see a Harvard on its belly, broken-backed, with black smoke billowing and flames licking at its engine. Her propeller had scoured deep rents in the concrete landing strip, like the curved black talons of a downed fire-breathing dragon.

Through the clear glass of the cockpit, Jox made out a shadowy form, struggling at the latticed hatchway. The figure managed to get it open, unbuckling his safety belt to tumble from the burning aircraft. Unconscious on the runway, he lay crumpled and still as a pool of aviation fuel caught fire before Jox's eyes.

Jox sprinted towards the crash scene, running straight into the flames to tug at the comatose airman, trying desperately to pull him from harm's way. He struggled with the man's weight, seeing that below the line of his goggles, his face was already badly burnt. His own hands were now alight as he heaved the dead weight clear of the flames.

Jox smothered the man's smouldering flying suit with his bare hands, his blistered fingers in agony when he lifted the airman's goggles. He recognised George Milne's cow-like eyelashes instantly. They were untouched by the flames, unlike the rest of his scorched body. Jox cradled his friend in his arms, rocking him gently as a clanging fire truck and ambulance screeched to a stop.

Milne died of his burns two days later. He was the first member of No. 12 Training Course to perish, but it was unlikely he would be the last. He had left their little gang of close friends but would sadly never be leaving Montrose. His funeral was at the Sleeping Hillock Cemetery, where he joined dozens of other airmen from this war and the last who'd met a similar fate, forlorn victims of the sea and her murderous wind.

The whole class and many of their instructors attended, Jox standing with his burnt hands wrapped in white linen. He felt very conspicuous as the class stood to attention and saluted. Jack Benzie played 'Flowers of the Forest' as a piper's lament. George Milne's family were all there, his father and numerous uncles, older but otherwise identical versions of their lost boy. These were uncomplicated men of the land, heartbroken by their loss, but sadly all too familiar with the cost of conflict, having lived through the bloody trenches of the last war.

Milne's mother and sister were crushed but stoic, putting on brave faces as they approached Jox and his devastated course mates. Morgan Chalmers, George Milne's best friend, had been flying on Milne's portside when the Harvard unexpectedly dropped to the ground. His was a grandstand view of his friend's death, just moments after speaking to him on the R/T. He sobbed in the arms of big Moose Grant.

'Pilot Officer McNabb,' said George Milne Senior. 'I wanted to thank you for your efforts in trying to save my son. May I shake the hand of a brave man?'

Jox raised his bandage, embarrassed, but dreading the farmer's firm handshake on his burns.

'Oh, I'm sorry,' said the older man. He stood bewildered for a moment, the vitality which Milne had inherited from him, draining away with grief. Jox hesitated before gently wrapping his arms around him. Milne's father began to cry, and Jox could feel the man's sobs through his solid farmer's shoulders. Jox was ill equipped to provide comfort to someone so clearly his senior.

'Come on now, Daddy,' said Milne's sister with a sad smile. 'You mustn't hurt Pilot Officer McNabb any more than he already is.' She had the same eyes as Milne, but on her feminine face they were things of beauty. George Milne Senior was ushered away by one of his brothers as she addressed the group. 'My brother Georgie thought very highly of you gentlemen. His letters were full of chatter about Mogs and Jox, Pritchard and Moose. He was particularly fond of you, Pilot Officer Chalmers.' Chalmers hid his face deeper in Moose's shoulder. 'I'm sorry, I don't mean to upset you.'

She smiled sadly, reaching into her coat pocket to retrieve a leather-bound notebook. 'I don't know if you knew this, but Georgie was a poet. He was very shy about it, but I'd like to read you something I found. It's for all of you, but especially for his dear friend Morgan the Rascal.'

She opened a marked page and began to read:

'If this day is when I die,
Remember me if you're still breathing,
I want a party at my wake,
No bawling, no greeting.
The tears on your faces must not be my fault,
And if I've gone before my years,
Let my brothers stand tall,
For this man's life was no cause for tears.
Laugh, my friends, and maybe cheer,
And think of old George who paid the price,
And I'll be laughing too,
Up here in rascal's paradise.'

She closed the notebook. 'I just wanted to say, my brother never felt more alive than when he was with you boys. He wouldn't want his passing to stop you from completing your task. You will be defending our nation soon; the protective shield against whatever evil may come. I need you to take my brother's place on those ramparts, and I expect each and every one of you to do it for my sweet darling Georgie.'

She approached Jox and fixed him with her gaze. 'Thank you, Pilot Officer McNabb, for what you did. Your flight leader, Flying Officer Carbury, told me your actions were foolish but incredibly brave. You're the bravest man I've ever met.' She reached her hand up and gently touched his face. She kissed his cheek and whispered, 'Thank you.'

Jox felt a lump of raw emotion in his throat. 'It was nothing, Miss Milne.'

'No, it was very much something, and please, I'm Alice, just Alice.'

CHAPTER FIVE

The first week of April 1940 was notable for two reasons. Across the frigid North Sea, the invasion of Norway began, with German forces landing at several Norwegian ports and swiftly capturing Oslo. At the same time, Denmark was also invaded and fell within six hours.

It was also the day when Jox and the surviving candidates of No. 12 training course reached the qualifying point in their advanced flying training. The occasion was marked by them receiving their RAF Pilot Wings; a brevet worn above the left tunic pocket of their uniforms. It was a machine-embroidered badge consisting of a pair of outstretched wings, a bit like those of a seagull, supporting a golden wreath encircling the RAF monogram, beneath the king's white crown and all stitched onto a black fabric backing. It was a simple enough thing, but represented the highpoint of their nascent military careers, after many months of study, intense concentration, anxiety and fear. It was in effect the announcement to the world that they were RAF pilots and could proudly wear these wings on their uniforms evermore. It was a big day but was tinged with sadness for those lost along the way.

For the first time in his life, Jox had achieved something entirely on his own. The intensity of the pride he felt when stepping forward to have the wings pinned to his chest by Wing Commander Robertson, RAF Montrose's Commanding Officer, surprised him. The CO shook his hand, leaning his creaky back towards Jox with obvious discomfort. A stiff smile appeared beneath his peppery moustache.

'You'll do, McNabb,' muttered Robertson.

Beside him stood their course leader and chief instructor, Flying Officer Brian Carbury with a self-satisfied look on his face. He nodded, his angled forage cap accentuating the movement. Over the last few months, this Kiwi officer had earned quite a reputation, not only for training No. 603 (City of Edinburgh) Squadron to combat-worthiness, but also for damaging a He 111 bomber in December and then destroying another east of Aberdeen in March. He was the model of a fighter pilot they all aspired to become.

Later, during the celebration in the mess, Jox was keen to catch the one man he most wanted to show his new wings to. Flight Sergeant Waugh was a guest of the mess for the celebration and silently sidled up to Jox, catching him unawares as usual. For the first time, Waugh was grinning. He still looked world-weary, but his sky-blue eyes glistened with pleasure. 'Congratulations sir. I'm pleased to have played my small part in getting you there.'

'You did a lot more than that. I'd be a wash-out if it wasn't for you. I'll always be grateful for your patience, Flight Sergeant Waugh,' beamed Jox.

'Ah, and there you have it,' replied Waugh. 'If I may give you a wee bit of advice, sir. Patience is exactly what you need if you're going to survive the coming storm. You have talent but must take the time to hone your skills. Be patient. A good fighter pilot must remain detached and calm. Haste, urgency and anxiety is what gets you killed. Professionalism and determination are the answers. Promise you'll work on it at your operational squadron.'

'Squadron assignments? We've not heard anything yet, Flight.'

'Oh, I think you'll be finding out soon enough. You've got yourself a cracking assignment, Mr McNabb.' He leant in conspiratorially. 'For me, flying the Hurricane is the pick of the bunch. There's an awful fuss made about those Spitfires, but I'll take the solid old Hurricane any day. Learn to handle that bird and she'll take care of you, getting you in and out of trouble all day long. The best of luck, sir.'

Hurricanes! Jox felt like he'd been whacked with a cricket bat. Months earlier, it had been the sight of a lone Hurricane swooping over his school that had inspired him to act. Now, he was on the cusp of climbing into one of his own. He needed to tell someone, anyone. He searched the assembled crowd of instructors and pupils and saw Moose towering above the others. Jox pushed his way towards the big Canuck, when he caught sight of Pritchard barrelling towards him. He was somewhat 'over-refreshed' and before Jox could react, his Cockney chum said, 'We're going sarf, mate! Leaving this bloody weather and heading home, Jox.'

'What are you talking about?'

'You haven't seen the notice board, have you? Squadron assignments are up. You and I are heading south with No. 111 Squadron. They're based at Wick, covering Scapa Flow, but thank God they are moving soon.' Pritchard was overjoyed, but it was unclear if he was delighted at the prospect of flying Hurricanes or the thought of escaping Montrose's diabolical weather.

The Treble Ones were the RAF's first squadron to fly the Hawker Hurricane and were recognised as masters at it. Flight Sergeant Waugh was right, it was a peach of an assignment. *Christ*, thought Jox nervously, *this is all getting rather real.* His excitement was tinged with an odd sinking feeling in the pit of his stomach.

The Treble Ones' recent CO, Squadron Leader Harry 'Broady' Broadhurst had recently been promoted to Wing

Commander at Training HQ for 11 Group, covering Greater London. His erstwhile squadron were following him south. Broady had famously opened the squadron's war tally by shooting down a Heinkel 111 on 29th November 1939. That was just a short month after the very first enemy aircraft brought down on Scottish soil by Archie McKeller of No. 602 (City of Glasgow) Squadron in October. At the time much was made of the downing of a He 111 bomber, the number being interpreted as a good omen.

The furore raised by Pritchard attracted Moose's attention. The big man parted the celebrating airmen like a snow plough through ice. He wrapped long arms around his friends. 'You boys sure are lucky, hey? Posted together. Good for you, fellas, I'm really pleased.' A mischievous grin spread across his chiselled features. 'Old Moose won't be too far away, though. I'm going to RAF Middle Wallop to fly Hurricanes too, before joining a new Canadian Squadron, No. 1 RCAF. We're all going to be flying Hurricanes, boys.'

The rest of the evening was spent discovering each other's assignments. Paddy would fly Spitfires with No. 65 Squadron at Hornchurch. As expected, Sally joined No. 603 in his hometown of Edinburgh on Spits too. Ginger was Hurricane-bound with No. 249 (Gold Coast) Squadron at RAF Church Fenton, as was Jack, but with No. 242 Squadron, there were mostly Canadians led by the formidable Squadron Leader Douglas Bader.

Most were happy with where they were being sent and it was generally accepted that those heading to squadrons in the south were fortunate, since they had more chance of action.

Others were less than delighted with their assignments. Pilot Officers Roy Callendar and Morgan Chalmers were posted to

No. 504 (County of Nottingham) Squadron based at RAF Wick, sixteen miles from frozen John O' Groats. They were determined to drown their sorrows and their enthusiasm for the task became infectious, with the evening developing into one of the most memorable and riotous parties ever enjoyed in RAF Montrose's wind-battered Officers' Mess.

The next day, all nursing fearsome hangovers, they were brought down with a bump with news of the Battle for Narvik. The wireless spoke of losses, a sobering thought as British forces landed at several sites and were heavily engaged by the enemy on land.

The goodbyes between men who had shared so much over the past few months was never going to be easy. They promised to stay in touch but knew the camaraderie of the course was being scattered to the four winds. They had survived the sodding system and appalling weather, though, to qualify as RAF pilots. The hangovers didn't help, but no-one really wanted to prolong the agony of parting. They left in ones and twos, a little depressed.

Chalmers was accompanied by his new best friend and No. 504 Squadron mate, Digger, who was rather green-faced as they approached.

'We'll be seeing you, boys. Think of us when you're out in London. Keep in touch. You know the address: RAF in the frozen middle of bloody nowhere.'

'It'll be all right,' said Digger. 'Tell you what, mate, let's make a little bet on who sees a whale first. Or maybe a U-boat. What do you think? The winner gets a bottle of whiskey. I'll bet a bottle of my Irish against your Scotch. How do you fancy that, Mogs?'

'It's a bet, Digger, my old friend,' replied an equally pasty, but game Chalmers.

'Let's meet up soon, Moose,' said Jox to the approaching Canuck.

'That would be great; just give me a couple of weeks to recover. I feel bloody awful.'

'I must admit, you don't look too clever,' said Jox. 'You'll be all right, though. In fact, we're all going to be fine. You know why? Because we bloody made it, boys. Now it's Jerry's turn to watch out.'

CHAPTER SIX

Jox and Pritchard arrived at RAF Northolt at South Ruislip, west of London, after an exhausting journey of road and rail trips. Northolt was one of the RAF's most important fighter airfields, with a brand new and 'forgiving' eight-hundred-yard-long concrete runway. The base was considered the centre of excellence for conversion onto Hurricanes and had been built beside a suburban neighbourhood. The expanse of the airfield and dispersal buildings were cunningly camouflaged to look like the nearby housing. There was even a fake stream painted across the main runway and hangars disguised as houses, gardens and allotments. At ground level the effect was quite comedic, but many aviators discovered to their chagrin that finding Northolt from the air was often a challenge, especially when obscured by cloud cover.

A number of famous pilots and squadrons were stationed at the airfield and as newly winged Pilot Officers, Jox and Pritchard felt very much at the bottom of the pile. They were paid the princely sum of fourteen shillings a day, six of which were deducted for food, lodging, laundry and the services of a long-suffering batman. The pair shared the services of Corporal Higgins, an aged native of Birmingham, who never seemed to be about when needed, but was supercilious and ingratiating the rest of the time. He did, however, know his way around the airfield and was a good deal better informed than the hapless newcomers.

RAF Northolt was serving as a makeshift OTU (Operational Training Unit), fast-tracking newly qualified pilots to gain a maximum number of hours before joining their operational squadrons, in their case No. 111 Squadron still in transit from Scotland. The Brummie corporal, in a good approximation of Uriah Heep, being 'ever so humble,' recommended the 'young sirs' strive for a maximum of training hours in Hurricanes, whilst they were here. He assured them 'learning on the job' here would be preferable to learning over France or the Low Countries, where Jerry was shooting at them.

Jox didn't really know what to make of Corporal Higgins, but appreciated his insights, realising he was a vital 'small cog' within the service to make the RAF work.

A few days after their arrival, Jox and Pritchard were ordered to report to the No. 111 Squadron adjutant, before meeting the Commanding Officer, Squadron Leader John Thompson. They were surprised by the summons from the CO but were reassured by Corporal Higgins.

'The boss likes to meet the new boys, to put a name to a face, in case he has to write a letter to family members.' The deadpan expression on Higgins's face was like a cold reflection on a coffin nameplate.

Spruced up and polished to a high gloss, and here Higgins was most useful, they presented themselves in the office block at the appointed hour.

'Come!' came the bellowed response to Jox's timid knock. He and Pritchard entered to find a pretty WAAF typing at a desk, behind which an older Squadron Leader was sitting at another desk, waving them over. He was the spitting image of Wing Commander Robertson, the Station CO at Montrose — perhaps a slightly younger version, but with the same 1914-18 ribbons on his chest.

'Ah, I've been expecting you. Where the devil have you been?'

They both tried to answer at once. Jox let Pritchard speak.

'We arrived two days ago, sir, but only received our orders to report to you at tea-time yesterday.'

'Right, fine,' said the grey-haired officer. He had a pale quiff at the front and darker hair at the sides. 'Which of you is McNabb?'

Jox took a step forward and saluted. 'That's me, sir.'

'So, you're Pritchard, then?'

Pritchard did the same. 'That's right, sir.'

The adjutant gave a curt smile and held out his hand. 'Your logbooks, please. Right, let's have a look.' He studied their documents. 'Where did you train?'

'No. 8 FTS at RAF Montrose, sir,' they parroted.

'What, both of you?' He didn't wait for their answer. 'Bloody chilly. My cousin's in charge up there. Bloody fool.'

Jox and Pritchard exchanged glances. They had both recognised the family resemblance.

'How many flight hours do you have?'

'A hundred and eighty,' replied Pritchard.

'A hundred and sixty-six,' said Jox. The adjutant looked up. 'I was injured for a week. My hands were burnt, sir.'

'Ah, yes. Well, you seem to have good marks and a commendation too, I see. Did you do something foolhardy, McNabb?'

'I'd say rather brave,' interrupted Pritchard.

'Would you now?' He flicked through the pages of the logbooks. 'How many hours solo?'

They answered ninety and a hundred respectively. He winced.

'Were they on Harvards?' They nodded. 'That's something, at least. Any chance either of you has actually been anywhere near a Hurricane? No, I don't suppose you have.' He leant back on his chair, sizing them up. 'Look, the interview with the old man is a simple formality. There's no need to worry. Just be polite, speak clearly and try to make a good impression. He's a decent chap really but has a lot on his plate.

'My name's Robertson, by the way, and I'm the relic from the last war he keeps around here to make sure the wheels keep turning like they're supposed to. Everybody calls me Badger, on account of this hair. My job over the next few weeks is to get you through a maximum number of hours in Hurricanes.

'I've got boys reporting to operational squadrons with less than six or eight hours. I saw what lack of training did during the last war and it doesn't sit well with me for that to happen again. I'll do my best to get you up to twenty hours, whilst you're here. It'll be bloody hard work and I'll need every effort from you, since it may well save your lives. Make no mistake, gentlemen; you'll be off to France within weeks and your training days will be over. There are real baddies out there who will be firing real bullets at you. Well, if you don't kill yourselves in the bloody aircraft first.'

They stood in awkward silence.

'Right, give me a sec and then let's get you in to see the CO. You first, McNabb.' He walked over to the frosted glass door across the room, catching the eye of the WAAF, who nodded. He knocked, opened the door and entered. He reappeared moments later and held it open. 'This is Pilot Officer Jeremy McNabb, sir. McNabb, this is Squadron Leader John Thompson. Your boss and mine.'

'Stop your bloody nonsense, Badger. Come on in, McNabb, let's have a chat.'

Jox's first sight of the Hurricane he would fly was something that would stay with him for the rest of his days. A Hawker Hurricane Mark 1, she was an older variant with a two-bladed propeller, used by the squadron as a trainer. The morning light reflecting off the varnished doped linen ran in stripes over her flanks and humped shoulders. Only the cockpit and engine cowling were protected by smooth metal panels.

Her paintwork was camo-patterned mustard and green, and she had no squadron identification letters. Jox knew the Treble Ones usually had the prefix JU, but this older aircraft only had the RAF roundel beside the number 111, painted in white and topped in red.

During his walk-round with the aircraft's rigger and flight mechanic, he was shown the high-mounted cockpit with the retractable latticed canopy for all-round visibility. It gave the bird its distinctive hump-backed silhouette. There was a stirrup at the base of the port wing and a handhold on the fuselage, to allow the pilot to get in.

The ground crew spoke lovingly of the Hurricane's composite construction of steel tubes, wooden battens and doped fabric, meaning enemy fire could often pass right through without exploding. Even if the steel tubing got damaged, repairs were usually quick and relatively simple, the crew cracking on and dealing with structural repairs within minutes.

Jox recognised the large radiator scoop in her belly from pictures he'd seen, distinct from the smaller twin ones on the Spitfire. It reminded him of the elliptical mouth of the river lampreys he would occasionally see when fishing the Devon, near school in Dollar. At the rear of the aircraft there was a single toy-like wheel and two larger retractable ones under each wing, protected by cowling which looked like the white spats worn by the drum major of the school pipes and drums. There were triple exhaust stubs running along either side of the nose, with varnished wooden twin-blades on a black spinner, giving her a mouse-like face.

The stocky, dark-haired fitter introduced himself as Corporal Black, or Blackie, as much for his oil-stained hands as for his name. In a strong Irish brogue, he said, 'This old girl still has a Rolls-Royce Merlin 1 engine, but you'll get plenty of life from her. Three hundred miles an hour easy. Manoeuvrable, reliable, sturdy and not too complicated; just how I like my women.' He grinned. 'You'll see for yourself; she handles like a dream.'

'Leading Airman Smithy is our armourer, but he's away sorting out a delivery of ammunition, sir,' added Flight Sergeant Barnes, a tall rigger, responsible for this aircraft's airframe and two others. He had a ginger mop of non-regulation length hair and buck teeth. 'He'd usually be the one to tell you all about the four .303 guns in each wing. They're zeroed in to cross streams at five hundred yards, but we can reduce it down to three hundred, if you'd like. Some of the foreign gentlemen like to get even closer before firing.'

He reached to stroke the port wing with a rag, then showed Jox the apertures of the gun muzzles, taped over with red linen.

'They're covered up right now, so nothing gets in there while you're taking off and so the guns don't freeze at altitude. When you fire, the rounds go straight through the gauze and the tatty bits tell us we need to re-arm when you land. I forget how many rounds you have exactly, but Smithy can fill you in. The thing to remember is you only have fifteen seconds of firing time. Short bursts, close-up and hopefully on target. You can't afford to waste rounds spraying the blue yonder, sir.'

Blackie linked his fingers together. 'Fancy a looksie in the cockpit, sir? I'll give you a leg up.'

It was higher than Jox expected, but he climbed aboard without too much trouble. He scanned the dashboard, recognising various dials and elements, but noted that the configuration was different to that in the Harvard. He looked up and saw the mirror above the windscreen, giving him a good view down the Hurricane's back to her tail rudder, elevators and beyond. Looking ahead, all round visibility was pretty good, except for what was hidden by the cockpit dash. It was less of a problem in the Hurricane than in the Spit, which was practically blind on the ground, requiring the pilot to sideslip at low speeds to see where he was going. Once travelling fast enough, the rear end would lift up to allow forward visibility.

The cockpit was roomy enough, but Jox wasn't a big man and he wondered how old Moose Grant was going to fit into this confined space. The dashboard was black and the interior of the cockpit was an almost jade green. Most striking was the control stick, topped by a black padded ring with a large brass button at eleven o'clock, to fire the guns with pressure from the right thumb. It was like a golden nipple of doom.

Jox wondered whether the controls would be modified for someone left-handed like Pritchard.

'Right sir, everything all right?' asked Flight Barnes, perched on the wing. 'These are for you,' he added, handing Jox a flying helmet and a pair of gauntlets. 'Orders from Squadron Leader Robertson, you should get an hour's flight under your belt before lunchtime. She's all fuelled up and your callsign is WAGON Red Two. The other gentleman is WAGON Red One. Please take your flight instructions from the tower: ASCOT Control. Let me know when you're comfortable and

I'll have Corporal Blackie hook up the starter trolley and we can get her going. Give me the thumbs-up when she's running smoothly and I'll pull the chocks away. Don't hang about once she's going or you'll damage the engine. She's an old girl and needs careful minding.'

Jox was filled with panic. 'Wait ... what? Don't I get some instruction or a briefing first? At least some guidance?'

Barnes grinned at him. 'Guidance? Not from me, sir. You're the one with the wings. I'm just a rigger. The tower will tell you what you need to know. We'll be here when you land, sir. Try to remember the number of the hangar,' he said, pointing to the nearest building. 'Don't get lost as you taxi out, and try to find your way back. Best of luck, sir. I'll have a cuppa waiting, if you like?' He hopped off the wing and stood back.

Blackie waited for the signal to fire up the accumulator trolley to coax the Merlin's twelve cylinders to life.

Jox looked around the unfamiliar cockpit and felt horribly alone. Everything he'd ever learnt about flying dashed from his head. He took a deep breath, pulled on his gloves and methodically touched each dial, lever and knob, naming them off, to reassure himself of what he was doing. He pulled on his flying helmet, plugged the microphone cord into the socket on the left of the cockpit and was relieved to hear Pritchard's familiar voice.

'Hello, ASCOT Control. This is WAGON Red One calling. Permission to start up and proceed to the runway? Over.'

Once Jox had taken off and the ground dropped away, the view over West London was breath-taking. To the south the mighty Thames snaked through the city, her shoreline dotted with silvery barrage balloons swaying clumsily on steel cables in the morning's breeze. Visibility was excellent apart from a few wispy clouds at high altitude. Given it was May, the only pluming steam and smoke came from factories, rather than during the winter months, when the fug of domestic coal fires would have marred the spectacle.

RAF Northolt was bound to the south by the Western Avenue, running from the centre of town westwards. The airfield was located between 11 Group Command HQ at RAF Uxbridge to the west, where Jox did his square-bashing, and RAF Bentley Prior at Stanmore, Fighter Command HQ. RAF Hendon was further to the east, the nearest other airfield, confirming Northolt's strategic importance.

Rising through the thermals over Perivale, Jox recognised the famous Hoover building; white towers with red highlights making it conspicuous against drabber urban surroundings. Gaining altitude, he saw extensive housing developments to the east and north of the airfield, and to the west, marshland, waterways and lakes which he identified as the Colne Valley Reservoirs, from the map provided by Flight Sergeant Barnes.

Taking position to Pritchard's portside, Jox followed his lead and began to take pleasure in what was effectively a joyride. They swooped low over Acton, where Jox made out the number 88 double-decker bus and the advertisement for Swan Vesta matches on the side, with a man with a flat cap and pipe. The purr of the Merlin engines caught the attention of the lady bus conductor, who waved at them enthusiastically. Heading towards the morning sun, they crossed North London, banking over the Thames estuary, above the Docklands, and then followed the river west. Spotting London's famous bridges, one after the other, was a joy for Jox and by the excited grin he spotted on Pritchard's face, he was feeling the same.

Battersea Power Station's twin chimneys reminded Jox of enormous white candles, stuck either end of a huge rectangular cake. Flying over the factories and moorings of Chelsea Harbour, four more chimneys in a row appeared on top of Fulham Power Station, like cricket wickets guarding the residential neighbourhoods of World's End and Fulham.

Putney flashed past, as the river chicaned left, then right, then left again, following the course of the Oxford and Cambridge boat race. Banking northwards over Chiswick, they headed for Acton to catch up the Western Avenue and to follow it home. Jox had been told this was where pilots unfamiliar with the area had difficulties finding Northolt, but he was quickly able to identify a sandy patch of land south of the airfield, which he pointed out to Pritchard.

Contacting the tower, they were given their headings and landing slots. Manoeuvring nervously, Jox landed first with a solid thud which couldn't in any way be described as elegant, but he was relieved he was down in one piece. He remembered to turn right off the runway onto the taxiway heading for the hangars. Pritchard wasn't far behind, as Jox followed the hand signals from Flight Sergeant Barnes, who appeared faithfully. He ducked beneath the aircraft, placed blocks under the wheels and his voice suddenly came over Jox's headphones. He had plugged his lead into the socket beneath the wing.

'Welcome back, sir. See, I told you, no problem. The Hurricane is a forgiving mistress, and I had every confidence. You were gone a little longer than anticipated. Always keep an eye on your flight time and your fuel reserves,' he added cheekily. 'I'm sure Squadron Leader Robertson will record two hours for you, so that's a bonus for your logbook.' Jox sensed him clambering about the aircraft, checking her over. 'Cut the power, sir; there's a good lad.'

As the propeller powered down to a stop, Sergeant Barnes's face reappeared alongside the cockpit. He had a flight helmet over his ginger mop and a mouthpiece covering his grin. 'Right, pull the latch and I'll give you a hand getting the lid back.'

Jox reached up, found the handle and pulled backwards over his head. The canopy slid backwards and Jox made a mental note to practise the movement a few more times, given the likelihood he might need to evacuate in a hurry in the future. For the time being, he was satisfied to stand on the cockpit seat, then clamber from the aircraft.

'Ruddy marvellous, Barnes. Thanks very much,' said Jox.

'My pleasure, sir, but you did all the work,' replied the rigger. 'Let me wish you a good flight and an equally safe return on every sortie.'

Jox looked across to see Pritchard strolling towards him. He still had his flying helmet on his head and was wearing a bulky wool-lined Irwin flying jacket. How he could stand to wear it in this heat baffled Jox, who was still sweating from the adrenalin rush of the flight.

'Come on, matey,' called Pritchard. 'This first flight deserves a celebration. I don't care if it's still too early, I need a pint after that.'

Jox couldn't agree more. He certainly needed something to calm himself down after the exhilaration of his first flight in a Hurricane. A flight over the bustling Capital of the Empire. London, the city he was now tasked with defending.

CHAPTER SEVEN

'Pull!' Two sharp cracks echoed across the still Sunday morning air, setting a flurry of roosting pigeons into panicked flight. They were a 'bird strike' threat around RAF Northolt, but this morning they were not the intended targets.

'Good shot that, man!' exclaimed Squadron Leader Thompson, who Jox soon learned was nicknamed Tommy. Black dust from the two clays drifted across the ribbed roofs of the deserted hangars west of the airfield. 'You've done this before, McNabb.'

'Yes, sir,' replied Jox. 'Took a game-keeping course at school, and I've also done a bit of shooting at Bisley.'

'At Bisley? I expect you're a crack shot then, my boy.'

'I wouldn't say that, sir, but I do have a reasonable eye.'

'Here, have another go,' replied Thompson, a challenge in his voice. He towered over Jox, as a former wing forward for the RAF's rugby team for four years.

Jox stood poised before saying, 'Pull!'

Two sharp reports and more clay dust drifted in the air.

'Excellent! You'll find this practice a lot more useful than static targets, McNabb. I like the boys to practice every weekend. The secret to success is to develop an instinctive feel for the deflection shot. Anticipating where the bird will be as your shot reaches it. Really no different than in your Hurricane. It's important to make your shots count, since you've only got about fifteen seconds firing time to make your mark. Spraying bullets is expensive and doesn't do anyone any good. Are you with me?'

'Absolutely, sir.'

'Glad to hear it,' said the handsome CO, his dark eyes twinkling with humour above a bushy moustache straight out of RAF central casting.

'Right then, give Pritchard a go.'

Jox handed over the shotgun with a wink.

Pritchard pulled a face and whispered, 'Girly swot.'

'Let me introduce you to a few people, Jox,' said Thompson. 'This is Flying Officer Mike Ferriss, who leads our "Yellow" Section. He's short of a man, so I'm going to let him have you.'

Ferriss was a serious-looking, thin-faced man not a lot older than Jox. His youth was rather at odds with the pipe clenched between his teeth. Removing it from his mouth, he smiled and extended a hand towards Jox. 'Delighted to meet you. What should I call you, McNabb?'

'My friends call me Jox, sir.'

'Jox it is, but please, I'm no sir. Mike is just fine, or the boys sometimes call me Wheelie, as in Ferris Wheel. They didn't dig terribly deep for that one. Where are you from, Jox?'

'I was born in India but I'm Scottish. Brought up in Clackmannanshire, near Stirling.'

'Come on then, I better introduce you.'

Ferriss had the most remarkable accent Jox had ever heard. He spoke like a member of the Royal Family. Jox smiled to himself as he was led towards two identical sergeant pilots, standing a little self-consciously amongst so many officers.

'I heard you talking to the CO about gunnery,' Ferriss said, 'so let me introduce you to the best shots in the squadron. You'll be happy to learn this fellow is in "Yellow" Section too. These are Flight Sergeants Cameron and Anthony Glasgow.'

The pair of squat men had sergeant's stripes topped by a crown on either arm; one was glowering and the other smiling disarmingly, but both exuded confidence and obvious competence.

'Pleased tae meet ye, sir,' said the smiling one, his Dundonian accent recognisable to Jox's attuned ear. 'This is my brother, Anthony. He doesnae say much, but he is useful if you're in a spot of bother.'

'Happy to pick up any knowledge you can share,' said Jox.

'Nae bother,' replied the glowering twin.

Both men had dark receding hair, fleshy noses and lips, and identical piercing grey eyes.

'You're from Dundee. I recognise the accent,' said Jox.

'Aye, that's right. How's it you know it, sir?'

'Oh, I'm Scots too.'

'Oh aye? No trace of an accent as far as I can tell.'

'Mark of a good education,' joked Jox, immediately regretting his words.

'Aye, well, we would nae know about that. We joined up as apprentices in '37 and then got a leg up with the war. An opportunity, you'd say, for us common fellas to improve ourselves,' said Anthony. 'Some call us "Trenchard Brats" but not to our faces,' he added with a dangerous gleam in his eye.

'Now, now, get back in your box, you raving socialist,' said Ferriss, patting Anthony's shoulder affectionately. 'Give the poor chap a chance to find his feet before you launch your revolution, comrade. Don't worry, Jox, Ant's bark is worse than his bite. Thankfully Cam's there to keep a muzzle on him and despite appearances, we're all terribly good pals.'

'Aye, best of pals,' repeated Cameron, but his brother didn't look entirely convinced.

Jox had the distinct impression he'd already done something wrong. *Christ, this promises to be an interesting few weeks*, he thought. *Where the hell's Pritchard when I need him?*

Jox searched for his friend, who was in animated discussion with a long-chinned flight lieutenant who had carefully pomaded shiny hair.

'There you are, Jox,' Pritchard said. 'Where have you been? This is David Bruce, known as David the Bruce, the A Flight leader.'

Jox shook his hand.

'Hey, nice to meet yah,' said Bruce. The look on his face indicated that he was expecting a reaction to his unusual accent. 'I was explaining to your friend, I was born in Trinidad, then spent time in New Brunswick, Canada and Boston, Massachusetts, before moving to Bristol. That explains my rather muddled accent. Welcome to the squadron. How do you know Pritchard?'

'We went through No. 8 FTS together.'

'Ah, you're lucky, my training lot was scattered all over.'

'Ours too, sir, but we do have one other pal, Moose, stationed with a new Canadian squadron not too far away. We're hoping to catch him in London sometime,' said Jox.

'I'm not sure how soon that will be. There's a rumour A Flight is lined up to be part of a composite squadron with boys from No. 253 "Hyderabad" Squadron, flying day missions over to France and coming home to roost in the evening back in Blighty. Things are heating up over there and they need reinforcements, but the powers that be are loath to commit more squadrons, since we'll be needed on this side of the Channel to defend the home islands when the time comes. Dowding has forbidden any Spitfires to be sent over, so I expect us Hurricanes are deemed more expendable. Can't say it sounds terribly promising. Rather an odd compromise, going in half-cocked like that. Bottom line, gentlemen, I'd get your affairs in order fairly pronto.'

The discussion was interrupted by a loud exclamation from Pritchard. 'Bloody hell! Wolfie McKenzie, is that you?'

'Pritchard! You old dog,' replied a baby-faced pilot officer. 'I didn't know you'd signed up. How the devil are you?'

'Just in for the duration, Wolfie. You look rather well. Put on a few pounds, I see.'

'Oh, bugger off! We can't all be Adonis like you. What are you doing here?'

'Same as you, I expect,' replied Pritchard. 'Let me introduce you to my chum Jox. You'll know David Bruce, of course, my new A Flight leader. You're in B Flight, I assume?'

'That's right,' replied Wolfie. 'Blue Three, flying with Jack Copeman, the tall chap over there chatting with the adjutant.'

'Jox!' called Pritchard. 'Come and meet Wolfie. We were at school together at King's in Wimbledon.'

'Just for sixth form, before I went off to Cranwell,' clarified Wolfie.

'Crikey, I had no idea you wanted to go pro,' said Pritchard. 'Going to make a career of it, Wolfie?'

'We'll see. Suits me for now.'

'So, how's your war been so far?' asked Pritchard.

'Not too bad. Still in one piece. Saw a little action up at Scapa Flow. Shared a probable He 111 bomber in April.'

'Wow. Tell us all about it.'

'Maybe another time,' replied Wolfie, keen to change the subject. He caught Jox's eye. 'Hello there, I'm John McKenzie. Don't worry about Pritchard, he gets overexcited.'

Jox laughed. 'Yup, I know, we trained together at Montrose.'

'He was like that at school, always getting into trouble. Actually, I'm not really from Wimbledon at all; it's only where my mother moved to. Originally, I'm from Aberdeen. The rest of my family are all still there.'

'Just what we need, another bloody Jock,' said Pritchard good-naturedly. He wrapped his arms around the necks of both men. 'I'm going to have a great time with my two best friends in the same squadron. What a laugh we're going to have. Here's to a great and glorious war!'

The following week Jox was put through his paces on the gunnery range. His Hurricane's guns were harmonised at Northolt's firing butts, supervised all the while by the monosyllabic Flight Sergeant Anthony Glasgow, who insisted the crossing point for the eight guns be shortened to 250 yards, rather than the prescribed 400 yards.

'We're under-gunned as it is with our .303s, compared to the cannons of the Bf 110 or Bf 109. We need to get in really close to be effective,' said Anthony. 'My tip for you is to use the rings of your illuminated sight to gauge your shots. A bomber should fill the entire sight before you fire. At 250 yards, both of its engines should fit inside the rings. Bombers generally fly reasonably straight, but don't count on it once they know you're there. Fighters are obviously smaller, much faster and the buggers simply won't stay still. You'll need to develop a sense of where one will be and fire there. Try to fit the fighter's wingtips in your rings before firing.'

Jox nodded. 'I appreciate your coaching, Flight. There's so much to learn and I don't want to hold the section back.'

Anthony fixed him with his flinty gaze for a long while, then said, 'You'll be fine. Just remember we'll be depending on you as much as you are on Mike and me. You need to use the eyes in your head, always looking and calling out anything you see. The slightest movement, we need tae know about it. Do you understand?'

'I do, Flight.'

'Fine. Now call me Ant,' said the flight sergeant. 'And one more thing. Your oxygen mask — use the damned thing. I've seen more crashes because pilots have blacked out for not wearing their masks than for any other reason. You'll have blacked out from the effect of G-force before, but that's only for a moment. Lack of oxygen will do that too but for a hell of a lot longer. We don't have the luxury of time up there. Good mask discipline is key.'

'Understood.'

'Good lad. Right, let's go for a spin. I'll take you over to Croydon, where we can do some practice attacks on the civilian passenger airliners as they come in. They don't like it much and we'll undoubtedly get complaints, but it's about the nearest you'll get to manoeuvring around something like a bomber, without the real thing.'

Jox put Ant Glasgow's coaching into practice when the newcomers to the squadron were sent on a four-day gunnery course in Wales. The evocatively named RAF Hell's Mouth was at Porth Neigwl on the Llŷn Peninsula in North Wales. Along the rocky coastline the Air Gunnery and Bombing Range provided painted targets on land, moored ones a mile offshore and then large cone-shaped target drogues were towed 1,200 feet behind Hawker Henley tugs. The students had the opportunity to develop their aerial gunnery skills, but Jox couldn't help thinking any Jerry pilot worth his salt was hardly likely to fly straight like the drogues nor remain static.

They were drilled on the accepted procedure when attacking bombers, the victim being played by a cooperative Wellington. They took turns to simulate shooting out its port engine first, followed by the starboard one, and finally the 'coup de grace', aiming for the bomber's body.

The Hurricane's principal role in an air battle was to attack the bomber stream, so there was little actual practice of fighter-on-fighter engagements. Apparently, this was the preserve of the Spitfires, which Jox found frustrating and somewhat worrying. What was useful, interesting and rather good fun, was reviewing his gun camera footage after simulated attacks and then being shown what best practice looked like.

Jox realised that estimating distance from a target was really key. Novices invariably fired too early, and when airborne he found himself repeating Ant's mantra of 'getting the enemy within your rings.' He also saw how rare it was for the enemy to fly parallel to your flight path, unless attacking frontally or directly from the rear. Otherwise, it was always vital to manoeuvre into a favourable position and range, and then know at what angle of deflection to fire. Firing in a straight line was almost always useless.

When they returned to RAF Northolt, the squadron mess was a-buzz with tales of recent sorties over France, whilst the 'youngsters' were off 'pretending' in Wales. They spoke of the catastrophic destruction of equipment and property they'd seen, and of the flames, smoke and carnage. Endless columns of terrified refugees had lined country roads, with panic-stricken ground forces retreating before the merciless Nazi *Blitzkrieg* or 'Lightning War'.

No. 111 Squadron had already made an impact on the enemy. Squadron Leader Thompson chalked up a Bf 110 heavy fighter and Yellow One, Wheelie Ferriss, brought down two He 111 bombers. He was cementing his position as the squadron's first ace, which was reassuring to Jox, as not only was he his section leader but also his guardian angel in the murderous skies. It was hard to reconcile the fresh-faced twenty-two-year-old, whose short curly hair was like a lamb's fleece, with the grim reality of a stone-cold killer.

The first time Jox and Pritchard went up with the entire squadron of twelve Hurricanes, it was to practice the tactics being developed by Thompson. He was determined the Treble Ones become the best squadron at bringing down the waves of bombers that would soon be targeting the United Kingdom. His approach was disarmingly simple and absolutely terrifying.

First one flight, then the next, would fly line abreast, charging headfirst at the enemy formation, all the while firing furiously into the cockpits of the oncoming bombers. They practised, one flight against the other, until Thompson roped in a friendly squadron of Fairey Battle light bombers to deputise as Jerry. What was effectively a giant game of 'chicken' usually resulted in spooked bombers scattering in all directions, often with several near-misses only just averted. As Yellow Three, Jox was positioned to the extreme port-side of the line, far to the left. He envied Pritchard as Red Three, tucked within the security of the line, until he saw how close he came to colliding with the bomber bearing down on him.

Once safely back on the ground, Jox was convinced the practice would surely be written off as a disaster, but to his utter incredulity both Thompson and Ferriss appeared delighted with the outcome. They were convinced the tactic would show real dividends when deployed against the Hun, despite the risks entailed.

Jox's war would begin on Friday, 17th May, 1940. A Flight were ordered to RV mid-morning above the Isle of Wight with a flight from No. 253 'Hyderabad' Squadron from RAF Manston. They were to refuel at Vitry-en-Artois airfield, 105 miles northeast of Paris, patrol the area and return to RAF Northolt before dark.

Jox had less than twelve hours to get himself ready for war. His first instinct was to take a solitary walk along the fence perimeter, after handing over his aircraft to the ground crew, who would spend the night readying it for the mission in the morning.

As a welcome to the squadron, and in collusion with Pritchard, who knew the 'inspiration' for Jox joining up, he would now be flying under the letters JU-X. JU was the prefix for No. 111 Squadron and the X was just for Jox. Pritchard's aircraft had also been resprayed with JU-P.

Jox took off his flying gauntlets and looked at his pale hands, still scarred with the burns from Montrose. His fingers were trembling, something he had never experienced before. *What am I scared of? The unknown or being fool enough to blindly agree to meet my fate? A lamb to the slaughter? Get a grip of yourself,* he thought. *Maybe I'm not a brave man, but I'll do my best. Please God, let me do my duty and not let anyone down.*

CHAPTER EIGHT

Take-off the next morning for A Flight was delayed by thick fog over London. The boys of No. 253 'Hyderabad' Squadron were unamused to be kept waiting, burning precious fuel as they circled uselessly over the Isle of Wight.

It was almost noon on the 17th of May by the time the tiered formation of the composite squadron approached Vitry-en-Artois airfield in the Pas-de-Calais department of northern France. They had flown high most of the way and, mindful of Anthony Glasgow's advice, Jox had carefully checked every connection of his oxygen mask. He could feel the warm condensation from his breath inside the chamois leather from wearing it for so long. It was a stark contrast to the chill of high-altitude flying and the ice crystals forming on the canopy.

Below them, France looked much like Kent and so far Jox had seen no signs of any aircraft, either friend or foe. From this height, only twirling towers of smoke carried on the wind from burning towns betrayed any signs of conflict.

Coming in to land, the damage on the ground became more visible. Country roads were clogged with scruffy refugees, travelling with what appeared to be the entire contents of their homes. Cars, vans, clapped-out lorries and even wheelbarrows and prams were filled to the brim. Those not crowding the dusty roads gathered in exhausted heaps in public parks and fields.

The aerodrome itself was a bumpy plain of grass when A flight landed. The French groundcrew indicated they should park up alongside a thick beech hedge, bordering a perimeter road clogged with refugee traffic. Parked opposite was a pristine row of Morane-Saulnier M.S.406 fighters shining in the noonday sun. Jox thought how very smart they looked, but also what a tempting target they would make.

Whilst the flight leaders searched for someone in charge amongst the camouflaged dispersal huts, a flaccid windsock spun lazily around a pole beneath a tattered tricolour. The pilots of the composite squadron de-planed and gathered along the hedge line for a quick cigarette, as petrol bowsers and ground crews swarmed over the aircraft, refuelling and wiping down the bug-splattered canopies.

Clambering from his Hurricane, Jox was called over by Ferriss, standing with Yellow Two, Anthony Glasgow.

'Right, Jox, here we have it,' Ferriss said a little breathlessly. 'We're wheels up in about twenty minutes, once the birds are fuelled up. Tommy's getting the gen and will let us know what's what. Now, listen, stick to Ant here like glue. He'll be following me.' He glanced over to the flight sergeant, who nodded. 'I want your eyes on swivels. Tell us the minute you see anything. Is that clear?'

Jox nodded nervously, as Anthony patted him on the shoulder. 'You'll be all right, son, just stick wi' me. I'm going to have a quick word with my brother and I'll be right back. Why not see how your pal Pritchard is getting on? It'll kill a bit of time, rather than dwelling on things tae much.'

Pritchard was peering over the copper-coloured hedge at the mass of refugees making slow progress down the country road. 'Christ, Jox, have you seen how many there are? Can you imagine how scared you'd have to be to grab the essentials and run, abandoning everything you know?'

'I wouldn't exactly say the essentials,' replied Jox. 'Look at that bloody great draught horse pulling that flatbed. There's a grand piano on there and an old dear in a rocking chair in the back.'

The magnificent grey beast snorted at the strangers, its long-haired black fetlocks straining in response to the driver's whip.

Jox noticed a little girl with blonde ringlets staring at them with big blue eyes. She was dressed in a smart red velvet tunic with a frilly collar, but her face was grimy, as were her boots and bare knees. She was holding up a tattered doll with a pale porcelain head and arms which matched her own wan complexion.

'*Bonjour*,' said Jox in his best schoolboy French. He pointed to the doll and asked its name. '*Ta poupée, comment s'appelle-t-elle?*'

'Marilyn,' replied the child hesitantly.

'*Je m'appelle* Jeremy,' said Jox. He asked her name and where she was from.

'Marguerite. *Nous venons de Wavre en Belgique*,' replied the little girl.

A voice from behind her called out, '*Marguerite! Viens la!*'

Jox saw a stout woman in a high-collared white blouse and a full skirt calling her. Beside her, an older man with a white walrus moustache pushed a wooden wheelbarrow filled with household utensils.

Jox smiled and waved as Marguerite trotted away.

The midday stillness was languid with buzzing insects, the dull clatter of chattels and snippets of conversation between weary refugees. The peaceful sounds were interrupted by the low throb of engines, then the sudden rolling shriek of sirens, rising one after the other into a gathering cacophony.

From a distance they looked like a ragged rookery of crows. They soon materialised into a mass of snarling aircraft with distinctive broken wings, wide throats and the solid legs of Stukas, the Junkers 87 dive bombers. Curious-looking aircraft, they had sown terror across Europe, always at the vanguard of the blisteringly paced German *Blitzkrieg*. Vulnerable to fighter attack without air superiority, with it they were a formidable asset, mobile artillery in support of advancing ground troops. Their presence immediately told No. 111 Squadron's pilots two things: first, their job was to deny that air superiority, and secondly German ground troops wouldn't be far behind.

Jox watched, horrified as a yellow-nosed Stuka dove vertically towards the cobbled road filled with refugees. It was beyond his comprehension to see innocent civilians cynically targeted like this, rather than the twin lines of fighters parked in neat rows across the aerodrome. The Stuka could reach 370 mph diving from a height of 1500 feet, to deliver a bomb load dead on target, so tales of accidental targeting of civilians was a myth.

Cowering behind the hedge, he saw an entire wing of Stukas take languid turns to dive onto their targets, delivering lethal bomb loads one after the next. The sharp rattle of rear gunners firing their guns into the devastation the bombs had wrought was equally shocking. The sounds of explosions and gunfire, mixed in with the wails of sirens fitted to the Stukas, created a cacophony which to Jox was the sound of hell itself.

Bombs fell from between their legs, projecting forward like the talons of a fish eagle reaching for its prey. Each bomb was fitted with a cardboard spinner which screamed as it fell.

Jox was punched hard in the arm.

'What the fuck are you waiting for?' bellowed Anthony Glasgow, as he dragged Jox towards their aircraft.

The men of A flight charged towards their Hurricanes like an ocean wave reaching a jetty. Ferriss was already strapping himself into his cockpit and to Jox's surprise so was Pritchard, who had been beside him seconds ago, witnessing the carnage.

Engines coughed and propellers began to spin, as the line of shiny Morane-Saulnier fighters were tossed into the air by mushrooming explosions. Others collapsed onto the ground, torn apart by cannon fire from swooping Bf 109s, presumably the Stukas' escorts.

It was a miracle any of them made it off the ground. One of the No. 253 Squadron lads was caught in the crossfire as he retracted his undercarriage. His Hurricane cartwheeled spectacularly, wingtip over wingtip, before crashing in a flaming heap against a tall line of poplars just beyond the airfield perimeter. Doused in aviation fuel, the towering trees burnt like giant matchsticks, scattering cindered leaves like black confetti, a whispering tribute to the young airman burning at their roots.

In his earphones, Jox heard Thompson's urgent voice: 'Right, WAGON Flight, this is WAGON Leader. Red and Yellow Sections on me. Let's get at those bastards.'

Thompson's Hurricane, identifier JU-T, banked up and to the right in pursuit of the Stukas, who had disappeared as suddenly as they had arrived.

'WAGON Flight, keep tight on me. VICEROY Leader, this is WAGON Leader. Sorry to see your chap go in. Can we leave you to deal with the Jerry fighters while we have a dekko for the Stukas?'

'Roger that, WAGON Leader,' came the curt reply from No. 253's own squadron leader, the emotion clear in his voice.

A Flight searched the vicinity for signs of the culprits until they ran short of fuel. One by one they returned to Vitry-en-Artois, carefully landing between the craters and burnt-out wrecks of the once proud French fighters.

Considering the airfield had been caught napping, casualties were light and most of the refuelling stations were still intact. What was missing, however, were the French ground personnel who had seen the attack as the excuse to evacuate. The pilots of the destroyed French fighters had also disappeared, leaving the RAF in sole control of the deserted airfield. The pilots refuelled their own Hurricanes, while a few of the boys from No. 253 Squadron went up the road to look for what remains could be found amongst the blackened row of poplars.

It was heavy work lugging the refuelling lines of the bowsers, with petrol splashing from the metal funnels inserted into fuel nozzles by clumsy aviators, unused to the task. Dancing vapour from spilt fuel wreathed the men and machines, dangerously enticing to nearby flames. The men of No. 253 Squadron returned with very little, their grim-faced squadron leader carrying a white fabric bag with the word FARINE printed on it. Inside was what remained of their comrade. His charred identity tabs were in his flight leader's pocket, a scant reward for grieving parents for the sacrifice of a son. In the bag, a dusty mixture of flour and human ash would be given a full military funeral in England, despite its dubious composition.

Jox was concerned for little Marguerite. He convinced Anthony Glasgow to join him in searching for her. Before they did, Anthony insisted they arm themselves with pistols. 'You never know what we might find out there. I'm nae taking any bloody chances after all this.'

The carnage which unfolded before them was beyond the darkest recesses of Jox's imagination. At every fresh horror, a grim-faced Anthony repeated, 'Those poor fuckers.'

The cart they'd seen earlier, loaded with a piano and the old woman in the rocking chair, had been hit by cannon fire across its entire length. The magnificent Belgian dray horse was dead in its harnesses, crumpled but upright on feathered fetlocks. Its huge grey nose pooled dark blood onto the cobbles. Behind, the piano was crushed and the rocking chair was smashed to kindling. There was no sign of the old woman until they edged past the cart, where they found her headless, heavy skirts blown up by the blast, a final indignity in death. Jox knelt to rearrange her dress to preserve her modesty, but the sight of the mangled mess above her neck made him turn and vomit violently.

'There, there, laddie,' soothed Anthony with a look on his face that told how appalled he felt too.

Scattered amongst the debris of a hundred households lay knots of the wounded and dead. Two kindly *bonne soeurs* whom Jox had seen earlier, herding exhausted children, presumably their charges from a Catholic orphanage or boarding school, lay together. Clasped to their breasts were beaded crucifixes and two infants who mercifully seemed undamaged in death, seeming asleep rather than slaughtered. The crimson blood splashed across white tabards was a shock to see, as was the close-cropped hair of one of the sisters, exposed as her headdress had been ripped away.

'Can you see your wee girl?' asked Anthony.

Jox surveyed the chaos with increasing desperation but could find no sign of Marguerite. He shook his head.

'I know it's rough,' said Anthony. 'But we've got to get back. We're not equipped to help these people and are much more useful defending them and making sure this doesnae happen again.'

Jox spotted something pale amongst the wild daisies growing by the roadside. He reached down and picked up the broken porcelain arm of a doll. He recognised it immediately as

Marguerite's. Delicate in the palm of his hand, it bore mute witness to what had happened here. He turned to follow Ant and quietly slipped the fractured toy into the breast pocket of his tunic.

Walking back to his aircraft, he realised with startling clarity what it was he was fighting for. He simply couldn't stand by and allow cynical attacks on innocent civilians like this. Not if he could do something about it, and especially if Jerry planned to bring this dirty kind of war to Britain's shores, to his homeland. He couldn't let that happen.

In the end, during this day in France they had been of little use. Exhausted, but mercifully intact, A Flight made its way back to Northolt. Jox felt frustrated, inept and impotent, feelings that were soon replaced with cold fury. Tomorrow would be another day, and he was determined this time to take the fight to the enemy.

On the morning of Saturday, 18th May 1940, before leaving for France again, Jox and the rest of the group were addressed by Thompson.

'Yesterday was a poor show, chaps. We were bloody lucky not to lose anyone, unlike the poor sods from No. 253 Squadron. Let's not kid ourselves, it was sheer luck. We were caught like sitting ducks.' He removed the cigar butt from his teeth and looked uncharacteristically contrite. 'That's on me, boys, and I'm sorry. I think, perhaps, all of us were a bit overexcited about being over there. It stops now. I want to see nothing but cold, hard professionalism, and that's what you can expect from me. Jerry gave us a kicking, and God knows those poor French civilians suffered. Today it's Jerry's turn.' Their usually effusive squadron leader was very measured with his words. 'Things aren't going well. We all saw it. The British

Expeditionary Force is pulling back from Belgium. Jerry isn't far behind, so there are a few key bridges which need to be taken out to slow them down. Our job today is to escort our bombers to get that done. There will be no free-for-all rhubarbs until the task is achieved. Are we clear?' He scanned the room for signs of dissent. 'Our base for today's operations is Lille's Marcq-en-Baroeul airfield. Overnight sitreps tell us yesterday's Vitry-en-Artois airfield has been abandoned. We land and refuel at Lille, then RV with the wing of Blenheim bombers heading for Valenciennes this afternoon. Is everything clear? Right, good luck, boys. Let's make it count.'

The flight to Lille passed without mishap. Landing at Marcq-en-Baroeul, they found it was significantly larger than yesterday's base of operations. They arrived in time for lunch. As befitting a substantial airbase, the field was protected by anti-aircraft defences and a flight of Polish pilots, serving with 1/145 *Groupe de Chasse Polonais*, lying on the grass near their aircraft in readiness. They flew somewhat dated Caudron C.714s, whose shortcomings were made up for by the Poles' reputed élan, flying skills and intense desire for vengeance on the invaders of their homeland.

The field also had an estaminet doubling as a mess for visiting British pilots. For some, though, French cuisine was rather beyond their modest British palate. The *patron de la maison* shared *la carte* with a flourish, featuring several dishes which to French eyes were very simple fare: cheese omelettes or *Quiche Lorraine*. The Glasgow brothers were having none of 'that fancy foreign muck'. They would accept nothing other than egg and chips. *Le patron*, whose English was somewhat patchy, explained the *patates-frites* were in fact chips. Finally, willing to compromise, Cameron agreed to an omelette, but Anthony remained adamant.

'All I want is bloody egg and chips,' he said, beginning to lose his temper. 'How difficult can it be? Mon-sewar, *je vous* bloody egg and chips. *Comprendez?*'

Le patron looked doubtful but nodded his head and walked off, muttering to himself.

A little while later, once everyone else had been served, Anthony's *déjeuner spécial* arrived. With a flourish, his egg and chips were revealed. Sitting on top of a nest of finely cut yellow *frites* was a fried egg with a bright yolk. A bright red yolk, with an eye, a rudimentary beak and translucent folded legs.

'*Voila pour monsieur, le* "bloody egg and chips",' said *le patron* proudly.

Anthony was furious, but it was unclear whether this was due to his squadron-mates' riotous laughter or the fact that he would be going hungry.

The first blood of the day went to Thompson. Whilst his men dined, he had decided to scout the surrounding area. His was an opportunistic kill, which added to his tally despite him being a little embarrassed to admit it was a slow, hedge-hopping Henschel Hs 126. A two-seat reconnaissance aircraft, lightly armoured and manoeuvrable, it was no match for his guns, but a valid target since they acted as artillery spotters and observers of troop movements.

The composite squadron departed from Marcq-en-Baroeul just after three. They were escorting twin engine Blenheim bombers, targeting the bridges over the Scheldt at Valenciennes. On the way, they were intercepted by a formation of nine Bf 110s from *Zerstörergeschwader* 26 (ZG 26). No. 111 Squadron's A Flight immediately set upon the raiders, allowing the bulkier Blenheims to make their way to the bridges, where they failed to destroy the targets and were savaged by fearsome German flak defences.

A Flight formed up, line abreast as they had been trained, and tore into the raiders.

Ferriss said to Jox, 'Yellow One to Yellow Three, keep tight on me. Same for you, Yellow Two.'

Ferriss launched himself at the first of the oncoming Bf 110 Destroyers, firing a three-second burst head-on into the aircraft's canopy. The shattered Perspex misted with bright blood, as the pilot's head exploded within.

As Yellow Three, Jox witnessed everything, but didn't fire his guns, so focused was he on holding in position for dear life.

Ferriss turned his attention to a second Bf 110, attacking it from a range of three hundred yards. He fired as he closed to two hundred. Catching it from astern, ragged hits stitched across the port engine, which began to smoke.

The enemy machine spun away, thick black smoke marking its descent earthwards until it thudded dully into the ground. Still unsatisfied and by now fighting mad, Ferriss engaged a third twin engine heavy fighter, firing a long burst into the wing, until panels began to fall off. Once again, smoke traced his victim's progress as it dove away, engines screaming as it sought refuge in a nearby bank of clouds.

Ferriss was still not finished and chased yet another Bf 110, scoring multiple hits until he ran out of ammunition. Flight Sergeant Anthony Glasgow, his Yellow Two, then took up the baton and finished the raider off, sharing the kill with his section leader.

Returning to Lille, the trio regrouped but were separated from the rest of the flight. This was when they were bounced by a foolhardy pair of fresh Bf 110s. Despite being short of ammunition, Yellow Section were able to frighten them off with bold attack feints. Frustrated, Jox, who still had plenty of ammunition, never got a clear shot as 'tail-end Charlie', nor was he quick enough to react when the enemy did blink across his gun sight.

He landed back at Northolt rather depressed. It had been a good day for the squadron, with five victories claimed in the morning and four more in the afternoon. The celebrations in the mess would undoubtedly be riotous, as the men tried their hardest to blot out what they'd witnessed 'over there'. Wheelie Ferriss had bagged three Bf 110s and shared another with Anthony Glasgow. Thompson added a Bf 110 to his shared Hs 126, and to top it all off even Pritchard had managed to wing a Bf 110, claiming it as a 'probable'.

It wasn't all good news, however, with F/L Charlie Darwood, one of the squadron's 'old-timers', reported missing in action. Butcher, his white Staffordshire Bull Terrier, searched frantically for his master around the mess, a sad sight.

On a fine day's hunting for the squadron, Jox was still languishing on a 'duck'. He hadn't even pierced the bindings of his guns by firing them. He put on a brave face for his carousing comrades, especially a jubilant Pritchard, but inside he was seething.

He knew, though, his time would come.

CHAPTER NINE

Rising through a cloudless Sunday morning sky in staggered Vic formations, A Flight tiered high above the endless green lattice of northern France's fields. It had been a clear trip from Northolt and there was no sign of life in the air or on the ground.

'WAGON Yellow Leader, this is Yellow Three,' said Jox. 'Single Bogey at four o'clock low. Estimate Angels Three or Four below.' Jox saw Ferriss's leather-clad head turn in the indicated direction.

'Where away, Yellow Three? I can't see him, are you sure?'

'Quite sure, Yellow Leader. We're above him in the sun, so he hasn't seen us yet. He's large and very low, maybe a transport, but I can see the crosses on his wings. Yellow Leader, permission to engage?'

'Roger that, Yellow Three. Proceed with caution. Yellow Two, stay high to ensure we're not flying into a baited trap.'

'Roger, Yellow Leader,' replied Anthony Glasgow, Jox's wingman.

'WAGON Flight, WAGON Leader here,' interrupted Thompson, the Treble One Flight Leader addressing the rest of the composite squadron. 'WAGON Yellow Section is engaging. Tallyho!'

Acknowledging the order, Jox replied, 'Roger, WAGON Leader. Yellow Three engaging. Tallyho, tallyho.'

He dropped altitude and swooped onto the bulky enemy aircraft, falling from the brightness of the sun. Getting nearer, from the three engines and bulbous nose he identified it as a Junkers 52, the Luftwaffe's principal transport, known by the

Jerrys as 'Auntie Ju'. Used to transport goods and personnel between air bases, they also served to deliver the *Fallschirmjäger*, Germany's elite paratroopers to their drop zones.

The Ju 52 had a distinctive corrugated aluminium metal skin, painted in a disruptive camouflage pattern. She was undeniably an unarmed 'soft' target, but if she was carrying a stick of paratroopers, they were undoubtedly on a mission, making it Jox's duty to disrupt them.

The prospect of downing the aircraft and ending the lives of up to seventeen helpless aircrew and troopers was, however, a daunting one for Jox, but the thought of what had happened to little Marguerite hardened his resolve. He reached for the hard lump of the doll's porcelain arm in his breast pocket, then leant forward to rotate the ring of his Dunlop firing button mounted on the spade-shaped grip handle of his control stick. Moving it clockwise with his thumb, he armed the trigger and all he needed to do now was press the push-button to fire eight harmonised .303 guns.

The Ju 52 flew on, unaware that Jox had tucked in tight behind her, ready to open fire. The rattling clatter of the guns took Jox by surprise, and he immediately registered several hits along the corrugated sides of the aircraft. It tipped sideways almost lazily as the portside engine exploded in spidery sparks, followed by flames. Jox had little trouble keeping up with his lumbering victim, swiftly glancing into the mirror above his head to check for any threat from behind. His heart leapt when he glimpsed movement, but he realised it was Yellow Two watching his 'six'.

He lined up the next burst carefully, keen not to waste ammunition. He knew the shells were at a premium and there would be plenty more sport this day. His second burst delivered more shuddering impacts and the central engine in her nose was alight. To reach it, Jox had fired through the pilots' compartment and they were most likely already dead, dooming anyone stranded in the back.

Jox fired a final burst and a long strip of cowling whipped past, narrowly missing him. The tough old transport was dead but didn't realise it. In a final display of defiance, she suddenly reared up, the twisting causing the burning engine to collapse her port wing, effectively folding the aircraft in two. She fell earthwards like the spinning seed of a sycamore, until consumed by a brilliant ball of flame.

Perhaps it was fuel she was carrying rather than men, hoped Jox, as molten metal rained like quicksilver onto the green valley floor. It was his first kill, but he felt no urge to celebrate. In fact, he was probably going to be sick. Mercifully, a calming voice distracted him from the bile rising in his throat.

'Good job there, laddie,' said Anthony. 'The first time is never easy. Now, form up on me and let's get back to the boys. We've got plenty more work. How are you set for ammo and fuel?'

Jox used the checks as a distraction as he reported back, powering up to catch Yellow Two.

They were soon back in position within the tiered formation and the rest of the flight. Pritchard asked how he'd got on, but the Red Section leader, David Bruce interrupted tersely. 'Concentrate on the task at hand, Red Three. There'll be plenty of time for chit-chat back at the mess. Let's focus now.'

A contrite Pritchard replied, 'Roger that, Red Leader.'

By four-thirty in the afternoon, the composite squadron of fourteen aircraft was on its second patrol over the Douai area. Squadron Leader Thompson was leading a flight of seven Hurricanes, representing half of the contingent, when a large formation of Heinkel 111 bombers was sighted at Angels One Zero or ten thousand feet.

Hitching up their chamois leather oxygen masks, the men switched on their oxygen tanks, angled for the climb and began positioning for a height advantage. In the contest that followed, the Treble Ones brought down three He 111 bombers, including one which spectacularly vaporised at high altitude, a lucky .303 round having set off the bomb load still rattling within its racks.

The fight wasn't a one-sided affair, though, with three of their number hit, one by a sharpshooting rear gunner and two falling victim to the bombers' escort, a dozen sinister Bf 110 Destroyers. It wasn't immediately clear who had gone down, but a single Hurricane was seen crash-landing in a farmer's field, gouging out a great scar in the spring crop before coming to a thumping halt against a hedge line.

Tasked with swooping low over the scene, Jox saw the pilot being helped from the wreckage by some soldiers on the ground, but it was unclear who it was or if the troops were friendly or not. What was very clear was that three 'Missing in Action' was a hefty price to pay in a single day.

During the fight with the He 111s and their escort, Jox and the rest of Yellow Section had stuck grimly together and had managed a few hits on the attacking Destroyers, whilst their comrades and the No. 253 Squadron flight dealt with the bombers.

Jox was delighted to register some solid hits on a hulking Bf 110 with a snarling shark's mouth painted beneath the cockpit, to his mind a much more honourable target than his earlier kill, the lumbering Ju 52 transport.

After what seemed like a matter of a few whizzing seconds and some snatched shots, he heard Ferriss say, 'Yellow Section, this is Yellow Leader. I have to pull out of the fight. My engine's running rough and the temperature gauge is right up. Yellow Three, fall back and let me know if you can see anything strange going on back there.'

'Roger that,' replied Jox, dropping behind and below Ferriss's aircraft, searching for any sign of the trouble.

'Yellow Section, this is Yellow Two,' said Anthony Glasgow. 'I'll keep an eye on things from up here, just to make sure we don't get jumped as you're checking things over, Yellow Three.'

'Roger that,' replied both Jox and Ferriss, as Anthony's aircraft first dropped, then soared elegantly away.

Jox watched the airstream bouncing behind Ferriss's wobbling Hurricane and recognised the white trail of a coolant leak. There was Glycol escaping in a thin stream where the tank had been perforated, and it wouldn't take long for the engine to start overheating, seizing up once the trailing vapour turned from white to acrid black smoke.

'Yellow Three to Yellow Leader, you've got a hole in your coolant tank. I can see the trail of a leak. Better get you down before things start overheating.'

'Roger, Yellow Three, but I think I already have. We're not too far from Marcq-en-Baroeul, so I should be able to make it back. Stick with me in case something goes wrong, so you can report back the location if I go down. I'd rather land, but if things get too hot in here, I'll take my chances with the chute, assuming I still have the altitude.'

Jox was struck by the weight of his responsibility as he watched over Ferriss. After the day's earlier losses, here was the real prospect of Ferriss, his section leader, also going down. Jox suddenly felt very alone and exposed in the deadly skies of northern France. He was grateful to hear the rough Scots burr of Anthony Glasgow coming through his earphones.

'Right, Yellow Section, I'm back. Let's see if we can't get old Yellow One back home in one piece.'

'Roger that,' sighed Jox with relief.

Between them they coaxed, cajoled and guided Ferriss's ailing aircraft back to Lille, talking him through every stage. Within sight of the airfield, black smoke streaked back from the overheating engine, then a sudden spray of boiling engine oil splashed up, obscuring the front canopy of the cockpit. Somehow Ferriss managed a textbook landing, in spite of flying with his leather-clad head, goggles down, poking out from the side of the cockpit. He had pulled the canopy lid back and had opened the emergency hatch as he desperately tried to clear the smoke and fumes billowing from within the aircraft's cramped cockpit.

He rolled to a bumpy stop in the middle of the landing strip and swiftly bundled out of the cockpit, tipping 'arse over tit' off the wing to land heavily in a puddle in the muddy grass. He rolled violently, as if trying to extinguish flames, and then lay worryingly still.

By the time Jox and Anthony Glasgow landed, taxied up to the side of the strip, jumped out and jogged over to him, the local ground crew had sprayed the ruined engine with foam and it was quietly ticking as it cooled, giving off the most appalling charred chemical smell.

Ferriss sat with a wet blanket over his shoulders, gratefully sipping from a canteen of water as he tried to clear his clogged nose and burning throat. He gave them a sheepish grin and croaked, 'That was a bit too bloody close for comfort. Thanks for sticking with me, boys.'

Jox bounded over and hugged him with relief but pulled away instantly at the overpowering reek of smoke and aviation oil. 'Bloody hell, Wheelie, you stink!' he said, covering his nose and gagging.

'Yup, it's horrible,' spluttered Ferriss, before breaking into a thick hacking cough and spitting copious black mucus onto the ground. Finally, able to catch his breath, he whispered, 'Christ, this is rough.' His grimy goggles were still perched on his forehead, with his nose and lower face smeared black with soot and splattered oil. Only his eyes and a bandit mask of pink flesh were unsoiled. Wet tears streaked the grime; tears of gratitude for having survived the ordeal, but also from the oil and fumes. Against the odds, Yellow Section had survived to fight another day.

Jox helped Ferriss up, holding him as they made their way back to Anthony's favourite eatery.

'By God,' Anthony roared. 'They better have some fucking beer. Any foreign muck will do. Today we certainly deserve a tall one!'

'I'll drink to that,' said Ferriss hoarsely.

'Aye, you bloody will,' replied Anthony, grinning ferociously. 'And by the way, it's your shout; officer's prerogative and all that, sir.'

After the fright of nearly losing Ferriss, a depleted A Flight made its weary way back to Blighty, home to safe suburban Northolt after the fiery chaos of France.

Ferriss got a lift home and a lie down aboard a Fairey Battle light bomber, lying prone in the bomb aimer's position.

The celebrations in the bar were subdued, given three popular members of the mess were posted 'Missing in Action, Presumed Dead'.

The biggest shock was the loss of Thompson, CO of the Treble Ones. Rumours were already circulating that he was the downed pilot who'd been spotted being rescued on the ground, but whether his rescuers were friendly or he was already languishing in a German POW camp was unknown.

Flight Lieutenant Charlie Darwood, the senior flight leader and 2ic would normally have stepped up to lead the squadron, but he'd been shot down the previous day. Butcher, his white Bull Terrier, was still haunting the mess, refusing all food or consolation from anyone. Some were beginning to find his mournful howling too harrowing, and he was eventually removed from the mess by Corporal Higgins, Jox and Pritchard's batman, who convinced the other corporals to adopt him.

Instead, it was Flight Lieutenant Bruce who stepped up as acting CO until someone permanent could be appointed by the station commander. It was also his dubious duty to let the others know the fate of the other two pilots lost during the day's operations. They were Flying Officer David Bury from Carlisle, former head boy of Eton College, and Pilot Officer Ian Moorwood from Boscombe in Dorset.

'David is ... er, was a really close friend of mine,' said Bruce, his voice catching. 'What a bloody waste. He was so full of promise. Only last week, he and I cadged a lift to visit his father's grave, Captain Edmond Bury of the King's Royal Rifles, killed in France in 1915. He's buried in Fleurbaix, twenty miles from Lille. It was the first time David had ever seen it.' Bruce looked at the faces of the men before him. 'I can't believe, a week later, he's gone too. He wanted to be a solicitor, like his father and grandfather.' Bruce began to quietly weep. 'He was so damned proud when he showed me his father's medal from the London Olympics in 1908. A silver medal for tennis. The family's Olympian taken by the first war and his son taken today. It's so utterly tragic.'

Bruce wiped his tears on the sleeve of his tunic, staining the sky-blue stripes of his rank. He composed himself. 'Right, we'll find out what we can about those we lost today and of course poor old Charlie yesterday. One or more may still turn up, but we can't really count on it.' He forced a smile. 'Next week, Yellow and Red sections will stand down. Blue and Green are rotating in, led by Jack Copeman and Pete Simpson respectively.'

Tall, lean Copeman nodded his head and Simpson lifted the pipe from his mouth. 'I'll step up as flight leader. Right-o, gents, let's carry on as best we can. I guess it must be CO's round at the bar, so get your orders in; my shout.'

It took Thompson five long days to make his way back from France. Jox listened eagerly to his tale of what had happened. Thompson was caught by cannon fire from a Bf 110 over Valenciennes, cutting his control cables, leaving his stick useless and resulting in a crash-landing in a farmer's field. He was in fact the chap seen being helped by soldiers on the ground. They turned out to be Jocks from the Argyll & Sutherland Highlanders, who, once convinced he was no Jerry — his RAF moustache helped — patched him up, fed him and sent him on his way to Boulogne. There he had little trouble cadging passage back to Blighty, aboard a filthy coal collier, which explained the sorry state of his uniform. Getting a rail warrant to travel back to London from Kent had proven more challenging, as he had no military ID and a face scratched to bits by the hedgerow he'd passed through, and he was generally too filthy to be taken seriously.

'Trust me to run into a bloody-minded bureaucrat, when all I wanted was to get back to my squadron and get back into the fight. Still, never mind, boys. I'm back now and raring to go. Sorry if I gave you a bit of a fright,' he guffawed. 'First off, I need a bloody bath!'

His usually magnificent RAF moustache was looking rather patchy and singed, presumably damaged during his travails returning from the continent. He was a little gaunt, but his spirits seemed undaunted. To the men of No. 111 Squadron, having him back was the tonic they needed, and their morale soared. They'd had a hell of a week, but now things were on the up. Good old Tommy was back.

CHAPTER TEN

No. 111 Squadron was withdrawn from the front line on the 21st of May, 1940, to spend a week at RAF Digby in Lincolnshire for rest and recuperation. They were given time to lick their wounds, mourn their losses and seek replacements to fill the gaps. RAF Digby was one of the RAF's oldest airfields, second only to Northolt, and Lincolnshire's flat land and open views were a big change from West London's busy skies or the carnage they'd seen in France.

During their brief time in the countryside, the battle for France was going from bad to worse. Lord Gort, Commander-in-Chief of the British Expeditionary Force, ordered a general withdrawal of British troops towards Dunkirk on the 19th of May, as German Army Group B approached through Belgium and Army Group A reached the coast to the south, after capturing Amiens and Abbeville. The BEF were effectively encircled and the battle of Dunkirk began in earnest on the 26th of May, with Operation Dynamo, the evacuation of British forces, beginning the next day. Belgium fell on the 28th of May, concluding the 'Campaign of 18 Days', followed by the fall of Lille, Ostend and Ypres in quick succession. The noose around Dunkirk was tightening.

Jox's squadron was sent back into the fray, this time based at RAF North Weald in Essex, callsign COWSLIP. They would be fighting as an independent squadron now. As Thompson put it, 'The gloves are most definitely off.'

To prove the point, previous restrictions on the use of Spitfires over France were lifted and the Hurricane's much vaunted but unproven cousins would finally be joining the fight. For No. 111 Squadron and other 'Hurricane-Jockeys' it was not before time, given what they had already endured.

Some 400,000 British and French soldiers were now trapped at Dunkirk with their backs to the frigid North Sea. It was the Royal Navy's job to get them off the beaches and back home, and the RAF's to keep the Luftwaffe off their backs.

The weather over Dunkirk on Friday 31st May, 1940, the Treble Ones' first day over the beaches, made for difficult flying conditions, but they knew it was certainly grimmer on the ground, down amongst the troops desperate for evacuation. The Luftwaffe's air attacks were more sporadic today than the previous few days, allowing for a record number of men, almost 70,000, to be rescued by the ships queuing up to help. It also meant Britain's fighters could concentrate their efforts on a reduced number of attackers and raids.

Using the line abreast attack formation, which was rapidly becoming their signature, No. 111 Squadron claimed thirteen enemy aircraft, downed with no losses. These included He 111 bombers, Stuka Ju 87 dive-bombers and a single Ju 88 fast bomber, destroyed by Sergeant James Robinson. He was wounded in the ankle by a cannon shell but managed to coax his damaged and bloody Hurricane back to England.

During the first patrol of the day, the squadron was lower than usual, allowing the men the full spectacle of the vast flotilla of motley vessels heading to France, then milling off the coast until they could access the crowded beaches. Standing instructions were for the squadron to stay above twenty thousand feet, keeping out of range of trigger-happy Royal Navy anti-aircraft gunners, but they soon realised enemy attacks on the troops were being launched from much lower.

Junkers 87 Stukas generally began their swooping bombing runs no higher than fifteen thousand feet, to allow them to visually aim their bombs onto targets.

It was just eight in the morning when a large formation was spotted harassing naval targets ranged below. They were being engaged by Boulton Paul Defiants, the first time Jox had seen them in action. They passed through the Stukas, as Anthony later described as 'shite through a goose' with devastating effect. The single-engined monoplane fighters were equipped with a Rolls-Royce Merlin engine like the Hurricane but carried a two-man crew, a pilot up front and a rear gunner. What was unusual about them was their greatest strength, but also their weakness.

The Defiants were let loose amongst them, dispatching half a dozen of the enemy in short order. Stuka crews, feeling comparatively secure with an enemy fighter flying alongside, were smashed to pulp by broadside volleys from quadruple firing .303 machine guns, fired at short range by the Defiants' 360-degree turrets. The grateful acknowledgement from the ships ranged below was heart-warming, praising the Defiants by the sounding their horns.

A trio of Stukas circled above what Jox later learned was the Royal Navy destroyer HMS *Keith*, off the coast at grassy Bray-Dunes, east of Dunkirk town. The Defiants had already cleared off after creating havoc, but more Stukas were coming in waves from inland. HMS *Keith* was attacked in successive bombing runs, the first of which were near misses, sending pluming great spires of foaming water into the air. Eventually one bomb did find its target, slipping down the ship's aft funnel before exploding deep inside a boiler room and taking out a large section of the ship's bottom. A black jet of smoke and debris was violently expelled up the funnel, shooting skywards like the exhaust of a giant firework. The crippled ship immediately listed, then settled in the water, still harassed by swooping dive-bombers.

'Right, I've had enough of this,' said Ferriss, for once forgetting his R/T protocol. 'Let's have a go at them.' Seething at what he was witnessing, the anger in his voice was clear. 'Yellow Section, this is Yellow Leader. All Yellow elements to attack enemy dive-bombers at estimated Angels Nine, below and descending. Tallyho, tallyho.' He banked his Hurricane onto a wing and dropped like a stone, followed closely by Anthony and Jox.

The floundering HMS *Keith* had been hit again. Beside her, a small motorboat tried desperately to transfer sailors from her sloping decks, whilst also pulling flailing men from the frigid water, covered in a thick oil slick from the dying Destroyer.

By ten o'clock, HMS *Keith* was below the waves and her crew, and those they had tried so hard to help, were left to their fates. From her ship's company, three officers and thirty-three ratings lost their lives, but thanks to brave MTB 102 that pulled alongside under fire, eight officers and 123 crewmen were rescued.

In the meantime, Yellow Section were determined to exact some measure of retribution. They pounced on the Ju 87 Stukas, diving like birds of prey, as they pulled out of their attacks on the stricken Destroyer and plucky rescuer.

The Stukas' wailing sirens were loud and distinct through Jox's flying helmet, as he caught one pulling away from the hapless men struggling in the water. A quick burst from his guns silenced the rear gunner, but not before a few hits, like crocuses of light, blossomed on his starboard wing. Checking for damage, he determined it was superficial and returned his attention to his target, by now desperately trying to escape.

He could see g-force's effect on the pilot's face, as his head strained against gravity. Eyes scrunched tightly shut, his mouth gaped open in what looked like a demonic laugh at the plight of his victims. It was of course an illusion, as the force encountered by the two-man Stuka crew when diving could make them black out, with the pilot's column specially equipped with a mechanism to automatically pull the aircraft from a dive when the pilot was incapacitated.

This one wasn't getting away. Thanking providence for the robust build of his Hurricane's wing, Jox dipped the nose and followed his prey, easily matching the Stuka's clumsy evasive actions. A second burst tore the heart out of the gurning pilot, before causing the explosive loss of the Stuka's kinked portside wing, sending the aircraft plummeting to the surface of the North Sea. It hit with a spectacular splash, not far from its recent victim.

Jox could hear nothing but the roar of blood in his ears, but as it cleared, the rush was pierced by the grateful whoops of ships' horns, celebrating the raider's demise. Jox waggled his wings in response, but quickly realised with a damaged wing, it wasn't the smartest of moves. Cursing his stupidity, he sheepishly regained his position within Yellow Section. He felt some small satisfaction at having avenged at least some of his countrymen, bagging himself a solid second kill.

Later, on patrol for the third time over Dunkirk, Jox faced the vaunted Bf 109 single-seater fighter, nicknamed 'Snapper,' for the first time. Small and almost delicate compared to the robust Hurricane, it turned less well than the Hurricane or Spitfire, but thanks to its fuel injection system it could easily out-dive both. It was elegant, swift and deadly in comparison to the Bf 110 Destroyers he had tangled with before, who although massively gunned, powerful and swift, lacked manoeuvrability, a weakness Ferriss had quickly learnt to capitalise upon.

The weather had cleared by early evening and sitreps of the evacuations achieved during the day had reached Luftwaffe fighter control. Late in the day, a 'maximum effort' was called for, sending massed enemy fighters into the tiger-striped, partially overcast skies. They were determined to harass the long-suffering British Expeditionary Force and their beleaguered French allies one more time before nightfall.

Yellow Section were on patrol northeast of Dunkirk, towards La Panne. They were at the rear of the squadron, in a holding pattern at Angels One Four, fourteen thousand feet up. Jox and Pritchard, as the relative novices, were assigned the 'weaver' roles, above and below the formation. Their job was to watch for sneak attacks from the rear, but as 'arse-end Charlies' they were also most at risk of being caught unaware and picked off.

The enemy were sighted at about two thousand feet above them; the classic attack position with the advantage of height. Turning to meet the threat, the formation braced for a swooping attack. Ferriss instructed Jox and Pritchard to close on Red Leader in readiness. Surprisingly, the scattered *Staffel* of delicate-looking but deadly Bf 109s remained high above them, on a vectored course passing directly overhead.

Jox watched nervously, expecting a swift half-roll and for the Bf 109s to fall on them like harriers on pigeons. He joined his comrades from Red and Yellow Sections as they climbed in pursuit of the retreating single-seaters. As they did, half a dozen twin engine Bf 110s were seen diving towards the crowded beaches down the coast.

Ragged lines of men contoured the tideline and spiked out into the water, where they stood in patient queues. Earlier, Jox had seen lorries and other vehicles being parked end to end, then lashed together to create improvised pontoons. At low tide, the wide-open beaches were extremely flat, and it was clear any sea vessel drawing more than a few feet would run aground. In an impressive display of Great British ingenuity, the 'Pongos' had used the low tide to build these pontoons of vehicles which were now swamped, allowing the little ships to moor up and the soaked, shivering men to clamber aboard. Several more pontoons were spaced along the beach, long, accusing fingers pointing the way home, but also at the larger ships, military and civilian, doing the heavy lifting to get the men there.

To the east of the burning town, a timber and concrete mole had been built during peacetime to protect the inner harbour from the sea's strong currents. Now, it was crowded with desperate men; right along the top of the mole itself, but also sheltering in between the crossed timbers holding it up.

Viewed from above, the crowded helmets made the mole look like an assembly line of egg boxes, but as the most obvious means of evacuating men directly onto the decks of larger ships, the men were just as vulnerable. Every enemy bomber targeting the beach used it as a rallying point, and it was hit several times, with untold hundreds of casualties suffered amongst the cowering men. Nevertheless, it still represented the best means for the majority of men to escape the hell of Dunkirk.

Observing from on high, Jox could see it was pretty ragged, broken in several places. Off the end of the pier, several ships had been hit, some damaged, but others sunk by the day's and previous day's actions. Just visible through the foaming grey water, they clustered like spectres, a ghostly collection of dead ships in a shallow naval graveyard.

Racing towards the Bf 110 Destroyers, Jox watched impotently as they strafed along the beach, scattering men like minnows pursued by predatory fish. Wet sand and water were churned up by machine gun fire, with impacts on the men remaining unseen beyond frantic movement, dark crimson spreading through the shallows and then chilling stillness. Frustratingly, despite gunning throttles to a maximum, they were unable to catch up with the raiders and had to call off the pursuit since their fuel gauges indicated worryingly low reserves.

The squadron were heading homewards over dark, churning seas, when a lone Spitfire was spotted, doggedly pursued by a Snapper on his tail. Yellow flight resolved to come to the aid of their little cousin, despite running low on fuel, and pressed an attack on the aggressive Snapper. He quickly realised he was outnumbered, falling away spectacularly, as if damaged and out of control, but then elegantly recovered, before racing for the French coast. He was clearly an *Experten*, who had 'played dead' to make good his escape.

Unable to chase after the wily bandit, a frustrated Ferriss said, 'Yellow Section, Yellow Leader. Little bugger's the one that got away today. Can't risk going after him. We'll be on fumes when we get back as it is. Time to go home, boys.'

One after the other, they turned towards the setting sun to complete their final patrol of the day. They would undoubtedly be back all too soon, but in the meantime the mess bar beckoned most sweetly.

CHAPTER ELEVEN

'I know, let's go to London and find old Moose on the way,' said Pritchard, his head lolling over the wooden expanse of the officers' mess bar.

'We can't, we're on duty tomorrow,' answered an equally inebriated Jox. 'Anyway, it's three o'clock in the morning. Far too late to go on an expedition!' he pronounced more loudly than he'd intended.

'What? I'm fine. A bit of fresh air and I'll be right as rain.'

'No chance, you've had a skinful,' said Jox, struggling to stay perched on his bar stool.

'Maybe you're right,' said Pritchard, suddenly rather moody. He'd gone quiet and Jox feared his friend was going to be sick. That wouldn't make them popular in the morning. 'It was bloody awful, wasn't it?'

'What was?'

'Dun-bloody-kirk,' said Pritchard. 'Poor sodding Pongos. They really copped it. I saw some poor bastards bursting wide open, splashing red jam everywhere.'

'That wasn't what got me,' said Jox, now also staring into the middle distance, reliving the horrors he'd seen during the day. 'It was the bodies in the water; hundreds of them drifting in the current like human seaweed.'

'How will we ever forget?' asked Pritchard.

Jox sighed and rubbed his eyes vigorously with his knuckles, as if trying to exorcise what was seared into them. 'I don't think we ever will.'

'I can't close my eyes without seeing them again,' said a teary Pritchard. 'How will I get any sleep?'

Jox peered at the finger of Scotch left in his tumbler, draining it in a single swallow. 'This'll certainly help,' he sighed. 'It has to. Come on, old chum, finish up. We've still got tomorrow to face.' He wrapped his arm around his tall friend's shoulders and lifted him from his stool. He was surprised at how heavy he was, steering him to the room they shared. 'Tomorrow,' he mumbled into Pritchard's already deaf ears. 'I can't bear to think of it.'

Pritchard was rather green around the gills the next morning, as the pair made their way unsteadily to their respective aircraft. Neither was really feeling up to it but had faith in the one sure way of perking up and instantly getting rid of their hangovers. Once settled into their cockpits, their chamois leather masks went straight on and the knobs were swiftly turned to release an invigorating blast of oxygen from their tanks. A few deep sniffs were just the thing to clear thick heads. It was a miracle how well it worked, and it wasn't the first time they'd depended on this gaseous morning regimen. Officially frowned upon by the powers that be, it had pretty much become standard practice amongst fighter pilots who needed to let off steam after trying missions, but also be in shape for what the following day would bring.

Feeling more or less human again, or at least alert enough to function, the friends were soon wheels-up, after a quick pre-flight check with the ground crew. Jox took up his position in Yellow Section's Vic, as the squadron settled in for the flight over southern England, the channel and onto Dunkirk. He was enjoying the cool solitude of the cockpit, the purr of the engine and the spectacle of 'the green and pleasant land' which he and his comrades had sworn to defend.

The tie around his neck felt rather tight, so he undid the top button to breathe more easily. Wearing it was an attempt to convince anyone observing that he was 'absolutely fine' after the excesses of last night. Jox leant back into his cockpit seat and cricked his head from side to side, checking his movement and vision were unencumbered. He heard the crunching of the bones in his neck, releasing the tension within. It sounded horrible and made his Hurricane wobble but was a daily part of his morning flight routine.

Jox reckoned he was somewhere between an average to fairly good pilot, no longer feeling like a fraud or parvenu within the squadron. He'd seen others taken through their paces and knew he definitely wasn't the worst amongst them. He wasn't so strong on certain technical aspects of aviation but had a good instinct for flight and a natural feel for it. The intricacies of how the power was generated by the Rolls-Royce Merlin engine's twelve cylinders still baffled him, but at least he was comfortable with the steps, processes and checks for sundry magnetos, booster valves, radiator shutters and other gizmos, which allowed him to get to the flying part.

On take-off earlier, with the engine running, he'd released the ground brake and had begun rolling forward. He sensed the airflow across the surfaces of the wings and felt the lift on the tailfin. Once the rattle of the wheels was silenced, he retracted them into the body of the wings and he felt released.

It was as natural to him as skating or skiing, both of which he excelled at. He didn't understand how or why, but instinctively he knew when to bank, dive or sideslip. He felt every bump, throb or twitch of the aircraft through his hands on the control column, but also through his feet on the pedals and even from the seat of his pants. He smiled, remembering the wise words of Newitt, his instructor at Fairoaks, telling him 'to feel the aircraft through your body and buttocks'. He could almost smell the 'Mellow Virginia' tobacco from the old chap's pipe.

It was a clearer day than yesterday and would undoubtedly be a long and difficult one, but he couldn't feel sorry for himself, compared to the lot of the poor sods still on the beach. He glanced over to Anthony Glasgow flying beside him, his face a picture of concentration. Actually, he couldn't see much of his face, covered as it was by his oxygen mask and goggles, but he could imagine the intensity of those pale eyes, scanning the horizon for movement as they approached the enemy coast.

Jox and Pritchard were called to their positions as top and bottom weavers by Thompson. Today, Jox would be up high and Pritchard down low. Jox really hoped the oxygen had done the trick for his hungover friend, otherwise it really would be a miserable day.

'WAGON Squadron, WAGON Leader here. Enemy coast ahead. Double check your masks as we climb to Angels One Five,' said Thompson. 'I want no repeat of yesterday when Robbie Powell passed out because of a mask failure. He's bloody lucky to have come out of it at Angels Five, otherwise there'd be bits of him all over *La Belle France*.' He paused, allowing them time to carry out the necessary checks. 'Right, let's go see if we can find some trouble.'

They didn't have to search for very long.

The sea was calmer, stretching away from them like a vast expanse of green marble. At this altitude, it reminded Jox of the billiard table he'd spent far too much time drinking Scotch over with Pritchard last night. Up ahead, a thick pall of black smoke rose from Dunkirk, which had been burning for days. Back at North Weald, Badger Robertson, doubling as intelligence officer until they found themselves a proper one, had said the town's industrial warehouses and manufacturing plants were full of chemicals, adding to the noxious fumes the poor sods on the beach were enduring, not to mention the inhabitants of the town.

'WAGON Squadron, WAGON Leader here. Vector 128, southeast by east. Maintain Angels One Five and keep a sharp eye out. We'll be crossing over the mole, then heading inland to find some trade. Weavers get moving. Acknowledge,' said Thompson.

'Roger that,' replied Jox, and began oscillating his Hurricane above and behind the formation. Below him and blending into the flecked green of the sea, he could see Pritchard doing the same. Jox glanced left to right, above and behind, in what he felt sure looked like some demented tic. He squinted into the sun's glare, then carefully scanned across the smooth sea surface once again. Whatever happened, he wouldn't be the one caught napping.

It was another sharp-eyed member of the formation who spotted a trio of Heinkel 111 bombers beneath them, intent on an anti-shipping target amongst the many scattered ships. Looming largest amongst them was an antiquated paddle steamer, a commandeered pleasure craft, far from its usual home. It left a distinctive churning wake as it manoeuvred itself near the mole. Beside it, a smaller vessel was painted white with an ostentatious red cross on its flat roof, clearly a hospital ship.

'Christ!' said an unbelieving voice. 'Can't those bastards see the bloody Red Cross?' Jox recognised the voice as Ferriss's.

'Of course they can,' replied Thompson. 'That's what they're ruddy aiming for. Gentlemen, this is your enemy. WAGON Squadron, WAGON Leader. Bandits at three o'clock low.

Estimated Angels Ten. Attack formation ... on my mark ... and break. Tallyho, tallyho.'

The squadron opened like a flower and bore down onto the unsuspecting bombers. Amongst the shipping, huge geysers of white water plumed as the first Heinkel's bombs exploded amongst them.

Jox watched, fascinated as Thompson's Red Section caught it. A brief trail of cordite smoke feathered from the wings of each Hurricane, as they fired at the enemy. First one, then the other of the Heinkel's engines started to smoke, before it began slowly sinking earthwards. Red Section's opening salvos were murderous, since there was no return fire from any of the bomber's four gunners.

A single white parachute blossomed in the smoky wake of its burning engines, etching a curving double parabola towards the sea. Yellow and Blue Sections were now engaging a second Heinkel.

Either Wheelie Ferriss or Anthony Glasgow fired a long burst into the bulbous egg-shaped cockpit, shattering Perspex panels like those of a greenhouse when pelted with stones. Suddenly exposed to high-speed airflow rushing in, more panels ripped away and the front of the bomber seemed to implode. The wind drag must have been too strong to fight, since once again only a single parachute escaped the stricken craft.

Jox spotted another airman trying to escape from the gaping front end, arms and legs flailing as he streaked away, but no chute opened as he fell silently and smashed into the sea, an afterthought to the earlier splash of the aircraft.

Jox looked to check Pritchard was maintaining his position and caught sudden movement to his rear. It only took an instant to recognise a pair of prowling Snappers, sleek Bf 109s sliding onto Pritchard's tail.

'Pritch, bandits on your six. Break, break!' he screamed into his mic.

Pritchard reacted instantly, banking sharply to first dip one way and then roll the other. A hungry tongue of tracer snatched after him, as he barrel rolled.

Jox dipped his own aircraft, straining to get after the second Snapper. Spots began to appear before his eyes, as he grunted with the centrifugal force bearing down on him. He managed to croak, 'WAGON Squadron, Yellow Three. Bandits to our rear. Two spotted, but there may be more. Break, break!'

The squadron were already in loose Vics, spread out and ready to take their signature line attack positions when required. They scattered like the final flourish of a firework, each radiating outward. Within seconds, aircraft were swooping in all directions. It was impossible to tell friend from foe.

Jox's Hurricane fell seawards, as he heard Pritchard's desperate voice screech, 'Jox, he's on me, get him off, get him off!'

'I'm on him, I'm on him,' replied Jox urgently. 'There's another one behind him. On my mark, draw him to the right. Ready, ready ... mark!'

Pritchard slid to the right, then pulled away even more sharply. His pursuer matched the movement and a beat later, so did the enemy number two. This gave Jox just enough time to sideslip his aircraft and let the second Snapper glide across the target rings projected onto the windscreen. He pressed the trigger and heard a reassuring roar of guns. Bright metal flew from the sleek Messerschmitt and within seconds he was tumbling, trailing a silvery wake like a child's sparkler. Jox had no time to watch, as he tightened onto the second bandit, chasing his friend's tail.

Pritchard jinked across the sky as if his life depended on it, but his pursuer was dogged and determined. He led them on a swirling, deadly game of follow the leader, grunting at the ever-tightening circles. Jox attempted a snatched shot, firing a burst as the bandit flashed across him. He missed completely but was horrified when Pritchard said, 'You've dinged me you damned fool!' A trail of smoke escaped from the starboard exhaust stubs on Pritchard's nose.

Seeing his prey winged, the bandit stopped weaving to line up a kill shot on Pritchard's struggling Hurricane. Perhaps it was the excitement of the moment, but he'd forgotten that Jox was still behind him. They fired at the same time. Pritchard fell away, trailing even more smoke, and the nimble Bf 109 burst into flames, a lucky tracer round striking the L-shaped fuel tank behind the pilot's armour plate and beneath his seat. The glow of the fire engulfed the inside of the cockpit until the canopy lid popped open and a flaming figure scrambled out. He tumbled away from the aircraft's burning wake, burning brightly until he too was extinguished by the cold water below.

Jox searched desperately for Pritchard, as he spotted two Hurricanes trailing smoke. One was falling towards the beach, the other towards England. He barely had a second to choose which to follow, when he felt several teeth-rattling thumps along the length of his fuselage. The stick became slack and unresponsive, but he still had some control through his foot pedals and the throttle lever in his left hand. He glanced up at his mirror and saw the twinkling flashes of someone shooting at him. The Merlin engine, usually so smooth, was now ragged, coughing and knocking, as it spluttered its life away. He knew he was done for and tried banking hard, to reach the beach.

The dials on his dashboard shattered before his eyes and paralysing fear gripped him, as the unexpected warmth of urine flowed down his leg.

The Hurricane hit the glassy surface of the water with a glancing blow and skipped like a pebble, bouncing several times before the belly radiator scoop ploughed deep, sending a capsule of frothing water over the canopy. Before banging his head on the shattered dashboard, Jox had the presence of mind to raise the propellered head, to ensure the tail and rear wheel struck first, so the aircraft didn't tumble arse over tit, before being pulled straight down by its engine-heavy head. Instead, its momentum cut a wake in the water like a giant duck landing. The prop thrashed sea spume until finally stopping, a single wooden blade pointing skywards like the black fin of an orca.

Panicking at the sight of all this water, Jox instinctively pulled the toggle of his yellow Mae West and immediately regretted it as it inflated, wedging him against the sides of the cockpit. Outside, a horizon of green water began climbing the windscreen. White water bubbled furiously up between Jox's knees, and he knew he didn't have long before she sank and took him down with her.

In a last desperate act, Jox reached above his head and tugged at the twin handles of the sliding cockpit cover with all his strength. The lid jerked back, releasing a further cascade of water into the confines of the cockpit. He undid his straps with difficulty, due to his foolishly inflated life jacket, then braced his feet against the bottom of the cockpit and pushed hard, making an almighty effort to stand upright.

He popped out of the cockpit like the proverbial cork, and duly inhaled a good deal of sea water. The buoyancy of his life preserver gently lifted him over a passing wave as he gagged.

He leant back, panting and looking up at the streaked sky. There were still aircraft buzzing noisily in all directions, with several spiralling smoke trails of those who had gone down like him.

The water wasn't as cold as he'd expected, but he felt heavy and encumbered by his clothing. He flung away his gauntlets, kicked off his boots, then whipped off his flying helmet. The wet oxygen mask and mic cable had been irritatingly flapping against his face.

The Hurricane was sinking fast and hot engine parts sizzled as the water reached them. It groaned in the current and Jox realised he had to get away or risk being pulled down by the vacuum of the aircraft sinking. He kicked a few thrashing strokes but didn't know which way he should be heading. He stopped, then using his arms to spin, he tried to get his bearings. Quickly exhausted, it dawned on him he could be here for a while.

Bobbing gently in the water, his mood darkened as he realised he might actually have shot down Pritchard's stricken aircraft. He was feeling rather sorry for himself when a deep, baritone voice called out from behind.

'Ahoy there, soldier! You wantin' a lift home, boy?'

Jox spun to glimpse hands reaching over the rough slatted sides of a timber whaler boat. The back of his life vest was hauled up by a boathook on the end of a pole, and he tumbled into a pool of brackish water at the bottom of the boat. He looked up to see a grinning black man, white teeth edged by a thick salt and pepper beard.

'Boy, you're lucky we're passin' and have space for you,' chuckled the sailor. He looked across to another burly black man wearing a navy donkey jacket under a kapok life jacket, who was handling the boathook. 'Curtis, come now. This boy needs a blanket.'

The other put down his pole, grabbed a felted grey blanket from a pile and threw it across.

'There now,' said the first seaman. 'You settle down here with them boys and wrap up with this blanket. Here, take me hat,' he said, removing a knitted woollen bonnet. 'My name is Oscar, and I'm glad we found you. We'll get back right now to the ship and maybe get a bit of rum inside you.'

Jox peered at the dozen or so other bedraggled soldiers huddled in the open boat. They were pale, filthy and hollow-eyed. One had no boots and another had his head wrapped in a soiled bandage. Some wore helmets but most had salt-encrusted hair or were smeared with congealed oil. They looked like they'd been through the grinder.

One, an angry-looking chap with a bald head, moustache and two pips said, 'RAF, eh? Where the bloody hell have you been?'

Jox glared at him, but replied steadily, 'Fighting, but up there. I just saw my best friend go down, before I got hit too.'

The other man bristled, desperate to find someone to blame for what he'd experienced. 'Never saw hide nor hair of you lot, did we, lads?'

A number of the others muttered their agreement.

'Hush now, boys,' interrupted Oscar, the greybeard. 'We've all done what we could. You sit down, get yerself warm and let old Oscar and Curtis get you back to Blighty. We're goin' back to the ship, to tie up and then get towed back to Hingland. The war is over for you boys, at least for a while.'

It took about half an hour to get clear of the tide off the beach. Oscar and Curtis rowed with a comfortable rhythm, as Jox peered at the windswept French coastline. Hundreds of ships were still waiting to collect men, but the beaches did seem emptier. The mole was still crowded and along the western dunes he saw what looked like flashes of lightning striking the beach, sending smudges of grey sand into the air, followed by the dull thuds of impacts.

'That artillery fire's coming in from Gravelines,' said the bald lieutenant, who, judging by his Royal Artillery tabs, would know what he was talking about. 'Jerry's *Blitzkrieg* has finally broken through to the east.' He gave Jox an embarrassed look. 'Sorry about earlier. It was simply frustration talking. No offence meant.'

'None taken,' replied Jox wearily. The cold in his damp clothing and wet stockinged feet was starting to bite.

Once the whaler was hitched alongside the merchant steamer *Tortola* by stout ropes, it took three hours before the familiar cliffs of the Kent coast were in sight. It was nearly dark when the weary men filed off the open boat onto the crowded quayside at Deal in Kent. By then many were thoroughly seasick, piling further misery onto men who had already suffered far too much.

Stepping onto dry land, Jox felt a little unsteady. Alone on the quayside, he reached for the pocket of his damp RAF tunic. There he found the hard porcelain form of the little Marguerite's dolly's arm. Somehow, it had become his lucky talisman.

CHAPTER TWELVE

A few days later, Jox was back at RAF Northolt.

'She's a real beauty sir,' said Flight Sergeant Barnes in a reverent voice. He and Corporal Blackie, the fitter, stood by Jox, admiring his brand-new Hawker Hurricane Mark 1A. 'That's a three-bladed Rotol airscrew there. She's got an all-hydraulic landing gear, leading edges skinned in sheet metal and a chuffing great Merlin III engine with a supercharger boost. Give you an extra thirty miles per hour when you need it to get in or out of trouble.'

'She's a beauty all right, sir,' agreed Blackie. 'Get you up to fifteen thousand feet in just over six minutes. That's higher than the tallest Alps, sir.' He rubbed a smooth cloth over the aircraft's new paint job, as if stroking the flank of a racehorse. 'Look at this,' he said, ducking under the portside wing. Jox dropped to his knee to see what he was pointing at. 'They've painted the underside of the wings a duck-egg blue. None of that black wing, white wing business anymore. It may have been useful in peacetime to be spotted from the ground, but with Jerry's anti-aircraft gunners trying to blast holes into you, best not to attract attention.'

'This "doghouse" is a lot roomier for you — begging your pardon, sir, I mean the cockpit,' added Barnes, whose long body was leaning against the new Hurricane's solid metalled wing. 'Bubble canopy for extra headspace and an armoured windscreen too. They've even added armour plating behind the seat. All clever stuff, this.' Barnes was clearly impressed, now shielding his eyes from the glare off the aircraft's freshly doped surface. 'She's a beauty, all right.'

Jox was keeping his own counsel as he looked over his new aircraft. Three of the new Mark 1As had been delivered that morning by Air Transport Auxiliary (ATA) pilots, fresh from the factory at Brooklands in Surrey. The pilots had turned out to be remarkably pretty women, who'd caused quite a stir when they had landed. One of the aircraft was destined for Thompson, who had crashed his in France. The next was for Ferriss, whose previous aircraft had proven too burnt-out to be salvaged, and finally this one was for Jox, a replacement for the late, great JU-X, lying at the bottom of the English Channel.

'I've been meaning to ask,' said Flight Sergeant Barnes. 'How's Mr Pritchard doing? The boys in the maintenance hangars were talking and told me he was injured.'

'Yes, that's right,' replied Jox gloomily. 'Thankfully, I think he's going to be all right. He made it back from France in one piece but with his Hurricane in trouble. He pancaked in some hop field over in Kent but got tangled up in all the plants and wires. He's hurt his leg and is convalescing by the seaside at RAF Hospital Torquay. I spoke to him on the telephone, and he said he's fine and will be back in about a month. He said not to worry and that he's giving the nurses merry hell.'

The ground crew laughed at the thought of Pritchard, who they knew was one for the ladies, chasing after the squealing sisters on his crutches. Jox joined in with their laughter, trying to mask his relief that Pritchard had made it home more or less in one piece. When they'd spoken, he'd apologised for hitting his aircraft, but Pritchard laughed it off.

'You seem to be forgetting the Snapper you got off my tail, just before you and the second chap decided to have a tickle. As far as I'm concerned, chum, you're the one who saved me, rather than putting me here. I owe you one, not the other way around.'

Earlier, Thompson had called Jox into his office. Jox had feared the worst, especially when he saw both Ferriss and 'Badger' Robertson waiting there too. They told him Pritchard was in hospital and would be fine, but that unfortunately Sergeant Anthony Glasgow was posted Missing in Action.

'Cameron isn't taking it at all well and after a discussion with the MO, we've decided to send him on a spot of leave,' said Thompson. 'That leaves us short of three men, on top of the three we lost earlier in May. It's an unsustainable rate of attrition,' he added bitterly. This explained their serious faces.

'We're having a shuffle around,' said Thompson. 'We're moving you up to Yellow Two with Wheelie and we've found a replacement for a new Yellow Three. It'll be your responsibility to watch out for him and get him trained up.'

'His name is Toby something double-barrelled and he's straight out of school, a bit like you, so the two of you should get on,' said Robertson. 'Tall fellow, bright blond hair and well built. He's waiting in my office and for goodness' sake, find him a nickname; I can't be dealing with that double-barrelled nonsense.'

'Look, I know you've not been with us for all that long,' said Thompson. 'But your performance in France was impressive. The two Bf 109s you got off Pritchard's back, which we're letting you have as one destroyed and one probable, brings your total up to three and half, well, almost four kills. That's almost enough to make you an ace, so congratulations, not too far to go.'

They gathered around to shake his hand and thump him on the back. Jox stood there getting winded and feeling like a bit of a fraud.

'Higgs, one of our old boys, is re-joining the squadron after completing a R/T course at RAF Uxbridge,' said Thompson. 'He'll step in as Red Two, but we'll still need to find a replacement for Pritchard. How long did you say he's out of action?'

'He said about a month. He's feeling well enough but can't bend his leg. He won't be much use in a cockpit until he can.'

'Not sure he's much use in any case,' muttered Thompson darkly.

'A bit harsh, chief,' said Robertson. 'Poor chap took one for the team.'

'Well, yes, I suppose so, but it was young McNabb who got those two bloody Snappers off his back and saved his bacon.'

Knowing what he knew, Jox felt an even greater fraud.

'We're also getting a few new kites and one of them will be for you. Personalise it if you want,' said Thompson. 'Perks of being an aspiring ace, what?'

Which explained why Jox was standing with his ground crew, trying to decide what to add to the paint job of the factory-fresh JU-X.

'Surely you must have a sweetheart, sir,' said Blackie. 'Some darling Coleen back home in Scotland, maybe?'

'Nope, afraid not. Nothing like that,' replied Jox.

'How about your mother's name, then?' suggested Barnes.

'She died when I was very young. I can barely remember her.'

'Come on, sir. We've got to think of something.'

Jox looked at the delicate porcelain arm of a little girl's dolly in the palm of his hand. 'I want you to call her "Marguerite". Write it in cursive handwriting, as if it was written by a schoolgirl. For each of my kills, I don't want a black cross, just a simple daisy, as in the flower.'

'A daisy? Are you sure, sir?' asked Barnes. 'I'm not sure Squadron Leader Thompson's going to like it much. Not exactly warlike, if you don't mind me saying.'

'He said I could have whatever I wanted, and that's what I want,' replied Jox.

'Right you are, sir,' replied the red-headed aircraft rigger. 'Begging your pardon for asking, but who's Marguerite?'

'Just someone who reminds me what I'm fighting for.' Jox tucked the toy arm back into his breast pocket. 'Tell you what, maybe you're right about the warlike bit. How about you add a bare arm holding a Scottish Claymore sword? There on the side of the nose, beneath the exhaust stubs? Should do the trick, don't you think?'

Pilot Officer Tobias Carmel-Connolly was a good foot taller than Jox, in an awkward 'I grew this tall over a single summer and haven't got used to it' sort of way. He had rowed at school, for the county and then inexplicably for Wales. Correspondingly, he was a bulky proposition with a shock of white-blond hair and rosy cheeks, adorable on a little boy, but not ideal on a fighter pilot who wants to be taken seriously. He'd come straight from training and was eager to please, brimming with puppy energy, which made Jox feel tired just looking at him.

'It's Toby, isn't it?' asked Jox. 'How many hours do you have?' Jox found himself asking the same questions that Robertson had asked what felt like years ago, but it had only been a few months. He concluded by saying, 'Stick with me. Do what I ask of you, and I expect you'll be fine.'

He paused, knowing he'd forgotten something. His name!

'Look, Toby, we try to keep things pretty informal. So, I'm Jox, our section leader is Wheelie, the adjutant is Badger and the Squadron Leader is Tommy; well, at least when you're not in trouble. I've been told to find you a nickname and I've come up with "Jugs", as in Toby Jug, and to be honest those ears are almost as red as your cheeks.'

'Er … right … sir.'

'I'm not a sir, I'm the same rank as you,' said Jox, enjoying the fellow's discomfort.

'I can live with Jugs,' Toby replied. 'But I don't fancy having to explain it to my mother.' In spite of his size, he was clearly a mummy's boy and the apple of her eye.

'Right, Jugs it is. Now, let's go have a spin. Get to know your old Hurricane.'

The battle for Dunkirk ended during the night of Tuesday, 4th June, 1940, when a final twenty-seven thousand French troops were evacuated, leaving almost twice the number to be captured. Over three and half thousand British troops died defending the perimeter and practically all of the British Expeditionary Force's heavy equipment was either destroyed or abandoned to the enemy. The Treble Ones were active over the beaches right until the very end, with Sunday, 2nd June being a particularly big day.

David Bruce, Pritchard's Red Leader, bagged a He 111, then damaged a Bf 109 and a Hs 126. Green Leader Pete Simpson got a probable Bf 110 and Canadian Pilot Officer Rob Roy Wilson destroyed a Bf 109, damaging a second over the beaches. Hit in the process, he managed to limp home to England, until fumes forced him to bale out short of the coast. His Hurricane crashed into the sea, but a useful onshore breeze drifted him inland, and he arrived unhurt a mile from RAF Manston in Kent.

The next morning the squadron were back to a complement of twelve and were relocated, this time to the civilian aerodrome of London Croydon, renamed as RAF Croydon for the duration. It was on the outskirts of southeast London and was a satellite station to RAF Kenley, call sign TOP HAT, controlling Sector B of Fighter Command's 11 Group.

Before leaving RAF North Weald, Thompson held a briefing to say he expected a tight formation as they flew to Croydon. He warned that he planned to take them through their paces on the way there.

'You old salts seem to be slackening off and our new bloods need to be brought up to speed, so I've decided to make you sweat. Our rate of losses is unacceptable, and I'm convinced it's because our formation is too loose for proper mutual protection.'

His faith in massed attacks on bombers, using the weight of numbers to break up the stream, remained unshaken, despite the squadron's recent losses and rather too many mid-air near misses. The men realised they were in for some hard-going attack drills, always within nerve-shattering feet of each other. The prospect of their flight to Croydon was already sounding terrifying.

They took off in a loose arrowhead, streaking across the wide-open grass of the airfield. A steep battle climb followed, scrabbling for altitude as they would under battle conditions. On the ground, each section of three had formed in a loose Vic, with Thompson leading Red Section, and Yellow and Blue positioned to their left and right, to create a larger Vic. Green Section formed up to the left again, but slightly to the rear. Facing into the light summer breeze, the entire squadron released ground brakes, opened up throttles and accelerated down the airfield. Gathering speed, their tails lifted as air flowed over the Hurricanes' stocky wings. Left hands on the throttle levers, they pulled back their central control columns to gently lift the aircraft, keeping them far enough apart to avoid propwash, but in position with their feet in the stirrups of the floor pedals.

Thompson's lead Hurricane was the first to fold away his wheels as he began his ascent. Straining to maintain their positions and harried by constantly barked instructions, the men followed through the morning haze and the scattered clouds forecast by the Met men. It was a hard slog, climbing at a rate of a thousand feet every sixty seconds, their ears popping with the altitude.

'WAGON Leader to Red Two; close up, damn you. Keep it tight,' barked Thompson.

The formation inched closer together. Jox was flying as Yellow Two and watched his section leader, Ferriss, obsessively, stationed forward of him and to his left. He also kept an eye on Red Three, just ahead of him, as well as the new boy at Yellow Three, to his left.

Jugs was always a little late executing any manoeuvre, wobbling dangerously after each move. He was often so close that Jox could count the rivets down the side of his cockpit. So focused was he on flying alongside the unsteady newcomer, that it dawned on Jox that he had barely looked around or considered any external threat out there. He resolved to have a serious word with the new boy before he got either or both of them killed.

'Flights by echelon will move to the starboard side ... on my mark... Go,' ordered Thompson.

Green Section swung away first, clearing the airspace behind them, just as Blue Section slipped in, wobbling in their propwash. Red and Yellow sections followed suit, until the entire formation had changed direction. They progressed from one evolution to the next, a peculiar murmuration of stocky metal and doped canvas birds, snaking across the skies.

Undoubtedly impressive from the ground, Jox couldn't help wondering how tactically useful it really was, panting and grunting with the exertion of each turn, loop and dip inflicted upon them. Every time the Vics reformed and closed up, he saw how perilously close they came to disaster. With sweat streaking down behind his mask, he wondered, after his own brief but intense experience of combat, what was really the point of all this. His fight had been pure chaos and nothing like the balletic precision of these acrobatics.

They were drilled repeatedly, changing altitude, altering course and changing positions, over and over again, and always with Thompson's voice nagging them to tighten up and move faster. The concentration required was exhausting, with any misunderstanding threatening catastrophe.

Having completed a series of stomach-lurching mock attacks, followed by steep power climbs to recover the dominant upper positions, Thompson finally relented and gave the bearing for Croydon, their new home.

Coming in to land, they followed the usual procedure, but were made to feel self-conscious by Thompson's Hurricane orbiting and keeping a critical eye on their landings.

Jox concentrated on reducing his speed to 150 mph; lining up the landing strip and deploying the undercarriage. He listened for the whirring of the hydraulics, then the solid clunk-clunk of each wheel locking into place. He checked for the green light on the dash, then reduced his speed further. Height was at 700 feet and descending.

Low enough to slide his hood back to get some fresh air after all the exertion, Jox gulped the cool breeze as he glanced at the windsock, making sure he was landing downwind. Flaps down, he was all set for the final approach. Dropping lower still, he came bumping down in what was a reasonable landing. Keeping his nose up, the wheels rumbled across the bumpy grass and applying the brakes, he swung her side to side, using friction to slow down.

Speaking in his headphones, a woman's voice that sounded oddly familiar said, 'Wheels down. Welcome to Croydon.'

He taxied to the position indicated by an airman waving white paddles and switched everything off when they crossed. Climbing down from his Mark 1a, resplendent with her new paintwork, he felt a rush of pride. There had been some gentle ribbing from the others about the flora adorning his aircraft, but once he'd explained the inspiration for the name and daisies, most were complimentary about the choice.

He was parked next to a pilot with an unfamiliar face. The man approached and introduced himself as Flying Officer Peter Higgs. He was from Oldham in Lancashire, had joined the University Air Squadron whilst at Merton College, Oxford and having just graduated, he'd joined up about the same time as Jox. Higgs was twenty-three, so had a few years on Jox, but was about the same height, with dark hair and a thin moustache unsuccessfully attempting to disguise a youthful face. He seemed friendly and self-deprecating, and Jox liked him immediately.

When he was introduced to Jugs, Higgs exclaimed in an exaggerated accent but with no trace of meanness, 'By heck, lad, by the look you, you ought to be on t'other side.'

And he wasn't far wrong. With his bright blond hair, blue eyes and rosy cheeks, the hulking Jugs was pretty much the beau ideal of a young Teutonic knight, beloved of National Socialist mythology. The red marks left by the mask on his face, after Thompson's manoeuvres, even provided the semblance of duelling scars. Jugs sniggered self-consciously with the others but was clearly glad to be accepted by the squadron.

CHAPTER THIRTEEN

It was early June 1940, when No. 111 Squadron first arrived at RAF Croydon. They were joined shortly afterwards by No. 501 'County of Gloucester' Squadron, flying in from St Helier in Jersey, where the 'Boar's Heads', as they were known, had regrouped after the fall of France. Following the subsequent invasion of the island, this group of experienced pilots were also familiar with what to expect from a pitiless enemy, pulling out in the nick of time.

They were to become dependable comrades to the Treble Ones and solid messmates. Both had been through the meat grinder of France and what the newspapers were now calling the 'miracle of Dunkirk'. Both waited with trepidation to see what the enemy would do next.

The new Prime Minister, Winston Churchill, was on BBC radio on the evening of the 18th of June, broadcasting a speech he'd made to the House earlier in the day. He was steely and forthright, expressing the hope and resolve the nation would need to make it through the dark months ahead. The usually boisterous mess quietened down to hear what he had to say, and the airmen huddled around the wireless set up on the bar:

'The Battle of France is over: the Battle of Britain is about to begin. Upon this battle depends the survival of Christian civilisation. Upon it depends our own British life, and the long continuity of our institutions and our Empire.

'The whole fury and might of the enemy must very soon be turned on us. Hitler knows that he will have to break us in this island or lose the war. If we can stand up to him, all Europe may be freed and the life of the world may move forward into broad, sunlit uplands. But if we fail, then

the whole world, including the United States, including all that we have known and cared for, will sink into the abyss of a new Dark Age made more sinister, and perhaps more protracted, by the lights of perverted science.

'*Let us therefore brace ourselves to our duty and so bear ourselves that, if the British Empire and its Commonwealth last for a thousand years, men will still say: "This was their finest hour".*'

Elsewhere in the speech, he referred to 'the darkest hour in French history,' but what was a little unclear to the assembled Treble Ones was quite when this hour ended and the 'finest hour' began.

On Thursday 6th June 1940, the squadron were escorting Bristol Blenheim light bombers on a raid over the Abbeville area, on the eastern flank of the beleaguered 51st Highland Division, still trapped in France. They were bounced by several *Staffel* of high-flying Messerschmitt Bf 109 fighters, resulting in the Blenheims scattering like panicked sheep. As their faithful sheepdogs, the Treble Ones did their best to keep them together, rather than get picked off one at a time by the marauding pack of wolves.

David Bruce, leading Yellow Section, claimed a Bf 109, adding to the probable Hs 126 observation aircraft bagged earlier in the day. Ferriss claimed two more Bf 109s, leading a few weeks later to official recognition when his name appeared in the *London Gazette* of 21st June 1940. He was to be awarded the Distinguished Flying Cross by His Majesty the King himself, as the first British fighter pilot to shoot down eight German aircraft in three successive sorties.

As for Jox, he was just pleased to still be in one piece, and grateful his ward, Jugs, was too.

At Green Two, Sergeant Ron Brown wasn't so fortunate. He was forced to bale out over what he took to be German-occupied France but was fortunate to be picked up by some Grenadier Guards, retreating south in good order, perfectly befitting the disciplined elite Household Division. Slightly wounded, he was taken to a field hospital, then packed off on a train, finally finding himself aboard a hospital ship bound for England. Yet another Treble One had made it home, taking the long way.

The German forces entered Paris on 14th June 1940, before which all remaining British troops in France were ordered to withdraw. The order came too late for the 51st Highland Division, encircled at St. Valéry-en-Caux, who surrendered en-masse on 12th June. This calamity affected central Scotland most heavily, and since this was where Jox had been to school, over the following weeks he learnt of several old school chums who were 'in the bag' and would remain prisoners for years to come.

Elsewhere, the evacuation of a second BEF was underway from several southerly French ports and on a scale similar to Dunkirk. The squadron flew defensive sorties over what became known as 'Operation Aerial'. They witnessed no end of chaos, carnage and the loss of many lives — most tragically, the Luftwaffe's bombing of a Cunard passenger liner called *Lancastria* with six thousand souls aboard, including many children and civilians, as well as wounded and evacuated troops. She sank off St Nazaire, with the loss of well over four thousand.

France finally surrendered on the 22nd of June 1940. To twist the knife in the wound, she was forced to sign the documents of surrender inside the very same rail carriage where Germany had surrendered in 1918.

This lull directly after the fall of France left the members of No. 111 Squadron and their messmates despondent and pretty low. The tonic they needed came in the form of the Canucks of No. 1 Royal Canadian Air Force. Assigned to becoming operational under the tutelage of the veteran Treble Ones, with them came Jox and Pritchard's training pal from RAF Montrose, Moose Grant. This was the lift Jox needed when he had been feeling convalescent Pritchard's absence most keenly.

Their reunion was typically embarrassing for Jox. Spotting his friend, the enormous Canuck came bounding over and scooped him up, then carried him back to his squadron mates like a babe in arms. Higgs and Jugs, whom Jox had been enjoying a quiet pint with, were worried they were witnessing kidnap, perhaps part of some dare, but were daunted by the size of the abductor. They scrambled after Moose, laughing but nervously concerned for Jox's welfare.

Sitting at a table nearby, Squadron Leader Thompson was in deep discussion with his section leaders: Ferriss, Bruce, Copeman and Simpson. They looked over, bemused but unconcerned.

'Hey, here he is!' boomed the big man. 'Fellas, say hello to my good friend Jox McNabb. Best damned fighter pilot I ever flew with and probably the bravest too. Remember, I told you about our pal, George Milne who died in training. Well, it was Jox here who ran into the flames to pull him out of the wreck. Brave, but pretty dumb too.'

The other Canadians in Moose's squadron seemed impressed. They were all extremely tall and bigboned in a 'grown on the prairie' kind of way, with good teeth and wide smiles. When Moose finally relented and put him down, Jox found himself looking up at them. Not one of them was less than a head taller than him.

Moose introduced a flurry of names: Si, Phil, Neil and Nick. They shook hands and nodded their heads from their lofty heights, and it occurred to Jox they would make big targets.

'Come and meet the boss,' said Moose. He grabbed Jox by the arm, dragging him towards an older gentleman in a squadron leader's uniform. There were CANADA patches on his shoulders and when he smiled, he revealed a gap between his front teeth. He had a chubby face with a thin moustache, and his bemused look told Jox he was used to Moose's exuberance and that of his Canuck colleagues.

'Squadron Leader Archie McNab of No. 1 RCAF, please allow me to introduce my good friend Pilot Officer Jox McNabb of No. 111 Squadron,' said Moose. He clearly thought this was the funniest thing he'd ever uttered.

'Nice one, Moose. Pleased to meet you McNabb, or may I call you Jox? Things will likely get a mite confusing if I don't. I can assure you; you don't want to be getting my tab at the end of the night at the rate my monsters drain a bottle.' He held his hand out to Jox, squeezing it hard, not in a display of strength but just in the manner of a man who judged others by their handshake. 'Get your friend a drink, Moose, and get yourself one too. Let's see if they have any decent whisky back there. Make mine Canadian if you can, but Scotch will do. Two fingers and remind me to get the adjutant to have a case of good stuff stashed behind the bar.' He turned back to Jox. 'I've heard a lot about you. Moose has good things to say. He was really delighted when he heard the Treble Ones would be here to meet us. He mentioned a Pritchard too. Is he around?'

'Pilot Officer Pritchard was wounded in France, sir. He's recovering in hospital, but will hopefully be back with us soon,' replied Jox. 'We could certainly do with having him back. Our replacements are well meaning but just don't have the experience.'

'Hell, son, we're replacements too. Give us a chance.'

'Oh, I didn't mean to imply, sir…'

'Take it easy, son. I'm kidding and please, call me Archie. My old man's a sir, not me. Let me introduce you to my 2ic, Flight Lieutenant Gordon McGregor. We're all Canadians here, but as you can tell from our names, we have a lot of ties to Scotland. Why, with Grant, McNab, McNabb and McGregor, it's a real gathering of the clans.'

Jox shook hands with McGregor, who had a receding hairline, dark eyes and the 'Desperate Dan' five o'clock shadow of a man with strong beard growth.

'Honoured to meet you,' McGregor said. 'I guess you all saw some action in France to be needing those replacements. I couldn't help overhearing.'

'Not at all. Yes, the squadron had a tough time of it,' replied Jox. 'Victories but also losses; both of men and machines. My Hurricane was shot out from under me over the water at Dunkirk. So was my section leader, the CO and of course Pritch.'

Moose returned with their drinks and handed them around.

'I see. Say, I wonder, could I ask you for a favour, Jox?' said Archie McNab. 'Could you point out your CO? I'm guessing he's either the big squadron leader with a large forehead and the big old moustache, or else the balding chap with the blond hair. I'm due to meet my opposite numbers tomorrow morning but reckon it's more neighbourly to meet for the first time here.'

'Squadron Leader Thompson is the chap with the moustache. I'd be happy to introduce you,' said Jox. He left Moose holding his pint and walked over to Thompson and the squadron's section leaders sitting at a circular table. They got to their feet as Jox introduced Archie McNab.

'I hope you don't mind, gentlemen, but I'd be happy to have a brief conversation with Squadron Leader Thompson here,' said an insistent McNab.

Jox and the four subordinates made to leave, but Thompson replied, 'I'm not terribly keen on talking shop in the mess, Archie. It's our one refuge from the daily grind.'

'Oh, no need to worry about that. Just wanted to get to know one another.'

There was a brief stand-off, as the junior officers made their excuses and retreated.

'Christ, what bee's got into Tommy's bonnet?' hissed Ferriss as they joined Moose, who by then had introduced his gang of lanky pals to Higgs, who wasn't exactly huge, and Jugs, who thankfully was, thereby preserving some modicum of squadron self-respect. The fact that he didn't really know one end of a Hurricane from the other was not considered relevant at this time.

The evening deteriorated or progressed, depending on one's perspective, and became increasingly riotous as mess games were introduced. At first, they were fairly standard high jinks like making your way around the room without touching the floor, while being pelted with cushions at best, pint glasses at worst. This game was surpassed by the 'footprint' challenge. The objective was simple: the squadron who could place a sooty footprint the highest up on the white domed ceiling of the mess bar room would emerge victorious. The Canadians had a height advantage, which set them out as early leaders, but once the Treble Ones began flipping the littlest and lightest amongst them, then propelling them up to the dome like a Highland caber, they snatched victory. It wasn't long before

Jox found himself barefoot, upside down and being propelled through the fuggy air of the bar. He jarred his ankle on the sloped ceiling but was safely caught by rugger-playing Thompson and young Jugs, the Welsh rower.

It was only once things quietened down that Moose pulled Jox aside. 'Let's have a sit down and catch up on the news from chaps at Montrose. You told me about old Pritch, and I'm real glad to hear he's more or less in one piece. I heard from Jack Benzie; you remember the Canuck who played the bagpipes at Georgie's funeral? He got wounded and baled out, south of Dunkirk, but was lucky like you and made it back. The Royal Navy did a hell of a job. Heard about anybody else?'

'I did get a letter from Paddy Finucane the other day,' said Jox. 'He got posted to No. 65 Squadron at RAF Hornchurch, which is not too far from here. Pritch would know. I think it may be somewhere in Essex. He sounded pretty chirpy in his letter. He's almost finished his conversion onto Spitfires after a bit of a rocky start and loves them now. He seemed quite upset about not having the chance to get a crack at Jerry in France.'

'There'll be plenty of time for that, he needn't worry,' replied Moose.

'How about you? Heard from anyone?'

'Yeah, I'm afraid I got a letter from old Mogs a few weeks ago. He's not in great shape,' said Moose. 'Digger bought it. Apparently, he went out on patrol in some pretty bad Highland weather and was reported missing. About a week later what was left of his aircraft was found on a mountainside. Mogs said he hit the hill like a drunkard walking into a wall. Flying in low cloud, straight into a Ben something or other.'

'That's what they call mountains in Scotland. Like Ben Nevis.'

Moose looked at Jox, not understanding. 'Mogs thinks he's cursed. Says anyone who he pals up with dies. Wants us to keep away in case it's contagious.'

'That's just dumb,' said Jox. 'I know he's upset, but he can't go on believing such nonsense. He's a fine pilot and needs friends.'

'Yeah, that's pretty much what I wrote back, but remember he was always sensitive. He was pretty messed up after George Milne's death.'

'We all were,' said Jox. 'But I'm afraid it's going to get worse before it gets better. We need to hold onto our friendships, not run away from them.'

Moose wrapped his bulging arm around Jox's neck. 'You're a wise little man,' said the chiselled Canuck.

'And you're squeezing me far too tight,' spluttered Jox.

Over the next few weeks, Croydon's three squadrons practised massed take-offs, power climbs to altitude and interceptions of feigned intruders of varying size, formation and number. They rehearsed progressions from one attack pattern to the next, with one flight always remaining 'on readiness' to defend Croydon's airspace. Occasionally, there were enemy reconnaissance flights probing overhead and a few small-scale raids on naval targets and southerly airfields like RAF Manston, Hawkinge and Lympne by the coast. It was becoming very clear, though, that the enemy were coming.

Yellow Section were on patrol one morning, when the female voice of one of the plotters at RAF Kenley, covering Croydon, spoke: 'WAGON Yellow Leader, this is TOP HAT control. Are you receiving me?' Jox listened idly, wondering why Anthony didn't answer. The voice asked again, 'WAGON Yellow Leader, this is TOP HAT, do you receive?'

Bloody hell! Jox thought. *That's me.* Ant was MIA, Wheelie was on leave after his DFC and he was flying as Yellow Leader, with Moose as Two and Jugs as Three.

'Er, yes ... TOP HAT Control. WAGON Yellow Leader. I can hear you loud and clear.'

'Acknowledged, Yellow Leader. Please be more attentive. We expect you to be responsive at all times.' She sounded irritated and yet somehow familiar. 'Yellow Leader, we have reports of bogeys approaching BEER Sector, vector 100 from your position, rising to Angels Eighteen.'

BEER Sector, that's Biggin Hill, south-east of Croydon, Jox remembered.

'Roger that, TOP HAT Control. WAGON Yellow Section complying,' said Jox. Without missing a beat, he went on, 'Yellow Section, this is Yellow Leader. Tight on me for vector 100. Possible trade at Angels Eighteen.'

Moose and Jugs acknowledged by giving a thumbs-up.

'TOP HAT Control. WAGON Yellow Leader. How many bogeys are we looking for?'

'WAGON Yellow Leader, this is TOP HAT. Will advise. Stand by.'

Yellow section continued to climb on their heading, rising through successive layers of cloud like thin wafers. The weak sunlight bathed them with a rosy glow. Jox told his section to keep a sharp eye out as they neared the vector point.

'WAGON Yellow Leader, TOP HAT here. Stand down, stand down. Bogeys reported as friendlies. Repeat. Stand down.'

Up ahead were a trio of bulky shapes, skimming the dimpled surface of the wafer clouds, their dark silhouettes standing out against the soft pink. From up here they could have easily been identified as either Heinkels or Blenheims. Catching them unawares would have been a disaster or a complete triumph, but either way there could have been a massacre.

Exhaling with the relief of carnage averted, Jox snapped angrily into his microphone, 'TOP HAT Control. This is Yellow Leader. Too bloody close for comfort.'

'WAGON Yellow Leader, TOP HAT Control. Error acknowledged. Please observe the radio procedure. Over.'

I'll give you proper R/T procedure, thought Jox furiously. Just then, it hit him like a ton of bricks; he knew who that voice belonged to.

CHAPTER FOURTEEN

Jox touched down beside Higgs, and then Jugs and Moose landed just behind. He taxied alongside one of Croydon's tarmac runways, then parked where instructed by the ground crew. He unplugged his mic cable and uncoupled the tube to his oxygen tank. The shut-down routine had become second nature to him, as next he unclipped his safety straps and hauled himself from the bucket seat. He was sweaty in the summer heat as he dumped his parachute onto the aircraft wing, nodding to an unknown rigger who would take care of it. He wondered where Blackie was.

'Mind you don't let the silk get wet on the grass. I don't want it sticking together if and when I need it in a hurry,' said Jox.

'Aye, no problem, sir,' replied the airman, who knew what he was about.

Jox glanced across the field, to see Higgs and Moose heading towards him. Jugs was chatting to his rigger, pointing something out beneath his ailerons. It was good to see the confidence with which he was managing his ground crew.

Croydon was the biggest aerodrome Jox had ever flown into. Officially classed as a satellite station to RAF Kenley, it was in fact a good deal larger. Fifteen miles south of London, it had been a civilian airfield since 1915, becoming London's main airport during the 1920s. Amongst aviators it had a reputation for fog, low-lying cloud and weak radio transmitter (R/T) reception. Still, it was a hell of a place to be posted.

Only recently taken over by the RAF, the conversion from a civilian aerodrome to working fighter station hadn't been straightforward. Apart from the rare luxury of having four separate runways, the terminal building had been converted into the admin block and the adjoining Aerodrome Hotel had become a luxurious mess and accommodation for pilots. Dotted around the airfield, fuel and oil was stored in huge circular tanks and several of the civilian hangars were being used as ammo stores. All of which meant it was a hell of a target for the enemy and liable to go up with a bang, even before its three resident fighter squadrons were thrown into the mix.

An oddly familiar silhouette was standing at the door of the pilots' dispersal and briefing room. He was small, almost petite, wearing an RAF peaked cap which was too big for his head and a non-regulation fawn mackintosh, like those worn by police detectives in the crime flicks. Jox recognised Sandy Bullough immediately and ran over to greet him, but he was surprised at his subdued reaction and somewhat sour demeanour.

In spite of dropping out of flight training at Fairoaks, Bullough had clearly made it up the greasy pole of promotion rapidly and was already a flight lieutenant. In contrast, Jox languished as a lowly pilot officer. Bullough looked at him expectantly, wanting some acknowledgement of their difference in rank. This perplexed Jox, since it ran counter to his every experience in a fighter squadron. Rank, airs and graces, boasting or any excess of bravado were all frowned upon. Hell, even Squadron Leader Thompson insisted on being called plain old Tommy.

'Hullo there, Sandy, what are you doing here?' said Jox, trying to break the ice.

Bullough answered with a rather clipped, 'Is it not customary for junior officers to salute their superiors, Pilot Officer?'

'Come off it, Sandy. We're old chums.'

Bullough removed his leather gloves, one finger at a time, still staring at Jox expectantly. Higgs and Moose joined them, giggling together about something.

'You glamour boys really think this war is a big joke, don't you?' said Bullough. 'Just a big jolly organised for your benefit. Well, you're going to learn the lesson the hard way.' He turned on his heel and strode off through the glass doors into the dispersal building.

'What was all that about?' asked Higgs, seeing the sour look on Jox's face.

'I've absolutely no idea,' he replied. 'Sandy was at flight school with Pritch and I but got washed out. He's obviously stayed in the service but seems to have become rather up himself. I was pleased to see him again, but he acted so strangely. How odd of him.'

'Don't worry about it, chum,' said Moose. 'He's a little man with a big hat, who thinks he's a big deal. As my old dad would say, "Does the mountain lion worry about what sheep think?" Forget about it and let's see if we can't rustle up some tea and biscuits. I'm starving.'

Jox was hungry too and the thought cheered him up, but he was still perplexed by Bullough's offish behaviour. He wondered what Pritchard would have made of it.

Later, Flight Leader Ferriss asked Jox to accompany him for a spin over to RAF Kenley to meet their plotters and the sector controller who would be directing their missions out of Croydon. He also wanted moral support for a mysterious hospital visit that he was dreading facing alone.

Jox was intrigued, but mainly agreed to come along because Ferriss owned a two-seater three-wheeler Morgan F-Series sports car, which he rather fancied having a go on. He'd been saving up his pay, plus the allowance his father was still letting him have until he turned twenty-one, and it was beginning to add up. He hoped to get himself a little run-around, once he'd passed his test of course. Jox was grateful for his father's continued generosity but found the idea of still receiving 'pocket money' rather at odds with his day job of fighting a deadly war.

As they roared down the suburban roads between Croydon and Kenley, Ferriss tried to explain the task before them. It appeared that when Flight Sergeant Anthony Glasgow was posted Missing in Action, his twin brother Cameron had had what could only be described as a nervous breakdown and was currently on medical leave.

'Cam has rather fallen to pieces over the loss of his twin,' said Ferriss. 'Ant was always the leader of the two, with Cam the more approachable and less fearsome one. We've not heard anything through official channels yet, so he could be all right, or maybe a prisoner, but of course it could also be for the worst. The uncertainty has rather unhinged poor old Cam.' His face was bleak. 'He's got himself in such a windy state, he's refusing to fly or go anywhere near a Hurricane. The squadron's so short of experienced pilots and this refusal is doing him no favours. The powers that be are taking a very hard line on this sort of thing, and there's a very real possibility of him being drummed out of the service for LMF.'

'LMF? What the devil's that?'

'Lack of Moral Fibre. The official term for cowardice,' said Ferriss grimly. 'It's a very serious accusation, especially for someone like Cam whose entire life has been the RAF. He and Ant joined as young apprentices, and their professional success is entirely down to being "Trenchard Brats". If he doesn't snap out of it, he'll be busted from flight sergeant to airman, then spend the rest of his career sweeping out hangars, digging trenches and cleaning latrines. The Air Ministry is really gunning for "shirkers and malingers" with the official party line being that we can't have them putting the wind up anybody else. Imagine what would happen if we all bottled it.'

'Cam's no coward,' said Jox, angered by the suggestion.

'I bloody know that,' replied Ferriss. 'It's why you and I are going to see him at the sanatorium they've got him locked up in. I need your help to snap him out of it, otherwise it'll be curtains. Christ, I wish we knew where Ant is.'

The iron gates to Cane Hill Mental Hospital in Coulsdon were every bit as forbidding as you might expect of a place chosen to give windy airmen 'a short, sharp shock to the system'. Built as Surrey's third 'Pauper Lunatic Asylum', it was an impressive Victorian complex housing male and female mental patients but was also now providing a programme designed to 'scare miscreants straight'.

Ferriss's three-wheeler skidded down the gravel driveway, flanked by an impressive avenue of horse chestnut trees. Several exhausted-looking men in khaki boiler suits were running laps around a muddy field, being screamed at by burly instructors.

Memories of his basic training at RAF Uxbridge flooded back to Jox, but he realised these men were going through something much worse. Everything unpleasant was turned up to a maximum, in volume, intensity and the sheer bloody-mindedness of the correctional staff. One or two of the sweating men watched as the RAF officers passed in their flash motor car. They were immediately harangued by screaming NCOs for inattention to their tasks.

'Get your eyes back on the job, you horrible little man,' screamed a particularly red-faced instructor, who looked set to blow a gasket.

Jox felt grateful he wasn't the 'horrible little man' in question and hurried after Ferriss, who was already halfway up the sandstone steps leading to the imposing reception area of the hospital. The brick surface of the portico was covered in red climbing ivy reaching up the sides of the three-storey clock tower with dials facing each of the Poles. The bright scarlet of the leaves seemed misplaced against the grimness of the buildings and the bleak atmosphere within.

Cameron Glasgow had been crying. He looked small, lost in an oversized boiler suit, his bare feet in clumpy soft-soled slippers.

'They dress us like this, so we can't get far if we run. That way, we're easily spotted in town,' said Cameron. 'I know I've tried.' The briefest glint of his old self gleamed through his raw-eyed, but glazed expression.

'For Christ's sake, Cam, running away will only make things worse,' said Ferriss. 'Going AWOL will only make them throw the book at you.'

'I've got tae go and see my ma,' sniffed Cameron. 'If we've lost Anthony, I'm all she's got left in the world. I can't have her fretting about me.'

'Look, we don't even know what's happened to Ant,' said Jox. 'Seems to me you're adding to her worry.'

'How so?' replied Cameron, his eyes narrowing.

'I'm pretty sure the single biggest thing your mum is proud of, is how well you and Ant have turned out — to have two sons defending their country. She'll be desperate about Ant, of course, but will still be proud you're doing your bit. When or if she learns that you're refusing to do what you've been trained to do, it seems to me she will have lost both of her perfect sons, not the one. What pride can she take from you being labelled a shirker due to LMF? What if you get cashiered or even worse?'

Cameron sat looking small and lost in his creased boiler suit. The familiar and formidable Glasgow glare had momentarily flared when Jox had started speaking, but had now been replaced by a hollow, haunted expression.

'I know you're not yellow,' said Jox, speaking even more bluntly. 'You and Ant are some of the bravest pilots I've ever seen. Ant has saved my bacon more than once and would expect you to do exactly the same. I know you want to stay alive for your mother's sake, but surely you must see it's the son who was doing his duty that she's proud of and deserves, not this one who is running from his responsibilities.'

'I can't help wondering what Ant would make of all this,' said Ferriss. 'Wherever he may be, it's the brother he left behind he'll expect to see again, if, God willing, he returns to us.' Ferriss's cut-crystal accent made him sound like an Anglican clergyman delivering a sermon, but his words seemed to be making an impact. 'I'm not sure he would recognise this version of his brother.'

Cameron hung his head as tears streaked down his cheeks.

'In practical terms,' said Ferriss, 'if you get the chop, you'll lose all rank and seniority. Your pay book will be stamped with a big red "W" for "Waverer" and wherever you go, people will know about your LMF rating. That's even assuming you'd be allowed to stay in the RAF. Whatever you and Ant have been earning and sending to your mother will also be hit. If the worst has happened to your brother, there may eventually be a pay-out, but given he's still MIA, it'll take a while until things are resolved. In the meantime, you're not contributing any more than he is. I'm sorry if all this sounds harsh, but you really need to understand the seriousness of what's happening. At a squadron level, we can only cover for you for so long, but things will soon be out of our hands.'

Ferriss stood and began to pace the room. 'It's not just that, Cam; we need you. The squadron's in a crisis. Jerry's coming and we all bloody know it. Those of us who were in France know how bad it can get, but the new chaps, the replacements, are lambs to the slaughter. Christ, even Jox is considered a veteran and he's been with us for less than a year. We've lost too many men. It's bad enough losing Ant, but we can't afford to lose you too.'

Ferriss and Jox left Cane Hill Hospital a few hours later. They left a quiet and withdrawn Cameron Glasgow and were unsure whether they had got through to him. The only glimmer of hope was the sad smile he gave when shaking their hands. 'Thanks for coming, lads. I've got a lot to think about. I dinnae want to let anybody down.'

The pair decided they really needed cheering up and deserved a pint after these last few grim hours. Ferriss suggested a quick drink at the Wattenden Arms, a pub close to RAF Kenley, before grabbing lunch at the officers' mess.

The pub was a squat building by the roadside, popular with local farmers as well as RAF personnel from the airfield. Walking towards the portico entrance, Jox noticed the sign above the door had a sword and bushel, perhaps meant to represent both types of clientele. Inside it was an odd mishmash of styles: oak panelled walls, a pair of ancient stone fireplaces with mantels greasy with accumulated soot, low ceilings decorated with art deco vines and grapes (appropriate for a pub, he supposed), plus oversized ceiling roses holding up what looked like Victorian street lighting. The walls were covered with pictures of aviators going right back to before the first war, and a large two-bladed wooden prop from a Sopwith Camel was hanging off a beam.

Despite the early hour, the pub was full of furry-cheeked yokels and boisterous off-duty aircrew, all competing for the attention of the two chubby barmaids with intricate hairstyles. The room smelt of fire ash, cigarettes and yeasty beer as Jox ordered two pints of Courage, somehow appropriate in the midst of the Battle of Britain.

'Do you think we got through to him?' asked Jox. They were seated at a corner table in the elegant dining room of Kenley's officers' mess, enjoying an excellent fish pie with what Ferriss called 'a half-decent *Pouilly-Fumé*' served by the attentive sommelier cum airman. It was the best glass of wine Jox had ever tasted, second only to the 'fine *Bourgogne Aligoté*' they'd enjoyed earlier with their buttered potted shrimp. It appeared Ferriss knew his way around a wine list, despite his youth. As they were towards the end of the lunch service, the neighbouring tables held only a few senior officers, a pair of WAAFs with their pilot escorts and a rather intense group of ops room controllers in deep discussion. Jox really hoped they weren't the same ones they would be meeting later, as the wine was rather going to his head.

'Look, we tried our best,' said Ferriss. 'It's really up to him to figure this out, but he does need to get a move on. This sort of thing saps squadron morale.' He took a sip from his fine choice of wine. 'I was chatting with Tommy yesterday, and he's at his wit's end. He's convinced our head-on tactics against the bomber streams are war-winning, but to make it work our pilots need to be brave as lions, to hold their nerve and not shy away with the wobbles.'

'That's rather harsh,' said Jox. 'Cam's as brave as anyone, with the kills to prove it.'

'That's not the issue, Jox. He's affecting morale. Tommy says to face what's coming, we all need to hold our nerve. Frankly, it's the only thing we have.'

'D'you really think so?'

'Look, Jerry has more of everything than us. All we have is our men and the belief we are defending our homes and way of life. It's the only way we can prevail. Personally, it's what I need to believe too or else I couldn't face climbing into my Hurricane every day.'

'You?' asked Jox. 'But you're the bravest amongst us. I mean, you've just been awarded the DFC from the king. Hell, I even know your citation by heart: *During two consecutive days in May, Flying Officer Ferriss shot down a total of four Messerschmitt 110s although heavily outnumbered. Later, he shot down a further three Messerschmitt 109s. In these combats he has displayed outstanding ability.* How many kills is it now? Nine? Hardly someone that's windy.'

'You'd be surprised,' he replied. 'All I do is get in close, then fire at the last minute. I just try to hold my nerve, then spray and pray.'

'It seems to be working. You're our highest scorer. Must be doing something right.'

'You know that score may well change too. All of our scores might,' said Ferriss. 'The Air Ministry is having doubts about our claimed kills. They've sent us a new intelligence-wallah, whose job it is to tease apart any claims. He's called Bullock or something similar.'

'Bullough, Sandy Bullough,' said Jox. 'I know him rather well. We were in flight training together. He's well-connected, but didn't make the cut, and now seems to have it in for pilots. I always thought he was a decent chap, a little self-important and a bit of a know-it-all, but essentially decent. I really hope he isn't going to be trouble. I mean, Christ, it's the last thing we need right now.'

CHAPTER FIFTEEN

The Kenley sector operations room, callsign TOP HAT, was a flurry of activity and yet every instruction was carried out in hushed tones and with calm efficiency. The chatter of airborne pilots and other sectors waxed and waned over the tannoy as interceptions and operations were controlled across southern England. Over a hundred RAF personnel were working in three-hour shifts here, providing around-the-clock 'Command and Control' for the sector. They had a direct link to Fighter Command HQ at Bentley Priory and also 11 Group Headquarters at Uxbridge, plus several lines to Observer Corps centres and Direction-Finding Stations across the sector. And yet, this vital nerve centre of RAF Kenley's operations was located in a modest single-storey brick building, protected by a simple earthen bank, just a short distance from a rather more imposing officers' mess.

The main ops room was painted a shade of hospital green, perhaps in an attempt to soothe the frenetic activity and frantic minds contained within, or simply because a surplus of it was available. The radiators, door frames and even the furniture were all green. Only the coloured wooden plotting blocks scattered across the large octagonal map table dominating the room provided any dissenting colour. One wall had a series of illuminated names with coloured lights to summarise squadron status and readiness, and on the other a raised viewing platform held a bank of manned telephones.

Roughly two thirds of personnel here were women. Women's Auxiliary Air Force plotters leant over the map table wearing light blue blouses, with sleeves rolled up to the elbows, headphones and speaking microphones slung around their necks. Bouffant hair was variously crushed by the headsets or pinned up out of the way. They were using long wooden batons to move plotting blocks across the table, to represent aerial contests as they progressed. More senior WAAF staff stood behind them or were on the dais supervising the plots or manning the various telephones alongside their male counterparts.

Each block on the map table of southern England was labelled with the letter H for Hostile, with details of the direction of travel, height and likely number of enemy aircraft. Friendly aircraft were labelled with their squadron numbers on bright yellow panels. If two squadrons were working together, both sets of numbers were placed on the same block. If the height and aircraft number were on a red panel, they were being controlled by Kenley; if white, another ops room was in control.

From the back of the gallery, Jox spotted a block indicating No. 111 Squadron was on patrol alongside No. 501 Squadron. They were over Tangmere Sector, west of Kenley, with twenty aircraft on high patrol at Angels Two Five, twenty-five thousand feet.

A tall blonde plotter leant forward and nudged the 111/501 block towards the south. She spoke deliberately into her neck mic: 'WAGON Leader, this is TOP HAT Control, are you receiving me?'

Jox recognised Thompson's voice instantly, a little garbled and high in pitch because of the high-altitude oxygen from his mask.

'TOP HAT Control. WAGON Leader. I can hear you loud and clear.'

'WAGON Leader, trade for you approaching SHORT JACK Sector, Vector 190 from your position. Thirty plus bandits at Angels One Eight,' said the cool and calm blonde.

Jox glanced over to Ferriss, engrossed in conversation with the scar-faced squadron leader they'd met earlier. He was the Kenley Ops Room Controller and had shown them around the facilities, introducing a bewildering number of faces. His name was Drummond, and he seemed keen for Jox and Ferriss to see the ops room in action and how they handled the shift change, due in about twenty minutes.

Drummond had pilot wings on his chest, plus the purple and white ribbon of the DFC, evidence he'd seen some real action. He had a scar running from his hairless eyebrow down his right cheek to the lip. There was a sort of double pleat in his face. Maybe it was the headache from too much wine at lunch, but Jox didn't like the condescending tone and unapologetic leering Drummond aimed at WAAF personnel trying to get on with their jobs. He and Ferriss seemed to be getting on, so Jox was happy to sit and observe, wishing he could get a glass of water.

He watched the blonde WAAF push a strand of hair behind her ear. Her face was flushed in the stifling heat of the room. 'SHORT JACK Control, this is TOP HAT Control. We have WAGON and MANDREL squadrons available to you. Currently vectored on 190 at Angels Two Five.'

'Roger that, TOP HAT Control. SHORT JACK have VILLA squadron on the bandits, believed to be thirty plus Dorniers. Request WAGON and MANDREL provide top cover and guard against fighter escort.'

'SHORT JACK Control, this is WAGON leader,' interrupted Thompson. 'Roger that, will comply.' A moment later, MANDREL leader from No. 501 Squadron did the same.

Jox, Ferriss and Drummond followed the action through intermittent Radio Transmitter messages, the plots moving across the map and the occasional exclamations through the ops room speakers. Pilots grunted as they strained against g-force, cheered with triumph, shouted stark warnings and there was at least one drawn-out scream in a Scottish accent, followed by deathly, crackling silence.

After a while the shift changed, and WAAF plotters were briefing their incoming counterparts on the lay of the table, before handing over plotting batons and unplugging their headsets. The tall blonde was talking to an equally striking WAAF, her curly hair pinned up in a complicated chignon. Her eyes and smile were unmistakable. It was Alice Milne, Georgie Milne's sister. She looked quite different in uniform, somehow seeming taller, but her eyes were the same. She glanced up at the gallery and did a double take as she spotted Jox. She then smiled shyly and gave him a little wave. It felt like a bomb had gone off in his chest.

She glanced at Drummond, who was making a show of himself, effusively waving back. She gave Jox a nervous look, then acknowledged the scarred squadron leader. Every instinct Jox had about the man crystallised in an instant. He had a reason now to dislike him, instantly recognising a rival. Drummond too realised that Jox had shown more than a passing interest in Assistant Section Leader Alice Milne. He immediately pulled rank at Jox's request to have a word with her, insisting, 'It is categorically out of the question that a WAAF plotter be disturbed while on duty.' Jox could see the logic, but knew it was nothing more than a blocking manoeuvre.

Confounded in his initial intention, whilst Ferriss and Drummond said their goodbyes, Jox asked to use the facilities before their drive back to Croydon. He scribbled a quick note to Alice, saying how pleased he was to see her again and that he had hoped to speak with her but realised she was on duty. He wrote that he was stationed with the Treble Ones at Croydon, so not really very far, and perhaps they could meet up? He would be in touch and in the meantime would be listening out for her over the airwaves.

Jox managed to convince a rather stern WAAF sergeant that he knew ASL Milne quite well, having been a close friend of her late brother George. The hard-bitten NCO had undoubtedly seen legions of lotharios trying to gain access to her women, but fortunately she knew about George's death and so agreed to pass on the note.

Jox thanked her profusely, before hurrying to catch Ferriss and Drummond outside the ops room hut. Squadron Leader Drummond sniffed as he reappeared, dismissing him with a nod of the head, but made a point of shaking Ferriss's hand. *Respect due to the DFC*, realised Jox, irritated by the thought.

At dawn the next morning, the squadron were on twenty-minute readiness. A Flight sat together in the dispersal. Ferriss, Jox, Higgs, Bruce, Jugs and Moose were lounging sleepily on the garish cushions of the cane chairs in what had once been a passenger lounge. Jox hated this waiting and dreaded the rattle of the dispersal telephone when it rang, followed by the clanging of the 'Scramble' bell. Outside, it was pouring with rain and the heavy cloud made it unlikely they would be called any time soon. Over the weekend, the Luftwaffe had bombed Plymouth for the first time and the previous week Cardiff, but unseasonal July rain promised some respite from more raids.

Badger Robertson entered the room, interrupting Jox and Ferriss's half-hearted attempt at a game of chess. At breakfast, the eggs had been swimming in a strange orange oil and now the whole flight were feeling rather queasy. Nothing to do with the shenanigans in the mess last night, of course, but many were looking forward to the restorative whiff of oxygen to blow away the cobwebs. Robertson didn't seem very happy.

'Cheer up, Badger. It might never happen,' said Ferriss.

Robertson forced a smile. 'How did things go with Flight Sergeant Glasgow yesterday?'

'Not too bad,' said Ferriss. 'What did you make of it, Jox?'

'I think we got through to him,' replied Jox. 'He said he had a lot to think about.'

'Well, he better get a bloody move on. I just got a note that the Air Ministry and Group are gunning for him. They want to make an example of malingerers and our silly little Jock apparently fits the bill.' He sighed. 'I'm really not sure whether this will make things better or worse. Here. His mother is receiving a copy any day.' He handed Ferriss a sheet of paper, a mimeograph copy of two sides of an original document.

'What is it?' asked Jox.

'It appears Ant is a prisoner of war in Germany,' said Ferriss. 'Says here he's been wounded but is alive and well. It's from the Red Cross in Switzerland.'

'They're called Red Cross Capture Cards,' said Robertson. 'He was at a transit camp, *Dulag Luft* near Frankfurt. Our Intelligence chaps say it's an interrogation camp where all RAF prisoners are sent for processing and questioning. "Slightly wounded" could mean anything really; they're hardly going to tell us if he's dying.'

'I think we should take this at face value,' said Ferriss. 'It's brilliant news. Proof he's alive, and that's got to be better than not knowing. I'd say it's just the news the twins' mother will want and our best bet of getting Cam shipshape and back with the squadron.'

'Right then, chaps,' said Robertson. 'Ma Glasgow is getting her copy shortly. With all this Jerry and Frog-speak, I don't suppose the old dear will make head or tail of it. I better get Tommy to send a follow-up cable to stave off the sting of the "Regret to Inform" telegram we sent a few weeks ago. You chaps sort out a copy of this and get it over to Cam with some note of explanation.'

'I don't mind doing it once we're off duty,' volunteered Jox. 'I'll drive it over to him, if I can borrow the car, Wheelie? I'll take Moose with me, so he can supervise my driving. After, we might pop over to Kenley and see how the sister of that chap we trained with at Montrose is doing. Moose knows her too. She's a WAAF in the ops room.'

Ferriss arched an eyebrow and chuckled. 'So, no ulterior motive then? Sure thing, chum, take the car, but I'm not sure a big lump like Moose will fit into the F-Series. Take it easy around corners with his weight; it's only got one back wheel.'

Robertson returned to his office, now distinctly chirpier.

'Actually, I was meaning to speak to you about the car,' said Ferriss. 'I've got an idea. I remember you said you've been saving up. I paid two hundred pounds for the Morgan, a few years ago, but don't get the chance to drive it much these days. Do you fancy going halfers?'

'Christ, I'd love that,' spluttered Jox. 'But a hundred quid is a bit rich for me.'

'Don't worry, we'll sort something out,' replied Ferriss. 'Seems a shame she doesn't get out much, and since you fancy her almost as much as that pretty WAAF, why not? I should warn you, though, Squadron Leader Drummond has also got his eye on her. I'd watch out for him if I were you.'

'Yup,' said Jox. 'Don't worry, I've got his number.'

'Be careful, you're playing with fire,' warned Ferriss. 'About the car: our arrangement will be somewhere between a bet and an insurance policy.'

'What do you mean?'

'Well, if you pay me half or whatever you can realistically afford, you'll own half and I'll own half, and we can share maintenance costs,' explained Ferriss. 'Then if either of us gets the chop, the other one takes the old girl. If we both get the chop, the squadron can have her. Are we agreed?'

'Sounds like a rather macabre arrangement to me, but needs must, I suppose,' said Jox. 'You're on, Wheelie. It's awfully decent of you. Thanks very much.'

'Not to worry, old chum,' replied Ferriss. 'Come on, it's your move.'

The dispersal telephone didn't ring until after midday. Croydon's Hurricanes were scrambled, along with those of No. 56 Squadron at North Weald and No. 32 Squadron at Biggin Hill. They were then joined by the Hornchurch Spitfires of No. 74 Squadron and a further six from No. 64 Squadron at Kenley. It had become the largest multi-squadron interception Jox or for that matter any of the Treble Ones had ever been involved in.

Robertson watched them take off by section. B Flight would follow, once A Flight was up and circling the airfield. The whole squadron would then head for Kent. On the ground, each section of three waddled into line, stopped, then pitched forward with exhaust stubs crackling bright flames before gushing black smoke was snatched away by gathering airspeed. Tails rose as engines warmed, pulling the aircraft along as they began to run more smoothly.

Ferriss was always the first off the ground, while Jox eased up gradually, building up speed before slowly climbing. Higgs retracted his wheels as soon as he was airborne, but David Bruce left his down until absolutely sure his engine was running smoothly and he wouldn't lose power. Moose wobbled on take-off, big feet twitching on the pedals and then Jugs, the new boy, always waved to his ground crew for luck and was slow to take off, having to strain to catch up with the rest.

Once A Flight were up, they circuited the airfield before Thompson and B Flight led by Stan Connors joined them; Jack Copeman was leading Blue Section and Pete Simpson led Green. Once up, the squadron banked by sections astern, all twelve aircraft in a covering formation.

They vectored towards a merchant convoy of twenty-five steamers codenamed BREAD. It had rounded North Foreland point earlier, bound for the Dover Straits, covered by six Hurricanes of No. 32 Squadron.

By the time the convoy and escort reached Folkestone, they had been spotted by a Dornier 17Z, a reconnaissance scout. A threatening raiding force was soon reported by the Observer Corps, consisting of twenty-four Do 17 bombers with an escort of thirty Bf 110s plus an estimated twenty Bf 109s. The Treble Ones and the other squadrons were being sent as 'the cavalry' to the convoy's aid, providing reinforcements to the vastly outnumbered No. 32 Squadron Hurricanes.

In their usual 'bomber busting' role, No. 111 Squadron were tasked with tackling the Dornier bombers. The squadron flew straight into the pack of oncoming aircraft, holding a shallow V-shaped Vic formation at a speed in excess of three hundred miles an hour. There was a high risk of collision, but they'd been trained exhaustively by Thompson and the effect on the bomber stream was extraordinary. Peeling it open like a banana, No. 111 Squadron's Hurricanes were right in amongst them. The glazed cockpits of several bombers crumpled under the weight of fire, and terrified enemy aircrew were seen scrambling backwards in their seats at the onslaught of the snarling fighters.

Jox later found out that the Spitfires of No. 74 'Tiger' Squadron, Hurricanes of No. 56 'Firebird' Squadron and No. 32 'The Royal' Squadron were clashing with the fighter escort. Lurking amongst the slow-moving bombers, though, was the German fighter ace and veteran of campaigns in Spain, Poland and France, *Oberleutnant* Walter Oesau.

Oesau caught the aircraft of Higgs, who, either damaged by Oesau's fire or trying to evade it, collided with the Dornier 17 he was attacking at the time. At a height of six thousand feet, the Hurricane's wing was sheared straight off, as was the bomber's. Both fell into the boiling sea below. Higgs was seen to successfully bale out, as did two airmen from the Dornier's crew of four. A rescue launch sent out from Folkestone was able to pick up the Germans, but no trace of Higgs could be found.

RAF Croydon's No. 111 Squadron claimed three enemy aircraft destroyed, with Fighter Command overall claiming three Do 17Zs, six Bf 110s and a Bf 109E during the air battle over the BREAD convoy. Just one ship was sunk during the day's attack.

CHAPTER SIXTEEN

'So, let's recap, Pilot Officer McNabb. Your tally stands at a Ju 52 transport destroyed on the 19th of May 1940 and a Stuka Ju 87 on the 31st of May, both in France. Then over Dunkirk, you were awarded a Bf 109 destroyed and a second probably destroyed on the 1st of June 1940. The probable seems rather generous to me,' said Bullough sourly.

'Come off it, Sandy. I get it. You've got the rank, but let's cut out the nonsense,' said Jox. 'You know me far too well.'

'Please answer the question.'

'After four sorties over various convoys today alone, I really don't need this,' said an irritated Jox. He was met with silence from Bullough, still waiting with his pencil poised. 'Sorry, what was the question?'

'Is that your recollection of the victories you have claimed over the enemy?'

'Not my recollection. The first two were claimed and witnessed by Tommy and Wheelie respectively. I was told about the Bf 109s when I got back from Dunkirk, after being shot into the drink. Actually, it was confirmed by Tommy again. Why is there any uncertainty about them?' asked Jox.

'I see, by Squadron Leader Thompson? No, no, there is no criticism implied. We just need to be thorough and check all claims retrospectively,' said Bullough. He changed tack. 'So, tell me, how have you been faring since the squadron was posted to Croydon?'

'Plenty of shouts, too many actually, but no more runs on the board for me, I'm afraid,' replied Jox wearily. 'Too busy trying to stay alive. We've been sent on a lot of wild goose chases, chasing phantom raids.'

'I see. Tell me about the operation over Convoy CW3, the BREAD convoy.'

'Bloody awful. A shambles, really. As usual, we charged at the bombers like a bunch of demented idiots. I'm fairly confident I got some good hits on one of those big Dorniers, but they can soak up a lot of damage. I was on Higgsy's tail when he suddenly reared up, smashing straight into the guy he was attacking. Chopped straight through the wing and before we knew it, they were both spinning towards the sea. There was no smoke or flames, just spinning wreckage, then a few chutes popped open and then huge splashes. It was a sunny day by then, with a little haze over Folkestone, and the convoy were below us, like toy ships with wakes like comets.' Jox tried to rub the grime from his sweaty flight gauntlets off his hands. 'They scattered in every direction when the bombers had a go at them. Then up came the flak from their destroyer escorts, making the sky a hazardous place for both us and the Huns. It was a swirling mess of aircraft, contrails from the mêlée twisting in all directions. Several bombs went off in the water, but I didn't see any ships get hit. You know what it's like: one moment a frenzy of planes in every direction, the next it's all over.'

'Well, no, I don't know, that's why I have to ask,' said Bullough. 'To get the intelligence sitreps right.'

There was an awkward moment of silence before Jox continued. 'I saw a Snapper go down, chased hell for leather by one of our Hurricanes. I recognised the JU prefix and think it might have been Wheelie.'

'Why do you say that?'

'He was very close and firing all the way. There were bits falling off the fellow like confetti at a wedding. He chased him out to sea and was going at a hell of a speed. The Hun was crabbing along very low, trying to get home. Wheelie poured short steady bursts into him, then the port wing dropped, the starboard reared and in a flash, he was in the drink.'

Bullough leafed through his notebook. 'Yes, Flight Lieutenant Ferriss has made a claim of a Bf 109 and a shared Do 17 on 10th July. He was also wounded in the foot.'

'Well, there you go, that's the squadron's three victories accounted for: the Dornier Higgsy pranged, Wheelie's Snapper and then a shared bomber. No sign of any over-claiming there, as far as I can see.'

'Look, it's not that we don't want you to make claims. We just need corroboration. Someone has to see it go down. Ideally with a map reference.'

'Map reference! Have you gone mad?' said an outraged Jox. 'We've got our hands rather bloody full up there without scrambling for map references.'

'I know that, but you must understand we need to get an accurate picture of what's happening. How else can we know how the war is going, other than fanciful supposition or wishful thinking? If there's no wreckage, no eyewitnesses, no location provided, how can we possibly verify the claim?'

'Well, they might have fallen into the sea. Higgsy and his Dornier certainly did. So too did Wheelie's Bf 109.'

'They can't all fall into the sea, Jox. At the current rate of claims, we'd need two thirds to end up in the drink to make things tally up. It's just not reasonable.' Bullough looked up to see Jox grinning. 'What?'

'You called me Jox. See, we're making some progress. Glad to have you back, old chum.'

Bullough closed his eyes wearily and shook his head, but he did smile.

'Come on,' said Jox. 'Now I've got you back, let's go have a drink. It must be after six. I can introduce you to some people and *be nice*. That way, you won't be such a bad smell when you question them and doubt their claims. I don't think you've even met Moose. He's a real laugh. You should meet the flight leaders too: Wheelie and Stan Connors, both of them with the DFC. Real Jerry killers both, but awfully nice chaps too. Must have fifteen kills between them. Then there's Squadron Leader Thompson with something like seven or eight.'

As they approached the mess, someone was singing and playing the piano — badly.

'Roll out the barrel, we'll have a barrel of fun. Roll out the barrel, we've got the blues on the run. Zing boom tararrel, ring out a song of good cheer. Now's the time to roll out the barrel, for the gang's all here.'

They pushed through the swinging door of the bar to find Pritchard propped up against the piano, pounding away at the keyboard and holding court to about half a dozen pilots from Croydon's three resident squadrons. A number of Moose's tall Canadian friends were enjoying the singalong, along with a couple of pretty WAAFs. Pritchard's leg was strapped up, like a gout-ridden old colonel from the Raj. He was in full song and bowed his head as he spotted Jox and Bullough. Jox noticed a walking stick hooked onto the back of the chair and his friend looked thin and tired, despite the forced bonhomie.

'Where the hell have you two been?' said Pritchard, once he had finished the chorus and acknowledged the applause from his crowd of admirers. He struggled to get up, as the other singers groaned that the impromptu singsong was over. Jox saw him wince, before getting up and hobbling over with a grin.

'Come on, girls, give me a hand,' Pritchard said to the WAAFs, one a brunette, the other a pretty redhead. 'Let me introduce you to some old chums, who by the look of things, could do with some cheering up.' Pritchard had a woman under each arm. 'Hello, boys,' he said, glancing first at one and then the other. 'This is Vi and Di. Ladies, meet my old friends, Jox and Sandy.'

Noticing the blue braid on Bullough's sleeves, the brunette smiled. 'Good evening, sir.'

'Never mind that sir business, Vi,' said Pritchard. 'We're all pals here.'

'Oi, darling!' said the redhead, prodding Pritchard's chest with her index finger, nails shining with scarlet nail polish. 'I'm Vi, she's Di. It's not complicated, Pritch.'

'You haven't changed a bit,' said Jox. 'But you're not exactly fighting fit, Pritch.'

The ladies released Pritchard, realising the conversation was taking a serious turn and they preferred the entertainment offered by the Canucks who were calling them back. Jox reached to catch him as Bullough grabbed the other arm, and together they manoeuvred the injured, but also slightly squiffy Pritchard to some armchairs where they could all sit and chat.

'Great to see you again, Sandy,' said Pritchard. 'I didn't expect it; I just knew Jox and Moose were here.'

'Yes, well, I'm flying a desk now,' replied Bullough. 'I'm the new IO for the Croydon Wing. Trying to make sense of the fantastical claims we're getting every day.'

'Rather you than me, chum,' said Pritchard. 'Sounds like a job, clipping other pilots' wings, and I can't imagine it makes you terribly popular.'

'War's not a popularity contest. As soon as we all get our heads around the fact that this is not some big jolly, the better.'

'You don't need to convince me,' said Pritchard. 'This leg is pretty much fused straight because of this damn war, and I've lost my right kneecap to boot. I can assure you, that's far from being jolly to me.'

'So, what *are* you doing back here?' asked Jox.

'Well, as lovely as the hospital in Torquay is, the Palace Hotel overlooking Babbacombe Bay, it does get rather boring. I managed to convince the doctors that I might as well recover back with the squadron, where I might be useful to the war effort. So here I am, still "Ineffective Sick", but hopefully I can help Badger on ground duties until I'm fit again. Anyway, Croydon's a lot closer to home in Wimbledon than Torquay.'

'Did the doctors say if you'll be able to fly again?' asked Bullough.

'I need to get more flexibility back into the leg. It'll take time, but if Squadron Leader Bader can fly with no bloody legs, surely I can with a stiff one!'

'If anyone can, it's you, Pritch,' said Jox, pleased Bullough was joining in the banter.

'Too bloody right!' replied Pritchard.

'You know,' said Jox, 'I'm really pleased you two have turned up. I've been meaning to find an excuse to get up to Kenley. You remember George Milne? I'm not sure if you heard, Sandy, but he was killed in a training accident at Montrose. His sister Alice was at his funeral, you remember, Pritch? Well, she's a WAAF officer based at Kenley now. She and I have been exchanging letters, and I was planning to go see her with Moose. Trouble is, one of us is always on duty. I'm off tomorrow, but he's got some training exercise with his No. 1

RCAF Squadron boys. Coordinating something with two ground wallahs should be much more straightforward.'

'Oh, thanks very much, that's just charming,' said Pritchard.

Jox looked to see if Bullough was offended and was relieved to see he wasn't.

'Right, sounds like a plan,' said Jox. 'Just to be clear, gentlemen, I have first dibs on the fair Alice. I've already got more than enough competition from a certain squadron leader up there, without any more interference from you two. Actually, Sandy, as the IO, you may be well-placed to distract the fellow for me. What do you think?'

Bullough smiled. 'I'm happy to help, but I'm not doing anything that's going to get us into any trouble. What's the chap's name?'

'Squadron Leader Drummond,' replied Jox.

Bullough winced. 'He's a crook one to pick a fight with. He's got a reputation as a hard-head and a bit of a pain.'

'Ooh, I knew getting back together with you chaps was going to be bags more fun than being stuck in Torquay,' said Pritchard. 'Bring it on, Jox. *Nil desperandum*, the Fairoaks massive are here!'

It took them a few days to get organised — time for Jox to get a note to Alice saying the three of them would be visiting and to check she wasn't on duty when they called. The two-seater Morgan couldn't take all three of them, but thankfully Pritchard had his father's four and a quarter litre 1936 Bentley Tourer, which they squeezed into quite comfortably, despite his leg.

The day before it had rained continuously, and this morning Croydon and the nearby airfields were wreathed in thick fog. The squadrons were officially 'confined to quarters', but in practice it meant they were free to make their way to Kenley, secure in the knowledge that Alice wouldn't be swamped by active operations. The Luftwaffe would be staying on their side of the Channel, and all sides could have a Saturday off.

'Who is this Marguerite you keep mentioning in your letters?' asked Alice, the challenge clear in her beautiful eyes.

Jox chuckled, flattered at the reproach that suggested a touch of jealousy. 'No one for you to worry about.'

'But who is she? She seems awfully important to you,' she insisted.

'She's no older than seven,' he replied with a sad smile. 'Marguerite was a little French girl I met near Dunkirk. I only knew her for the briefest moment, before the horror of a Stuka dive-bomber attack. I lost sight of her, and I'm afraid she may not have survived. All I could find was a piece of the dolly she was holding. It's become a lucky charm for me.' He reached into his tunic pocket and showed Alice the porcelain doll's arm he always carried with him. 'I named my Hurricane after little Marguerite; that way, at least someone remembers the little French girl. Her namesake seeks vengeance for whatever may have happened to the real Marguerite.'

'You've named your Hurricane after a little girl?' whispered Alice, clearly touched.

'Yes, I've got a photograph of me with my Marguerite.' He reached into his pocket and took out a photo. 'I thought perhaps you might like it.'

'I'd like that very much,' Alice said, blushing a little. She looked at the photo of a grinning Jox, standing beside the wing of a large hulking aircraft, his finger pointing at the cockpit. Looming above his head were propeller blades and a trio of stubby engine exhausts. Along the edge of the cockpit were a row of four painted daisies, and across the Hurricane's oil-streaked nose was the name 'Marguerite'.

'You seem very happy together,' she said.

'Not exactly happy,' replied Jox. 'Relieved to still be alive. We'd just landed after a huge shout over a convoy near Folkestone. Not all of us made it back. That's pure relief you're seeing there. I was still trying to catch my breath, when my rigger thought it might make a good snap. If you look closely, you can see I'm dripping with sweat and the marks of my goggles are still on my cheeks.' A little embarrassed, he added, 'I've signed it on the back.'

Alice turned it over. In neat, but spidery handwriting it said: *To Miss Alice Milne, with fondest affection from Jeremy 'Jox' McNabb, Summer 1940.*

She looked at him, blinked those eyes and said, 'I'll treasure it.'

Jox could feel his heart thumping in his chest and could only muster a rather banal, 'So, how have you been?'

'Oh, being kept pretty busy, but you know that. I was on duty during the BREAD convoy mission. I knew No. 111 Squadron were up but wasn't sure if you were with them. I kept listening for your voice.'

'I was there,' replied Jox. 'And I was doing the same.'

She smiled and lowered her gaze in a way that reminded him of George. Emboldened, Jox reached for her hand, and she let him have it. He leant in nervously and kissed her. She didn't pull away, so he put his arms around her. His mind had been racing earlier, but now he felt at peace. He'd found somewhere to belong.

Jox couldn't stop thinking of Alice, of her scent and the warm pressure of her body against him when they'd kissed. He shook his head, trying to banish the distracting thoughts, since he needed to concentrate. It was only their second sortie of the day.

Earlier, after a glorious sunrise, the striped mackerel sky appeared to be lit with fire. Great corrugated expanses of orange and pink were edged with gold, glistening as if molten. It was a 'blitzy' morning, beautiful but portending nothing but fair weather, blistering action and undoubtedly some death. The morning patrol was a non-event, but back in the saddle for a second time, Jox couldn't shake off a feeling of dread.

He focused on taking his Mark 1A through her paces. The propeller blades were set at a fine pitch, so they cut through the air, allowing him to throttle up generously on take-off. He left the ground in less than half the distance of *Marguerite*'s predecessor and was fifty feet up by the time it would have taken the old one to get to ten.

Waiting for the rest of the squadron, he circled the airfield, testing the controls, changing the pitch from fine to coarse. It was like changing gears on the Morgan, with the three blades on the spinner biting deeply into the air, driving the aircraft's performance forward. It flew faster, climbed harder and manoeuvred more easily than what he was used to. Whatever aerobatics he wanted to pull, throwing the aircraft about the sky, her sturdy wings remained reassuringly solid. The creaks, groans and complaints during manoeuvres with his old fabric-covered Hurricane were a stark contrast to the silence of the Mark 1A's airframe; the only sound he could hear now was the throaty purr of her engine.

Once the squadron were formed up, they vectored towards Kent, where trouble was brewing.

It was becoming increasingly clear the Ju 87 Stuka was vulnerable to British fighters and that the vaunted *Zerstörer*, the Bf 110, whilst fast and packing a terrifying weight of fire, was also susceptible due to its lack of manoeuvrability. Meanwhile, evidence was accumulating that the RAF's Boulton Paul Defiant fighters were outclassed and being dominated by their opponents.

Relatively inexperienced and having just arrived from RAF Turnhouse in Scotland, the turreted fighters of No. 141 Squadron were to operate from West Malling in Kent. Three aircraft had mechanical issues, so only nine squadron aircraft were left to patrol the English Channel, south of Folkestone at about lunchtime on this first sunny day for about a week.

There was no warning from the sector ops room as the squadron was suddenly attacked by a *Staffel* of Bf 109s from III/JG51, led by the veteran *Oberleutnant* Hannes Trautloft. The Defiants could only defend themselves if attacked from the side or the rear, as they lacked any forward firing guns.

Six of the helpless Defiants were shot down, with three falling immediately to the sea in flames. Only the late arrival of Thompson and No. 111 Squadron saved them from complete destruction.

The squadron hit the swarming Snappers like a wave swamping a beachside picnic, swatting several down and scattering the rest. Only three Defiants escaped, one with a mangled gunner lying in the rear, so damaged it would never fly again.

The 'butcher's bill' for No. 141 Squadron was ten killed from six aircraft lost. The Treble Ones claimed four Bf 109s, all confirmed kills, including a definite for Stan Connors, B Flight Leader.

Jox knew *Marguerite* had hit several Bf 109s but had nothing definitive and certainly nothing which would pass Bullough's stern inquisition.

CHAPTER SEVENTEEN

'Bloody hell, you're a sight for sore eyes,' said Badger Robertson, taking the little round spectacles off his nose, before rising from his desk. Standing in the doorway was a slightly dishevelled, sheepish-looking Cameron Glasgow. Jox looked on happily.

'Flight Sergeant Glasgow reporting for duty, sir,' Cameron said nervously.

'Welcome back, my dear boy!' said a delighted adjutant. 'One of our prodigal sons is back in the fold.'

Jox and Cameron caught up properly the next day, over breakfast in the mess hall. It was the usual fare of powdered eggs, sliced spam, a choice of marmalade or plum jam, margarine and as much square white toast as they wanted. It was cut straight across for the airmen and diagonally for officers, but all washed down with lashings of strong tea from the tin canteens burbling in the corner. For Jox it was fuel for the day, but Cameron seemed to be making up for lost time. He already looked healthier than the last time Jox had seen him, but still rather twitchy.

'Thanks for coming tae see me the other week,' he said, masticating furiously.

At school, Jox had been taught not to speak with his mouth full, but it wasn't a lesson taught in the rough Dundee quarter where the Glasgow twins were from. He took a swig of his tea.

'I appreciate you bringing that paper about Ant being a prisoner too. I received a letter from our mammy and she's had another yin, more recently. Apparently, Ant's in Austria now.

The main thing is he's alive and in one piece. Aye, it's a hell of a weight off my mind.'

'Glad to hear it, Cam,' said Jox. 'How are things going with you?' He searched for clues about Cameron's state of mind in his restless eyes and erratic movements.

'Fine, I'm fine,' replied Cameron, chewing once more. 'I've been to see Tommy and then got debriefed by Pritch. I understand he's grounded until his leg gets better. I hope it does, he's a sound fella. I've also been looked over by the MO and he's given me the green light. So, in theory, I'm all clear to take poor old Higgsy's place as Yellow Two. After all, it was mine in the first place. By the way, who's got my brother's spot as Red Two?'

'I have,' said Jox. 'A replacement called Jugs is Red Three now. He's pretty green, but he'll get there.'

'You're not exactly a veteran yersel, Jox. I can remember you arriving at Northolt wi' Pritch not so long ago. The both of youse were pretty damned fresh, as I recall.'

'Right enough, but we've had to learn fast since then.'

'Aye, my brother always said you had a good eye,' said Cameron. 'What's your kill count?'

'Still just the four from France. I can't seem to get any decent hits on target.'

'You'll be fine. Concentrate on staying alive and the odds are in your favour. The opportunities will always come along.'

'I'm not so sure, Cam. You've been out of action for a bit. There're bloody hundreds of them every time we're up. It's absolutely terrifying. There's so many and we're so few.'

'Ach, well, I'm back now and I'll be keeping an eye out for you. My brother would want me tae dae that.'

Jox chuckled. 'I always thought he felt I was a bit of a pain.'

'Aye, well, maybe, but that disnae mean he wasn't watching out for you. Anthony doesn't suffer fools, and he didn't think that of you. It's as good as friendship tae him.'

'So, when are they letting you back up?'

'I've got a couple of practice sorties with the Canadian boys from No. 1 Squadron today and then if everything is all right, I'm operational.'

'So, back with us tomorrow?'

'Aye, well, that's the plan. You no gonna eat that fancy toast?'

On Thursday, 25th July 1940, Convoy CW8, codename PEEWIT, consisted of twenty-one coal ships heading east off Southend under Royal Navy escort. Past Margate and approaching the Strait of Dover, German radar installations on the coast of France detected the fleet and sent several fighter formations after it. They were initially met by Spitfires from No. 65 Squadron from RAF Hornchurch, but as the afternoon progressed, more and more aircraft were sent into the fray by either side.

Some sixty fighter aircraft were wrangling over the convoy, with casualties falling and weary survivors limping homewards to refuel, re-arm and return. By mid-afternoon the airspace above the convoy was fairly clear, as sixty Stuka Ju 87s arrived and attacked unopposed. Five of the panicked sea vessels were rapidly sunk and a further five damaged. As the force of Stukas withdrew, only then did the Spitfires of No. 54 Squadron at Hornchurch arrive, followed by those of No. 64 Squadron from Kenley.

They were confronted by a veritable armada of enemy aircraft appearing over the hazy horizon, including thirty big-engined Ju 88 dive-bombers and an escort of over fifty Bf 109 fighters. The rest of No. 64 Squadron and No. 111 Squadron were immediately scrambled, as the combined British force faced odds approaching five to one.

The engagement drew on into the afternoon, with squadrons dropping out, returning to their bases, then re-joining the fight. By the end of the day, Convoy CW8 had lost eleven coal ships from the total of twenty-one, in addition to the loss of two Royal Navy destroyers. They had been hounded relentlessly from the air, but also harassed by swift torpedo E-boats and pounded by the monstrous explosions of heavy artillery guns on the French coast.

When the PEEWIT convoy finally reached its destination of Portland, only two coal ships had survived. It had been a very bloody day for both the Royal and Merchant Navies.

During the fourth sortie of the day, A Flight, led by David Bruce, headed for the coast where rain clouds were finally forming after a clear and murderous day. Whilst still over land, Jox spotted a solo Spitfire in trouble, trailing dark smoke. On his tail was an aggressive yellow-nosed Snapper, intent on finishing the job he'd started.

'WAGON Flight Leader, this is WAGON Red Two,' said Jox. 'Single bandit at three o'clock, in pursuit of a struggling Spit. Estimate Angels One Three, below.' Jox saw the rest of the flight's leather-clad heads turn in the direction indicated.

'Where away, Red Two?' asked Bruce. 'I can't see them, are you sure?'

'Quite sure, WAGON Flight Leader. We're up in the sun. The Snapper hasn't seen us yet. WAGON Flight Leader, permission to engage?'

'Roger that, Red Two. Proceed. WAGON Yellow Section, let's head up to provide top cover and make sure this isn't a trap. Red Section, stay on with Red Two.'

'Roger that, WAGON Flight Leader,' said Ferriss, as his Hurricane dropped in behind Jox, with Jugs on the other side.

'TOP HAT Control, WAGON Flight Leader here. WAGON engaging. The Snapper is all yours, Red Two. Tallyho!'

Jox acknowledged the order. 'Roger, WAGON Leader. Red Two engaging. Tallyho.' He swooped onto the attacker from the brightness of the fading sun. He fired only once he was tucked in behind him, slightly to the right to avoid being seen in his mirror. He took careful aim, avoiding firing through the target onto the Spitfire beyond, which was now smoking dramatically.

His first burst hit the Bf 109, with thudding impacts sparkling along its cowling. The pilot immediately pulled up and away very skilfully, jinking hard to the right.

Jox had been taught by Anthony Glasgow that most right-handed pilots instinctively looked left when first hit and then pulled left to evade. This pilot did exactly the opposite and Jox was struggling to keep on his tail. As his opponent turned, the kill tallies on his rudder became visible, and Jox banked sharply to follow. It was the tail of an experienced ace.

Jox felt the metallic taste of fear rising in his mouth, as *Marguerite* pitched in pursuit. He glanced sideways and saw the Spitfire making good its escape, as its erstwhile aggressor had found a new dance partner. The ace twisted and turned, but Jox held on grimly, grateful his opening burst had winged his opponent. He recognised the thin, white trail of a coolant leak when it appeared and knew the engine would start to seize once the trailing smoke turned black.

In a desperate attempt to throw Jox off, the ace rolled sharply one way, then pitched violently the other, then attempted an Immelmann loop to first gain altitude, flip over and then bring his guns to bear as he charged at Jox head-on. Unfortunately for him, the ailing engine lacked the power, and the anticipated black smoke traced the manoeuvre, making it both visible and obvious.

Any other pilot may well have sheared off, when confronted by an enemy fighter swooping at him head-on from altitude, but the Treble Ones had been well trained for just these assaults. Thompson had made it their bread and butter with constant cries of 'Turn and face them!' Ferriss had drilled Jox tirelessly to fire his way through frontal attacks.

The Bf 109 roared towards the Hurricane, expecting it to veer away and so overshoot the mark, just as Jox's powerful blast of fire flew straight into the yellow cowling of the spinner and into the black heart of the already struggling engine. The aircraft reared up, the canopy shattered and misted red with the ace's blood. It flipped back on itself, then fell like a stone.

Jox pulled hard against the g-force, greying out for a moment, with his vision clearing in time to see his victim slam into a cow pasture outside Hawkinge. At first, he was convinced he must have been hit himself, but miraculously appeared to be unharmed. He laughed nervously, sick with relief. That was when it dawned on him: he was finally an ace, a five-kill ace.

In his ears, he heard the congratulations of Bruce and then Ferriss saying, 'Good kill.' Even old Sandy Bullough wouldn't argue with this one.

Once back on the ground, there was very little fuss made of Jox's change in status. Perhaps everyone was just too tired to make a big deal of it, not least because they all knew they were back on duty tomorrow. The weather boffins said that fair conditions were set to continue, which could only mean more enemy incursions and more merciless action.

Jox felt he needed to tell somebody and by the evening was resolved to get a line through to Kenley. He waited impatiently to be 'put through' by one telephone post after another, presumably dotted around the crowded operations room. As he waited, he felt anxious and guilty for using an official line for what was a distinctly unofficial purpose. A hesitant voice came on the line.

'Assistant Section Leader Milne. How can I help you?'

'Hello, darling,' said Jox, trying out the term for the first time. It felt rather odd and contrived, and he was embarrassed. 'It's me.'

There was a long pause.

'How did you get this number?' Alice whispered. 'You could get me into awful trouble.'

'I know, I'm sorry. I just needed to hear your voice.'

'Why? What's happened?' He could hear the alarm in her voice, and it made his heart leap. 'Are you all right?'

'I'm fine. No, really, I am,' he replied. 'It's just … well, I've been on operations all week. It's been exhausting, but today I finally bagged another Bf 109. It's no big thing, but technically it makes me an ace. I'd rather expected the chaps to make a fuss, but it's all been a bit of a damp squib. I just needed to tell someone. I haven't really got any family, other than my father in India and my Auntie Jane in Scotland, so I thought I'd tell you.' He suddenly felt rather foolish. 'I'm sorry, I shouldn't have called. I don't want to get you into any trouble.'

'Don't be silly, Jox,' said Alice. 'I've been thinking about you too and wondering when we might see each other again. Especially, well, how we left things…'

Now it was his turn to sense her embarrassment.

'We're not really doing a very good job of this love affair business, are we?' he said. 'Look, how about lunch at the Wattenden Arms? It's not far from Kenley, and I'm fairly sure they can pull together a decent Sunday lunch. It might not be a roast like before the war, but hopefully it'll still be good. How about I pick you up in the Morgan and we go for a spin afterwards?'

'That sounds marvellous,' she replied, sounding genuinely excited. 'But don't you think the Wattenden is rather public? A lot of Kenley people are regulars there.'

'I'm not worried about who knows we're together. The more the merrier. Why, are you embarrassed to be seen with me?' he blurted out, not really thinking.

'No! No, please. It's not that,' she said, but clearly worried about something. 'It's just Squadron Leader Drummond. He's being quite persistent, and I wouldn't want to antagonise him. He could well be there, and I really wouldn't want to cause a scene.'

'We have every right to be seen together,' said Jox indignantly. 'It sounds like I'm going to have a word. I'm not afraid of him. I'm a bloody ace, for Christ's sake!' He was losing his temper, but also knew he was overreacting. 'I'm sorry, Alice, but I'm not having Squadron Leader bloody Drummond dictate where I go with my girl.'

She was silent and he wondered if he'd lost the line.

'Is that what I am? Your girl?' she asked.

'Why, yes,' he spluttered, then wondered if he had pushed things too far.

'Good. I rather like the sound of that. Sod Drummond! Pick me up at the gates on Sunday at twelve. I must go, darling. I can't wait to see you.'

There was a click then a constant tone, quite unlike his thumping pulse rate. She had called him darling.

The morning of Saturday, 27th July 1940, the weather over the Dover Straits was fair, but remained cloudy out in the Channel. Luftwaffe dive-bombers, escorted by Bf 109s were harrying Convoy BACON off Portland Bill's lighthouse and were intercepted by Hurricanes and Spitfires from various squadrons throughout the morning, resulting in the loss of a Ju 87 and a Spitfire. At two-thirty, the specialist fighter-bombers of 3./Erpr. Gr. 210 attacked Dover harbour, damaging the Royal Navy destroyer HMS *Walpole*, before No. 111 Squadron arrived to chase them back to France with no losses.

By the evening, the weather had cleared and the squadron were on their fourth sortie, as six minesweeper trawlers accompanied by the destroyers HMS *Wren* and HMS *Montrose* were attacked off Aldeburgh by He 111 bombers. HMS *Wren* floundered, and HMS *Montrose* was badly damaged. The Treble Ones arrived too late to fend off the attackers but were witnesses of the carnage amongst the proud Royal Navy ships. With a grandstand view from his cockpit, Jox boiled with frustration at the ops room incompetence which had allowed these brave men to die beneath his wings.

Dover was attacked again half an hour later. Moored within its harbour walls, the destroyer HMS *Codrington* had the depot ship HMS *Sandhurst* moored alongside. The former was sunk, and the latter was badly damaged.

By now, though, No. 111 Squadron were in position to seek some retribution. They got swiftly in amongst the waves of Ju 88 fast bombers, before the escort of Bf 110s and Bf 109s had time to react. Flying solo, the *schnell* bombers were often too fast to intercept, but hemmed together in a massed Circus, they sacrificed speed for bombing accuracy, and presented a perfect target for No. 111 Squadron's signature line abreast assault.

Lined up with his squadron mates besides him, Jox picked out his intended victim and settled his targeting rings as they approached one another on a collision course. He slowly pressed the gun-button and counted, one and two and one, as converging streams of fire blasted into the oncoming bomber.

The forward air-gunner took a hopeful squirt at him before he was even in range, but stopped firing as soon as *Marguerite*'s eight guns reached him, devastating the inside of the Ju 88's cockpit. Inside, four crewmen sat in close proximity and the effect of the fire was murderous. Just the pilot escaped unhurt, soaked by the blood and gore of his *Kameraden*. The bombardier on the forward gun was slumped in his seat as if asleep and behind him, the radio operator was missing the top of his head. *Marguerite* was knocked off track by the powerful recoil of her guns, hitting the turbulence in the bomber's wake and bouncing through it like a fairground attraction.

Struggling with the bucking, Jox tried to get his guns back on target. He strained at the control column, hauling *Marguerite* brutally, but overdid the manoeuvre. His vision fogged as centrifugal force sucked blood from his brain towards his extremities. It took a few long seconds for him to recover and see clearly again. By then, his target was far off to the portside, fast and low, desperately seeking France's friendly skies.

'Right, he's mine,' said Jox, throttling up his engine after it. He positioned himself above and behind, seeing the crippled bomber was struggling to stay airborne, losing altitude steadily above the swelling surface of the sea. *Marguerite* accelerated like a gannet pursuing a silvery shoal, but Jox fluffed the shot, firing too early and for too long, registering only a few solid hits on the portside engine and to the rear of the cockpit.

Shards of shattered Perspex fell, reflecting light like tinsel in the bomber's wake. The stricken engine was smoking, leaving a long, oily smear across the hazy evening skyline. Jox drew in closer and fired again.

The big bomber shuddered under the renewed impacts and immediately changed its angle of descent, falling steeply towards the cliffs on the French coast ahead. If the pilot had hoped to crash-land the flying wreckage onto the heathland above the cliff, he almost made it, but was just too low and hit the vertical chalkface with a thunderclap boom, followed by a billowing plume of flame. An oily black mark marred the chalky white as burning debris slid down the rock face like treacle, settling in burning lumps on the narrow beach below, before being extinguished by the lapping waves.

Peering at the chaos he had created, Jox was distracted by a dark reflection on the sea surface. He sensed a looming presence in his mirror and acting purely on instinct, he wrenched *Marguerite* skywards, up and over the cliff top, then pulled starboard as cannon fire streaked beneath him, exploding amongst the chalk and sparse vegetation. He barrel-rolled, before giddily glancing back to see a huge twin engined aircraft chasing after him. The beast was above him now and fired a burst which stitched through the Hurricane's starboard wing, thumping several rounds into the armour protecting his back. He felt like he'd been punched in the kidneys.

Jox pulled *Marguerite* into ever tightening circles, knowing the big Destroyer was less manoeuvrable, but had massive fire power and greater speed. There was little chance he could outpace him, but he could dance and pirouette far better. For what felt like a long time, the two aircraft curved around each other, trajectories twisting like mating snakes. Jox felt his vision greying out several times and the exertion on his clobbered back was agony. He hoped the Destroyer was feeling it too, but he knew he was weakening and *Marguerite* had taken a lot of damage. After another series of teeth-rattling thumps, a hole the size of his head appeared in the already damaged wing. The rudder was unresponsive and he was desperate.

The Bf 110 was gaining on him, angling for what would prove to be the killing blow. Without thinking, Jox allowed his Hurricane to drop and the Destroyer cast a dark shadow over the top of him as he passed overhead. Jox jerked the column violently back between his knees, hitting the firing button with his thumb. His eight guns roared for the briefest moment, before clicking impotently. He'd run out of ammunition!

Jox craned his neck, desperately trying to locate the big beast. He searched above, but realised it was now actually below and seemed to be falling. He levelled off, then followed it cautiously. The big fighter seemed to be in trouble, yet showed little sign of damage. The back hatch of the Bf 110 lifted and then something fell away, followed by the flailing figure of the rear gunner. His parachute blossomed open as Jox circled, and he was pleased to see the wind was pushing the airman towards the beach. It took him a while to orient himself until he spotted what was left of improvised pontoons of submerged vehicles, which told him he was over Dunkirk.

Jox dipped his battered wings in a quick tribute and turned for home. His engine was in a bad way, howling like a hound on the scent of a fox. There was boiling white glycol tracing rivulets over the canopy, filling the cockpit with its stench. He didn't have much time before *Marguerite* would overheat. He lifted her nose, trying to gain altitude as flames began to flare from the exhaust stubs, too close for comfort to the fuel tank behind the instrument panel. Death, it seemed, was just an arm's length away.

'Come on, *Marguerite*,' he grunted, wrestling with the column. It was a question of muscle over gravity, sheer will over grim reality. He cleared the white cliffs of Kent with a few feet to spare. She was going too fast but was low on fuel, so not as combustible as she might have been. He crash-landed wheels up and tail first, skid-bouncing a good thirty feet over concertinaed barbed-wire at the top of the cliff. *Marguerite* spun like a cartwheeling gymnast, before landing upside down, held up in a thicket of yellow flowering broom.

Jox hung groaning from his straps. He reached for the handle of his canopy but was confused since it was below him. He was surrounded by a sea of yellow and as he slid it back, the glycol stink was replaced by aviation fuel and inexplicably the fragrance of flowers.

I must have bumped my head, he thought, pulling the pin from his straps.

He fell, then felt his head violently jerk back, tugged by the oxygen tube and radio lead that were still attached. He landed face first, feeling the crunching impact of the ground through his aching kidneys and the dry crack of the porcelain doll's arm in his pocket.

While the cooling engine ticked, inky blackness rushed in.

CHAPTER EIGHTEEN

'Come on, Jox, be serious. Look at the state of you,' said an exasperated Pritchard. Clustered around the foot of the bed were Ferriss, Moose and Bullough.

'Are you seriously suggesting that we sneak you out of here, so you can meet up with your bit of fluff?' asked Ferriss.

'To be fair,' said Moose, 'she's certainly not that. Alice is a grade A girl and certainly worth the displacement.'

'That may well be,' said Bullough, increasingly the voice of reason. 'But we'd be breaking at least a dozen regulations, not to mention seriously putting your health at risk. I mean, for goodness' sake, have you seen yourself in the mirror?'

Jox shook his head then tried to smile, regretting it immediately as it tugged at his split lip, which began to bleed again.

'Oh Christ, more claret,' said Pritchard, rushing to the bedside with a clean handkerchief. 'Hold this against it and then have a good long look at your boat when you're ready.' He handed him a compact mirror. 'Brace yourself, chum, it's not pretty.'

Jox wondered why Pritchard had a woman's compact in his pocket, but figured it was better not to ask. It could have belonged to any number of girlfriends amongst the WAAFs at Croydon, or for that matter Kenley. If nothing else, his friend certainly knew how to work a crowd.

The face in the mirror was certainly a vision, but the question was of what? He had two enormous black eyes, with some green and yellow thrown in, and it was a wonder he could see out of them at all. His nose was scraped raw where his oxygen mask had been snatched away as he fell to the ground and his split lip, two broken ribs and aching kidneys were all thanks to his less than gentle landing on Kentish chalk.

He considered himself lucky on three counts: *Marguerite* was a write-off but thankfully hadn't burst into flames; the big yellow bush he'd landed in had slowed him down and stopped him from scraping bloodily along the chalk, and most importantly the big hits from the Bf 110 Destroyer had smacked into his back armour like sledgehammers to the kidneys, but he had no serious wounds. A few inches either way and it would have been a leg, an arm or his head. A single 20mm cannon shell would certainly have taken any of those right off. He'd been fortunate and he knew it.

'Where's the arm?' he asked. The others looked at him as if he'd lost his marbles. 'The porcelain doll's arm that was in my pocket. It's my lucky charm. When I fell, I heard it crack.'

The others were now taking him very seriously. Fighter pilots were a superstitious lot, and no one messed with a man's lucky charm.

'I'll ask the doctor,' volunteered Bullough. 'You three stay here and try to dissuade him from this madness.' He pushed through the ward's glass doors, searching for some medical staff on duty. Here, the extra bit of blue satin braid on his sleeves might come in useful.

'He's not such a bad bloke, that one,' said Ferriss, turning his attention back to Jox. 'You're lucky Cam stuck with you, when you went tearing off after that bloody great Ju 88. He's confirmed the destruction of the kite, so even Sandy's satisfied, and thankfully he spotted you limping back to Blighty. Radioed in the position of your prang above the cliffs. That's why they got to you so fast.'

'Did he see the Bf 110 go down?'

'Didn't mention one. Why, what happened?' asked Pritchard.

'Well, how do you think I got bashed up like this?' replied Jox. 'The Jerry bomber was on its last legs when I went after it, but then I got bounced by that big bugger. Knocked seven shades of shit out of me. He had me, he really did. I felt like a tiddler on the end of a line being reeled in. I wriggled like fury, trying to execute the right twitch trick you taught me, Wheelie, but nothing seemed to work. He must have been over-keen or over-confident because he then overshot, just as I tipped my nose up and fired off a few rounds. To top it all off, I ran out of bloody bullets. I was dead and then he suddenly gave up and began to fall. I circled around as best as I could in my knackered plane and saw a single chute. The pilot must have copped it. I tell you, it was the damnedest near-run thing.'

The others listened with grim faces, realising their friend had had a miraculous escape. They had all lost enough friends to know you didn't often get a second chance.

Pritchard broke the brooding silence that had settled upon them. 'Right, Jox, you've seen the state you're in. You must know if you turn up looking like chopped liver, you'll scare the life out of Alice. Moose and I can run up to Kenley and let her know what's happened. She'll recognise us and will know we're not mucking her about.'

'I can't do it, Pritch,' said Jox firmly. 'I promised to be there. It's important to me. I'm going to do this with or without you boys, but I'd really appreciate your help, because I'm kind of sore.'

'Christ, we're gonna need a wheelchair and will probably have to carry him too,' said Pritchard, immediately switching to practical mode. 'My car's big enough for us all, but it's not going to be easy. You up for this, Moose? Wheelie?'

They both nodded.

'Thanks, boys, I'm really grateful,' said Jox, wincing as pain shot up his back. 'Make sure you cadge some painkillers off the doc,' he added breathlessly. 'It hurts every time I move.'

Bullough came bursting through the doors, rather pleased with himself. 'Aha, my boy,' he said. 'Ask and you shall receive.' In his hands were four broken pieces of Marguerite's dolly's arm. 'It shouldn't be too difficult to stick it all back together again with some tape and glue. It may be a little damaged, but aren't we all? Good job I asked when I did; they were about to chuck it out. They couldn't understand why anyone would want to hold onto something like that. One of the nurses said it reminded her of a dead baby's arm.'

'That's the point,' said Jox wearily. 'The doll belonged to a little girl who Ant and I met in France. She was in a refugee column bombed by Stukas near the airfield we parked in for lunch that time; remember where we lined up like a bunch of idiots? Pritch? Wheelie? You were there. We couldn't find the little girl, Marguerite, afterwards. Just the arm of her dolly.'

'That's why your Hurricane is called *Marguerite*, isn't it, Jox?' asked Bullough, his eyes blazing with emotion.

'Yes, it was. But not anymore. She's a pile of junk now,' said Jox.

'Oh, I wouldn't worry about that, Jox,' said Bullough. 'Between us, I'm pretty sure that by the time you're back on your feet, there'll be a *Marguerite III* painted up and waiting for you. Right, fellas? In the meantime, I'll take care of getting this dolly's arm all back together again.'

'Great idea, Sandy,' said Pritchard. 'But first, perhaps we need to help put old Humpty Dumpty over here back together again. After all, he's got an important *rendezvous* with a lady tomorrow, and what else are we if not "All the King's men"?'

The sole concession Jox was willing to make was that Ferriss would go ahead and pick Alice up at the gates of RAF Kenley in the Morgan. That way, he could warn her Jox was not in the best of form, but he was still determined to make their first date. He would meet her at the Wattenden Arms, where he would find a table so he could sit comfortably, despite his injuries. In the meantime, Pritchard, Bullough, Moose and Wolfie McKenzie, Pritchard's school pal who he'd dragooned in for good measure, would get Jox to the pub and get him set up. They would then make themselves scarce, keeping a discreet eye on things to make sure that Jox was all right.

It should have run like a military operation, but trouble started when Ferriss went to the wrong gate, so was late in arriving. Then, as it was a mild day, he had the roof down. This normally should have been fine, but since Alice was in uniform and so had no scarf for her head, her carefully coiffed hair was blown to bits by the time they got to the pub.

In the meantime, after a good deal of pushing and shoving, during which the poor fellow was dropped a few times, Jox was set up. In the end, Moose insisted on carrying him on his own, like a babe in arms — and not for the first time, he pointed out, to the acute embarrassment of the long-suffering Jox before the other patrons of the pub.

The boys then retreated to the bar, leaving Jox waiting rather self-consciously in the pub's beer garden, having already drawn the attention of pretty much everyone with their 'push-me pull-me' antics.

Alice came running into the garden, searching for Jox, and then froze when she spotted him, propped up with his elbows on the table. She stood staring, with tears filling her eyes, then rushed over and tried to give him a hug. He groaned and she stepped back. Ever so gently, she raised her hands to his swollen face and held it. She then kissed each of his cheeks as gently as a butterfly landing on a flower petal, and then his torn lip. He winced.

'Oh, darling, you really have been in the wars,' she sighed. 'Please tell me you're all right. Mike says you'll be fine, but you look so awful. Are you in a lot of pain?'

'The pills help,' he croaked. 'But it's not really my face that hurts so much, it's my back. It feels like I've been punched by Max Schmeling.'

'I've no idea who that is.'

'Never mind.' He smiled weakly, splitting his lip, yet again. 'Please sit down. I'll get one of the boys to get us some drinks.'

'You've got such a loyal bunch of friends,' she said as Pritchard hurried over.

'They're good chaps,' agreed Jox. 'But that's squadron spirit for you. We watch out for each other, in combat and in life. I was born an only child and have never had any siblings; now I feel I have many brothers.'

Alice looked at him with glistening eyes. 'Oh, I so wish Georgie could have experienced this, what do you call it? *Esprit de corps?*'

'But he did. These chaps are as much his friends as they are mine. You met many of them at his funeral.'

'I'm sorry, Jox. I'm not really thinking straight. The shock of seeing you hurt has left me a bit emotional.' She took his hands in hers and stroked the burn scars on them.

'And there I was thinking you were particular about who you stepped out with, Miss Milne,' said a smirking Squadron Leader Drummond, the scar on his lip stretching. Taking a liberty, he leant over Alice and placed both hands on her shoulders, as if giving her a neck massage.

Jox's battered face was a picture of undisguised fury. Alice glanced at him and shook her head. He tried to get up but struggled as jolts of pain shot up his back.

Alice shrugged Drummond's hands off and said, 'I am, and now you know why I have steadfastly refused you, Squadron Leader. I'll remind you I am an officer in the Royal Air Force, just as you are, so kindly address me as such.'

'Just like me? I say, there's spirit in the little filly after all,' laughed Drummond. 'No accounting for taste, I suppose, but I really can't see how your chosen beau is going to be of much use to you, if you know what I mean. What the devil happened to you, McNabb? Slip in the shower?'

'Fighting for his king and country,' replied Alice. 'You should try it sometime, rather than pawing every poor WAAF you can get your slimy hands on.'

'Oh, you know, I've had no complaints,' leered Drummond.

'Well, you're bloody well going to get one now,' said Jox, trying to get up again. Drummond stepped up to him and forced him back into his seat. Jox groaned at being manhandled.

'Stay down, sonny,' said Drummond. He pointed to the purple and white DFC ribbon on his chest. 'Come back when you've earned some stripes.'

Just then, Bullough appeared with a platter of drinks. He put the tray down on the table, right between the three of them. He stood up straight, then looked at the scar-faced squadron leader, who was a good foot taller than the short and comparatively frail-looking intelligence officer.

'Ah, you must be Squadron Leader Drummond. I've been hearing some interesting rumours about an officer who's been making a nuisance of himself to several of the WAAFs at RAF Kenley. As IO for both of our airfields, you must know it's the sort of thing that would come across my desk. It's a question of whether it harms morale and provides potential for blackmail, thereby encouraging espionage and other such murky stuff,' said Bullough breezily. 'Now, where do you suppose a complaint like that might end up? Right at the top, I'd say. I was just discussing the point with Squadron Leader Robertson, our adjutant and the station wing commander, this very morning as it happens.' He tapped a bony finger on the DFC ribbon on Drummond's chest, as if spotting it for the first time. 'It's the sort of thing that could rather spoil a chap's otherwise unblemished copy book, don't you think? A black mark, if you will, say on his stripes? It would certainly mar the rest of his career. Now, that would be such a pity, don't you think?'

'Are you threatening me, Flight Lieutenant?' asked Drummond, as a puce colour rose to his scarred face and his eyes bulged at the effrontery of this lowly junior officer.

'Oh, I wouldn't say that. You're quite at liberty to sit elsewhere, but I do think it's time for you to leave us,' said Bullough, with an odd flinty smile on his face.

'You and whose army, little man?' sneered Drummond. 'And I should warn you, there are consequences to threatening a senior officer.'

'Oh, I'm not threatening you,' smiled Bullough as Jox watched, horrified by how the situation was evolving. 'But I do think perhaps he might be.' Bullough nodded towards the imposing bulk of Moose, who had appeared behind Drummond.

'I'd say it's time for you to go ... sir,' said Moose in a low whisper.

'So would I,' said Pritchard and then Wolfie McKenzie, each standing either side of Moose. None of them were exactly small men and had the same determined glare as Moose, who took a step towards Drummond.

Like most bullies, he backed right down when confronted, but even if he hadn't, there was no way Drummond could have coped with so many burly opponents. His superior rank would undoubtedly have protected him in the long run, but not before he had received a good kicking, and his nefarious reputation would have been exposed and discussed at great length during the court martials of the 'mutinous' subordinates. Their threat undoubtedly constituted 'conduct unbecoming,' but then again, his reputation did too. Drummond glared back at them, the realisation slowly forming in his mind. He turned abruptly on his heel and marched off, muttering to himself with indignation.

Jox felt an immediate wave of relief and then deep gratitude for the support of his friends. They had truly had his back, and as a lonely schoolboy who'd had to grow so swiftly into a man, it was something he truly valued. He was deeply grateful for these friends, his comrades and brothers.

They gathered round and ensured he was comfortable, then made themselves scarce by retreating to the bar. After all, Jox still had a luncheon date with a beautiful woman and despite a poor start, it was a rare occasion in wartime and not one to be squandered.

Leaning painfully back in his seat, Jox smiled at Alice, but knew that one day soon there would be a reckoning. He would need to take care of Drummond once and for all. Behind his forced smile, deep within, he was already relishing the prospect.

CHAPTER NINETEEN

It took Jox several weeks in hospital to fully recover from his ordeal over Dunkirk, but rather longer for his fury at his treatment by Drummond to subside. He brooded as he healed, as in the skies overhead the Luftwaffe was beginning to switch focus from attacks on convoys in the English Channel to targeting RAF airfields across southern England.

The newspapers were full of the derring-do of the nation's dashing fighter pilots, reporting on how they were 'single-handedly holding back the tide of the Nazi invasion'. As for No. 111 Squadron's contribution, Squadron Leader Thompson shared the key points of his official sitrep on the squadron's performance, which stated that to date they had been responsible for fifty-six enemy aircraft being confirmed as destroyed, one unconfirmed and nineteen others damaged. Four pilots and ten aircraft had been lost, and three, including Jox, had been injured.

Trying to kill his boredom between visits from Alice or the other chaps, Jox wrote letters and tried to catch up on the progress of the other fellows he'd trained with at Fairoaks and Montrose. Flight Commander Brian Carbury and Andrew Salvesen were still up in Scotland with No. 603 Squadron, defending the city of Edinburgh. Likewise, Morgan Chalmers was at the Royal Navy anchorage at Scapa Flow, sadly now without Digger Callendar, the second of their training flight to die. On a group photograph he'd had taken at Montrose, Jox marked a tiny biro cross in the space above both Digger and George Milne's faces.

The Irish charmer, Paddy Finucane, appeared to be making a name for himself, flying Spitfires with No. 65 Squadron out of RAF Hornchurch. According to the papers, he had shot down five Bf 109s over the last few weeks, with two destroyed, two probables and one damaged. Jox was struck by how quickly he was scoring, in contrast to his own slow and rather tortuous progress. Ginger Neil and Jack Benzie were stationed at RAF Church Fenton, the latter with the Canadian No. 242 Squadron led by the fearsome Squadron Leader Douglas Bader, a keen exponent of big wing multi-fighter formations.

After a tedious and infuriatingly long week, Jox was visited by Robertson and Ferriss. They updated him on how things were going at Croydon and how the chaps were coping with the relentless daily sorties and shifting focus of attacks. There had been no new losses and replacements were arriving. Pritchard's leg had improved enough for him to be back in training and Cameron Glasgow was also operational. He had been given the responsibility for Jugs Carmel-Connolly's training but was apparently much more cautious than Jox. The blond-haired, baby-faced Jugs was often heard bleating, 'If the RAF can trust me to do it, Cam, why the devil can't you?' Jox laughed, as it reminded him of his own tough apprenticeship under the watchful eye of Cameron's brother Anthony.

Wonder how he's doing cooped up in Austria? thought Jox. *No doubt giving them hell.*

After circling around the issue for a while, Ferriss finally raised the incident at the pub. There had been no immediate fallout, but both he and Robertson had been fully briefed and were keeping an eye out for trouble. The fact that Jox was out of the way was probably fortuitous, giving Drummond a chance to cool down. Once Jox was back on his feet, they said it would be wise to keep out of the vengeful squadron leader's way for a bit. Jox nodded but knew the day would come when he would go looking for the man.

'There is one bit of good news for you, though,' said Robertson. 'It's been six months since your little lot became pilot officers, so the powers that be have decided forthwith you will be known as Flying Officer Jeremy McNabb. Moose and Pritch too, God help us.'

'Congratulations, Jox,' said Ferriss. He handed him a pair of flying officer's braids, a light blue strip between two darker blue ones, to replace the thinner pilot officer ones currently on his uniform. 'Please be sure you are correctly attired the next time you report for duty,' Ferriss added with a wink. 'I heard about Drummond's crack regarding stripes and although these aren't really the ones you wanted, it gives me pleasure to present them to you. I'm smart enough to realise you and Ant saved my bacon back in France, and there are more than a few of us grateful to have had you around, not least that pal of yours, Pritch.'

'Thank you,' replied Jox. 'It means a lot, especially from you, Mike. You've always been a mentor to me.'

'Piece of cake,' he replied.

'Right, now that you two young ladies have quite finished flirting, perhaps we might rustle up some lunch?' said Robertson with a twinkle in his eye. 'Is the canteen any good here, young McNabb? Oh yes, I almost forgot. I've got something for you from old Mother Glasgow. She heard about how the pair of you talked Cam back to his senses and she's sent you a little gift. Mike's got his, a blue and green confection, but this one's yours. I'm told it's McNabb tartan.' Robertson held up a bright red woollen scarf with a bit of green.

'Oh yes,' said Jox. 'That's McNabb tartan all right. One of the more garish ones out there. The founder of my school was a McNabb, and I've had to wear a kilt this colour every Sunday for as long as I can remember. What's yours like, Mike?'

'Not as loud as yours, but just as scratchy,' he replied.

'Scratchy?' laughed Jox. 'In my experience, pretty much everything from Scotland is scratchy.'

'Well, according to Mother Glasgow, "This is to keep you sweet boys warm as you defend our skies. It comes with the love and gratitude of a mother".'

'If I ever needed motivation for what we do, that's all I'd want to hear,' said Ferriss.

'Quite agree,' said Jox. 'Help me up. You know how grumpy old Badger gets if he isn't fed regularly.'

'Less of the old, you whipper-snapper,' protested Robertson. 'I was fighting the Hun when the two of you were still in your nappies.'

'Exactly. Now, there-there and do come along,' said Ferriss, ever the peacemaker.

Jox went back to ops within a week. His first day back was Sunday, 11th August. The day before had been squally and thunderous, with thick cloud cover over the Channel. He would later learn the day had been earmarked by *Reichsmarschall* Hermann Göring himself to be the start of *Adlertag*, or Eagle Day, but was postponed due to the poor weather. It was rescheduled for the 13th of August when fairer conditions were expected, but in the meantime the 'fat one's' frustration meant he demanded a full rehearsal on this Sunday.

The morning was fine and clear with some thick clouds up high, threatening to bring rain on as the day progressed. The first raid of the day was again over Dover, but RAF plotters believed this was a feint and No. 111 Squadron were not called to readiness. It wasn't until about 10:00 that the radar monitoring station at Ventnor on the Isle of Wight reported a heavy raid assembling over the Cherbourg peninsula in Normandy. All of 11 Group's squadrons were put on alert, followed shortly thereafter by those of 10 Group to the west. The day was developing into one of maximum effort for both belligerents.

At first, only six squadrons were scrambled and the Treble Ones were left on the ground at Croydon. The Observer Corps then reported a mixed Circus of over a hundred and fifty aircraft, including He 111 and Ju 88 bombers, escorted by Bf 109s and Bf 110s, heading for Portland in Dorset. Their most likely target was the Royal Navy base there or the gasworks and the oil storage tanks at nearby Weymouth. A further six squadrons were scrambled, but again No. 111 Squadron were left out.

What was now approaching was the largest single air raid ever launched against English shores. Row after row of enemy aircraft advanced, a mass of menacing black crosses of varying sizes, ranged in sinister serried ranks, or in familiar Vics or the Luftwaffe's preferred *Rotte* or 'finger-four' formation. Fighters circled the bomber formations, trying to draw out their British opponents so the bombers could have a clear run at ground targets unharried. Some were successful in their intent, others not, but a dogfight of epic proportions was soon raging in the Dorset skies. In the meantime, Jox and his squadron mates fumed in clammy cockpits, still waiting in readiness. They followed the drama on the R/T in their headsets, desperate to join the fight.

It was a peculiar experience for Jox. He was no longer sitting in the familiar embrace of the old *Marguerite*, rather her latest incarnation as *Marguerite III*. She was ready and waiting on his discharge from the hospital, freshly painted in his own particular flowery livery. She was, however, utterly new and alien to him and he found it troubling. Everything was where it should be, but he was nervous about flying an unproven aircraft for the first time.

The squadron was dispersed amongst the many bomb-proof pens scattered across Croydon's plain, all waiting for the Very pistol signal to release them. They were listening to the Kenley ops controller, and Jox bristled as he recognised Drummond's voice. He forced himself to bury his animosity and concentrate on the task at hand.

He was flying as Red Two to Wheelie Ferriss, with Jugs Carmel-Connolly at Red Three. He saw Ferriss wagging his finger at him in response to Drummond's voice. Jox glanced over to Jugs, who was pulling on his leather flying helmet over the bright shock of his white-blond hair. He caught Jox's eye and waved. A Flight was led by David Bruce, with Pritchard and Cameron Glasgow in his section. Pritchard's school friend Wolfie was in Blue Section, led by tall, thin Jack Copeman, along with Sergeant Ralph Carnall. Canadian Rob Roy Wilson flew with another Rob, a Scots Sergeant Robert Sim from Ayrshire, led by B Flight Leader Stan Connors. Leading the squadron was Thompson, who was roaring at the ops room with frustration.

The scramble was finally called just after midday and as they rose up through blue-grey clouds, green mist was coming off the sea. There were occasional streaks of sunlight peeking through the clouds, providing an ephemeral accent of pale russet. Jox was reminded of the colours of Scotland and felt the pull of home more strongly than he had for months. Wading up through a murky ten thousand feet, the squadron left a trail of turbulence in the moving wasteland of dirty clouds, leaving behind dark traces of their passage through.

They found their foes amongst this shifting jumble with some difficulty. Dornier 17s of 9/KG2 were attacking a merchant convoy off Harwich, protected by Bf 110s of ErprGr 210. Three other fighter squadrons were already involved in the fight, which quickly developed into a deadly game of peek-a-boo between the angry moving clouds. The convoy of shipping escaped unharmed, but the RAF lost three fighters. No. 111 Squadron emerged unscathed and returned home to refuel and rearm.

Their turn-around was immediate and Jox was already feeling more confident about the *Marguerite III*, now their maiden flight was over. Next up, the squadron were vectored to a build-up of enemy aircraft over the Thames Estuary, threatening a convoy of merchant ships leaving London's docks.

When the enemy were first spotted over the muddy waters of the Thames, the entire squadron seemed to twitch with nerves and pent-up anticipation. Before them were a sleek mass of long, twin-tailed Do 17s, a *Staffel* of Ju 87 Stuka dive bombers and a surprisingly light escort of only about fifteen single-seater Bf 109 Snappers. The heavy bombers were spaced as if on parade, with escorts tiered in fours as if reviewing it. The number of bombers for such a small escort seemed preposterous, but the appeal of the wonderful target for hungry fighter pilots overcame reservations.

'WAGON Squadron, this is WAGON Leader,' said Thompson in their headsets. 'Concentrate on the bombers. Attack by Section, all clobbering the same Heavy. TOP HAT Control. WAGON Squadron attacking. Tallyho. Tallyho.'

Red Section tightened on Ferriss, and it struck Jox again how very odd it was that so many bombers should be so lightly defended. A little bunch of Bf 109s were bobbing about between the lumbering giants, as if freelancing for trade. They seemed unburdened by the restraint of flying in formation, and it occurred to Jox that they might be *Experten*: senior men who knew how to take care of themselves and didn't follow anyone's orders. Autonomous and moving freely, they scattered and reformed seemingly at whim. This was a complete contrast to No. 111 Squadron, who charged down onto the bombers in their usual regimented manner: headlong and line abreast to get in amongst them.

Today, their trademark tactic didn't work. Or at least it didn't have time to work, as they charged in straight and level and were jumped by at least two dozen Snappers with blood-red nose cones, attacking in double pairs from a towering mass of dark cloud hanging above them. Two Hurricanes were swatted down in quick succession, one disintegrating soundlessly at altitude, a momentary flash followed by falling metal components. The other left a long streak across the pressing clouds like the stroke of an ink pen, straight and dark, and down into the swirling brown waters. The squadron scattered; the hunters were now the panicked prey.

Jox immediately feared the exploded Hurricane was Pritchard's friend, Wolfie. He'd caught sight of his chubby face at Blue Three, just moments before they'd followed Thompson's orders and charged like demented cavalry trying to break an infantry square. Jox banked sharply to escape the thudding turbulence of the explosion but dipped his wings in time to see the falling debris, like black rain peppering the churning dark waters.

He was trying to keep on Ferriss's tail, as he twisted and turned up ahead, in desperate pursuit of a fleeing Dornier. Bumping along in his wake, Jox tried to line up a shot and fired a solid burst into the bomber's open bay, the deadly payload already jettisoned in panic.

A double file of Bf 109s flashed between them. The lead pair were chasing a falling Hurricane and the second peeled off towards him as he was spotted. Winking hot fire was aimed in his direction and he pulled up hard and to the right, to avoid the swirling tracers. The Snappers split left and right, arching hard over as they tried desperately to get after him.

Jox was panting into his mask with the exertion of the Gs he was pulling. His vision blurred, but he knew he had to get away. He feared these two had hunted as a pair before and was determined not to become their prey. He reached blindly for the lever on his dash which would awaken *Marguerite III*'s powerful new Merlin engine. The effect was like tapping a conductor's baton before an entire orchestra begins to play. The powerful surge was a solid shove to his still sensitive back and he saw the needles and dials on the panel before him, jumping and quivering. He had tugged the override booster, accessing the emergency power that could help him escape his deadly predicament.

The engine was being brutally abused and roared like a wounded animal, but it delivered the burst of power which added twenty miles an hour to his already impressive speed, pushing him from harm's way. If held too long, the Merlin would tear itself apart and *Marguerite III* would have been very short-lived indeed. Within the vibrating capsule of the cockpit, Jox's body shook so violently that his teeth clattered, and he couldn't focus his eyes. By sheer instinct he corkscrewed his aircraft, then pulled up as his vision gradually began to clear.

He jerked his head back to check if he was still being pursued. He was on his own.

One instant, the sky roared with angry aircraft swirling and snarling around one another. The next, Jox was alone, before the panorama of twisted white, black and grey contrails reaching out like the tentacles of a monstrous Portuguese Man o' War, the brooding clouds above providing a lumpy head. He was short of fuel and could see neither friend nor foe. The furious R/T chatter from moments ago was replaced by harsh static. He didn't know if his set was US, unserviceable in technical speak, but he felt very alone and exposed.

He searched for movement or signs of life but could see nothing but the sinister tentacles. Navigation home was made easy by the position of the Thames, but during his flight over London he couldn't shake off a deep sense of foreboding. His head was on swivels, constantly moving, so anxious was he not to get jumped again. He knew at least two of his comrades were down, but feared the final tally would be higher, given how badly the squadron had been mauled by the red-nosed Snappers' perfectly executed ambush.

The Treble Ones lost five pilots that Sunday: Pilot Officer Jack Copeman, aged twenty-seven, went down in the Channel, posted Missing in Action. Wolfie was the pilot killed in the catastrophic explosion witnessed by Jox. Pilot Officer Rob Roy also failed to return and was presumed to have crashed into the sea. His good luck over Dunkirk — when fumes had forced him to bale out far from the English coast, but he had still safely drifted inland — had clearly run out. The last two lost were Sergeant Robert Sim and Pilot Officer Toby 'Jugs' Carmel-Connolly, both disappearing into the murky waters of the Thames Estuary.

That Sunday, 11th August 1940 the RAF lost twenty-five fighter pilots. Worse was to come in the following days, but the loss of over a third of the squadron was a devastating blow to the battered survivors of No. 111 Squadron. At least two other RAF squadrons suffered as heavily, and there were few within 11 Group who escaped unscathed.

CHAPTER TWENTY

'Five pilots lost and not a single body to bury! How can they just have disappeared? How do you expect the boys to mourn them?' asked Jox.

'I don't know,' replied an exhausted Ferriss. They were at the bar of the mess and looked up as Squadron Leaders Thompson and Robertson came in through the swinging doors, equally tired and grim-faced. Trooping in behind them were the squadron's veteran sergeants: Cameron Glasgow, Ralph Carnell, Harry Newton, Bill Dymond and Ron Brown.

'Right, gather around, chaps,' said Thompson. Addressing the leader of B Flight, Stan Connors, he said, 'Stan, have a quick dekko in the snooker room and then upstairs. I want everyone here. I'll get some drinks in. What's your poison?'

'Pale Ale, if that's all right, Skip,' said Connors, before slipping from the room.

A short while later, the surviving pilots of No. 111 Squadron, plus the adjutant and Bullough, their intelligence officer, were gathered to hear what Thompson had to say. Normally ebullient, brash and full of confidence, this evening he stared at the parquet floor before sighing and clearing his throat.

'Well, there's no two ways about it, we took a hell of a beating yesterday.' There was an uncharacteristic wobble in his voice. 'We've lost men before, but not this many all at once. It's a hell of a blow.' Tears were forming in his eyes. 'Jack Copeman was one of our originals. He joined the squadron back in '38. Rob Roy and Wolfie have only been with us since May, but both had seen action in France and Norway.' He looked for Pritchard, knowing he and Wolfie had been to school together. 'I'm so sorry, son.'

Pritchard nodded sadly.

'Sergeant Sim was only with us for about a month and young Carmel-Donnolly even less, but they were still an integral part of this squadron.'

'Carmel-Connolly,' said Robertson.

'What?'

'His name was Carmel-Connolly, not Donnolly. I think it's important to get it right.'

Thompson was irritated and a little embarrassed. 'Quite so. Carmel-Connolly. Lovely young chap. Always making such a fuss over his ground crew. I dare say they'll miss him too.'

Robertson frowned but nodded his encouragement for Thompson to keep going and get out what they'd obviously rehearsed.

'Yes, sadly missed,' said Thompson, trying to find his train of thought. 'We'll get letters to their families in due course. God, I hate writing them. Anyone who wants to add a note, let Badger know and he'll let you have the address, once he's checked you haven't shared anything sensitive or too upsetting. We'll organise a proper memorial when we can, but for now we're still in the fight of our lives.' He stood before them, his hands on his hips, making an already impressive bulk seem even larger. 'I'm afraid things will get rather bloodier before they get better. We must steel ourselves for the fight ahead and the likelihood of more losses. Badger has been onto the Air Ministry about replacements, but the truth is there are many other squadrons hit as hard as us. For now, we need to pull our belts in and cope. Bulldog spirit, boys.' He searched their faces. 'Any questions?'

Jox surprised himself by putting up his hand. 'Aren't there any lessons we should be learning from the clobbering we took yesterday? Shouldn't we at least be changing our tactics or something? Those red-nosed Snappers certainly seemed to know we were coming and properly bounced us.'

The glare from Thompson was murderous, and both Robertson and Ferriss also shot Jox nervous glances. Perhaps it was his youthful lack of tact or simply the indignation he was feeling, but Jox kept going. 'Charging in like that, in a straight line, may have worked when Jerry didn't know what to expect, but they certainly seem to know now. Shouldn't we at least adopt their finger-four formation, rather than lining up like clay pigeons at some weekend shoot?' His question hung unanswered, as Thompson continued to glare at him.

Robertson decided to intervene. 'Look, I know we're all upset. The tactics we use have been developed by the very best specialists in the RAF. This squadron has the honour of being considered the service's premier bomber attack specialists. Look at the numbers we've achieved. Why, Tommy, Wheelie and Stan have all brought down a dozen kills apiece and you're an ace now with, what, half a dozen? Surely, we must be doing something right.'

'But at what cost, Badger?' asked Jox. 'At least if our guns were upweighted, we'd stand a better chance of getting the job done and taking down more of those big bombers. I saw what happened to Wolfie. I was right there with him when he got hit by a cannon burst from one of those red-nosed bastards. He simply exploded as if a grenade had gone off in his cockpit, reduced to tiny fragments in an instant. One second he was there, the next gone.'

'This isn't helping, Jox,' said Thompson, a dangerous edge to his voice. 'You're upset, I'm upset, we're all bloody upset. You may be raising some valid points, and I assure you there are people looking at improving things all the time. Take your cockpit armour, for instance, which by the way saved your life when you decided to go stooging after that Ju 88 over France. Well, it didn't even exist when we were fighting over Dunkirk, now, did it?' Thompson took a deep breath. 'We're in the fight of our lives. We will be called to defend these islands again tomorrow and the next day and probably the day after that. Until we either stop those bastards or are nothing but stains on the grass or slicks on the water. We need to accept the limitations we face and do the best we can to get the bloody job done.'

His gaze slowly panned across the youthful faces gathered before him. He acknowledged each one of them in turn, before finally settling on Jox. 'I know you, Jox. You've got what it takes. You've already proven it. This is the wobbles talking. We all get them, but I need you to dig deep. All of you must dig deep. We're far from done here, and I will never accept anything other than the Treble Ones being right in the middle of the fight. I'm bloody proud it's our job to bring down the bombers crossing our shores. Those bastards who come to bomb our cities, our homes, our people and even our children. They will not pass, not on my watch, gentlemen, and bloody well not on yours. Do I make myself clear?'

There was a murmur of agreement.

Thompson asked again, this time more forcefully, 'Are you with me?'

He was looking directly at Jox now, no longer glaring, but rather pleading. Tears were running down the sides of his great hooked nose, disappearing into the dark hair of his impressive RAF moustache. Moisture hung like beads of distillate on the hairy tips, before fat drops fell onto the varnished parquet floor. Not unlike the scattered fragments of Wolfie's plane which sprinkled the muddy surface of the Thames, thought Jox bitterly.

'Yes, Tommy, I'm with you,' he finally replied.

'Good lad, because we need you,' said Thompson, as the rest of No. 111 Squadron applauded, thumping one another on the back.

There wasn't a dry eye in the house, but throats suddenly seemed extraordinarily parched. The night was going to become a long one, a wake for their missing brothers. Tomorrow would take care of itself but would undoubtedly be bringing further challenges.

CHAPTER TWENTY-ONE

On Thursday 15th August 1940, the Luftwaffe's largest air deployment of the Battle of Britain was launched. The day began with extensive raids across the north and west of 11 Group, but the radar stations along the south coast were soon also picking up signs of a massed Circus heading for the Kent coastline, specifically RAF Manston and RAF Lympne. So many aircraft were airborne over the Channel that individual formations were no longer discernible on the radar scopes, and the armada was estimated at well over a thousand aircraft bound for southern England.

By 1130 the radar stations at Dover, Rye and Foreness were demolished, with all power lost and their towering radio masts felled. Fighter Command was blind and reliant on the eyes of the Observer Corps, well-meaning but with limited ability to see the coming threat.

By mid-afternoon several more airfields had been bombed and the fighter cover sent up to protect them had been completely overwhelmed by the massed enemy raiders. Seven fighter squadrons from 11 Group, including the Treble Ones and totalling a mere eighty fighters, were confronted by over three hundred enemy aircraft.

Considering the odds ranged against them, it was miraculous it wasn't until the third sortie of the day that the squadron had its sole casualty, over Selsey Bill. Tragically, watched by his own brother, old Etonian F/O Basil Fisher first brought down a Ju 88 bomber, but was struck by return fire from the bomber's doomed gunners. Circling protectively, his brother Anthony saw him escape the flaming cockpit of his stricken

Hurricane, but watched in horror as the parachute caught fire, flaming to nothing as Basil plummeted to his death amongst the smoking ruins of Selsey's devastated gasworks. A deeply traumatised Anthony returned to Croydon but was back on patrol within the hour.

After a very long day, the main combat area shifted westwards, giving 11 Group a degree of respite and the opportunity for 10 Group to join the fray.

Just before seven in the evening, No. 111 Squadron's nine surviving Hurricanes took off yet again on the fifth offensive sortie of the day. They climbed to ten thousand feet, awaiting their next vector, when they were alerted by the Kenley ops room that Croydon itself was under attack.

Twenty-two specialist Bf 110 dive-bombers from the elite *Erprobungsgruppe* 210, or Test Group 210, had been tasked with bombing RAF Kenley, but in the fading evening light had struck Croydon by mistake. They were undetected by Drummond's ops room at Kenley, since they had shadowed a formation of Do 17s attacking RAF West Malling in Kent, before streaking off at great speed towards London with a small escort of Bf 109s.

Approaching low through the hazy clouds, they were lit by the weakening rays of the setting sun as they delivered their bomb loads with precision, albeit onto the wrong airfield. The Hurricanes from No. 32 Squadron at Biggin Hill and the Treble Ones were patrolling at Angels Ten and so were perfectly positioned for an interception. The unexpected onslaught scattered the Bf 109 escort, who abandoned their Destroyer comrades to their fate. Forming a defensive circle against the harrying Hurricanes, many of the panicked fighter-bombers released their bombs indiscriminately, then tried to slip away in twos and threes, hoping to use their superior air speed to streak home to France through the evening cloud cover.

Dropping through the haze, Jox spotted a lone Messerschmitt Bf 110 flying very fast and hugging the contours of Croydon's shattered cityscape. He was furious that his home airfield had been sneakily attacked while the squadron's back was turned and was determined to make this raider pay. Approaching the twin-engined aircraft from behind and above, he dropped to chase him down what he recognised was Purley Way, running parallel to the airfield heading south.

At this low altitude, Jox was able to keep up with his normally faster opponent, dodging between buildings and firing snatched bursts which struck his target, but also the tarmac on the carriageway below. The familiar roof of a pub frequented by the squadron flashed by, as he bounced through the Bf 110's twin propeller wakes.

The urban landscape gave way to the lusher hues of England's 'green and pleasant land' as they now raced and dodged between trees and over hedges and bubbling streams in a deadly game of cat and mouse. By the time they reached the tiny village of Crockham Hill in Kent, the raider was ablaze, his ruptured fuel tanks spreading flames over the wings and along the aircraft's long body. A fiery plume trailed behind him as he lost altitude, with Jox still tight on his tail.

He suddenly clipped the tip of a towering elm and cartwheeled straight into the ground. A huge ball of fire rose from the wreck, immediately cremating the crew of two and pushing up thermals which lifted Jox like an autumn leaf floating above a bonfire.

Jox was now low on fuel as he circled the airfield. He couldn't raise the Croydon tower, nor the ops room at Kenley to get permission to land. Wreathed by pyres of grey smoke, all he could see were bright fires burning in buildings around the airfield perimeter. He had no option, though, but to attempt a landing amidst the devastation. He did so with a bump, taxiing gingerly between the craters and scattered debris until reaching his alloted blast-proof pen.

He was relieved to see his usual fitter, Irish Corporal Blackie, who guided him into the E-shaped pen. As he pulled in, he noticed the adjoining space held the burnt-out remains of a Hurricane, the result of a direct hit. Blackie looked pale, grimy and absolutely terrified as Jox switched off his engine.

Stepping down from the cockpit, he was surprised to find himself alone. Blackie had simply disappeared, probably back down into the shelter at the back of the pen. It could take up to twenty and Jox knew the ground crew sometimes slept there, when on standby to refuel and rearm quickly, and to tackle any repairs required. He unclipped the central buckle of his straps and heaved the parachute onto *Marguerite III*'s smoke and grime-streaked wing. She stank of burnt oil and cordite from her fired guns, but the smell was mixed with burning Croydon, the swirling combination rising into the cooling air of the summer's eve.

Jox trudged wearily towards a group of personnel he could see clustered around the next pen along. There was a deep crater gouged out of the pen's grassy protective slope and the concrete and brick facings of its shelter were shattered. Jox recognised Cameron Glasgow, his wingman with whom he had lost contact during the melee over the airfield. Damp and sweaty, with hair standing on end, he had a wild expression on his face, pale grey eyes betraying the strain of combat. Beside him, almost unrecognisable, was a shaky Sandy Bullough, covered in a mantle of brick dust, having just emerged from the shelter which had taken a direct hit.

'You boys look awful,' said Jox, alarmed by Bullough's listless expression.

The South African turned and walked away without saying a word. Cameron replied wearily, 'Aye, we're all right. Unlike these poor sods.'

Arranged in a ragged row were about a dozen bodies, sprawled in the grass before them. Most wore RAF blue and had their faces covered with grey blankets. Nearest was a rigger or fitter in baggy work overalls, the word CANADA just visible on his shoulders.

'One of Moose's lot?' asked Jox, already knowing the answer.

'Aye,' replied Cameron. 'Johnny Cox, one of No. 1 RCAF's armourers. Really nice fella. Three kids and a wife back at home. He was just telling me the other day.'

Jox nodded sadly. Lying beside Johnny were the tan-coloured legs of a WAAF, poking at unnatural angles from beneath her blanket. He was first struck by the folly of going to war in a skirt, then noticed she only had one shoe on. The big toe of her foot was poking through a hole in her regulation tan tights, and the toenail was painted a vivid scarlet that somehow seemed familiar. He knelt beside her and picked up a cold hand, recognising the nails which had previously been immaculate, but were now chipped and ragged, still with the vestiges of the same bright colour.

How did he know her? It suddenly came to him. She was one of Pritchard's lady friends, a WAAF they'd met the other night. What on earth was her name? Jox wracked his brain. Was it Di or Vi? The clever brunette or the brash redhead? He lifted the corner of the blanket gingerly and immediately regretted the impulse. Her ruined face was propped up at an awkward angle by the Tommy helmet still strapped to her head, looking like meat on a plate. He dropped her hand in shock and tasted sour bile rising to his throat.

He rose unsteadily to his feet and glanced down the rest of the line. Another airman in overalls had half of his leg blown away. The ragged raw gore was open to the air, where flies were already buzzing. Next to him, a sodden red mess seeped through the fibres of the blanket covering another. Jox couldn't face any more. He got to his feet and then was violently sick onto the grass.

Cameron put an arm around him as he began to weep. He rubbed his back, whispering, 'I ken it's bad, Jox, but we're going to be all right. We can take it.'

The two Scotsmen surveyed the devastated plain of Croydon, smoky columns twisting through the air as muffled explosions of munitions cooking off were heard across the airfield. The devastation was extensive and widespread. Hangars, workshops and airport buildings were ablaze. Bombs that had been released indiscriminately in a panic had also hit factories, commercial properties and the suburbs of the town. The terminal housing Croydon's fine officers' mess, where the squadron had toasted the memory of their comrades just a few days ago, was completely destroyed, as were some forty training aircraft, burnt in their hangars. The armoury had also been hit in a booming explosion of spectacular pyrotechnics and clattering ordnance. The plain of the airfield itself was heavily pockmarked, and for all intents and purposes Croydon was out of commission. War had finally come to London.

CHAPTER TWENTY-TWO

'Where the hell have you been?' asked Jox at the sight of a bedraggled Pritchard standing with a blanket around his shoulders, filthy socks on his feet and a trouser leg torn to shreds.

'Visiting the delights of the East End. Poplar, to be exact,' replied his fed-up-looking friend.

It was the morning after the raid on Croydon and the airfield was in chaos, but the Treble Ones were on standby again. Their makeshift dispersal was a canvas tent, dating from the last war or maybe even earlier, pitched opposite the NAAFI caravan that was doling out steaming mugs of tea and fried egg sandwiches to the pilots.

'What happened to your breeks?' asked Cameron, seeing Pritchard's ruined trouser leg and the angry red weals running down his calf.

'I baled out over the city and ended up in a back garden. Landed in a hydrangea bush, as I recall,' replied Pritchard.

'What, a plant did all that damage?' said Jox.

'No, it was the bloody dog in the garden. Must have taken me for a Jerry, invading his own private patch of lawn that is forever England. The beast was massive.'

'How did you end up there?' asked Jox. 'Last time I saw you, we were piling in when all of this happened.' He waved his NAAFI tea mug, indicating the devastated surroundings.

'Well, I was with you, but then got too close to one of those enormous Bf 110s. He didn't have time to have a proper go at me but did clip me with his props. Before I knew it, the damned thing had chewed off most of my tail, not unlike that bloody dog and my trousers!' He laughed, despite his weariness. He had obviously been through a lot.

'What took you so long tae get back?' asked Cameron.

'You try walking all the way from Poplar in your bloody socks! I only managed to get a lift this morning from some firemen but had already walked most of the way.'

'What happened to your shoes?'

'Damned things flew off as soon as I jumped. My fault, really. I'd loosened my lace-ups because my feet were swollen from all of our sorties yesterday. The laces were untied and then suddenly whish, they were gone and I was hanging from my parachute in just my socks. Bloody good brogues they were too.'

'Glad you made it down in one piece,' said Jox. 'As you can see, the place got the stuffing knocked out of it.'

'Yeah, it's a right mess. What's the damage? Any casualties?'

'Really not good,' replied Jox. 'The squadron's lost six of our airmen: Adams, Halley, Couling, Dell, Hurley and Mills, and I'm afraid old Charlie Darwood's dog, Butcher, was killed too. Poor thing's been missing him so much. Maybe they're together now.'

'Corporal Higgins will certainly miss him,' said Pritchard, thinking of the batman they shared, who had adopted the orphaned English Bull Terrier.

'Moose's Canadians lost one of their armourers too,' added Cam. 'Nice laddie called Cox. Hasn't been in the country very long. Their ground crews only got here a few weeks ago.'

'There's worse, I'm afraid,' said Jox. 'There were over fifty civilians killed in town, and many are still unaccounted for. With all these fires, many bodies are unrecognisable.'

'Christ, that's grim.'

'And I'm sorry to say, mate, there's more. One of those WAAFs you introduced me to last week has also bought it,' said Jox as gently as he could. 'I saw her myself.'

Pritchard went pale, the stubble on his chin and the shadows under his eyes instantly ageing him. 'Who was it? Di or is it Vi?'

'I'm not sure. I recognised her bright red nail polish. I'm afraid she was in bad shape.'

'That's Vi,' said Pritchard with unnerving certainty. He covered his eyes with dirty, scratched hands, another legacy of the mutt defending its back yard. 'She was so sweet, full of life and then just snatched away. I don't think I can stand this, Jox, I really don't.' He wept silently, the trauma of the night and this morning's news etched on his haggard face.

Jox and Cameron exchanged glances, but neither could find anything soothing to say. They were both as numb and traumatised.

There was the screech of tyres on tarmac outside the tent and the raw gunning of an engine. They stepped out through the flaps of the tent to investigate the source, passing the 'Scramble' bell hanging from a tripod. Outside, an excited Ferriss waited.

'Good, I found you, Jox. Hop in, I've got something to show you.' He was at the wheel of their jointly owned Morgan F-Series three-wheeler and revved the engine impatiently. Spotting Cameron and Pritchard behind Jox, he added, 'Cadge a lift off someone, boys, and head over to where the erks usually park the fuel bowsers. You know, outside the firemen's hangar. It's worth the trip, I guarantee. Come on, Jox, hurry up!'

Jox got in, mystified, and they roared off.

'We're bloody lucky this little beauty is still in one piece,' said Ferriss. 'I usually park her opposite the mess, beside the flagmasts. Well, during yesterday's attack, one of the bloody things, the big one with the yellow windsock, was blown over. Damned thing missed the car by mere inches. Can you imagine the state the old girl would be in, if the bloody great pole had landed on her? Lucky escape in my book, considering the state of the airfield.'

Ferriss seemed remarkably cheerful considering the devastation they were driving through. He kept to tarmacked areas and concrete parking aprons, navigating around bomb craters, charred bits of unidentified debris and several burnt-out vehicles.

They screeched to a halt beside the burnt-out hulk of a refuelling bowser. The reservoir tank on the back of the vehicle looked like a giant hand had chopped into it, splitting it open like fruit. The gushing aviation fuel had burst into flames and the grass around it was scorched black, marking a charred perimeter, with the smouldering remains on oxidised wheel rims, the tyres long since burnt away.

Ferriss jumped from the car while it was still moving and ran towards the scorched remains of a large aircraft. It too was burnt, probably igniting when it had struck the bowser, but having bounced off, it had come to grinding stop by the firemen's hangar. This proximity had presumably meant it was extinguished before being entirely consumed.

The area reeked of aviation fuel, melted metal and burnt rubber. Jox recognised the downed aircraft as a Bf 110, a twin-engined *Zerstörer* or Destroyer. The characteristic fish tail was intact, but the long sides of the aircraft were reduced to a lattice of rib struts. The black blades of the twin propellers were bent like the talons of some great beast. The pilot and rear gunner's cockpit, usually encased in a greenhouse-like glass capsule, was little more than a blackened hole. Visible on the cowling below it and just ahead of where the pilot had sat was the red outline of the British Isles under the yellow crosshairs of a bombsight. This was the emblem of *Erprobungsgruppe* 210's fighter bombers.

'Give me a hand to get this panel off,' said Ferriss, breathless with excitement. 'I'm not having any ground erks or the chaps from No. 32 Squadron nabbing this. It's ours.'

'Is that what this fuss is all about? A trophy?' asked Jox incredulously.

'Well, not just that,' replied a now slightly embarrassed Ferriss. 'It's also a chance to have a dekko at the enemy, up close and personal.'

Jox glanced into the blackened rear-gunner's cockpit. It was filled with thick black ash and smelt like what could only be described as a very burnt Sunday roast. There was a figure hanging from blackened straps that seemed too small to be a fully grown man. Jox knew fierce heat could shrivel the human body, but there was no mistaking the bulbous shape of a skull, yellow and shiny like tooth enamel. Mercifully, the head was hanging at an angle that meant he couldn't see what was left of the airman's face.

No such luck with the pilot. His clawed hands were still on the flight column, bony digits gleaming through fissured, carbonised flesh. Booted feet were still perched on metal pedals, and the heat had pulled the flesh from his face. It was held up by the strap of his radio mic, revealing the screaming grimace of ivory teeth beneath the points of jutting cheekbones. In the black waste of the face, the eyes had shut in death, but had since opened like boiled mussels as they had cooled. Sky-blue and undoubtedly considered Aryan, they stared reproachfully at Jox's intrusion.

'Poor bloody sod,' he muttered, his fragile stomach churning.

'Don't feel sorry for them,' replied Ferriss. 'They attacked us. We did our jobs and took care of things.'

'He's still someone's son. A brother or lover, Mike.'

'They should have thought of that before attacking when our backs were turned.'

'I can't agree. We can't lose our humanity, otherwise we're no better than animals.'

'Look, Jox, we're fighting for our survival, but we can't be fighting each other over this. Let's agree to disagree. Give me a hand with this panel and watch out; it's probably still hot and I don't want the paint to fall off. We need to preserve the map and bombsight.'

'Why are you so intent on getting this trophy? It's not like you, Wheelie.'

'Don't you realise this attack was a milestone? I want something to mark the day.'

A grey utility vehicle, an Austin Tilly, pulled up. Pritchard and Cameron jumped from the cab, followed by a bemused airman who'd been dragooned into driving them over from the dispersal. The battered truck had obviously been left out during the attack and was peppered with ragged shrapnel holes through its bodywork and the canvas-covered rear cab. They approached, intrigued by the sight of a downed enemy.

'What milestone?' asked Jox. 'I'm not following you.'

'Don't you see? By attacking London, Jerry has made a big mistake. We're much further north than the south coast, where their attacks have been devastating. We've been struggling to keep them contained down there.'

Cameron, Pritchard and the driver stopped poking through the wreck and were listening.

'Now they're having to fly further to get here and to get back to refuel — all the while using up precious fuel. Any Jerry fighter that gets to us here at Croydon probably has no more than ten minutes over London. Which means fighter escorts have to abandon their bombers earlier, exposing them to attack unprotected. We have more time now to detect them and intercept once found.' Ferriss was warming to the theme. 'So far, it's mainly the squadrons of 11 Group that have been doing the heavy lifting during the enemy's raids in the south. Over London, though, they're in range of 12 Group based to the north, which means we have twice as many fighter squadrons to throw against them.' He grinned. 'Wouldn't you call that a milestone, Jox? I think Jerry's decision to switch to attacking London will be decisive. It'll allow the squadrons of 11 Group to catch their breath, recover a bit and bring in replacements, while the northern squadrons can finally get stuck in. Strategically, Jerry has made his first major blunder and that, to me, is worth commemorating.'

They prised their trophy off the carcass of the Bf 110 and hauled it back to the dispersal, where it was proudly displayed between two tent poles. They had time to grab some lunch from the NAAFI van before the 'Scramble' bell was rung frantically by an anxious airman. They sprinted to waiting Hurricanes dispersed across the pitted airfield, but it took longer than usual for the squadron to get airborne, given the obstacles and craters they had to negotiate first.

It had been a quiet morning for the WAAF plotters, but now the radar screens identified three heavy raids boiling up. One was seemingly targeting the Thames Estuary, another was off

Dover and a third was massing over Cherbourg, heading for the Portsmouth-Southampton area. Between Yarmouth and Portland there were an estimated three hundred and fifty plots on the radar screens simultaneously.

Twelve different squadrons were scrambled to meet them from 10, 11 and 12 Groups, but several bombers still managed to get through to targets in the Croydon area to cause extensive damage. The London boroughs of Sutton and Merton were badly affected, with Beddington, Carshalton, Mitcham and Wimbledon all suffering too.

Their 'home turf' was being attacked again, whilst No. 111 Squadron were vectored elsewhere, en-route to RAF Hawkinge. They were then redirected towards Dungeness on the Kent coast, between Folkestone and Brighton, intercepting some two hundred aircraft, with the Biggin Hill Hurricanes of No. 32 Squadron and Wittering's Spitfires of No. 266 (Rhodesian) Squadron.

Over Marden in Kent, the enemy formation was principally Dornier 17 bombers escorted by Bf 109s. No. 266 Squadron led by Squadron Leader Rodney Wilkinson attacked the high-flying escort, whilst the two squadrons of Hurricanes went after the main bomber stream.

Jox and Cameron, flying at Red Two and Three, stuck close to Ferriss as they angled for their attack. Ferriss picked out a pair of the bombers who were a little out of position at the starboard rear of the group. As the two Dorniers throbbed beneath them, Ferriss carefully lined up his shot on the twin tail of the rearmost of the pair. He glanced at his wingmen, who would pick up the baton, each firing in turn into the bomber's long fuselage. Experience had taught Ferriss that the Dornier 17 was remarkably difficult to kill, unless attacked from the front. No other Treble One had as much experience at this as Ferriss, bar perhaps Thompson. Now attacking from up high and from behind, there was only the slim body and wide expanse of the wings to aim for, rather than his usual target of choice.

Behind him, second in line, Jox watched as Ferriss dipped his nose before firing. The pair of bombers were silhouetted against the mosaic of the Kentish fields below. To Jox it brought to mind the fat trout he had once guddled for with his hands in Dollar Burn, as a boy at school. Warm summer days had been spent in the bitter cold of the bubbling waters. Distracted, he was brought back into the moment by the sound of Ferriss firing, seeing twinkling tracers striking the lean flanks of the laggard bomber. It was now in Jox's sights, camouflaged dark green on top and dove-grey on the sides, with propellers on yellow-nosed spinners and squared black crosses picked out in white by the wingtips.

The leader of the pair didn't react when his companion was fired on by Ferriss, but he did when Jox started. The reaction was like touching the slippery flanks of one of those boyhood trout; if he'd failed to pin it against the rocks with his fingers, he would see it shoot off across the gravelled burn. This was no trout, but the instinct for self-preservation was identical.

Ferriss took out the lead Dornier without having to fire a shot. It reared up, reacting in panic to Jox's attack on its companion, and flew straight into Ferriss's Hurricane, which was directly overhead. Jox was already clear, as Cameron fired in turn at the second bomber when he saw the blur of collision in the corner of his eye.

The Dornier had a full bombload onboard and the explosion was catastrophic. Jox and Cameron were swept aside by what felt like a giant's hand, barrel-rolling away in opposite directions to escape the blast. Their sturdy Hurricane wings cleaved through the turbulent tendrils of boiling hot air, the surge of their Merlin engines just powerful enough to haul them from harm's way. In their wake, the gutted remains of Ferriss's aircraft fell, locked in an embrace with its hulking victim. The second Dornier fell too, trailing smoke and popping four neat white parachutes.

No. 111 Squadron's leading ace was gone, his life snatched away in a mid-air collision and the resulting catastrophic explosion. His squadron mates had no time to dwell on the loss, engaged as they were in furious air combat with multiple fighters and bombers.

Friend and foe weaved through the Kent skies, a teaming mass of black crosses manoeuvring, twisting and spinning in a spectacular but murderous ballet. Here, a Hurricane fell, flames engulfing the cockpit as the pilot baled out. There a Spitfire was attacked by a hunting pair of Bf 109 Snappers, colliding with a third as he tried to escape their withering fire.

Friday the 16th of August cost No. 111 Squadron dearly. In exchange for three Dornier 17s and a Bf 109, Flight Sergeant Ralph Carnall was left badly burned but alive. It also cost the irreplaceable Flight Lieutenant Henry Michael Ferriss DFC.

Jox had many friends and the war had already taken several. None, though, was as important to him as Mike Ferriss, a father-figure despite only being twenty-two, a role model to emulate, a trusted mentor, but most of all a big brother to this lonely only child.

CHAPTER TWENTY-THREE

The day after Mike Ferriss's death, Jox was summoned to the squadron office. To call it an office was perhaps an overstatement, given that it was simply the corner of a hangar not completely wrecked by the Luftwaffe's recent attention. A handwritten sign on a bit of cardboard read '111 Squadron' and there were two blackboards hanging on the wall, one headed A Flight and the other B. Ferriss's name had already been rubbed out from one board and wounded Sergeant Carnall's from the other. Jox was mystified to see his name was on neither.

He announced himself to the WAAF sergeant typing furiously on a large black typewriter. He watched as she pulled a document from the roller, then started the whole operation once again, inserting triplicate sheets of paper interwoven with well-used blue carbons. Whatever else was happening at the ravaged airfields across England, the RAF's bureaucracy plodded on unhindered. The sergeant had large brown eyes which squinted short-sightedly as she concentrated on her work. It made her look grumpier than she actually was. Jox had met her before socially, as ever introduced by Pritchard, and she was actually very sweet, rather shy and unsure of herself. Now, the sole sign of nerves was the tin helmet perched on her head, which wobbled as she typed. To Jox she seemed like some sort of mechanical mushroom, potentially amusing, but he was in no mood to see the comedy.

He did smile, though. Looking up, she smiled back.

'He shouldn't be very long, Flying Officer McNabb.'

The last time they'd met, it had been Jox, but she was being professional now and he'd clearly been summoned on official business. Reaching nervously into his tunic pocket, he retrieved his lucky talisman, the porcelain doll's arm. He held it in his hand, still scarred but fading, rubbing the smooth surface with his thumb. He could feel the repaired fissures and found them soothing.

The tarpaulin sheets hanging on a wire dividing the 'office' space rocked gently in the breeze that whistled through the bomb damage to the hangar roof. It was going to take a while for Croydon to get patched up and return to some semblance of normality, but then again, what was normal in wartime?

From the other side of the sheets, Jox could hear the parade ground voice of Thompson speaking on the telephone. There were also occasional whispered prompts from Badger Robertson, the adjutant, interjecting.

'Yes, six, that's right,' said an exasperated Thompson. 'Yes, I know it's tight everywhere, but it's rather hard to meet the squadron's commitments with just six pilots. Yes, including me.' He paused, listening to what the person at the end had to say. 'You can? Marvellous! Yes, of course, we don't expect them all at once. How many? Well, three would be a good start, I suppose. What's that, all of them foreigners? Well, I suppose so. A Frenchman, a Pole and what? A Czech? I don't really know what that is, but can he fly? Oh, I see, quite experienced then? How about his English? Right, so he's fluent, but the rest are still learning.' He was quiet again. 'What about the Frenchman, can he *parlez-vous*? He's not a Frenchman? I assumed by the sound of his name. Oh, I see, a Belgian. He's a count?' He listened, then replied, 'Well, we've never had one of them before, but we've had several old Etonians, so I suppose it's not all so different. Righto, sounds like a start. Keep us in mind when you have any more. We need to get back to strength. Yes, Badger will be in touch regarding the details. When can we expect them? Next Tuesday? Well, it'll have to do. Let's just hope that Jerry is as exhausted as we are and lets us have a quiet weekend. Yes, we'll be in touch. Cheerio.'

There was the quiet rumble of conversation behind the curtain. The WAAF sergeant smiled again. 'They shouldn't be much longer.'

Jox nodded as her name suddenly popped into his head. 'That's all right, Maureen,' he said. 'I'm in no great hurry. It's rather nice to sit quietly for a bit.' She seemed pleased he'd remembered her name.

The tarpaulin parted and Robertson's head popped through.

'Ah, Jox, there you are, come on in. We're just finishing up.' He looked weary, his grey hair and sallow skin betraying his age.

Jox got to his feet, quickly popping the doll's arm back into his pocket. He gave Maureen a quick smile and followed Robertson. He found the bulky body of Squadron Leader Thompson sitting behind a makeshift desk, scratching at some papers with a fountain pen that was dwarfed in his fleshy hand. He looked tired too, the deep furrows of the crow's feet around his eyes accentuating his droopy moustache.

'Thanks for coming, Jox,' he said, after taking a deep sigh. 'I'm really sorry about what happened to Mike. I know the two of you were close. I was very fond of him too. We're really going to miss him. He was one of our old boys, one of the best from before the war. Bloody shame to go like that.'

They stared at Jox for so long he began to feel self-conscious. It was Robertson who decided to break the silence.

'We want you to take over Red Section. David the Bruce will continue to lead A Flight, but you'll be his number two. The rest of the men trust you, and it's what Wheelie would have wanted. He thought very highly of you.'

This wasn't what Jox had expected, and he didn't really know what to say. Dealing with his own grief was one thing, but adding that to new responsibility? He was feeling exposed and starkly aware of his youth. He was just nineteen years old, and they were asking him to lead men into battle.

'Cam Glasgow will stay put as Red Two and we'll swap Pritch in as Red Three, as you move up to Red One,' said Thompson. He was eyeing Jox carefully. 'They're both good men and you know them well, so there shouldn't be any issues. That way, at least I have a Red Section which is complete and dependable. But remember, Jox, you're the lead now. Bruce and Connors will deal with the headache of bringing on the new replacements when they arrive, but I want your section to be combat-ready.' He glanced down at the sheet on his desk. 'We've got three new chaps arriving next week, so try to make them feel at home. They're all foreigners, I'm afraid. Not colonials like Moose or old Rob Roy Wilson, but proper ones with unpronounceable names. Could you find them something shorter and more memorable, Jox? You did a rather good job on young Jugs. Gosh, what was his full name again?'

Before Jox could answer, Robertson replied, 'Carmel-Connolly. The boy's name was Carmel-Connolly.'

'Yes, that's it! Lovely young chap. Pity how things turned out. It's their lack of training, you see; they just don't have enough hours before we send them up. Still, can't be helped, we must move on. It's not as if Jerry is backing down any time soon.'

'What are their names, sir? The replacements,' asked Jox. 'So I can let the chaps know who and what to expect.'

'Their names?' said Thompson, momentarily thrown. 'Oh yes. Let's see. The Czech is called Miroslav Mansfeld. He's been with the Czech Air Force since 1930, so is an older chap and really quite experienced. He served with the French Foreign Legion, then flew during the Battle for France. He's completed his Hurricane conversion course at 6 OTU Sutton Bridge. The second chap is from Belgium and is a count, apparently. His name is quite a mouthful, *Chevalier* Olivier de Ghellinck. In the Belgian Air Force from the beginning of the war, two recorded kills, then made his way to Gibraltar via North Africa. Last chap is a young Pole called Janusz Macinski. He fought Jerry in Poland, then made his way to Blighty via Romania and has a bit of combat experience too. All three are straight from 6 OTU, so they should know each other, which may come in useful.'

It was a lot of information for Jox to take in and he was struggling to keep up. On the names, he only caught Miro-something, Olive-something else and then Mack. That would do for a start, he thought: Miro, Olive and Mack. Short and easy to remember.

'One more thing,' said Thompson. 'I want you to work with Badger to arrange Mike's funeral. I've sent a telegram and more or less the standard letter to his parents, but they've been in touch and want to arrange a local funeral. His father is a pharmacist in Chislehurst in Kent, so not far from here. I expect a full squadron turnout — well, at least everyone that's left. It'll be our opportunity to say our goodbyes to Mike, but also the other chaps we lost over the Thames Estuary. I know you felt quite strongly that they needed to be commemorated somehow. The section leaders will help you rustle up enough airmen for an honour guard. I want this done properly. Mike deserves it, and so do the others. I know I can count on you for this, Jox.'

When Jox slipped back through the curtain, he saw his name had been chalked up on the blackboard as Red One. It was reassuring to see Cameron Glasgow and Pritchard's names scribbled beneath his name, but the weight of responsibility pressed heavily on his shoulders. Whatever else, this war was certainly making him grow up fast.

Jox crossed the shattered airfield, heading for the dispersal tent. Parked outside it was Ferriss's three-wheeler, still waiting for its master like a faithful hound. It dawned on him; the car was now his.

'Here's to Wheelie Ferriss,' said Pritchard, raising a pint of blond lager beer. Jox, Bullough and a few others were toasting the memory of their fallen comrades. They were in The Propeller, a big brick-built pub on Purely Way in Waddon, Croydon. It was an appropriate place to hold an impromptu wake, with its three-bladed Merlin propeller mounted outside. Since 1936, it had been a solid presence along the A23 Purley Bypass, the road down which Jox had chased his latest Bf 110 kill during the attack on Croydon the previous week. He recalled firing bursts at the big Destroyer, as it swung between the roadside buildings. His misses had stitched up the tarmac roadway and pinged off the red bricks. Debris and damage still lay on either side of the pub, but The Propeller seemed unscathed.

The lager held aloft by Pritchard was blond and bubbling and was sometimes referred to as 'Jerry Juice' for its Germanic origins. Barclay Perkins, the pub brewery, was one of the first in London to brew the lager, as early as the First World War.

The Treble One boys enjoyed the irony of toasting their erstwhile leader with this particular brew.

'Here's to Wheelie,' they all parroted.

After long pulls on their beers, Sandy Bullough asked Cameron Glasgow, 'How's Sergeant Carnell doing? Badger mentioned that you and Sergeant Brown went to see him. How's he holding up?'

'Nae good,' replied a grim-faced Cameron. 'He's got burns to his face, neck, hands and legs. He's in the best place for treatment, and it's amazing what they can do these days, but I've got tae tell you it's an awful hellhole.'

'What do you mean?' asked Jox.

The rest of the gathering had turned to hear what the tough Scots flight sergeant had to say.

'Ralph's in a lot of pain,' said Cameron. 'His face and hands are charred black. They've got his arms encased in saline-filled bags, trying to hydrate the burnt flesh. Every day they put him in countless baths, trying to clean his burns and prepare them for grafts. He's a tough laddie, but there's a lot of suffering and pain in his eyes.'

Cameron took a swig of his drink, steeling himself. 'He's in a bad way, but nothing like as bad as some of the chaps in there. You wouldnae believe the faces of some of them. Charred, peeled, skull-like heids, often with nae hair left and missing noses or lips. Some are blind and others speak in a hideous rattle through exposed teeth. Ralph says the technical term is "Airman's burns", but the damage is horrific. The surgeon in charge is called McIndoe, and those poor boys call themselves "McIndoe's Guinea Pigs". I don't know how things will turn out for Ralph, but it'll take a long time. I know if I ever go down in a flamer, I'm taking a pistol tae my heid, because that's no life. No life at all.'

They became pensive as Jox said to no one in particular, 'You know, they're calling us heroes, but they've really no idea what it's like. They see us high up in the sky and think the fight is clean and bloodless. We kill at arm's length and never get splashed by our victim's blood, but it's still bloody, all right.' He rubbed his hands together as if trying to get them clean. 'The things I've done would have had me judged and rightly condemned as a callous murderer in peacetime, but now they try to call me a hero, a righteous killer. It makes no sense to me.'

He looked at his comrades, hoping someone would have an answer to the torment he was feeling.

'The weapons this war has given us mean our ability to destroy goes way beyond our humanity. The guns, aircraft and bombs have allowed us to create chaos and destruction. The democracy of this destruction means the littlest man can easily kill the biggest and strongest. Size no longer matters, just your will to do it.'

He wasn't sure anyone was listening, nor did he really understand what he was saying. They all stared sightlessly at their own private ghosts.

'In reality, war is very boring. We do the same thing over and over again. We hurry, then wait long hours until we are suddenly faced by minutes of sheer terror, then go off and do it all over again. It's so very dull and utterly exhausting, and yet is also the greatest endeavour of my life. We'll never be more tested and will no doubt look back at this time as the best of our lives. It all seems so utterly pointless and a terrible waste.'

'Oh, come on, Jox,' said Pritchard. 'You do speak some prime bollocks.' He had a big grin on his face. 'It's not because you're our new section leader that Cam and I have to put up with you spouting this nonsense. What it does mean, though, is you need to get the next round of drinks in.'

Once Jox had returned from the bar, Pritchard raised his glass again. 'Come on, let's get this wake going. Gentlemen, I give you the eternal memory of my dear old school chum, Wolfie McKenzie. Here's to him!'

They went through the names of all the pilots the squadron had lost recently, one after the next: Higgs, Copeman, Wilson, Sim, Carmel-Connolly, Fisher and then the six airmen lost during the raid: Adams, Halley, Couling, Dell, Hurley and Mills. As each was toasted and raucously cheered, in his mind's eye, Jox saw them appear and seem to join the party. Even the airmen, some of whom he didn't know very well were there, a little out of focus, perhaps, but still there. Front and centre was Mike Ferriss, his mentor and friend, lustily joining in the fun.

Pritchard strode over to the piano in the corner of the room. He sat down, cracking his knuckles. 'This one is for our dearly departed. It was one of old Wheelie Ferriss's favourites.'

Pritchard played and began to sing. Around him, his companions joined in as they recognised the words to the old Great War favourite, 'The Dying Aviator'. In Jox's imagination, their dead comrades joined in:

'A poor aviator lay dying, at the end of a bright summer's day,

His comrades had gathered around him, to carry his fragments away.

The crate was piled on his wishbone, his Lewis was wrapped 'round his head.

He wore a spark plug in each elbow, 'twas plain he would shortly be dead.

He spat out a valve and a gasket, and stirred in the sump where he lay,

And then to his wondering comrades, these brave parting words he did say:

Take the manifold out of my larynx, and the butterfly-valve from my neck.

Remove from my kidneys the camrods, there's a lot of good parts in this wreck.

Take the piston rings out of my stomach and the cylinders out of my brain

Extract from my liver the crankshaft and assemble the engine again!'

The song went on and Jox joined in too. Tears streamed from his eyes and he caught sight of Mike Ferriss, who nodded and raised a ghostly glass.

CHAPTER TWENTY-FOUR

No. 111 Squadron was scrambled in response to a desperate cry for help from Squadron Leader Drummond, the ops controller at Kenley. No-one else was available and the airfield was under imminent threat of attack. Once off the ground, their vector was immediately confirmed as the airfield of RAF Kenley itself.

'WAGON Leader, this is TOP HAT Control. Vector on this location at height one hundred feet, repeat one hundred feet.'

'Are you bloody mad, TOP HAT Control?' replied Thompson. 'I could prune the trees at that height.'

'I repeat, yes, repeat ... vector on Kenley ... patrol at one hundred feet ... thirty plus low-level bandits approaching.' Drummond's distinctive voice then added, 'Please hurry.'

It was a Sunday morning which had started slowly for the Treble Ones, as their airfield was still being put back together again and the debris of the week's attacks cleared. After the early morning mist, the skies had brightened to a wide, blue expanse that was expected to last well into the following week. Under normal circumstances, it would have been the makings of a perfect Sunday, but it seemed unlikely the Germans would cooperate.

Three distinct formations of enemy aircraft were detected on the Cathode Ray Tubes of the signal monitoring services that were increasingly playing a role in giving the RAF fair warning of their foes' intentions. Sometimes referred to as RADAR (Radio Detection and Ranging), the plots appeared at first to be heading for London, but given the Luftwaffe's recent focus on RAF airfields, the analysts' views were that Kenley and

Biggin Hill were the likeliest targets. Both had significant sector operations rooms, vital for the coordination of the RAF's fighter response and interception of enemy excursions.

The Kenley sector controller sent his No. 615 Squadron to intercept the raid over Hawkinge, and then No. 64 vectored onto a high-altitude plot threatening the airfield. His desperate call to nearby bombed-out Croydon was an urgent plea to meet a new as yet unidentified group of bombers approaching at a very low level.

Croydon and Kenley were less than five miles apart, and there was no opportunity nor apparently any need to gain altitude, since the squadron were within sight of the airfield in minutes. Kenley was on a large flat plateau surrounded by trees, wedged between the villages of Coulsden and Whyteleafe. It had two tarmac runways that crossed like the folded sleeves behind a freshly ironed shirt and a ring of distinctive E-shaped blast-proof pens budding off the perimeter taxiway, designed to protect Kenley's resident fighters. From the air, the outline of the airfield somewhat resembled a teddy bear's head.

Low and approaching from the north, Jox could make out the various hangars and maintenance sheds, and on his portside the large, pointed roof of the officers' mess, where he'd enjoyed his memorable meal with Ferriss. In the foreground, there was a smaller building looking rather exposed on its own, although protected by an embankment around it. This was Kenley's sector ops room, where Drummond, the WAAF plotters and controllers, and in all probability Alice, operated. Jox dipped his wing to get a better view as Stan Connors, at the head of the formation, said, 'Tighten up, WAGON squadron.'

There were only eight surviving aircraft flying in two finger-four formations, an idea pinched from Jerry and a concession from Thompson given their depleted numbers. Connors's flight consisted of David Bruce, Pete Simpson and Sergeant Ron Brown, whilst Jox was tucked in tight on Thompson's portside, with Cameron Glasgow and Pritchard on the other side.

From his position, Squadron Leader Thompson could make out nine Dornier 17 bombers pretty much flying straight at his squadron, but at tree height. They were coming from the south and he made the spot decision to sweep around the airfield to catch them from the rear. This was a departure from the classic head-on attack, usually No. 111 Squadron's signature approach.

'WAGON Squadron, WAGON Leader,' said Thompson. 'All aircraft on me, repeat, on me. We're going to swing around the perimeter and hit them up the arse. On my mark, break!'

Was he trying something new or running shy because of the recent run of devastating losses? Jox wondered. Most likely, it was just that he'd realised the squadron had never attacked at such a low level and was very aware the airfield's anti-aircraft defences would be opening up at any moment. The depleted squadron swept anti-clockwise, seeing the approaching formation spreading out and their bomb bay doors opening. Bombs began falling at twenty past one and Kenley's ordeal had truly begun.

At low altitude, every building and hangar on the aerodrome was perfectly visible to the Dornier crews and the explosions began to blossom amongst them with unnerving accuracy. As the Treble One Hurricanes assumed their positions behind the enemy, alarmed rear gunners began firing desperately at the threatening British fighters, who began to fire back. With the bombers directly over the airfield, Kenley's ground defences added to the cacophony of noise as sandbagged Bofors gun positions around the airfield opened fire.

As the lead bombers approached the northern fence line, at the top of the 'teddy bear's head', the airfield's parachute and cable defences were activated. Spaced at sixty-foot intervals, they consisted of rockets which when fired, pulled five hundred feet of steel cable skywards, where they then hung suspended beneath a deployed parachute, in the hope of snagging a passing bomber. Any aircraft that became entangled immediately risked being dragged down by the heavy cable which now had two deployed parachutes holding it back.

The theory was simple enough and proved remarkably effective, with Jox first hearing the whoosh of the rockets, the squeal of cables unrolling and then the grinding screech of at least two enemy bombers getting caught up and tumbling to earth. It was hard to tell whether this success was due to ground fire, the PACs or the impact of No. 111 Squadron's opening assault. This combination of threats was by no means discerning, as Jox saw a hapless Hurricane up ahead in the squadron formation, gutted by groundfire and spinning off, trailing smoke.

The bombers dropped their one-hundred-and-ten-pound bombs, in batches of twenty, across the airfield. They'd been fused for low-level release and many found their mark amongst the airfield's hangars, mess rooms, administrative buildings and parked aircraft. Smoke, flame and devastation were widespread, with the officers' mess, station headquarters and the sector ops room all being hit. Jox watched in horror as great lumpen iron bombs bounced and skidded across the tarmacked surface of the runways before exploding spectacularly.

Within ninety seconds, Kenley was reduced to ashes and ruin. Jox's every instinct told him to peel back to check the damage to the ops room building, but Thompson ordered, 'Let's get after those damned Dorniers. WAGON Squadron, close-up on me. Now, let's make them pay for this.'

Jox pulled on his control stick and reluctantly chased after his squadron mates, who were already amidst the raiders. The Do17s had sacrificed speed and altitude for accuracy, but now desperately tried to claw back height after their bombing run. They were easily caught by the vengeful fighters and the clear blue sky meant there was no cloudy sanctuary to escape into. Their pursuers lined up behind them, firing carefully considered bursts of fire into their retreating forms. Rear gunners who had survived the Treble Ones' initial onslaught fired hopeful squirts back at their attackers, but Jox's chosen victim remained mute, the gunner already dead at his post.

Sandwiched from below by No. 111 Squadron and from above by No. 615 Squadron, the beleaguered survivors of the first wave of bombers scattered like fish targeted by hungry gannets. Jox's aircraft bumped in their turbulent wake, then was jostled by the recoil of his own guns. He felt a grim satisfaction at seeing the hits registering across the expanse of the Dornier's wings and into the fuselage.

A Hurricane flashed across his nose, firing as it passed, and he just had the time to register the KW squadron code on the side of the aircraft, identifying it as a No. 615 Squadron Hurricane, 'stealing' a half share of his Dornier. Their joint victim unexpectedly and spectacularly lost a wing, before plunging earthwards. Not very far below them, it smacked into a neighbouring cow pasture, scattering the terrified bovines, who were fortunate to escape the flaming 'barbeque' that landed on top of them.

Jox's attention was already on other things as he banked the Hurricane and headed back to decimated Kenley, now facing a second onslaught of bombers.

'WAGON Squadron, WAGON Leader here. Regroup on me and await further orders,' said Thompson. 'TOP HAT Control, WAGON Squadron is awaiting your instructions.'

Jox glanced over his shoulder; his wingmen, Cameron and Pritchard were still with him.

'Red One, this is Red Two,' cried Pritchard. 'Where the hell are you going? Our orders are to regroup on WAGON Leader.'

'I've got engine trouble, Red Two,' lied Jox, perhaps for the first time to Pritchard. 'I've got to pancake this kite pronto.'

'Negative, Red One,' Pritchard replied. 'Can't you try to make it home? We're really not far.'

Jox didn't reply as he swung over Kenley from the east, where an enormous pall of black smoke was rising vertically, until it was caught by the breeze in the upper reaches of the sky and began drifting towards the Thames Estuary. Several Kenley-based aircraft had returned home and were circling the devastated aerodrome, plunging in and out of the dirty funnel rising from the battered remains of the airfield. Most were short of fuel and desperately looking for somewhere to land on the cratered and pitted moonscape below. The fact that it was crawling with emergency personnel firefighting and bringing aid to the wounded didn't help the matter. In his headphones, Jox heard the calls from Croydon's tower directing Kenley's Spitfires to land at RAF Redhill and for the Hurricanes to head for Croydon.

Despite his orders, Jox was determined to get down at Kenley. He had to see that Alice was safe and couldn't live with the idea of simply flying off and leaving her to her fate in the carnage below. He circled the flat expanse of the airfield, searching for a clear stretch of grass or tarmac. He glanced nervously at the gun emplacements, recognising he was at the mercy of any trigger-happy or vengeful anti-aircraft gunner on the ground.

'WAGON Red One, this is WAGON Leader. Damn it, Jox, where the bloody hell are you? Report!' demanded Thompson furiously.

'WAGON Leader, this is WAGON Red One. I've got trouble with my engine.' The lie was becoming easier. 'I need to pancake at TOP HAT location. TOP HAT Control, this is WAGON Red One. My aircraft is damaged. Permission to land?'

He got no reply from the Kenley ops room. The static in his earphones was ominous and with his mind racing, he was imagining the worst case amongst the fire and flames. Worrying about Alice made up his mind and he reached for the lever to lower the undercarriage, as he scanned for a clear patch. The cratered runways were out of the question, but surely somewhere on the expanse of the airfield there must be some unblemished strip of turf.

More by luck than skill, he kissed the Hurricane onto the grass, the wheels rumbling as friction slowed him down and he pumped the brakes. Suddenly, his nose was pitched forward and he cracked his head against the dashboard. The roaring Merlin engine powered the propellers deep into the soft ground, dredging up a fountain of brown soil and turf that battered against his canopy. With a final groan, *Marguerite III* rocked back onto her rear wheel, pitching his head back violently against the headrest of the seat. Instinctively, he reached for the lucky talisman in his breast pocket and gave the ceramic surface a reassuring rub. His breath rasped in the mask, ears pounding, and then all he could hear was the ticking of his aircraft, broken and cooling, but mercifully not alight. *Marguerite III* had brought him down safely and in one piece, but he couldn't say the same for her.

He quickly unclipped his mask, slipped the leather flight helmet from his head, then reached up to pull back the canopy. Pulling himself up, the first thing that hit him was the blast of heat and the smell of Kenley burning. It was like he'd landed in the mouth of a volcano — smoke, fire and burning chemicals a toxic nightmare of heat and odour. He clambered over the side of the cockpit, tumbling onto the grass and raw earth ploughed through by the Hurricane coming to a grinding stop. He touched his forehead and winced as he saw blood on the fingers of his gauntlet. He unwound Ma Glasgow's tartan scarf from around his neck and carefully wrapped it around his damaged head in a makeshift bandage.

I'm like some Highlander fleeing the defeat at Culloden, he thought grimly. He looked over his wrecked aircraft, realising she was beyond repair.

'I'm sorry, old girl, this is on me.' He ran an affectionate hand over her grimy wing. 'I just had to get us down.' He turned his attention to his surroundings. Nearest to him, two aircraft had been parked within a protective pen, but were unrecognisable as they burned fiercely. Some Jerry bomb-aimer had dropped the pickle smack on, he acknowledged grimly. They must have been parked fully fuelled and ready to go, by the ferocity of those flames.

He saw a pair of firemen in leather jerkins, thick gloves and rubber boots, doing their best to douse the flames with a hose. As he trudged towards them, the rearmost of the two called over to him.

'Mind how you go there, son,' he said in a Cockney accent. He wore a large white helmet emblazoned with the word FIRE and was pointing at a burning building. 'Keep away from that hangar. It's full of paint and thinners which are going off like rockets.'

As if on cue, Jox heard a series of loud pops, like mortar shells leaving their tubes. A flaming pot arched high into the air, landing with a clatter on the concrete apron before them. The entire area was splattered with paint of different colours, some of it burning and giving off a thick, cloying stench.

'Cover your nose, son,' advised the burly fireman. 'You don't want to be breathing in that muck. Here, I'll give you a hand.' He checked with his mate that he could handle the hose on his own, then strode over to Jox. 'Cover your mouth and nose with that scarf and I'll pop a quick bandage on the bump on your head.' He pulled a linen pad from his jerkin pocket, then pressed it to Jox's forehead, winding the two attached strips around it. 'There you go; the bleeding has pretty much stopped, and now you look like a proper wounded soldier.' He smiled to reveal white teeth, bar the one missing at the front, bright against his smoke-grimed face. 'Here, you're not one of ours, are you? What are you doing here?'

'No, I'm down from Croydon. Had some trouble with my engine, so I needed to land.'

'You've got more problems than that, my old china,' said the cheery fireman. 'Look at the state of your bird now. Mind you, she's not as knackered as some around here.'

'Thanks for your help,' spluttered Jox, desperate to get to the ops room.

'No problem,' he replied. 'Like I said, keep away from the hangars. There're all kinds of hidden nasties stored inside. Plus, all of the roof frames are made of timber and covered in tar paper. The whole bloody lot's a tinderbox.'

Jox began to run towards the eastern edge of the airfield, where he knew both the mess and the ops room were located. The pall of black smoke seemed to be thickest right above his destination.

'One last thing, son,' shouted the fireman. 'For God's sake, keep clear of any UXBs. The whole place is littered with them. Half of Jerry's bombs didn't go off. Maybe they dropped them too low, but watch out — they could go off at any moment.'

Jox ran along the perimeter taxiway, passing by two more hangars, one burning fiercely and the other crushed, as if by a giant's foot. There were electrical and PAC steel cables strewn everywhere amongst the wrecks of several aircraft and vehicles. He came across the crumpled forms of several bodies, dead airmen lying on the grass as if caught in the open by the attack. The lone body of a charred German aviator was lying on the tarmac of the taxiway, his parachute strewn behind him, deployed too low to save him when he'd jumped from his burning aircraft.

Approaching the ops room, Jox's heart was in his mouth. A bomb had struck the building's protective bank, hurling soil and gravel onto the roof and against the windows. Every pane of glass was shattered, and the roof was partially staved in. A thick pall of red brick dust hung over the area as he picked his way through the debris, hoping to gain access. The ops room had been hit, but not as badly as he'd feared. There was hope Alice would be all right. He just had to find her.

CHAPTER TWENTY-FIVE

'What the Devil is that man doing in my ops room? McNabb, get out!' screamed Drummond, his scarred face turning puce as his attention was diverted away from the chaos of the devastated ops room.

A wooden beam supporting the roof had crashed down through the plaster ceiling, painted a vile hue of hospital green, crushing the map room's octagonal plotting table and scattering coloured blocks like the playthings of a bad-tempered toddler. Every surface was frosted with red brick dust, every face and uniform with a rusty hue.

An injured WAAF plotter lay with her legs trapped beneath the crushed table, tears carving rivulets in her grimy cheeks as she writhed and groaned. Elsewhere, a panicked colleague screamed in hysterics as the pre-recorded air raid warning blared from the tannoy on a loop: 'Attention all personnel. Attack alarm. Attack alarm. Formation Attack. All personnel take cover immediately.'

'I can smell gas, sir,' said a dishevelled but calmly professional flight sergeant standing beside Drummond. 'We should evacuate all personnel. The comms are all out anyway, and she could blow at any second. What are your orders, sir?'

Drummond stared at him, as if emerging from a trance. 'Right … right you are, Flight,' he said, now back in the room. 'Don't just stand there — everybody take cover! Evacuate the room, there's nothing more we can do here.' Seeing Jox still before him, he roared, 'And get this bloody man out of my ops room. He has no place being here. This is a restricted area.'

Jox stood, unimpressed by the sight of his nemesis overwhelmed and panicking.

'Where is she?' he asked Drummond's perpetually sneering face with its covering of brick dust. 'I won't ask you again.'

'How dare you! Who d'you think you are?' said Drummond, looming large over him. He jabbed a stiff finger at Jox's chest. 'And what are you going to do about it anyway, you pathetic little man?'

Jox had never really been taught to fight properly but had played a lot of rugby. He knew he had a hard head. It was still sore from the bang on the kite's dash, but he reasoned that at least he had some padding from the bandage. He launched his forehead at the taller man's face, aiming for the bridge of Drummond's nose. It connected with the sound of a boiled egg landing on the floor. A bright splash of blood spread through the bandage, but also down the front of Drummond's dusty tunic.

Jox had delivered a classic 'Glasgow Kiss,' of which the twins would undoubtedly have been proud. He grabbed Drummond's lapels and cocked his head again. He snapped forward for a second time, catching Drummond mid-forehead. Every ounce of anxiety, worry, anger and frustration within Jox propelled him forward. The big squadron leader collapsed in a twitching heap, as a light-headed Jox stood over him. The gash to his forehead had reopened and was bleeding, bright droplets splattering to the dusty floor and adding contrasting hues to the brick dust.

'Angela, will you see to the squadron leader's nose?' the flight sergeant asked a senior WAAF NCO. He then turned to his duty corporal. 'Wickes, this flying officer appears to be wounded. Kindly escort him to the first aid centre, where they can get him patched up. No, don't tend to his wound here. Get him out of here to the medi, now!'

Jox was still dazed as he was strong-armed from the ruined Ops Room. On his way out, he spotted the tall blonde WAAF who had handed over to Alice the last time he was here. Over lunch at the Wattenden Arms, she had told him she was her closest friend and was called Rosemary. Jox dug in his heels and struggled against the corporal's grip.

'Rosemary!' he called out.

She raised her dust-grimed head, blond locks dishevelled and a swollen black eye on her face. She peered at Jox through her puffy eyelid. 'Do I know you?' she asked.

'Yes! Well, no. I'm Alice's friend. Alice's boyfriend, Jox. Jeremy McNabb.'

Rosemary recognised the name, if not the face.

'Have you seen Alice? Is she safe? Please tell me she's safe,' pleaded Jox.

Rosemary ran her fingers through matted hair before answering. 'I don't know. She was hurt when the roof caved in. It was chaos in here, but I think she was one of the first taken to the first aid post.'

'Come on, son,' interrupted Corporal Wickes, taking a firmer grip on Jox. 'You be a good officer and don't give me no more trouble. That's where we're going, anyhow. Get you fixed up and maybe we'll find your friend.'

The carnage at the medical post was even worse than in the ops room. The dead and the wounded lay scattered on the grass in front of the damaged hospital block.

Confronted with chaos, Jox searched the badly shaken faces for Alice. The 'All Clear' sounded across the shattered airfield as he spotted a ragged row of bodies lying in the grass, sadly reminiscent of what he'd witnessed at Croydon. His heart sank but found some hope when he realised the twisted ankles of the fatalities were all in trouser legs and wearing masculine boots.

It was a fluttering bandage that caught his eye. There she was, holding a canteen to the lips of an airman with both arms in slings. On her left cheek, an outsize wad of gauze had been clumsily taped and he could see a red spot seeping through the centre. Her hair was loose, grimy with brick dust and blowing in the hot wind from the fires on this already blazing August day. She had never looked more beautiful.

The wounded soldier she was helping nodded in his direction to let her know that someone was staring. He was a touch resentful that someone was stealing her away but respected the officer's uniform and fighter pilot's attire.

The full beam of Alice's gaze made Jox's heart leap. She flew across the space between them, straight into his arms. They held onto each other very tightly, long enough for others to notice and for some wag or other to start whistling, as soldiers did. She pulled away, a little embarrassed, but Jox held on to her, then kissed her. He'd been through far too much to be distracted by some petty whistling.

Very gently, he took her hand and asked, 'Is there somewhere we can go?'

She nodded and led him towards the grand façade of the officers' mess, looking rather battered after the day's ordeal. Most of the windows were shattered and the building's signature ivy hung like tattered garlands after a stormy New Year's Eve. Stepping through the main entrance, the sandstone columns were streaked with smoke from the roof, burning at the other end of the long mess building.

'We've got our own little sitting room,' said Alice. 'No one will be there with all this going on.'

Broken glass crunched beneath their feet as they crossed the parquet floor. The WAAF officers' sitting room was small but cosy, with pink drapes at the windows and large salmon damask-covered sofas and armchairs. Someone in procurement had probably decided these were appropriately feminine colours. On the walls 'Careless Talk Costs Lives' and 'Keep Mum, She's Not So Dumb' posters were somewhat at odds with a framed WAAF recruitment poster featuring a pretty, smiling sergeant imploring readers to 'HELP THE R.A.F. JOIN THE WAAF'. Otherwise, a bookcase was filled with well-thumbed paperbacks, inexplicably mainly westerns and a tattered pile of *Picture Post* periodicals. They sat at either end of the large sofa, both looking like they'd been through the wars: him with a bloody bandage around his head and her with a gauze pad on her cheek.

'Don't look at me,' she said, suddenly self-conscious. 'I must be hideous. It was flying glass that cut me, but I think I was lucky. A sick bay nurse put two stitches into my cheek, but said it was a clean cut. I'll probably end up with a scar, like some ugly pirate.'

'You could never be ugly,' said Jox. 'Anyway, I'm a fine one to talk — the state of me!'

'Oh, I don't know, you seem rather roguish. I think I like it.'

Jox smiled, overwhelmed by a sudden sense of relief. 'I was so worried about you, darling. I had to be sure you were all right. You are all right, aren't you?'

'It's been awful. I've never been so scared in my life. It all started so innocently. We'd just finished lunch here at the mess and I was heading down to the ops room to begin my shift. The tannoy started shrieking that "Attack Alarm" business and then the sirens came on. The wailing has always given me the willies, but thankfully there was no panic in the ops room. We put on our tin helmets and got on with the job.' She looked at her dirty hands, rust-coloured with brick dust, but also dried blood. Jox could see they were shaking, so he moved along the sofa and took them in his.

'I heard the bombers' engines above us, through the timbers of the ops room roof. Then the crump of bombs going off, at first well away across the airfield, then getting louder and nearer. The noise of our ack-ack blasting away at them and the sound of those infernal rockets going off was the most terrifying. All of a sudden, it felt like someone had lifted the roof off the ops room, then slammed it back down. The ceiling caved in and there were people screaming everywhere. It was complete pandemonium. The squadron readiness panels shattered and glass flew across the room, with a piece smacking me in the face. Before I knew it, I was being bundled off to the medi, but things were much worse there. They patched me up and once I was sorted, I thought I'd better lend a hand, since it was the nurses and doctors who were the worst hit. I heard Doctor Cromie was killed and poor Mary had a terrible cut to her leg. She was so brave, smiling through it. I would have been simply terrified.' Alice sat silently, reliving the terrible things she'd seen. 'How about you? Are you all right?' she asked.

It was dawning on Jox what he'd been through to get to her and be sure she was safe. 'To be honest, I've got myself into some terrible bother. I was just so worried.' He rubbed his eyes, catching the bloody bandage around his head and making the wound throb.

'What do you mean?'

Jox took a deep breath. *In for a penny, in for a pound*, he thought. 'I needed to know you were all right. I disobeyed my orders, feigning an engine failure to land here at Kenley. I was ordered not to, but landed anyway, risking my aircraft. I managed to get my perfectly sound aircraft down in one piece, but then pranged it straight into a crater. That's how I bumped my head and wrote off a Hurricane worth thousands of pounds. Or at least, that's when I hurt my head the first time.'

She wasn't following him.

'I ran to the ops room to find you and it was in a complete mess. Drummond caught sight of me and started having a go. I just wanted to know you were safe, but he was poking and prodding me. After everything we've been through over the last few weeks, I dunno, I'm afraid I rather lost it.'

She looked at him, wide-eyed with alarm. 'What did you do?'

He sniggered nervously. 'I biffed him … with my head … twice.'

'Oh my God. You've assaulted a superior officer.'

'Yes, I'm rather afraid I have.'

'If I know Drummond, he'll be coming after you.'

'Yes, darling, I rather suspect he will.'

Alice stared at him for a long while and then gathered his face in her hands. 'We do get ourselves into a terrible pickle, don't we? But you must know, I'd rather face the music with you than with anybody else.'

Jox smiled at her, with the roguish sticking plaster and gauze on her face. He could see his own bandage on the periphery of his vision. 'Look at the state of us,' he laughed, before giving her a gentle kiss. He leant back on the salmon-coloured sofa, closed his eyes and considered for a moment. Then he got up and dropped onto one knee before her. Some shattered glass crunched beneath him.

'Never mind that, darling,' said Jox. 'I should have organised things better than this. Well, organising anything at all would have been a start, but sitting in this ridiculous pink room with you, with the war raging outside, I've realised I don't ever want to be without you.' He smiled. 'Alice Milne, would you make me the happiest of men and agree to become my wife?'

CHAPTER TWENTY-SIX

'The great air battle which has been in progress over this island for the last few weeks has recently attained a high intensity. It is too soon to attempt to assign limits either to its scale or to its duration. We must certainly expect that greater efforts will be made by the enemy than any he has so far put forth. Hostile airfields are still being developed in France and the Low Countries, and the movement of squadrons and material for attacking us is still proceeding. It is quite plain that Herr Hitler could not admit defeat in his air attack on Great Britain without sustaining most serious injury...

'The gratitude of every home in our Island, in our Empire, and indeed throughout the world, except in the abodes of the guilty, goes out to the British airmen who, undaunted by odds, unwearied in their constant challenge and mortal danger, are turning the tide of the World War by their prowess and by their devotion. Never in the field of human conflict was so much owed by so many to so few.'

'That was rather nicely put by the Prime Minister,' said Robertson. 'I quite like the idea of being one of "The Few".'

He was sitting on a scratched leather armchair in the lounge bar of the officers' mess at RAF Debden. Either side of him in equally battered seats were Jox and Pritchard. The IO, Sandy Bullough was up at the bar getting some drinks. No. 111 Squadron had relocated to Debden the previous day, as the repairs to Croydon continued but seemed to be taking longer than expected. Debden had also been bombed, suffering five fatalities, but as a smaller airfield it had resumed operations more quickly than the spread-out Croydon.

The Treble Ones had bagged this corner of the lounge as 'theirs', and with much good grace the resident No. 17

Squadron had ceded their place in comradely recognition of No. 111 Squadron's recent harrowing losses.

'Bit too bloody few of us, if you ask me,' said Jox. Pritchard nodded bleakly in agreement.

'You're in luck,' said Robertson. 'Those three new chaps are joining us tomorrow. It would have been Stan Connor's job to get them up to speed, but with him copping it after that Kenley fiasco, I'm afraid you two need to step in.' He hesitated before continuing, glancing at Jox, then Pritchard. Jox just nodded. 'Tommy and David the Bruce are up at the Air Ministry, trying to sort out that spot of bother you got yourself into with Drummond, behaving like a complete lunatic. Look, we really can't afford to lose any more experienced pilots. You will of course receive an official reprimand, but you're bloody lucky it wasn't worse. If it wasn't for the fact you are a damned good pilot, you would have been up for court martial. Ah, here come the drinks!'

Bullough approached unsteadily with several pint glasses wobbling on a tray. They each reached for a pint, then raised their glasses.

'To us and those like us,' said Robertson.

The other three replied, 'The Treble Ones.' They took deep swigs of their drinks.

'We mustn't forget to toast the delectable soon-to-be Mrs Alice McNabb,' said Pritchard. 'You're a lucky man, my friend.'

Jox blushed but knew that Pritchard was right. He was lucky on many counts, not least since the squadron had inexplicably rallied around him after he'd got into that mess with Drummond. He was still shocked that he had managed to get away with it.

'To Mrs Alice McNabb,' they parroted.

'It's a shame that old George Milne isn't here to see it,' said Bullough ruefully. 'It would have been a really special day for him. Seeing his sister wed one of his best friends.'

The next morning it was raining, and it continued for the rest of the day. Instead of the massed attacks of the previous weeks, single enemy aircraft or small formations were sent over, seeking targets of opportunity. Almost six hundred sorties were logged by Fighter Command intercepting these 'tip and run' incursions, and thirteen enemy aircraft were brought down at the cost of a single British fighter. The Treble Ones were not needed, which was just as well; the night before had turned into a long one, as Debden's resident squadrons were keen to welcome their new messmates properly.

Jox was snoozing under an old copy of the *Daily Mirror* when he was nudged awake by Pritchard's foot. He was slouched beside him in an equally peaky state.

'Jox,' he said, nudging him again. 'There are some gentlemen outside asking to see you.'

Jox lifted a corner of the newspaper, daubed with graphic images of blitzed buildings and the wrecks of several downed Luftwaffe bombers.

'What do you want?' he asked irritably. 'Can't you see I'm trying to sleep?'

'Duty calls, my friend,' replied Pritchard. 'The replacements are here and we're on.'

Jox sighed and got up. He shuffled across the dispersal room, blinking in the brightness of the hallway. Outside the door were three uniformed men that came to attention, a reaction he hadn't expected. He looked them over and was struck by how very different each of them seemed.

Miroslav Mansfeld, the Czech pilot, was obviously the oldest and yet was the only sergeant. He had dark, piercing eyes, set beneath a high forehead with wavy hair tucked unconvincingly into an RAF forage cap. He had the squat physique and broken nose of a boxer, with a pronounced gap between his front teeth when he smiled.

Pilot Officer *Chevalier* Olivier de Ghellinck, on the other hand, was tall, fair and slim, with an aristocratic air about him. He had a long neck with a prominent Adam's apple, which bobbed as he spoke, half-strangled by the tie he was wearing. He spoke in a soft French accent and when he saluted, Jox noticed he was wearing brown leather gloves, which he kept on even when he gave Jox a somewhat effeminate handshake. His smile was friendly and seemed genuine enough.

Finally, Polish Janusz Macinski was about the same height and build as Jox. He had a handsome, youthful face and a similar widow's peak, although he was prematurely greying on the sides. He clicked his heels together and gave the Polish salute, touching the peak of his cap with two fingers. It reminded Jox of the boy's scout salute, which somehow seemed apt given Macinski's boyish looks.

The three of them had the VR initials of the 'Voluntary Reserve' on their lapels, in addition to RAF wings and shoulder patches, like those of Moose and Bullough, identifying their home nation. Macinski's additional adornment on his chest was a set of Polish pilot wings, known as *Gapa*, consisting of a silver metal badge of a flying eagle holding a laurel wreath in its beak.

'Good morning, gentlemen, I'm Flying Officer Jeremy McNabb,' said Jox wearily. 'Welcome to the Treble Ones. We're very glad you've joined us. Right, where to start? I won't soft-soap things; we've been through tough times recently and have lost a few good men. You have big shoes to fill.'

The blank expressions on their faces made it clear they had no idea what he was talking about. It occurred to him that despite speaking English well enough to fly, these were foreign pilots unlikely to understand British expressions. Proving the point, Mansfeld asked, 'What soft soap, please, sir?'

'Never mind,' replied Jox. 'Listen, we're pretty informal within the squadron, so we give each other nicknames. You can call me Jox. My friend over here is Flying Officer David Pritchard, but we all call him Pritch. I've been asked by the adjutant to find you nicknames, something easier for the rest of us to remember and pronounce. Olivier, you'll be Olive, Miroslav you're Miro and Janusz, how about Mack? Everyone happy with that?'

'I'm happy,' said Miroslav. 'My mother, she calls me Miro. My friends too.'

'Good stuff,' replied Jox. 'We're your friends now, Miro.'

The burly Czech beamed.

'How about you two? Happy?' asked Jox.

Mack clicked his heels and replied, '*Tak pan!*' then, 'Sorry, yes sir. Mack is good.'

'What about you, Olive?'

The Belgian count had a pained expression on his face, halfway between a sulk and embarrassment. 'I am sorry *Monsieur* Jox, but Olive is not the *nom de guerre* I had hoped for. I was expecting something, how you say, *plus guerrier*, more warlike.'

'What do you suggest?'

'I do not suggest. It is not for me to decide.'

'All right, how about Ghillie?' said Pritchard. 'Your surname is de Ghellinck, right? That's not too far off, now, is it?'

'What is Ghillie?'

'A gamekeeper who teaches you how to catch salmon in Scotland.'

The count shrugged, with the rather Gallic expression of a downturned mouth, but nodded agreement. '*Bon ça marche*, Ghillie. I like it. I like the fishing too.'

'Right, that's settled,' said Jox. 'Pritch will take you over to the hangars now and introduce you to your ground crews. Please treat your rigger and fitter with the utmost respect. Your armourer too. Your life depends on them. Once that's done, each crew will show you to your new, or at least new to you, Hurricanes. You'll find some of their accents a little difficult to understand, but I dare say they'll struggle with yours. Make the effort with them and they'll take good care of you. It goes without saying, you should get to know every inch of your aircraft. She's your mother and lover. Take care of her and she'll take care of you.'

He clapped Pritchard on the shoulder. 'Thanks, matey. While you're doing that, I'll catch up with Bruce and Badger to see how they want the flights and sections divvied up. These new bodies should more or less get us back up to strength. Hopefully you and I can still fly together, but let's see what the higher-ups have in mind.'

Entering the squadron office, Jox found David Bruce, the sole surviving flight leader in deep discussion with Robertson and Thompson. Thompson looked pale, his dark moustache stark against his skin, like a large slug across his lip. Robertson was sucking on his unlit pipe. Before them was a chalkboard and a list of names divided into three.

'Ah, Jox, perfect timing. We were just talking about you,' said Robertson, his hand dusty with chalk. 'We're having a bit of a squadron re-org, given our losses and the replacements.'

'I'm shuffling the pack,' interrupted Thompson. 'Spreading the experienced chaps out with the new bods. Thankfully, they're not entirely green and have seen some combat, but we'll need to see how their language skills hold up.'

'They seem fairly fluent to me,' replied Jox. 'Miro the Pole is probably the roughest, language-wise, but he looks like a real scrapper with the most combat experience.'

'Good. Here's the thing,' said Thompson. 'We're also going to divide ourselves up differently. I know I've been wedded to my ways before, but given our losses, I've been convinced that Vics of three leave us too exposed. I think Jerry is onto something with their "finger-four" formations, so we're going to copy.'

Jox nodded his approval, happy to hear it.

'We're going to split up into three sections of four pilots, rather than the three-man sections we had before. I'll lead Red Section, with Sergeant Dymond as my wingman. He's an experienced chap and has been with the squadron since '38. The second pair will be led by Pritch, supported by Count whatshisname.'

'We've agreed to call him Ghillie.'

'Ghillie? That's not bad. Even I can remember that. Right, so that's Red Section. David, do you want to take us through Yellow Section?'

'Righto,' replied Bruce. 'I'll have Pete Simpson as my number two. He was a bit shaken up by his crash landing on Epsom golf course the other day, but he seems well enough now. He's a solid chap. My second pair will be Ron Brown and Sergeant Tom Wallace, who joined us in July. He's got himself into a bit of bother over a girl; he was an officer but was busted down to sergeant. A romantic South African, but he seems to know his way around a Hurricane.'

'Who's leading Blue Section?' asked Jox.

'You are,' said Thompson, fixing him with a challenging gaze. 'Think you can handle it?'

'Me? Strewth, surely I can't be the most senior.'

'It's not about being senior,' replied Thompson. 'It's about being up to the job and capable of leading the men. You'll have Cam Glasgow as your number two, so that's business as usual, and then the two new boys. Miro will lead the pair, with Macinski as his number two. That should pretty much bring us back to full operational strength and so I suspect we'll be straight back into the fight, if the weather clears a little.'

Thompson's attention had already moved onto something else, as Robertson said, 'Right, Jox, better get your boys up to speed. We're going to need them. Oh, and by the way, for when have you arranged Mike Ferriss's funeral with his parents?'

His mind was already racing with what he needed to do to get Blue Section up and running, so Jox had to stop and think of the answer.

'Friday, 30th of August at two o'clock,' he replied. 'St Mary's Church in Chislehurst, Kent. Mike's parents will meet us there at one. I've arranged transport for the honour guard, and I'll take my car with Sandy. Pritch has got his too, which can take a lot more than mine. Anyone that is off duty will be expected to attend. I've also organised a fly-past with Moose and Squadron Leader McNab of No. 1 RCAF.'

'That's a nice touch,' said Thompson. 'I'm sure Mr and Mrs Ferriss will appreciate it. By the way, how have our Canadian friends been doing since they left us?'

'All right, I suppose,' replied Jox. 'I spoke to Moose yesterday, to get things arranged. No. 1 Squadron RCAF is fully operational now, flying out of North Weald. They've been in a few scraps and bagged a trio of those new Dornier 215s on the 26th of August. They lost one of Moose's tall friends. I can't quite remember which one, they're all so bloody tall, but I think it was Phil. A lovely, gentle chap.'

'The more new squadrons we have joining the fray, the better,' said Thompson. 'Please send Squadron Leader McNab my compliments and my sincere thanks for No. 1 RCAF's service to the Treble Ones.'

'I've also arranged for some named wreaths from the squadron for the chaps we lost on the 11th of August, who'll have no known grave. I thought it would be nice to place them on Mike's grave.'

'Good idea,' said Thompson, a haunted expression crossing his face. 'Our lost brothers all together. I sincerely hope they've found some peace.'

CHAPTER TWENTY-SEVEN

Ferriss's funeral was held during the height of the Battle of Britain. The 'Butcher's Bill' for the day ended up as thirty-nine RAF fighters destroyed, with No. 222 Squadron alone losing eight Spitfires. Over fifty pilots were killed with a further thirty-nine badly hurt. Two hundred civilians were killed, with enemy losses amounting to forty-one aircraft. For once, though, No. 111 Squadron escaped with no losses.

'Funeral party will slow ... march,' Jox ordered as commander of the bearer party. He was following six airmen, led by his rigger Flight Sergeant Barnes, carrying Ferriss's flag-shrouded coffin to the graveside. They were bare-headed in the summer breeze, wearing slate-blue RAF uniforms, black ties and blancoed white webbing belts. Jox had Ferriss's RAF accoutrements in his arms, as he glanced sideways to check that Pritchard was on standby with the firing party, six more airmen armed with SMLE (Short, Magazine, Lee-Enfield) rifles.

As he approached the gloomy rectangle cut in the sod, Jox ordered, 'Halt. Bearer party, inwards ... turn.' The bearers turned to face the coffin. 'Prepare to lower ... lower.'

They lowered their precious cargo until it rested on supports across the grave.

'Shun.'

The bearers' arms cut to their sides, as they knelt on their right knees.

'Wreath.'

The right-hand bearer took the wreath from Jox and placed it on the coffin. The next one placed Ferriss's belt and side arm beside the wreath. The same happened with his Distinguished Flying Cross, with Jox finally placing Ferriss's peaked cap on top of the coffin.

The padre mumbled a few words which were punctuated by the sobs of Ferriss's mother. The stillness of the suburban church yard was then shattered by the sound of gunfire: the salute from Pritchard's firing party. A flock of terrified pigeons roosting in the church roof scattered, circling as a lone bugler sounded the 'Last Post'.

Growling in the background came the roar of approaching aircraft. Every eye at the graveside turned skywards at the distinctive sound of Merlin engines. Low on the horizon, just above the village rooftops, came a Vic of four Hurricanes in 'finger-four' formation, like the fingernails on a right hand. Once directly over the churchyard, the second aircraft on the long side of the formation pulled dramatically skywards, leaving a gap to represent the fallen man's space. Climbing almost vertically, the aircraft appeared to be ascending to heaven as the remaining formation circled the village, before disappearing from view.

Once Ferriss was lowered to his final resting place, Jox ordered the funeral party to replace their headgear. He called, 'Funeral party will salute ... salute.'

The arm of every serviceman and several retired ones went up, as the bearer party placed six tribute wreaths beside the graveside. One each for Flight Lieutenant Henry Michael Ferriss, Pilot Officer Jack Harry Hamilton Copeman, Pilot Officer John Woffenden McKenzie, Sergeant Robert Black Sim, Pilot Officer Robert Roy Wilson and Pilot Officer Tobias Carmel-Connolly.

After the ceremony, Jox approached Ferriss's grieving parents nervously and self-consciously. He needed to offer some words of comfort but didn't really know what to say. The best he could manage was, 'My sincere condolences, Mr and Mrs Ferriss. Mike meant a great deal to me. He was my brother, teacher and mentor. He was the bravest and most selfless brother in arms I have ever served with.'

Mr Ferriss fixed Jox with a tearful but determined stare. 'How remarkable. You all called him Wheelie, didn't you? To the family, he was always Michael. He was such a different person with you, living a completely different life. My dream was for him to become a doctor, but he wanted to serve his country first. I told him, don't worry; you've got plenty of time. He was only twenty-two, you know, but you're even younger, aren't you, son?'

'Yes, sir, I am,' replied Jox, feeling himself welling up. 'We'll keep flying for him.'

'I know you will,' replied Mr Ferriss. 'I know you will. Thank you and God bless you all, boys.'

Ferriss's parents commissioned an intricately carved gravestone for him, with bronze RAF wings above the motto 'PER ARDUA AD ASTRA'. His headstone was inscribed:

TO THE MEMORY OF
F/LT MICHAEL FERRISS D.F.C. R.A.F.
WHO GAVE HIS LIFE IN THE BATTLE OF BRITAIN
AUGUST 16TH 1940 AGED 22 YEARS
LOOKING FOR THE RESURRECTION OF THE DEAD
AND THE LIFE OF THE WORLD TO COME

CHAPTER TWENTY-EIGHT

No. 111 Squadron had been vectored over Brooklands in Surrey, where the Vickers Armstrong aircraft factory produced Wellington bombers and the nearby Hawker factory produced replacement Hurricanes. Fortunately for Fighter Command, on this occasion it was the Vickers plant that the attacking Dornier 17s targeted, delaying production for vital weeks.

By five o'clock in the evening, the squadron was again on a sortie intercepting a fresh raid over the terrifyingly familiar waters of the Thames Estuary. It had been yet another bad day for Fighter Command, with every 11 Group squadron engaged, some as often as three or four times. Over seven hundred and fifty separate sorties were flown. The death toll was heavy, with thirty-five German aircraft destroyed for thirty-three RAF fighters shot down, thirteen of which were destroyed.

As the evening sun set on another torrid day, the weary survivors returned to RAF Debden. Trying to find an upside for the day, they conceded that at least the squadron's replacements had been blooded and Jox was impressed by how aggressive and keen to join the fight both Miro and Mack had proven to be. They stuck together like good wingmen, but he did have to explain there was no need to get quite so close to the enemy before opening fire. They told him that this was how they were taught, and they wanted to be sure of a kill. Between them, the pair had scores to settle for what the Nazis had done to their homelands. It was chilling to see how determined they were to exact revenge, the broken-nosed boxer as much as the boyish Pole.

Over in Red Section, Pritchard reported that Ghillie had also performed well and had brought down a confirmed Do 17, witnessed by several others, and solid enough to meet Sandy Bullough's stringent claim criteria. That evening, when Jox congratulated him, he smiled slyly before saying, 'You see, *Monsieur* Jox, the Ghillie, he can catch the big fish.'

Later, as they gathered at the Debden mess, they were joined by Thompson, who was again looking tired. 'Not a bad day, chaps. Some good solid kills. Congratulations, Count Ghillie. Just a damned shame we lost old Bill Dymond. Another one of our originals gone. It's never easy, chaps, but we need to shake it off. I'm afraid we're going to be busy again tomorrow.' He nodded towards Bullough, who was busy collating claims in his notebook. 'Our intelligence boys tell us Jerry is still after our airfields, but is also increasingly attacking factories, warehouses and docks. London is likely to be targeted in particular, so we're heading back home to Croydon in the morning to act as protection. The aerodrome is still fairly bashed up, but it'll be good to be back on familiar turf, in spite of Debden's excellent hospitality. Right, that's it for now. Have a good evening. David. Jox. Section leaders briefing in the morning at 0700, before we head off. Sandy and Badger, you too, please.'

The next day, No. 111 Squadron had just landed back at the still cratered Croydon, when the familiar patterns of bomber formations were seen bubbling up over Calais on the cathode-ray tubes of the radar monitoring services at Dover. By eight o'clock their targets were identified as the RAF airfields at Hornchurch, North Weald and Debden, which they had only just vacated. Quickly scrambled back over the station, the Treble Ones repaid their debt to the generous resident squadrons with a series of disjointed dogfights over the airfields, resulting in only RAF North Weald being seriously damaged, but not put out of action.

The pace of operations was relentless and exhausting, with each sortie becoming a gamble as to whether a pilot would return and see his squadron mates and friends again. New losses were always sudden, unexpected and utterly devastating.

The Luftwaffe continued to target Fighter Command's airfields, but also ramped up operations against the British factories that manufactured aircraft, engines, propellers and other vital ancillary components.

The first big attack of Wednesday, 4th September concentrated on several airfields, with escorted bomber formations coming in from both the Thames Estuary and also in the direction of Dover.

By nine o'clock in the morning, No. 66 Squadron's Spitfires from Kenley and Croydon's No. 72 Squadron Spitfires and No. 111 Squadron Hurricanes had been pitched against the ominous mass of Bf 110s and Bf 109s coming in over the estuary. By nine fifteen, after a short and brutal engagement with several single seater Bf 109s, both David Bruce and Janusz Macinski were shot down off Folkestone. Bruce's aircraft was seen to crash into the sea, whilst Macinski reportedly baled out. There were persistent but unsubstantiated rumours that he was machine-gunned by the enemy whilst descending and then when bobbing on the surface of the water.

Jox and his squadron mates had no time to grieve for these fallen comrades, as they were immediately vectored to the Dover area mid-morning, then back to Surrey after lunch, with a quick turnaround for refuelling and rearming. Fourteen different squadrons were engaged across 11 Group's sector, and yet fourteen Bf 110 specialist fighter-bombers from 5/LG

1 were able to slip through the screen to bomb the Vickers Armstrong factory at Brooklands again, where two-thirds of the RAF's Wellington bombers were produced.

This time, just six 500kg high explosive bombs found their way to the target, but with devastating impact. Hundreds of factory workers were killed or seriously injured, principally by flying shards of glass. By the day's end, Fighter Command had again put up almost seven hundred sorties, losing seventeen fighters. The balance was only just tipping in the RAF's favour, but not from No. 111 Squadron's perspective.

The day's operations and sorties ground on with relentless intensity. On the 5th of September, they were once again despatched to Dover, and in their absence, five different airfields including Croydon were hit. Biggin Hill was severely damaged, with very little of the airfield left standing. 'Biggin on the Hill' was effectively out of commission.

Returning with a reduced section of three to their newly cratered and smoke-wreathed home, Jox felt a weariness he'd never experienced in his young life. Once he had landed and trundled to a halt, he sat in his ticking and cooling Hurricane. He was enjoying a rare moment of quiet and before he knew it, he was sobbing. He couldn't stop himself as tears streamed down his cheeks, still creased with the pressure marks from his goggles and mask. He reached into his tunic to find the doll's arm; the only thing that seemed to soothe his shattered nerves. He rubbed the cool, hard ceramic surface with his thumb feverishly, until the sobs subsided. He sensed a shadow cast across him from outside the cockpit canopy. Through the distorting Perspex he made out Flight Sergeant Barnes and Cameron Glasgow, his number two. Cameron wrenched back the canopy and peered in.

'You all right, Jox? Christ, you had me worried. I thought you were hurt, not just sitting here greeting like a wee girl. Come on, pal, suck it up. Me and Barnesy will give you a hand.'

Moments later they were walking across the pitted field, and Cameron had his arm around Jox. 'It's all right, Jox. Sometimes, it all gets too much. You know it happened tae me and you got me out of it. Well, I'm here now to do the same, whatever it takes, laddie. You got that?'

Jox didn't have the energy to answer but nodded gratefully.

Flight Sergeant Barnes came running up behind them, having checked over Jox's *Marguerite IV*. 'Sorry to bother you, sir, but there's a call from the tower for you. The CO wants to have a word. He's waiting in the dispersal tent.'

'What now?' said Jox wearily.

Thompson, Robertson and Bullough were waiting for him. He dumped his Irvin flight jacket, goggles and flying helmet onto a tattered yellow armchair and crossed somewhat petulantly over to the tea urn kept permanently on the go by an orderly. He grabbed a chipped enamel mug, filled it with brackish tea, then poured in a lot of sweet, condensed milk. He felt sure he would need the sugar to face whatever music was coming his way.

'Take your time, why don't you?' said Thompson brusquely, but with good humour. He looked pale and drawn, as they all were, but seemed to be in a good mood.

What have you got to be so chirpy about? thought Jox sourly.

'Here, read this, in the order of the tabs that Sandy has numbered.' He handed Jox a newspaper the size of a pamphlet. Jox saw it was a copy of *The London Gazette*, the official newspaper where promotions and awards were announced. This edition was dated 6th September 1940, which was actually tomorrow. He opened it at the page indicated by Bullough with a big red 1.

The KING has been graciously pleased to approve the undermentioned awards in recognition of gallantry displayed in flying operations against the enemy:—

Awarded a Bar to the Distinguished Flying Cross.
Acting Flight Lieutenant Stanley Dudley Pearce CONNORS, D.F.C. (40349), since killed in action. This officer has led his flight in all its operations against the enemy with great skill and courage. In a week of almost continuous action, he shot down at least four enemy aircraft bringing his total successes to twelve.

Awarded the Distinguished Flying Cross.
Squadron Leader John Marlow THOMPSON (34185). This officer has commanded a squadron since January, 1940, and has operated over various areas in Northern France. He has taken part in nearly every patrol and, under his leadership, eighty-one enemy aircraft have been destroyed, twelve probably destroyed and at least forty-four damaged. He has, himself, shot down eight and damaged at least six enemy aircraft.

Jox looked up at Thompson, who seemed rather pleased with himself. So too were Robertson and Bullough. 'Congratulations, sir, that's marvellous news. Very well deserved,' said Jox. 'It's really great Stan Connors has been recognised posthumously. At least that's something for his family to cherish and hold on to. I believe he had a wife and a little daughter.'

'That's right,' said Robertson. 'Living up in the Borders.'

Why are they making such a song and dance about this? wondered Jox.

'Turn to the second tab now, please,' said Bullough, a glint in his eye.

Jox turned the page over to read:

Awarded the Distinguished Flying Cross.
Flying Officer Jeremy Argyll Easton McNabb (41276). This officer has shown himself to be a keen and steady pilot and has displayed magnificent courage in the face of superior numbers of enemy aircraft. Since the middle of May he has shot down at least eight enemy aircraft. His magnificent spirit has been of the highest order and he has ably upheld the fine work of his squadron.

Below his entry, Jox recognised another name. His heart sank when he realised it had only been four days since Bill's death.

Awarded the Distinguished Flying Medal.
580059 Sergeant William Lawrence Dymond. Since May, 1940 this airman pilot has accompanied his squadron on nearly all offensive patrols over France, and its engagements over this country. During this period, he has shot down eight enemy aircraft, and probably destroyed a further three. Sergeant Dymond has displayed a fine fighting spirit.

Jox looked up at the trio but was a little surprised they weren't making a fuss of him. A Distinguished Flying Cross was a big deal and he'd put a lot of hard work into earning it. The least they could do was congratulate him, he thought.

'Back to the front and the third tab, please, Jox,' said Thompson, visibly excited.

Jox wondered what the hell was wrong with them. Perplexed, he turned to the page as instructed and read:

The KING has been graciously pleased to approve the award of the GEORGE CROSS to the undermentioned:—
Flying Officer Jeremy Argyll Easton McNabb (41276).
In March 1940, a Harvard training aircraft crashed at RAF Montrose and immediately burst into flames. At this time, Acting Pilot Officer McNabb was undergoing training as a candidate pilot and was first to arrive on the scene. Despite the severity of the conflagration before him, Acting Pilot Officer McNabb's first and only thought was for the welfare of the pilot in the burning aircraft. At great personal risk to himself and ignoring the fact that his own clothes were already ablaze, he approached the flaming wreckage to pull the unconscious pilot clear. The stricken pilot, Acting Pilot Officer George Milne, subsequently died from his burns, but this in no way diminishes the supreme gallantry and devotion to duty shown by Acting Pilot Officer McNabb's actions on this day.

The trio were now cheering as Jox peered at his scarred hands holding the slim pamphlet. Thompson seized the right one and began pumping it up and down. Unable to contain himself any longer, he gave Jox a big bear hug, lifting him off his feet. The other members of the squadron now came streaming into the tent and gathered around Jox.

Cameron, Pritchard, Ghillie, Miro and the rest were all cheering and talking at once. Wise old Badger Robertson had the last word. 'So, Flying Officer Jeremy A.E. McNabb GC DFC. How does it feel?' He gave a wry smile, then added, 'That's an awfully big medal you've got there, my lad. There's only one better than that, but relax, my boy. You've still got plenty of time.'

CHAPTER TWENTY-NINE

After four months of continuous frontline combat, it was time for Jox and the few surviving members of No. 111 Squadron to return to Scotland, to rest, refit and recuperate. It was time for others to pick up the sword. They had earned their rest and were initially posted to RAF Drem on the outskirts of Edinburgh. The citation of Squadron Leader Thompson's DFC quoted a figure of eighty-one enemy aircraft destroyed by the Treble Ones, with a further twelve probably destroyed and at least forty-four others damaged. By any measure this was an extraordinary achievement but was one that had cost the squadron dearly.

Jox and Alice arrived at Buckingham Palace early to meet Squadron Leader Thompson and his wife, Sylvia. Both men were dressed in their finest dress uniforms, and as a wing commander, Thompson was now sporting three new braids around his sleeves, compared to Jox's paltry one. They had a joke about it, but Thompson quickly closed the discussion by saying that by day's end, Jox's George Cross would far eclipse anything he had on his uniform. Beside them, Alice was in her WAAF uniform, whilst Thompson's wife, a rather short lady compared to her burly husband, was in a sombre black dress and a voluminous fur stole made of some unidentified animals, perhaps foxes. She chatted amiably to Alice as Thompson fussed over Jox's uniform, tugging at his tunic belt, straightening his black tie and smoothing down his lapels.

He fussed how Jox imagined a father might have, but he knew his was far away in India and frankly he wasn't really that kind of a father. More a distant presence who he had rather lost touch with, but to be fair the war in Europe and the advance of Japan across Asia hadn't exactly made communications between them easy, even if they'd wanted to correspond. Jox took some satisfaction from knowing his father, who read *The London Gazette* religiously — since he was always keen to keep tabs on the progress of other civil service mandarins — would undoubtedly see his wayward son had done well and been decorated, twice.

In the meantime, Thompson was an excellent substitute. This burly, rather overbearing man had at first rather intimidated Jox, then frustrated him with his intransigence and unwillingness to adapt tactics to the changing face of combat, but now he saw him as a brusque but paternal figure. He was a man who cared deeply for his men and had taken the harrowing rate of loss very much to heart. Thompson's promotion was well-deserved, but the new training role was a tacit acknowledgement that he was exhausted, a husk of his former self, who needed time before taking on a new operational command.

His Majesty the King was taller, thinner and more softly spoken than Jox had imagined. Pinning the George Cross on Jox's chest, he stammered, 'H-How d-does it f-feel to be a hero, M-McNabb?'

'Oh no, I'm no hero, Your Majesty,' replied Jox. 'I just did my duty and sometimes things turn out that way.'

'N-Nonsense, my boy,' replied the king in his reedy, somewhat breathless voice. 'I can s-see the right stuff w-when it's before m-me.' He shook his hand. Jox saluted and was dismissed.

It didn't seem like much time had passed when he was before the king again, this time to receive the Distinguished Flying Cross.

'M-McNabb,' said the king, his eyes glinting with humour. 'Y-You s-see, I was right. I can t-tell you've been m-making quite a n-nuisance of yourself to the enemy.'

'Just doing my duty, sir.'

'That's all w-we can ask for,' replied His Majesty George VI. 'Your country is in your d-debt.'

Jox appeared before the king for a third and perhaps most poignant time. Both he and Thompson, having received their own awards, accepted the decorations of fallen comrades in their stead. On behalf of No. 111 Squadron, Thompson collected the Bar to Stan Connors' Distinguished Flying Cross and Jox, Bill Dymond's Distinguished Flying Medal, only four days after his brutal death.

'You again?' asked the king. 'It seems m-my instincts are right.'

'It's not for me this time, Your Majesty,' replied Jox. 'It is my sad duty to accept this on behalf of a fallen comrade.'

'A solemn duty indeed, b-but I f-feel you are worthy of it. I f-feel sure, we will meet again, McNabb.'

King George may be right, for there were other battles to be fought and other awards to be won, but for now Jox had done enough. He had faced the fury of the enemy's lightning war and had survived being one of the few. He'd lost many friends along the way but found a vocation where he could make a difference. He was loved and there was hope for a brighter future, a promise of life with a cherished wife.

There would be more trying times to overcome. He knew he would be back guarding the sky from dark raiders — now with experience on his side, and on his chest, the cross of his king.

EPILOGUE

London, April 1990

Melanie McNabb rushed past the formidable ship's cannons standing guard outside the Imperial War Museum in Lambeth. She skipped up the sandstone steps between the columns of the main entrance to the museum, giving the security guard at the doors a quick smile.

Entering the central atrium, she glanced at the display of warplanes suspended from cables above her head, marvelling not for the first time at the weight they carried. Her recent experience in Dunkerque had taught her just how heavy those warbirds were.

Melanie reached her dark office, hidden deep within the recesses of the building, tucked away from the public spaces of the museum. She switched on the table lamp on her impressive mahogany desk. The light cast twisting shadows across the book-lined walls and lit floating dust particles like miniature bombers caught in a Blitz searchlight. This was her sanctuary, far from the chattering school children who peered at exhibits that meant very little to them. Or the middle-aged military enthusiasts, mostly men, giddy at the sight of vehicles they had fantasised over whilst still in shorts. Or even the hollow-eyed veterans and survivors, who were really the only ones who understood the pain and suffering the suspended pieces of ironmongery had wreaked on a war-torn world.

Melanie emptied her coat pockets onto the table. Amongst the paper hankies, a lipstick and the keys to her flat was a clear plastic bag. She carefully tipped its contents onto a square of blue velvet material spread flat on her desktop. Amongst them glistened delicate silver oak leaves, still attached to the stubby black pendant of the Knight's Cross. If she was right, this was all that remained of *Hauptmann* Otto Werner's unique decoration for valour, received directly from 'The Fat One' himself, *Reichsmarschall* Hermann Göring.

The lamplight reflected off the other item lying on the patch of velvet. It was the coppery remnant of a spent .303 round. She had extracted it from what was left of the front seat of the Messerschmitt *Bf 110 Zerstörer* that she and Bobby Brown-Stuart had excavated from the beach at Dunkerque last month. He was still in France, navigating his way through the paperwork required to get what was left of the aircraft back to the UK. With any luck, it would be in Blighty at the IWM facility at Duxford by the end of the following month.

Melanie peered at the innocuous lump of metal and wondered if it might explain how an inexperienced boy-soldier of barely nineteen had bested a fighter ace, acknowledged as one of the enemy's best. She rolled the spent round in the palm of her hand, seeing it cast eerie reflected patterns across the military paraphernalia which crowded the room.

On top of a filing cabinet was an air-gunner's helmet, the light shining through a ragged hole the size of a fist, where the wearer's frontal lobe had once been. Next to it was a Norden bomb sight, to all appearances a lump of metal covered in dials and aluminium knobs, but at one time it had been the most closely guarded military secret. This far from impressive-looking piece of optical equipment allowed American bombardiers to recalculate impact points when on a bombing run, factoring in flight conditions, to deliver deadly munitions on a target as never before. In the half-light, a fertile imagination might have identified it as a giant robot's heart, and if that was the case, then the most secret of typewriters beside it must surely be the brain.

The Enigma machine was a cipher-encoding device developed by Germany during World War Two. It had been entrusted with the very highest level top-secret commercial, diplomatic and military communication by the Nazis, believing the constantly changing code was unbreakable. From data originally provided by Polish and French patriots, then from captured machines, the geniuses of Bletchley Park did in fact break the 'unbreakable,' to provide indispensable intelligence which did more to shorten the war than any other breakthrough could have achieved. The innocuous-looking black keyboard, a mass of rotors and keys, sat almost malevolently, as if still aware of the terrible knowledge it had once possessed.

None of this was what preoccupied Melanie. Her mind was still focused on the spent bullet. She placed it carefully on the desk alongside the Knight's Cross, then crossed the darkened room to the filing cabinet, barely giving the mangled helmet a second glance. She opened the middle drawer to retrieve an old-fashioned cassette player, then began searching through the top drawer amongst dozens of audio cassettes, all carefully labelled. She found what she was looking for and grunted with satisfaction. Back at the desk, she inserted the cassette, sat down, took out a pen and notebook, and pressed play.

After a series of clunks, a man's voice said, 'Session 18876, Reel 3.' There followed a long beep, and then Melanie heard her own voice.

'Interview with *Gefreiter* Rudi Watmacher, 9th *Staffel* of *ZG 26*. The date today is the 26th of June 1988. The interviewer for the Imperial War Museum, London is Doctor Melanie McNabb, and the interpreter assisting *Herr* Watmacher is *Herr*

Otto Schwarz.' There was another bleep and again her voice. 'Rudi Watmacher Reel 3. Good morning, *Herr* Watmacher. I hope you are comfortable.'

'Yes, no problem, young lady. Please continue.' The interpreter translated between each exchange.

'Thank you so much for sharing your memories of the *Kanalkampf* with us. It is an important testimony to record for posterity. I wonder if we might begin by asking you to focus on the morning of the 27th of July 1940. The day I believe you were shot down and injured. I hope the memories are not too painful to recall.'

'No problem. It was all such a long time ago, you know. Sure, my leg hurt like thunder for many years, but once they chopped it off, I was in much better shape. I move faster now than even when I was flying!' The sound of his rumbling laughter echoed on the tape. 'So, *der Chef* and I with the rest of our *Zerstörergeschwader* 26 were returning from escort duty for Junkers 88s raiding shipping off Aldeburgh, Suffolk in England. The weather that morning was terrible, but we were lucky; it cleared by the afternoon. On our way out, the radio reported on the British destroyer HMS *Wren*, which had been sunk in the morning by our He 111s. This was big news because she was an important ship. All of this was only nine weeks after Dunkirk, so our preparations for Operation Sealion, the invasion of England, were still underway. It was a happy time for us, and we still thought we were invincible!' Rudi chuckled.

'The Junkers 88s had been successful too. The bombers attacked Dover in two separate raids. Anchored in the submarine pens of the harbour, they found another destroyer, later identified as HMS *Codrington*, moored alongside a depot ship, HMS *Sandhurst*. *Codrington* had her back broken by our accurate bombing. She ended beached on the seafront near Dover's White Cliff Hotel, where she remained for the rest of the war, becoming a landmark for our crews returning from raids. It was a bad day for the Royal Navy.

'Over Dover, *der Chef* and I shot a Hurricane into the water. We'd both saw it plunge into the sea beyond the harbour wall, so I was confident it was a confirmed kill. He was keen to find more trade, so we left the rest of the *Staffel* when we approached the French coastline. The rest were heading home to Lille, but we went for some free hunting. I spotted a line of smoke out to sea and we went to investigate, soon recognising one of our bombers in trouble. Perhaps it was even one of the Ju 88s we'd been escorting earlier.'

'I'm sorry to interrupt, *Herr* Watmacher, but when you refer to *der Chef*, you do mean *Hauptmann* Otto Werner?'

'Yes, of course. He was my *Staffelkapitein*, but to me *der Chef*. It was an honour for me to be his *Bordfunker*. I was a simple *Gefreiter*, and it was unusual for a high-ranker to choose someone like me to be his radio operator. He always said he wanted me for my eyes, calling me *Blitzableiter* Rudi. Later in the war, when the Bf 110s became night fighters, there were three sitting in the cockpit, but at this stage we were just two: me and him.'

'So, you spotted an aircraft in distress and decided to investigate?'

'Yes, that's correct. One of the Ju 88's engines was smoking, and it was clear she'd been in a fight. The fuselage was streaked with oil and the cowling was tattered in many places. The best way to say it is she was trying to limp home, but was losing altitude and leaving a long oily streak across the sky. That's when we heard the sound of the machine guns.'

'Where was it coming from?'

'Not clear at first, but we soon found a Hurricane attacking our wounded friend, *die Auto*. That's what we called our bombers. *Der Chef* says, "That's not very sporting, Tommy. I think we need to teach this trespasser that he is not welcome in France. He should pick on someone of his own size. *Rudi! Pauke-Pauke*, Attack!"

The Hurricane hadn't seen us yet, he was so focused on his victim. He took a long run at the Ju 88 and began firing from too far away and for too long. I doubted he would have much ammunition left when we attacked.' *Herr* Watmacher took a deep breath, audible on the tape.

'*Der Chef* positioned our Destroyer behind the Tommy and was about to open up with our guns and cannons, when the little Hurricane suddenly twisted up and away. I had never seen a manoeuvre like it and if the swearing that came from the front cockpit was anything to go by, neither had the *Hauptmann*. He was an ace, you know, and together we had seen a lot of fighting, but this Tommy pulled something new on us. He must have spotted our silhouette in his mirror or sensed our shadow. Anyway, during several stomach-churning minutes, I tried to get my gun onto him, but to be honest, we rear gunners were only of any use when being pursued or flying straight and level. For maybe twenty minutes, we curved around each other, engines roaring and grunting with the G-force, each desperately trying to gain an advantage. In the meantime, the crippled Ju 88 *Schnellbomber* crashed into the cliffs at Cap Gris-Nez in a huge plume of flame.

'We seemed to be winning more than our Tommy and *der Chef* got several rounds into him. A big hole appeared in one of his wings and his tail was ragged. I really don't understand why he didn't fall apart. *Der Chef* was roaring with laughter as we chased him this way and that across the sky, closing in to deliver the *coup de grace* and then, once again, he would manage to slip away. *Der Hauptmann* was losing his temper as the Hurricane suddenly dipped below us, then abruptly lifted its nose. I heard what sounded like two or three rattles, not really bangs, more like gravel thrown at a car. Suddenly, everything stopped. *Der Chef* was silent, and I could feel our Destroyer was tumbling. The G-force crushed me into my seat as we tipped forward. I realised I had to get out; our big bird was falling towards the earth. I glanced over his shoulder and could see *der Chef* was slumped with his head lolling. I lifted the hatch and heaved the gun out to make room for me to bundle out of the aircraft. Let me tell you, describing it like this sounds a hell of a lot easier than it really was.'

'So please, what happened next?'

'Well, I fell out of control for a while before I reached for my cord and the parachute opened with a bang. I was worried that we were still over the sea, since I'm not a very strong swimmer. Thankfully, I'd lost track of our position during the fight and realised we were eastwards along the coast and the wind was blowing me landward. Terrified, and remember I was only twenty-one, I searched for our Destroyer. Dangling from my parachute, I could see it falling towards the sand dunes. The Tommy pilot circled around me, waved and dipped his wings, before pointing his battered Hurricane towards England. Below me our Bf 110 wasn't burning, until it hit the ground very hard and a huge ball of flame rose from the beach. Then it burned fiercely and I was ashamed of losing *der Chef*, as I hung limply from the straps. I braced myself for landing and was cheered by the thought of the soft dunes behind the beach. Soft bloody sand, *mein arsch*,' he laughed bitterly.

'You see, *Fraulein*, I shattered my leg on those dunes. No bullet, no combat wound, just French sand. I lay in agony for a whole night, raging with thirst and watching *der Chef* in the wreck burning not so far from me. It wasn't until the next morning that some French school children, accompanied by some nuns, found me. In my delirious state, all I can remember was their black robes and their white headdresses blowing in the wind like seabirds. The next thing I knew, I was waking up in hospital with my leg in traction and plastered. My recovery was a long, painful story, but I never flew again.

'Thankfully, I was invalided out of the Luftwaffe honourably, so I didn't have to face the Russians. I consider myself lucky to have made it through the war working in a state woodwork *Fabrik*, hobbling about on my crutches. I've tried to put those memories behind me, you see, trying to concentrate on living and surviving. It wasn't until after the war that an *Amerikaner Doktor* told me my leg was *kaput* and would never heal. I would be better off without it. Eventually I agreed and haven't looked back since. This tin leg has been my companion ever since.' The sound of something being struck could be heard on the tape.

'Finally, *Herr* Watmacher, I wonder if you can remember where your aircraft crashed?'

'Oh, that's easy, *Fraulein*,' replied Rudi's good-humoured voice. 'It was in the dunes behind the beach at Dunkirk. Tommy's abandoned vehicles were littered everywhere from the evacuation. Where I was lying, I could see a row of trucks that had been driven into the sea to make a pier to reach the boats. By then, they had been submerged by the tides dozens of times and were half buried in the wet sand. There were abandoned helmets, clothing and weapons everywhere, and some bodies too, all slowly being covered by the windblown sand. I lay there thinking what a waste to leave it all to rust and rot away. But maybe it's best to leave those war things to do that.'

The tailor's dummy at the back of Melanie's office stood as a mute witness as she examined the charred German decoration and spent round on her desk. The whirring cassette of Rudi Watmacher's testimony clunked to an abrupt end.

Its flat, featureless face of varnished wood and yellow articulated fingers poked from the collar and sleeves of a slate-blue Group Captain's No. 5 Mess Dress jacket. Each sleeve had four thick bands of gold and seven brass buttons with a crown and an eagle, forming a rough W across the chest. It was a short jacket, worn over a low-fronted waistcoat with more buttons, a white dress shirt and a black bow tie. A matching pair of trousers with razor-sharp creases completed the uniform. On the left of the light grey silk facings were a set of miniature RAF pilot's wings, embroidered in gold, white and red thread. Below that were pinned a colourful row of miniature dress medals of every conceivable colour, shade and hue. These were the gallantry and campaign medals of Group Captain Jeremy A. E. McNabb GC, DSO, MC, DFC & Bar, Melanie McNabb's darling Grandpa Bang-Bang.

In the half-light of the darkened office, she glanced at the exquisitely dressed sentinel. Walking over, she brushed her fingers over the dozen medals, which had fascinated her since she was a child. What all the colours represented had always intrigued her: the man on a horse on the silver cross with a blue ribbon, the white enamel cross with a red flower on a red and blue ribbon and then the one on a striped purple ribbon with a winged cross and silver clasp.

She'd paid too much money for the mannequin, from some closing down sale on Jermyn Street, but she wanted to display her grandfather's uniform properly. Bobby Brown-Stuart had told her this was home to London's finest shirts and with a name like his, he really ought to know. Melanie smiled, realising the dummy was about the same size as her grandfather too. Never terribly tall, she remembered his pride at seeing her grow beyond his height, saying, 'You see, before the war, all we ever ate was rubbish. When I was growing up, school dinners were pretty awful, so I ended up a rather half-pint sort of fellow.'

Standing with the mannequin dressed in her grandfather's best, it was almost like having him right there. She leant her face into the material of the jacket and could smell his sandalwood scent, rather than the whisky and breadcrumbs she usually associated with Scotsmen of a certain age. Not her Grandpa Bang-Bang, she thought defiantly, not ever; he'd never smelt old. Her breath caught in her throat, a surge of raw emotion reminding her how much she still missed him.

'Was this down to you, Grandpa?' she asked the dummy, opening her hand to reveal the spent .303 round. 'Did you do this and if so, how the hell did you manage it? This man was a real killer, and you were just a boy.'

Melanie unclipped the group of miniature dress medals and laid them on the desk. The full-size ones, the real ones, had been tucked away in a bank vault ever since she'd been offered the best part of two hundred grand for them by an opportunistic medal auctioneer who had read Jox McNabb's obituary in the newspapers. It seemed inconceivable that they could be worth so much, almost enough to pay off the mortgage on her London flat. Not too shabby for 'a half-pint sort of fellow.' Whatever was in that glass must surely have been fiery stuff.

She ran her fingers over the stars, crosses, ribbons and clasps of the medals as a sudden thought struck her. She crossed the room and began rifling through a new filing cabinet. Getting frustrated, she slammed the metal drawer with a clatter, then muttered, 'Damn it, where did I put it?' She closed her eyes to concentrate. *Bloody well think, where might it be?* Inspiration struck and she returned to the desk, sliding open the bottom drawer, the repository of anything lying on the desk when she needed to clear it quickly.

She pulled out a pair of wartime binoculars in a battered leather case, then a Glengarry with a silver stag head badge. Next, a swastika armband, blood-red cloth with a white circle and the broken black cross, encapsulated in a transparent sheath of plastic to protect it. Finally, she found what she was looking for: a well-thumbed blue canvas notebook, an RAF pilot's logbook filled with her grandfather's spidery handwriting. She opened a page at random and spread it out. An envelope of photographs fell onto the desk. She would have a look in a minute, but first examined her grandfather's scribblings. In precise, unemotional, almost clinical words, he'd recorded every day's flights and the associated combat.

The record for 16th May, 1940 had a few opening lines, detailing:

AIRCRAFT NO: Hurricane N2555
PILOT DUTY INCLUDING RESULTS AND REMARKS:
Self; R/T Test to Hendon

Melanie scanned the page and realised it was the record of her grandfather's first four days at war, his first victory in France and the terrible losses No. 111 Squadron had incurred. His handwriting was small, almost infantile, mostly scribbled in pencil, but occasionally in blue biro. The first victory and subsequent ones on later pages were marked with a red swastika and usually an annotation. She ran her finger down the column, imagining the horrors so blandly described:

MAY 16
Hurricane N2555. Self; Attack Formation Drill to Northolt

MAY 17
Hurricane N2555. RV 253 (A Flight) to IoW
MAY 17
Hurricane N2555. Offensive Patrol to V-en-A FRANCE
MAY 17
Hurricane N2555. 1230 Ref column attacked Stukas; No. 253 pilot lost.
Offensive Patrol to Vitry-en-A
1500 Offensive Patrol Vitry
1830 Offensive Patrol to Northolt

MAY 18
Hurricane N2555. Self; Patrol to Lille. 1300 Lunch; F/L Darwood lost
1800 Return to Northolt

MAY 19
Hurricane N2555. A Flight; Patrol to Lille 1030 JU 52 FIRST BLOOD!! (Confirmed)
1630 Offensive Patrol to Douai
HIT Me 110 (Probable) 1800 to Northolt
Tommy, Bury & Moorwood all lost.

Melanie knew Squadron Leader John 'Tommy' Thompson had eventually made it back to Britain and had gone on to survive the war, but the others mentioned were all lost; a terrible toll after just four days of battle.

She turned her attention to the faded C5 envelope full of black and white photographs. She shook out the contents. These weren't modern-day snaps, rather the sort of thing taken by an official photographer to mark a special occasion. All except two. These were smaller, brown and white rather than black and white and a little faded, with unevenly serrated edges.

The first photograph was an informal snap of five airmen, none of whom she recognised. Their arms were wrapped around each other, horse-playing for the camera. They were in RAF uniforms of various guises, one in a light tan Sidcot suit, two with semi-inflated Mae West jackets on and, somewhat confusingly, the tallest of the group in the middle was wearing a peaked Luftwaffe cap. The shorter ones at either end of the group had pipes in their mouths, and Melanie noticed they all had carefully styled hair, entirely appropriate for a group of 'Brylcreem Boys'.

Along the white edge of the photograph, each individual's name was scribbled in biro: Carnall, Brown, Copeman, Bruce and Simpson. Copeman was the tall one in the German cap, and they were all grinning at the camera. Behind them was the distinctive silhouette of a Hurricane on an open field of flat grass. In the foreground there was the tongue and groove wooden dispersal hut. The men were carefree, full of good humour and life, but chillingly there were two small crosses marked above two of the heads: Copeman and Bruce. Above Carnall were the words 'WIA BURNT'. The implicit sixty percent attrition rate was a shock to Melanie.

The second snapshot was a portrait of a smiling Jox, sitting in the cockpit of a Hurricane. He had a dog on his lap, which Melanie recognised as a Border Terrier, the breed her grandfather had favoured all his life. Bizarrely, the lower edge of the cockpit had a stencilled row of flowers along it and on the aircraft's nose was the name *Marguerite III*. Below it was what looked like a raised arm holding a sword.

Melanie had never noticed these markings before, despite having seen the photo many times. Her grandfather looked happy and every bit the dashing fighter pilot. On the back of the photo was inscribed: *Self, Georgie and Marguerite III*. Turning it over again, she spotted frost on the grass, so reasoned it must have been after the Battle of Britain, but still early in the war as he was still a flying officer.

The largest photograph in the set was another group shot, this time the sort of thing taken of sports teams or school boarding houses. The wording on the chalkboard held by the individual sitting in the centre of the middle row made it clear this was No. 12 training course at RAF Montrose. Melanie counted forty faces, many with moustaches, ranging across four rows of ten. She recognised her grandfather, second from the left in the second row, smiling at the camera alongside a few familiar faces. Some she had seen in photographs, others she had met as old men. Still others she recognised by reputation, for example the handsome faces of Thomas 'Ginger' Neil and Paddy Finucane, both famous Battle of Britain aces. Ginger Neil survived the war, having shot down fourteen enemy aircraft, whilst Paddy was officially credited with twenty-eight kills, but may have achieved rather more. He was killed in 1942, a wing commander at just twenty-one. Besides Finucane's head there was a little cross, as well as by about a dozen others in the photograph, including the men on either side of Jox. One was tall, with a kind smile and large cow-like eyes and the other slim with a thin moustache and a toothy grin.

The final photographs in the envelope were a set of two: one of her grandfather receiving a medal from a tall, thin and slightly sickly looking man, which it took Melanie a moment to recognise as King George VI. Her grandfather wore a familiar nervous smile on his face, as the king was concentrating on pinning the decoration onto the lapel of his uniform. The second photo must have been taken later the same day and showed her grandfather standing beside a squadron leader, whom Melanie recognised as John Thompson, one-time Commanding Officer of No.111 Squadron.

Melanie was distracted by the phone ringing. She picked up the handset.

'Y'allo, this is Melanie,' she said.

'Hi Mel, it's Bobby. Just thought I'd give you a quick bell to let you know how things are going since we got Werner's Destroyer back to the restoration hangars at Duxford. The crates cleared customs last week and were delivered on Monday. I let Oli and his conservation team unpack everything, then have a good ferret about before telling me what they thought. I've just got an email from him saying he's got mixed news. Less good is that it's in a pretty lousy state, but he says he has been able to lift some good serial numbers off the chassis, dating the rig from the right time period and factory production run. There are some portions of it which can be lifted off and can maybe be preserved as good examples of various bits and bobs. The wreckage itself won't ever come together as a recognisable aircraft again. The 9th *Staffel* white cockerel emblem from the nose and the kill tallies off the tail rudder can be saved, so that's a good start.'

'Sounds promising,' said Melanie. 'Anything on the contents of the forward cockpit? I know it was in a hell of a mess, but we did pick up some promising bits and pieces.'

'Yeah, the French police have released what they are calling the *reliques organiques*, basically the teeth and a few bone fragments, and I'll get them to the lab for genetic profiling. Maybe we can find a direct descendent to make a positive ID. Should take a couple of weeks to get their results, so can I leave it with you to try to find a cooperative descendent?'

'I'll see what I can do,' replied Melanie.

'How did you get on with the bits you, shall we say, purloined?'

'Yeah, well, the less said about that the better. I was probably just a bit over-excited.'

'Understandable. I would be too if I had such a close family connection to the history before us, but how'd you get on?'

'Well, the calibre of the round in the remains of the cockpit seat is, as expected, a .303 and is right for a Hurricane's guns, but that's hardly conclusive given the number of those rounds being fired at the time. If we could match the guns from my grandfather's Hurricane, that would be something else, but it was wrecked on the white cliffs of Kent a long time ago.'

'What about the Knight's Cross?'

'Well, that's more interesting, but again the evidence is pretty much circumstantial, and any conclusion drawn would only be through a process of elimination.'

'What do you mean?' asked Bobby.

'Well, this EK definitely has oak leaves attached so in itself is extremely rare. There is no discernible numbering on the medal itself, but the timing of the wreck and the timing of when the oak leaves were first created are both compelling. The challenge is to link the medal to Werner, the teeth should do that, but then in turn we need to link my grandfather to Werner's wreck.'

'What have you got that could do that?'

'So far, I've scanned his logbook and found reference for the 27th of July 1940, of a probable kill of a Ju 88 and then a Bf 110, but with no witnesses, so not confirmed. Not much to go on.'

'Look, I know we don't have the wreck of Jox McNabb's aircraft, but I wonder if any of it might have been preserved by a museum or something. After all, it was a spectacular crash and right above the White Cliffs of Dover,' said Bobby. 'One other thought: I remember you telling me it was his seat armour that saved his life. It was quite a new bit of kit just after Dunkirk, so I imagine some boffin or other, in the Engineering Department of the Air Ministry, for example, would have been interested in proof that the kit worked. Let's investigate that.'

'I don't understand, how would that help?'

'Well, you said we don't have your grandfather's guns to match against the single round found in the cockpit seat and which presumably killed *Hauptmann* Werner, but what we do have are Werner's guns and cannon. So, should we find any rounds which match these guns in Jox's Hurricane, then we have the connection we need, only the other way around.'

'Bloody hell,' said Melanie. 'Why didn't I think of it?'

'That's why we're a team, dearie,' replied Bobby. She could tell he was pleased with himself, but frankly so was she.

'Okay, you clever sod, crack on and I'll have another look at Grandpa's records. I'll give you a call in a couple of days. Let me know if you uncover anything on the armour idea and please keep on top of Oli and his team. You know they're like a bunch of magpies, always interested in the latest shiny thing put before them. Make sure Werner's Destroyer remains suitably "shiny". Okay, better go, I'm running late. Bye, lovey.'

Melanie followed up on Bobby's idea and logged into the War Records website of the National Archives. She was a habitué of the enormous digital records of the nation. She soon found what she was looking for, a copy of the Combat Report which her grandfather had completed for his mission of the 27th of July 1940, providing the what, where and how of the final sortie of that day. Importantly, it provided the serial number of the Hurricane he crashed in and also more specific details of the location. She marvelled at how she had been able to find the facsimile of what was just a scrap of paper, typed up long ago and still with her grandfather's signature and those of his superiors. She recognised both names as others within No. 111 Squadron's ranks.

Handwritten across the top was 'Manuscript Copy of Pilot's Combat Report forwarded by H.Q.F.C. on 20/9/40.'

SECRET
FORM F - COMBAT REPORT
(Numbered: 105A; Stamped: 213)
Sector Serial No. (A) B.2
Serial No. of Order detailing Flight or Squadron to Patrol (B) (Blank)
Date (C) 27.07.40
Flight, Squadron (D) R3;'A' Flight; Sqdn 111
Number of Enemy Aircraft (E) 30-50
Type of Enemy Aircraft (F) Ju 88 + Me 110 & Bf 109 escorts
Time Attack was delivered (G) Approx. 1730
Place Attack was delivered (H) Dover, Kent; Dunkirk, France
Height of Enemy (I) 15,000 ft down to 1,000 ft
Enemy Casualties (J) Probable Destroyed 1x Ju 88; Unconfirmed 1x Me 110
Our Casualties Aircraft (K) A/c Hurricane R4187
Personnel (L) Pilot with injury to the back

Searchlights (N)(I) N/A
A.A. Guns (N)(II) N/A
Range (P) 250 to 150 yds Closing
Short bursts; Ammo exhausted

GENERAL REPORT
111 intercepted E/A over Dover, Kent. Self in pursuit over the Channel of Ju 88, reaching Dunkirk, France; 2x Enemy A/c destroyed; Own A/c Damaged; Return to Kent; Pancake St Margaret's Bay. Aircraft R4187 U/S

Signature (F/O J.A.E. McNabb)
O.C. Section (F/L J.M. Ferriss)
O.C. Squadron (S/L Thompson) Squadron No. 111

This would certainly give Bobby what he needed to start searching for any surviving parts of her grandfather's aircraft.

A few weeks later, Melanie answered the phone to a very excited Bobby.

'It's a match!' he exclaimed.

'What's a match?' she replied.

'The ballistics and composition of the metal alloy. As I suspected, the fragments from the bullets I told you about last week, those we found at the Royal Engineers Ballistic Centre, turned out to be what we've been looking for. They only have thirteen fragments left, retrieved from the wreckage of Hurricane R4187,' said Bobby breathlessly. 'That's our Hurricane, Mel! Jox McNabb's aircraft. The catalogue even references the name *Marguerite* on the wreckage. I didn't think there could be any doubt, as long as the ballistics matched, and they do.'

Melanie was trying to catch up. Bobby was perplexed by her lack of reaction.

'Thirteen,' he added. 'Unlucky for some, but not your grandfather, Mel.'

'Explain what you're saying, Bobby,' said Melanie. 'Remember I'm a historian, not a scientist like you. Baby steps, please.'

Bobby began to explain, a little more calmly. 'We have fragments of bullets and cannon shells retrieved from the wreck of your grandfather's Hurricane. I've had tests run. One to check the composition of the metal alloys — there can be remarkable regional variations, depending on which armament factories the ammunition was manufactured in. Now the 7.92 mm rounds from the forward firing MG17 machine guns are very common, but the 20mm MG FF cannon ammunition less so. We have samples of unfired rounds retrieved from the wreckage of *Hauptmann* Otto Werner and his *Bordfunker Gefreiter* Rudi Watmacher's Bf 110B, which have the name of the armament works stamped on their casings, but it is the composition of the metal that never lies.' He paused to check she was following. 'We also have the Destroyer's guns, where we have been able to match the groove pattern of the rifling to the few more or less undamaged bullets retrieved from the Hurricane's back armour. The grooving on fired rounds is as unique as fingerprints.'

Melanie glanced at her fingers, remembering her grandfather's own scarred hands, which he always dismissed as 'bumpy from the war'.

'Is this evidence plausible enough to make the connection between the two aircraft and therefore the two, or should I say three, men?' she asked.

'It's rock-solid, Mel,' replied Bobby. 'This evidence puts Jox and *Hauptmann* Otto Werner in the same French sky at the same time, and that, dear lady, is what our French friends call "*Un beau résultat!*"'

Melanie sat back. She'd done it, finally proven the connection between Jox McNabb and the German fighter ace Otto Werner.

She glanced across to the immaculately dressed tailor's dummy in her office, wearing her grandfather's finery. The deadly combat she'd unravelled had happened before any of Grandpa Bang-Bang's medals had even been won. When he was still just a scared boy.

What further horrors did those bright ribbons and shiny metal hide? And how had he managed to grow to the measure? She hoped to find out one day.

A NOTE TO THE READER

Jox McNabb is a fictitious character, an amalgam of real historical figures, people I've met and known, and ultimately, with a typical author's conceit, perhaps there's a bit of me in there too. In order to keep myself engaged with my stories, it is a habit of mine, perhaps a bad one, to use the names of friends and relations in the fiction as a sort of in-joke. They are never meant to be true to life, nor is it ever my intention to misrepresent anyone.

I also like to use the life stories of as many real individuals as I can, but always as a homage and in awe of their deeds, and hopefully treating their story with the utmost respect. It is an advantage of writing historical fiction that your characters live in the past, even if they were once real. It is therefore possible their descendants may recognise them and once again, I hope they can see the respect with which I have told their stories.

Some readers may wonder where the truth stops and the tale begins, but I can't help believing this is the joy of historical fiction. I will leave it for you to decide and hope the adventures of Jox McNabb will allow you to do just that, as they have me.

No. 111 Squadron lost a staggering twenty men during the course of 1940, the first full year of the Second World War. They would lose many more in the years to come, but never so many in a single year.

After the Battle of France, Flying Officer Thomas Higgs was killed in combat on the 10th of July 1940 and was in fact the first RAF pilot lost during the Battle of Britain. He was only twenty-three years old, and his body took a month to wash up on the Dutch coast on 15th August 1940. He is buried at

Noordwijk General Cemetery in the Netherlands, the first of The Few to be lost, but tragically far from the last.

Six other No. 111 Squadron pilots are listed as Missing in Action with no known grave. Their five names can be found with over twenty thousand others on the grey stone panels of the hauntingly beautiful Air Forces Memorial, which stands on the crest of Coopers Hill, overlooking the River Thames at Runnymede in Surrey. One is on the Polish Air Force Memorial at Northolt.

The missing 'Treble Ones' from 1940 are:

P/O John Woffenden McKenzie 33461, aged 20, MIA 11/08/40

Sgt Robert Black Sim 742609, aged 23, MIA 11/08/40

P/O Rob Roy Wilson 41513, aged 20, MIA 11/08/40

Sgt William Lawrence Dymond 580059, aged 23, MIA 2/09/40

F/L David Campbell Bruce 39853, aged 22, MIA 4/09/40

P/O Janusz Macinski 76721, aged 24, MIA 4/09/40

Fifteen more of their comrades are buried in cemeteries across the British Isles, as well as in France, Holland and Belgium:

F/L Charles Sidney Darwood 37085, aged 26, died 18/05/40, France.

F/O David Stuart Harold Bury 72077, aged 25, died 19/05/40, France

P/O Iain Colin Moorwood 42253, aged 21, died 19/05/40, France

Sgt Edward William Pascoe 740424, aged 27, died 19/06/40, U.K.

F/O Thomas Peter K. Higgs 36165, aged 23, died 10/07/40, Holland

P/O Jack Harry H. Copeman 41257, aged 27, died 11/08/40, Belgium

AC2 Samuel Adams 978577, unknown, died 15/08/40, U.K.

AC1 Alfred George Couling 749792, unknown, died 15/08/40, U.K.

LAC John William George Dell 610506, unknown, died 15/08/40, U.K.

LAC Peter Harland Hailey 517019, aged 24, died 15/08/40, U.K.

AC1 Bernard William Mills 749734, unknown, died 15/08/40, U.K.

F/O Basil Mark Fisher 72382, aged 24, died 15/08/40, U.K.

F/L Henry Michael Ferriss 40099, aged 22, died 16/08/40, U.K.

F/L Stanley Dudley P. Connors 40439, aged 28, died 18/08/40, U.K.

Sgt Jack Burall Courtis 391343, aged 26, died 5/12/40, U.K.

The airmen included on the list were killed on the 15th of August 1940 when RAF Croydon was mistakenly bombed rather than RAF Kenley. The raid was led by the Swiss-born commander of *Erprobungsgruppe* 210, *Hauptmann* Walter Rubensdörffer, the first *Luftwaffe* officer to violate Adolf Hitler's specific orders that London was not to be targeted. If he had made it home, he would undoubtedly have faced a court martial for unwittingly launching a deadly new phase of the Battle of Britain. I have attributed his downfall to Jox McNabb.

During the low-level bombing raid on RAF Kenley endured by Jox and Alice on the 18th of August 1940, Flight Lieutenant Stan Connors was hit by ground fire and subsequently crashed to his death. It was a 'blue on blue' incident that deprived No.

111 Squadron of its second DFC holder within a week, the first being Flight Lieutenant Henry Michael Ferriss DFC.

This novel is respectfully dedicated to the memory of these brave Few.

Per Ardua Ad Astra (Through Adversity to the Stars)

I hope you enjoyed reading my first novel. More in the series are in the pipeline. Reviews are important to authors, so if you enjoyed *The Lightning and the Few*, it would be great if you would post a review on **Amazon** or **Goodreads**. Readers can also connect with me on **Twitter (@P33ddy)** or **via my website**. Also, for anyone who may be interested, I have loaded some images on **Instagram (jox_mcnabb)** that inspired me to write the story of Jox's remarkable war.

Per Ardua Ad Astra.

Best regards,

Patrick Larsimont

patricklarsimont.com

Sapere Books is an exciting new publisher of brilliant fiction and popular history.

To find out more about our latest releases and our monthly bargain books visit our website:
saperebooks.com

Made in United States
Cleveland, OH
16 May 2025